THE RANCHER RETURNS

BRENDA JACKSON

To the love of my life, Gerald Jackson, Sr.
My first. My last. My everything.

To everyone who loves the Westmorelands,
this book is for you!

To the 1971 class of William M. Raines High School,
Jacksonville, Florida. Best wishes on our
45th class reunion. Ichiban!

Plans fail for lack of counsel,
but with many advisers they succeed.
—*Proverbs* 15:22

Prologue

"Hey, Viper, your cell phone was going off upstairs."

Gavin Blake, known to his SEAL teammates as Viper, nodded as he set his coffee mug on a side table in the barracks' common area. Standing, he stretched the kinks out of his body and felt his aches all the way to the bone. Their last covert operation had been risky as hell, but they'd succeeded in destroying yet another ISIS stronghold.

In two days they would officially be off duty and most of his teammates would be heading for home. However he had other plans. Getting laid was at the top of his agenda. It had been too long since he'd shared a woman's bed and he'd already made plans with a beautiful bartender he'd met in Mississippi while helping his teammate Bane out of a fairly dangerous situation several months ago.

Gavin raced up the stairs toward his berthing unit and retrieved his cell phone from the gear in his bunk. He'd missed a call from Sherman Lott, the man who'd lived on the neighboring ranch for years. Panic floated through

Gavin's belly. Had something happened to his grandmother?

Since his grandmother lived alone when he was away, Gavin had given their closest neighbors his contact information in case of emergencies. Of course the foreman was there, running the ranch in Gavin's absence. Surely if something was going on with his grandmother, Caldwell would have contacted Gavin. But what if this was one of those times when Caldwell had gone to Saint Louis to meet with one of their beef distributors?

Gavin quickly pressed the redial button and Mr. Lott picked up on the second ring. "Hello?"

"Mr. Lott, this is Gavin. Has something happened to Gramma Mel?"

"No, Gavin, your grandmother is fine physically. Not sure what's happening to her mind, though."

Gavin frowned, wondering what the man meant. Although she was nearing her seventy-fifth birthday, Gavin had never known a day in all his thirty-two years when Melody Blake hadn't been sharp as a tack. He'd spoken with his grandmother two weeks ago and she had sounded just fine to him. "What makes you think something is wrong with her mind?"

"She's allowed some fast-talking college professor to convince her that the outlaw Jesse James buried some of his loot on the Silver Spurs, and they plan to start digging up parts of her land next week."

Gavin refrained from correcting the man. The land was *their* property since Gavin legally owned all eight hundred acres jointly with his grandmother. Instead he concentrated on what Lott had said. His grandmother had given someone permission to dig on the Silver Spurs?

"There must be some mistake, Mr. Lott. You know my grandmother as well as I do. There's no way she would allow some man to—"

"It's a woman. A professor by the name of Dr. Harris."

Gavin drew in a deep breath. Who the hell was Dr. Harris and how had she talked his grandmother into agreeing to a dig on Blake land?

Rubbing a hand down his face, Gavin knew he would be flying home and not making that pit stop in Mississippi after all. *Damn!*

"Gavin?"

"Yes, Mr. Lott, I'm here."

"I hated to call you knowing you're probably somewhere doing important work for our country, but I felt you needed to know what's going on."

"And I appreciate you doing so. Don't worry about a thing. I'll be home in a couple of days."

Gavin hung up the phone and cursed in anger. He then placed a call to his ranch foreman, Caldwell Andrews. The phone was answered on the third ring.

"Caldwell? What's going on at the Silver Spurs? Sherman Lott just called and he thinks Gramma Melody has gone loco. He said something about her allowing some professor to dig on the ranch?"

He heard Caldwell curse under his breath before saying, "I wish Lott hadn't called you, Gavin. Your grandmother is fine. She likes the professor. They talked and according to Ms. Mel she read the professor's report and it's legit."

Viper rolled his eyes. "Caldwell, you know as well as I do that there's no buried treasure on the Silver Spurs. If you recall, when I was in my teens, Dad allowed this outfit to come in and dig up parts of the land when they convinced him there was oil somewhere on it. Not a drop of oil was found."

"I remember. But I guess Ms. Mel figured a little digging wouldn't hurt anything since it's a small area, away from the main house and far away from where the cows are kept. It's the south pasture."

"The south pasture?"

"Yes. Nobody ever goes over there."

Nobody but me, Gavin thought. He knew everyone thought of the south pasture as wasted land since it had compacted soil, little or no vegetation and unsuitable irrigation. However, that part of the ranch was where he could escape and find solace whenever he needed to be alone. For some reason, going there always renewed his spirits. It was where he'd gone as a kid whenever he would miss his mother, where he'd gone after getting word about his father being killed in the Middle East. And last year he had camped out there a couple of days after returning from his mission and believing his teammate Coop was dead. It was there in the south pasture where Gavin had dealt with the thought of his good friend dying.

"Like I said, Gavin. Your grandmother has everything under control."

He wasn't so sure of that. "I'll find that out for myself since I'll be home in a few days. Don't mention my visit to Gramma Mel. I want to surprise her." When he hung up the phone, he rubbed a frustrated hand down his face.

"Viper? Hey, man, you okay?"

Viper turned to see four sets of eyes staring at him with concern. His SEAL teammates. They were Brisbane Westmoreland, team name Bane; Thurston McRoy, team name Mac; Laramie Cooper, team name Coop; and David Holloway, team name Flipper. The five of them had survived all phases of SEAL training together and were not only teammates, but like brothers. More than once they'd risked their lives for each other and would continue to have each other's backs, on duty or off.

"Viper?"

He heard the impatience in Mac's voice and spoke up before Mac's edginess got the best of them. "It's my grandmother."

"What about Gramma Mel?" Flipper asked, moving closer. Each of them had at one time or another gone home with Viper and met his grandmother.

"Is she sick?" Bane asked.

Viper shook his head. "No, it's nothing like that. My neighbor called to let me know that Gramma Mel gave some college professor permission to dig on our property. This professor has convinced my grandmother that Jesse James buried some of his stolen loot on the Silver Spurs."

The worried expressions on his friends' faces switched to relief and then amusement. "Is that all?" Coop asked, grinning, resting his broad shoulder against a wall.

"That's enough. Nobody has permission to dig on the Silver Spurs."

"Evidently your grandmother gave it," Bane pointed out.

"Well, that permission is being rescinded, and I'm going to make sure Gramma Mel and this professor know it."

"Did you talk to Caldwell?" Flipper asked.

"Yes, but he'll go along with anything my grandmother says. Now I have to head straight home instead of making that pit stop in Mississippi like I'd planned. Hell, that means I'm giving up a chance to get laid for this foolishness."

Mac grinned. "But what if Jesse James did hide some of his loot on your land? If I recall, he and his gang robbed a number of banks in and around the Missouri area."

Gavin frowned as he zipped up his gear and faced his friends. "There's not any loot on the Silver Spurs and nobody can convince me otherwise."

One

Layla Harris smiled as she accepted the plate of cookies. "Ms. Melody, I wished you wouldn't have gone to the trouble."

She said the words out of politeness, knowing they weren't true. Nobody could bake like Melody Blake and she was glad the older woman not only liked doing so but also enjoyed sharing her baked goods with Layla. Especially when the snack included a delicious tall glass of milk that had been produced right here on this ranch.

"No trouble at all," Melody Blake said, smiling. "Besides, I enjoy your company. It can get lonely in these parts."

Layla knew the Silver Spurs was a good half-hour car ride from town. At least Ms. Melody had neighbors living fairly close who checked in on her regularly. Layla had discovered the land owned by the majority of the people in this area had been in their families for generations and most of it was used for ranching cattle.

There was something special about the eighteen hundred acres encompassing the Silver Spurs and the spacious Blake family ranch home. Layla had felt welcomed the moment she had driven into the yard. The sprawling ranch house was massive and Layla figured it had to be over fifty-five hundred square feet. What she liked most was the wraparound porch with a swing that faced a beautiful pond.

Ms. Melody, a retired librarian, had said she didn't mind living in the huge house alone because she was used to it, and reading and baking kept her busy. The kitchen alone was massive and it was where the older woman spent a lot of her days, creating mouthwatering treats. In addition to the huge main house, there was a spacious guest cottage located within walking distance.

When Ms. Melody had agreed to let Layla conduct her archaeological dig on the property, she'd also kindly invited Layla to stay in the main house, but Layla preferred the guesthouse. She could come and go without disturbing the older woman.

According to Ms. Melody, the Silver Spurs had been a prosperous cattle ranch for years. It had even survived when the majority of the men, including Ms. Melody's husband, left to fight in the Vietnam War. When her husband and son became full-time military men, they'd hired a foreman to keep things running smoothly. Ms. Melody also explained that although her grandson was active in the military as a navy SEAL, whenever he returned home he reclaimed his role as a rancher.

Layla met Caldwell Andrews, the ranch foreman, and found the man pleasant and capable. The same held true for the men who worked for him. They appeared to be hard workers who were dedicated and loyal to the Blake family.

There was so much about Melody Blake that reminded Layla of her own grandmother. Both were independent, in the best of health for women their ages and were active in their churches and communities. Only thing, Gramma Candace wasn't a baker. She preferred spending her time with a knitting needle instead of a baking pan.

"I thought I'd bake chocolate chip cookies this time. They're Gavin's favorite," Ms. Melody said, breaking into Layla's musings.

At the mention of Ms. Melody's grandson, Layla couldn't dismiss the shiver that went through her body. Gavin Blake was a hunk. Although she'd never met him in person, she had seen enough of the man to judge his looks thanks to the numerous framed photographs that hung on several walls in this house. Layla knew it wasn't the man's ego that was responsible, but the grandmother who loved her grandson and was proud of the fact that, like the father and grandfather before him, he was a navy SEAL.

From all the photographs she'd seen, Layla could tell just how well built Gavin Blake was, how drop-dead gorgeous. He was definitely eye candy of the most delectable kind. Any woman would be hard-pressed not to feel some kind of sensual pull whenever she feasted her gaze on his image.

Layla had studied one of the close-up photos, which showed dimples when he smiled, a blunt nose, stubborn jaw and full lips. His angular face made him look so much like the warrior she'd heard him to be. She'd also heard he was quite the ladies' man. That bit of information had been shared by some of the locals she'd met at the café where she occasionally ate lunch. Once they'd heard she was about to dig on Blake property, they didn't hesitate to give her an earful.

According to a very talkative waitress whose eyes lit up whenever she spoke of Gavin, Layla had learned he had been a local football hero who had put Cornerstone, Missouri, on the map after leading his high school team to the state championship. No one had been surprised when he'd gone to the naval academy since he'd come from a military family. His father had been killed in the Gulf War and very little was known about his mother. Rumor had it that she'd been pretty, a few years younger than her husband and the two had married within a week of meeting in New York. Apparently, she'd never adjusted to being a military wife or living out on a ranch and had packed up and left. To this day she had never returned.

"Your grandson and I have something in common," Layla said, returning her thoughts to the conversation, "since chocolate chip cookies are my favorite, as well."

As she bit into a cookie, she thought that chocolate chip being their favorite was *all* she and Gavin had in common. Unlike him, she hadn't spent much time enjoying the opposite sex. She'd spent most of her life in school, getting her advanced degrees and working toward tenure with little time for male companionship. She had doctorates in History and Archaeology, and at twenty-six she was the youngest professor at Flintwood University in Seattle. That position had come with sacrifices such as limiting her social life, especially when it came to dating. The only people bothered by her decisions were her parents. They were hoping a man would come along and put a ring on her finger and a baby in her belly. She was their only child and they didn't hide the fact they wanted grandchildren.

Nor had they ever hidden the fact they weren't happy with her career choice. They were both gifted neurosurgeons and they'd expected her to follow in their footsteps by entering the medical field. They hadn't been pleased when she'd chosen not to do so. The thought of someone digging a hole in the ground instead of saving lives didn't make sense to them. But she'd never felt the calling to be a doctor, and she knew history was important, too. Understanding the past kept people from repeating their mistakes.

"So, Layla, what's the game plan for today?"

Layla smiled. She liked Ms. Melody's attitude. When Layla had shown up on the Blakes' doorstep over a week ago she hadn't known what to expect. She definitely hadn't been prepared for the older woman to believe her story about hidden treasure. She'd faced so much cynicism from colleagues regarding her research she'd come prepared to argue her points. Ms. Melody had listened and asked intelligent questions. Plenty of them. The older woman had also taken two days to review Layla's research, which had resulted in more questions. It was only then that Ms. Melody had agreed, with a request for periodic updates.

Ms. Melody had told Layla that her grandson would most likely not support her decision, but she'd also promised she would deal with him when the time came. Besides, she didn't expect him to return home for a few months, and it was highly likely the treasure would be found by then. Layla hoped that was true. Her creditability with the university was on the line. The possibility of tenure was riding on the success of this dig and publication of her findings and techniques.

She'd participated in several excavations, but this would be the first one she'd spearheaded. Funds from the university hadn't been as much as she'd requested, due to budget cuts, but she was determined to make good use of what she'd been given and show results. The head of her department, Dr. Clayburn, hadn't offered much support. He'd even tried shifting the funds to another project. Lucky for her, he'd been out of the country when the vote had been taken.

She'd worked all her life for this chance to prove she was an archaeologist of note. If her research was correct—and she knew it was—she'd be the first one to find any of Jesse James's treasure, and she'd be the first to use some of the latest technology on a successful dig.

"Since all the permits are in order, I contacted the members of my team," she said, smiling. "They will be arriving in a week." Her excavation team consisted of students from the university, some from her classes and some from Dr. Clayburn's. She had spoken with every one, and they were as anxious as she was to get started.

"You have to be excited about that."

"Yes," she answered, though she knew that's when the pressure would begin. "The equipment will start arriving on Monday." Layla took another bite into her cookie before adding, "Again, I really appreciate you letting us dig on your property, Ms. Melody." It showed Layla that Ms. Melody believed in her work.

"There's no need to thank me. Anyone who took the time to read your research with an open mind would reach the same conclusion. It's historically documented that James and his gang robbed a bank in Tinsel and then headed to east Missouri before a sheriff posse drove them south. I think you're right. Given how fast a horse can travel loaded down with a cache of gold bars, it makes perfect sense that the gang holed up somewhere in this area before taking a chance to continue east. And it makes even more sense that they got rid of some of their loot before heading toward the state line. Like I said, your research was thorough."

An inner glow filled Layla. Although others had read the same documentation they couldn't forget her age or inexperience. Because of that, they assumed Layla was on a wild-goose chase, wasting university funds that were needed to finance more important archaeological projects.

At that moment they heard the sound of a vehicle pulling up in the yard.

Ms. Melody glanced over at the clock on the wall. "It's not even noon yet. I wonder who that could be."

Getting up from the table, Ms. Melody went over to the

window and glanced out. When she turned back around, a huge smile covered her entire face. Layla heard the love in the older woman's voice when she said, "It's Gavin. He's home. The rancher returns."

Gavin grabbed his duffel bag from the truck before closing the door. He tilted his Stetson back on his head and looked at the car parked in front of what his grandmother called the guest cottage and what he called the party house. It was where he and his teammates would hang out whenever they visited.

Gavin hoped that his grandmother hadn't extended an invitation for the woman to stay on their property as well as dig on their land. If that was the case, he intended to send her packing quickly. He didn't want anyone taking advantage of his family.

He thought about what he was missing in Mississippi. He'd looked forward to being in bed with that bartender about now. Calling to cancel had been hard. Promising to head her way as soon as he'd taken care of this unexpected family emergency had satisfied her somewhat.

Walking around his truck, he took a deep breath of the Missouri air. This was home and he'd always enjoyed returning after every covert operation. Silver Spurs meant a lot to him. To his family. It was his legacy. It was land that had been in his family for generations. Land that he loved. He enjoyed being a rancher almost as much as he enjoyed being a SEAL. *Almost.* He would admit that being a SEAL was his passion.

Gavin appreciated having a good man like Caldwell to keep things running in his absence. The older man had done the same thing during Gavin's father's time. And Caldwell's father had been foreman to Gavin's grandfather, so Caldwell and his family also had deep history with the ranch.

While he was home, Gavin intended to return to ranching. He couldn't wait to get back in the saddle and ride Acer as well as help Caldwell and the men with the herd. And he needed to go over the books with Phil Vinson, the ranch's accountant.

However, the first thing on his agenda was a discussion with his grandmother about her giving someone permission to dig on their land. Hopefully he'd have everything settled by next week and he would hightail it to Mississippi. All he needed was one night with a woman and then he'd be good for a while.

He had taken one step onto the porch when the front door swung open and his grandmother walked out. She was smiling, and when she opened her arms, he dropped his duffel bag and walked straight into the hug awaiting him. She was petite, but her grip was almost stronger than that of a man. He loved and admired her so damn much. This was the woman who'd been there for him when his own mother had left. The woman who'd been there for him when he'd laid his father to rest sixteen years ago. She had, and always would be, his rock. That's why he refused to tolerate anyone trying to take advantage of her kindness.

"Welcome home, Gavin," she said, finally releasing him so she could lean back and look at him from head to toe as she always did when he returned from one of his assignments. "I didn't expect you for a few months yet. Did everything go okay?"

He smiled. She always asked him that knowing full well that because of the classified nature of his job, he couldn't tell her anything. "Yes, Gramma Mel, everything went okay. I'm back because I understand you and I need to—"

He glanced over his grandmother's shoulder and he blinked, not sure he was seeing straight. A woman stood in the doorway, but she wasn't just *some* woman. She had to be the most gorgeous woman he'd ever seen. Hell, she looked like everything he'd fantasized a woman to be, even while fully clothed in jeans and a pullover sweater. He didn't want to consider what his reaction would be if she was naked.

His grandmother sensed his attention had shifted. She turned around and smiled at the woman. "Layla, come out here. I want you to meet my grandson."

Layla? Where had she come from? Was she the granddaughter of one of his grandmother's fellow church members or something? He recalled Mrs. Cotton had a granddaughter who visited on occasion from Florida and her name was Layla…or was it Liza? Hell, he couldn't remember. He wasn't thinking straight. When this Layla began walking toward him, he ceased thinking at all. She was wearing stretch jeans and a long sweater and had an eye-catching figure with curves in all the right places.

Gavin fought for air as she neared. He studied her features, trying to figure out what about them had him spellbound. Was it the caramel-colored skin, dark chocolate eyes, dimpled cheeks, button nose or well-defined kissable lips? Maybe every single thing.

Wow! Was he that hard up for a woman or did this Layla actually look *that* good? When she stopped beside him, a smile on her lips, he knew she actually looked that good. He kept his gaze trained on her face—even when he really wanted his eyes to roam all over her.

Not waiting for his grandmother to make introductions, his mouth eased into a smile. He reached out his hand and said, "Hello, I'm Gavin."

The moment their hands touched, a jolt of desire shot through his body. It's a wonder he hadn't lost his balance. Nothing like this had ever happened to him before and he touched women all the time. From the expression that had flashed in her eyes, he knew she had felt it, as well. Yes, there was definitely strong sexual chemistry between them.

"It's nice meeting you, Gavin," she said softly. He even liked the sound of her voice. "And I'm Layla. Layla Harris."

Harris? His horny senses suddenly screeched to a stop. Did she say Harris? Was Layla related to this Professor Harris? The woman's daughter perhaps? Was she part of the excavation team? She looked young, around twenty or twenty-one. Now he had even more questions and he was determined to get some answers when he had that little talk with his grandmother. "It's nice meeting you, too, Layla."

It was only when she eased her hand from his that he realized he still held it. She turned to his grandmother. "Thanks for the cookies and milk, Ms. Melody. I enjoyed them. I need to run into town to pick up a few items. Anything I can get for you while I'm there?"

"No. I've got everything I need."

Layla nodded. "Okay. I should be back in a couple of hours."

"Take your time."

Giving Gavin one last smile, she quickly walked down the steps toward the parked car. He stood and watched her every move until she was inside the car with the door closed. It was then that he turned his attention back to his grandmother. Not surprisingly, she was staring at him.

"For a minute I thought you'd forgotten I was standing here, Gavin Timothy Blake III," his grandmother said in an amused tone.

So he'd been caught ogling a woman. It hadn't been the first time and he doubted it would be the last. "What can I say, Gramma Mel?" He grinned sheepishly. "She's awfully pretty."

He decided not to mention how he appreciated that

sway to her hips when she walked, or how nice her breasts looked beneath her sweater.

"Yes, she is pretty. Come inside. Just so happens I baked some chocolate chip cookies this morning."

That made Gavin smile even wider as he picked up his duffel bag. His mouth watered just thinking about the cookies. Now if he could only get that image of Layla Harris's backside out of his mind…

"How are the rest of your teammates?" his grandmother asked, leading him through the front door. "You guys were together for over two months on this mission."

He glanced around as he entered. Everything looked the same. However, instead of smelling like vanilla, his grandmother's favorite scent, the house smelled of woman. Namely Layla Harris.

"Everyone is fine, just anxious to get home. Bane and his wife are renewing their vows in a few weeks and I plan to attend the ceremony," he said, placing his duffel bag on the sofa for now. "This was Coop's first covert operation after being rescued and he's good as ever."

The only reason Gavin shared that much info with his grandmother was because when he'd come home last year before the holidays everyone had believed Coop had been killed on assignment. The entire team had taken Coop's death hard. Then right before Christmas, they'd found Coop was alive and being held hostage in the Syrian mountains. Gavin and his team had been sent in to get Coop, as well as other hostages, out alive.

"This was Bane's first time back, too, right?" his grandmother asked.

Did his grandmother not forget anything? Bane, being master sniper, had been recruited to work in DC for six months teaching SEAL recruits. "Yes, we were glad to have him back as well. And before I forget, I plan to head for Mississippi next week. I've got important business to take care of there." His grandmother didn't need to know that the important business was getting laid.

As soon as he entered the kitchen, he went straight to the sink to wash his hands and then quickly headed for the coffeepot. After pouring a cup, he turned and watched Gramma Mel arrange a half-dozen cookies on a plate for him. He smiled. Anyone else would eat just one or two, but his grandmother knew him well. He needed at least a half dozen to get things started. "You need a fresh cup of coffee?" he asked her.

"Thanks. That would be nice, Gavin."

After pouring another cup, he moved away from the counter to sit down and she sat across from him. He placed her coffee in front of her and grabbed for a cookie. She slapped away his hand. "Say grace first."

He chuckled, recalling the protocol she expected of him. After quickly bowing his head in silence, he grabbed a cookie and almost swallowed it whole. He loved his grandmother's chocolate chip cookies.

She shook her head as she took a sip of her coffee. Now was as good a time as any to bring up what had brought him rushing back to the Silver Spurs. "What's this I hear about you giving some professor permission to dig on our land?"

Gramma Mel raised a brow over her cup of coffee. "And you know this how?"

He held his grandmother's gaze. "Sherman Lott called. He thought I had a right to know."

She frowned. "As far as I'm concerned, Sherman needs to mind his own business."

Gavin stared at this grandmother as he bit into another cookie. "The way I figure it, Caldwell is the one who should have called me. He's paid to keep me informed about what's going on around here. But he wouldn't call because he'd think doing so would be disloyal to you. And we both know what you mean to him."

His grandmother didn't say anything. She just stared into her cup of coffee. There really wasn't anything to say. Gavin had known for years that his grandmother and Caldwell had a thing going on. He wasn't stupid. Nor was he insensitive. He wanted the two people who meant the most to him to be happy. He figured that one day they would stop trying to be so damn discreet. In the meantime, what they did was their business. He'd only brought it up now to make a point.

"Caldwell would have told you had he thought it was important," his grandmother finally said.

"Whatever." He took a sip of his coffee. "So what about it? Did you give permission for a dig to take place on our property?"

She leaned back in her chair. "Yes, I gave my permission and I see nothing wrong with it."

Gavin kept his cool. "Well, I do. Honestly, Gramma Mel. You actually bought into this professor's tale about Jesse James's buried treasure?"

"Yes, I read her research and found it thorough and convincing. I have a copy, if you want to read it for yourself."

"I don't need to read anything to know the research is false. There's no buried treasure on our land, and I'm against the idea of anyone digging around for nothing."

His grandmother leaned forward in her chair. "And I happen to disagree. But what you believe is a moot point since I've given Layla permission and from what she told me this morning, her equipment will arrive in a few days—"

"Hold up," he said, giving the time-out sign with his hands. "Why did you give Layla Harris permission? It's her mother who's running things, right?"

His grandmother look confused. "Her mother? I never

met the woman. Layla is in charge or should I say Dr. Layla Harris is in charge."

Surprise made Gavin raise his eyebrows. "Layla is the professor?"

"Yes, and a very competent one."

Gavin shook his head, not believing such a thing was possible. "She's young."

"She's twenty-six. However, I admit she does look younger."

Twenty-six? That was still young and yes, she definitely looked younger. He drew in a deep breath, trying to force back the memories of just how she'd looked... in her jeans and sweater. And then the thought that she'd deliberately oozed her way onto his grandmother's good side made him mad.

"You might have given your permission, but I have not given mine. Something that major means we need to be in full agreement."

"No, it doesn't. If you recall, we agreed that any time you were away on military business, I could make decisions in the best interest of the Silver Spurs."

"I don't consider digging up our land to be in the best interest of anything."

"I disagree. I'm excited about what Layla might find. And I also gave her permission to stay in the guesthouse."

The line of Gavin's jaw tightened. He'd figured as much. Melody Blake was stubborn, but then so was he. He ate the last of his cookies, drained his coffee and stood. "I'm tired and need a full day of sleep. But we will talk about this again, Gramma Mel. In the meantime, I suggest you tell Dr. Layla Harris to hold up on bringing any type of equipment to the Silver Spurs."

And without saying anything else Gavin walked out of the kitchen.

Two

Layla pulled her car off on the shoulder of the road, unable to drive any farther. Once she killed her vehicle's ignition, she forced herself to breathe deeply a few times. Never in all her twenty-six years had any man wreaked havoc on her senses like Gavin Blake. Never had any man left her in such a mind-blowing sensuous state. Who would have thought a man could have her nerves dancing, her mind racing, her stomach swirling and her nipples actually feeling like they'd been stroked? She had been tempted to glide her hands over every inch of his sexy, sculpted body.

She had known he was the epitome of male perfection from all those photographs she'd seen. To be honest, that's where her troubles had started…with those photographs. In one, his lips had curved a little at the corners as he stared at her as if to say he knew exactly what she was thinking. She knew it was her wild imagination, but every time she glanced at that particular photo it was as if he was checking her out with those intense dark eyes of his. As if he knew her fantasies included him. Even in his photo, his muscular power had nearly overtaken her senses.

Pretty much like he'd done today. She hadn't counted on the real thing being even more explosive than his pictures. Before he'd realized she was in his grandmother's doorway, she had stood there spellbound as a rush of emotion made her body ache with desire. Then, when he'd noticed her, those eyes had made her yearn for something she didn't need. Something she had never needed. A man.

Gavin Blake had stood on his grandmother's porch wearing a pair of faded jeans and a T-shirt with his military tag hanging around his neck. Even wearing her sweater, she found the air cool, but the temperature hadn't seemed to faze him. Was he as hot-blooded as he looked?

The one thing she did know was that he was a big guy. Tall. Muscular. Built. She could imagine him as the football hero she'd heard he used to be, tackling players with little or no trouble. And she could definitely imagine him as a SEAL, taking on the bad guys to protect his country.

And she couldn't help but imagine him naked in bed… with her. Unfamiliar sensations raced through her just thinking about it. When he had touched her hand while staring into her eyes, she'd forgotten all about Ms. Melody standing there and had all but purred out loud. Blood had pounded through her entire body. She doubted she would ever use her hand again without remembering the feel of him. If her body reacted from a single touch to her hand, she didn't want to imagine him touching her anywhere else…her breasts, her stomach, between her legs. And when he smiled at her, she'd been a goner. She could still feel the impact in the pit of her stomach.

She had never experienced this kind of need in her life. She didn't even have a battery-operated boyfriend like some of her single female colleagues joked about owning. Sex was something that had never been on her must-do list. She'd put her energy into her academic career. But there was something about Gavin that made her think of heat and desire. Something that made the area at the juncture of her thighs quiver. Made her hormones sizzle.

Drawing in another deep breath, Layla admitted she needed to get a grip. She wasn't in Cornerstone, Missouri, to lust after the man who jointly owned the land she needed as an excavation site. All she wanted to do was stay on schedule and have a successful dig. Besides, Gavin Blake probably looked at other women the same way he'd looked at her. Hadn't that waitress in town enlightened Layla as to just what a ladies' man he was? Now seeing was believing.

Seeing was also a warning to keep her common sense intact and be on guard. An involvement with Gavin Blake was the last thing she needed, even though her body was trying to convince her otherwise.

There was something else she should be concerned about, something she just remembered. Ms. Melody had said that her grandson might be against the idea of a dig on the Silver Spurs. Although Ms. Melody had given the okay, would Gavin's return change anything? The thought of losing the permission she'd gained sent nervous jitters through her.

Maybe she should talk to Gavin Blake herself. She would present her research to him the same way she'd presented it to Ms. Melody. Layla wanted to believe he was reasonable. It wasn't as if she would be digging all over his property. She had narrowed it to one location.

Yes, she would talk to him herself, but only after she talked to Ms. Melody—and after Layla convinced herself she could talk to him without every part of her turning to mush.

* * *

Gavin's eyes flew open and his entire body went on full alert. His ears picked up the sounds around him and it was then he recalled he was back in the United States and not in some godforsaken country where he had to be on guard 24/7.

It was always this way for the first few days after he returned home. He had to regroup and get his mind back in sync with normal life, deprogram from battle mode and ease back into the life of a rancher.

Glancing at the clock on his bedroom wall, he saw it was ten at night. He wasn't surprised that he'd slept nearly nine hours straight. His ears perked up at the sound that had woken him. Was that a harmonica? Granted it was far off, but he could still hear it. His teammates teased him about having sonic ears, because of his ability to hear a sound over a hundred feet away.

He wasn't sure if that was a blessing or a curse when he involuntarily eavesdropped on conversations he wished he hadn't. Like the time Mac was outside the barracks and downstairs in the yard talking to his wife on the phone, telling her in explicit sexual terms what he planned to do to her when he returned home from their mission. Gavin had heard every single word and the details had nearly burned his ears. They had definitely made him horny as hell. For a fleeting moment it had made him wish he had a wife or an exclusive woman he could return home to instead of a little black book filled with names of willing women.

Gavin pushed the whimsical thought from his mind as he lay in bed and listened to the music. It sounded pretty damn good. He sat up and rubbed his hands across his face as if to wipe away the sleep. Pushing the bedcovers aside, he eased out of bed. Not bothering to cover his naked body, he strolled over to the window, pushed aside the curtain and looked out. The October air produced a chill that would send shivers through a normal person's body. But because of his SEAL training, Gavin could withstand temperatures of the highest and lowest extremes.

The way the moonlight crested the rocky bluffs, dissecting the valleys and rolling plains, was simply breathtaking. There was nothing more beautiful than Silver Spurs at night. For as long as he could remember, he'd always been moved by the grandeur of the land he was born on.

The harmonica stopped and he knew the sound had come from the party house where Layla was staying. Since the woman was still in residence, he could only assume his grandmother had not delivered his message. Had she done so he was certain Professor Layla Harris would have left by now.

Maybe he should talk to Layla Harris himself. Make it clear where he stood. He moved back toward the bed. Instead of getting into it, Gavin ignored the voice of reason saying he should wait and talk to Layla in the morning and grabbed his clothes off the chair. After sliding into his jeans he tugged his T-shirt over his head. He put on his socks and boots and headed for the door.

The music from the harmonica started up again.

Layla placed her harmonica aside. Playing it relaxed her and she would always appreciate her grandfather for teaching her. She could vividly recall those summers when she would sit on the front porch of her grandparents' New Orleans home and listen to her grandfather play his harmonica, then beg him to teach her how. When Grampa Chip passed away ten years ago, his request had been that she play the harmonica at his funeral and she had.

Thoughts of losing the grandfather she adored always made her sad and that was the last emotion she wanted to feel right now. Even when she had no idea what would happen with this dig, she wanted happy thoughts. Earlier, Ms. Melody assured Layla that all was well. Her grandson was too exhausted to think straight and he needed a full day of sleep.

Layla hoped that was good news considering she had all that machinery on the way. She figured Ms. Melody knew her grandson better than Layla did. She would wait for Gavin Blake to get his full day of sleep. Hopefully, after another discussion with Ms. Melody, he would see things the way his grandmother did.

Layla glanced around the guest cottage, thinking how much she liked it here. The place was larger than her apartment in Seattle. She definitely didn't have a huge living room with a fireplace or a spacious master bedroom with a large en suite bath with a walk-in shower and Jacuzzi tub. The cottage also had a loft that could be used as additional sleeping space, and an eat-in kitchen. She loved the wood floors throughout and the high ceilings. And because it sat a distance away from the main house, she could play her harmonica without worrying about disturbing anyone. That was something she couldn't do at her own apartment.

She stood to stretch and was about to head toward the bedroom when she heard a knock on the door. Glancing at the clock on the wall she saw it was after ten. Usually Ms. Melody was in bed every night by eight since she was such an early riser. Had something happened? Had the older woman decided not to butt heads with her grandson and didn't want Layla and her team to dig on the Silver Spurs after all?

Layla moved toward the door. It didn't have a peephole so she leaned against the wooden frame and asked, "Who is it?"

"Gavin. Gavin Blake."

Her gaze widened and heat swirled around in her lower belly. She tried forcing the sensations aside. Why would Gavin seek her out at this time of night? Had something happened to Ms. Melody? From their talks, she knew the older woman suffered occasionally with migraines.

She opened the door and the man stood there, almost bigger than life, and looking as yummy as a chocolate sundae. He was dressed as he had been that morning. Jeans. T-shirt. Western boots. But her brain wasn't computing *what* he was wearing as much as *how well* he was wearing it.

Although it was cold, he wasn't even wearing a jacket. He leaned in the doorway looking exactly like any woman's dream. Hot. Sexy. And then some. He was one of those can't-get-to-sleep nighttime fantasies that left you hot and bothered with no relief in sight. It was those thoughts that had her unable to speak, so she just stood there and stared at the penetrating dark gaze holding hers as her heart beat violently in her chest.

She knew SEALs stayed in shape, but the body of the man standing before her was simply ridiculous. She knew of no other man whose body was so well built. So magnificently toned. His jeans appeared plastered to him in the most decadent way. He made her think of wicked temptation and sinful delights.

Doubting she could stand there much longer without going up in flames, even with the blast of cold air, she swallowed deeply and then forced her voice to ask, "Is something wrong with Ms. Melody?"

From the look that quickly flashed across his features, she could tell he was surprised by her question. "What makes you think something is wrong with my grandmother?"

Layla sighed deeply. "What other reason would bring you here?"

That, Gavin thought, was a good question. Why *was* he here? He had heard the harmonica. And had quickly figured out the source was Layla in the party house. So what had driven him out into the night? He definitely could have waited until morning to talk to her about the dig. Had he come here just to stand in the doorway to try and get his fill of looking at her?

"Gavin?"

And why did the sound of his name from her lips send desire throbbing through him? In his horny state, it wouldn't take much to push him over the edge. "Yes?"

"If nothing is wrong with Ms. Melody, why are you here?"

He crossed his arms over his chest. "I heard you playing a harmonica."

Layla's jaw dropped in surprise. She must have been shocked that he heard her. The guest cottage was far away from the main house and on the opposite side of the bedrooms. Gramma Mel had probably told her he would be sleeping hard for a full day.

But he wasn't sleeping. He was here. He rubbed his hand down his face in frustration. He needed to get to Mississippi fast or else…

Or else what? He would begin thinking of Layla Harris in his bed? Too late. His mind had already gone there. More than once. Those thoughts had pretty much settled in the moment he'd laid eyes on her. Having her at the party house wasn't helping matters. Typically, all he had to do was snap his fingers to get any woman he wanted. Why were his fingers itching to be snapped? With Layla Harris, would it be that easy? Why didn't he think so?

"I am so sorry," she said now. "I didn't mean to wake you. I know you need to get all that rest and—"

"You didn't wake me."

"But you said that you heard me playing."

"I did, but that's not what awakened me." Gavin figured there was no reason to tell her how disrupted his sleep patterns tended to be during his first few days back home. Which still left her question unanswered. Why was he here? Why had he sought her out? In the middle of the night? "You play very well," he said.

Gavin thought she was even more beautiful than she had looked this morning. He blamed the easy smile that touched her lips.

"Thanks, but I'm sure you didn't come all this way just to give me that compliment."

No, he hadn't. He'd actually come to give her hell for feeding his grandmother a bunch of crock about buried treasure on their land. So he needed to say what he had come to say. "We should talk. May I come in?"

It was funny he would ask. After all, she was the visitor on his land. This was his house. Ms. Melody had told her that Gavin and some of his SEAL teammates had built it a few years ago as a place to hang out whenever they visited.

Gavin and his friends could get loud and rowdy here at the cottage without disturbing his grandmother. That accounted for why the place was so spacious with the cupboards bare—except for a refrigerator stocked with beer and wine coolers. Not to mention that a deck of cards seemed to be in every room.

"Yes, of course you can come in. You own the place."

"But you're my grandmother's guest."

Had he said that to remind her she wasn't *his* guest? To remind her that her presence on the Silver Spurs was something he didn't support? Layla would find out soon enough.

She moved from the door and he followed, closing it behind him. "Would you like something to drink?" Grinning brightly, she said, "There's plenty of beer and wine coolers in the fridge."

Gavin chuckled. "I'll take a beer."

She nodded. "One beer coming up." She felt his gaze on her backside.

"Here you are. I feel funny doing this," Layla said, coming back into the room carrying a cold bottle of beer.

He lifted a brow. "Doing what?"

"Serving you your own beer."

"No reason that you should. You're my grandmother's guest."

That was the second time he'd said that, Layla thought. Not one to beat around the bush, she crossed the room to hand him the beer, and then wished she hadn't. Their hands had only briefly touched so why was heat filling her? And why was he looking at her as if that same heat filled him?

She quickly took a step back and wiped her hands down the sides of her jeans.

"You think that will get rid of it?"

She met his eyes. She knew what he'd insinuated, but she wanted to be sure. "Get rid of what?"

"Nothing."

He then opened the bottle and took a huge gulp. Afterward, he licked his lips while she watched. Her chest tightened. He lowered the bottle from his mouth and held her gaze. "Want a sip?"

She drew in a deep breath to clamp down on her emotions. Was he offering to share his beer? For them to drink from the same bottle? Doing something like that was way too intimate for her. Evidently not for him. A distinct warmth coiled around her midsection. The way his eyes darkened wasn't helping matters.

She should call his bluff and take a sip. But that might lead to other things. It might give him ideas. The same ideas floating crazily through her head. The last thing she needed was an involvement with a man. Any man. Especially him. Her work was too important to her. The idea of an October fling was not. "No thanks. I had one earlier and one was enough for me."

Instead of saying anything, he nodded and raised the bottle to his lips to drain the rest. She watched his throat work. When had seeing a man drink anything been a turn-on?

When he finished the bottle and lowered it, she asked, "Want another one?"

He smiled at her. "No, one was enough for me."

She couldn't help but smile back at his use of her words. "I don't know, Gavin Blake. You seem like the sort of guy that could handle a couple of those."

"You're right, but that's not why I'm here."

His words were a reminder that he hadn't shown up tonight for chitchat and drinking beer. "Yes, you said you wanted to talk. Is there a problem?" Layla knew there was and figured he was about to spell it out for her.

"Who taught you to play the harmonica?"

She'd expected him to just dive in. His question threw her. "My grandfather," she said, angling her head to look up at him. "He was the best. At least most people thought so."

"And who was your grandfather?"

"Chip Harris."

Surprise made Gavin's jaw drop. "Chip Harris? *The* Chip Harris?"

Layla nodded. "Yes," she said, intentionally keeping her voice light. Very few people knew that. It wasn't something she boasted about, although she was proud of her grandfather's success and accomplishments. He'd been a good man, a great humanitarian and a gifted musician. But most of all he had been a wonderful grandfather. Her grandparents had helped to keep her world sane during the times her parents had made it insane.

Layla saw Gavin's dark, penetrating eyes suddenly go cold. "Is anything wrong?"

"So that's how you did it."

She raised a brow. "That's how I did what?"

"How you were able to talk my grandmother into going along with your crazy scheme of Jesse James's treasure being buried on my property. You probably heard she's a big fan of Chip Harris, and used the fact that you're his granddaughter to get in good with her. Get Gramma Mel to trust you and—"

"You jerk." Anger flared through her. His accusations filled her with rage. "How dare you accuse me of doing something so underhanded, so unethical and low? You might not know me but you know your grandmother. How can you think so little of her to imagine she has such a weak mind she could be taken in by anyone? How can you not trust her judgment?"

Layla drew in a disgusted breath and then added furiously, "For your information, I never once mentioned anything about my relationship to Chip Harris to her. Ms. Melody's decision was based on my research, which she took the time to read. And she asked questions and found some of her own answers. So regardless of what you believe, her decision was based on facts, Gavin Blake. Facts and nothing more."

Gavin was stunned by Layla's rage. When her words sank in, he regretted accusing her of manipulating Gramma Mel. He'd crossed the line and he knew it. He owed her an apology. "I'm sorry. I should not have accused you of that."

"But you did. Save your apology for your grandmother. She's one of the most intelligent women I know. But tonight you made her out to be a woman who can be influenced easily by anything, especially name-dropping. Like I said, you should know your grandmother better than that."

Gavin didn't say anything. Probably because he knew she was right. His grandmother was as sharp as a tack. She'd told Layla so many stories of how he'd tried to pull one over on her…unsuccessfully. Maybe he should do what his grandmother had done and read Layla's report for himself.

"I should not have come here tonight," he finally said.

"No, you should not have, especially if you came to talk that kind of BS. I don't have time for it."

Layla's words seemed to irritate him. "You don't think I have a right to question why you're here?"

She didn't back down. In fact she took a step closer. "You have every right. But you already know why I'm here. If you don't agree with your grandmother or you want to question why I feel a dig on the Silver Spurs is warranted, I can understand that. But what you did, Gavin, is question my integrity. I take that personally."

"You have to admit the idea of buried treasure on my land is pretty far-fetched."

"Maybe to you but not to me. You're a SEAL. I'm sure there are times when you engage in covert operations where the facts lead you to believe your assignment will be successful…although logically it doesn't seem possible."

He frowned. "It's not the same."

"I think it is. I did my research on the life of Jesse James. Five years' worth. I studied his life, specifically that bank robbery in Tinsel. That's what led me here. If you took the time to read my research, you would see it's all there. All I'm asking is for you to give me the same courtesy Ms. Melody did and take the time to read my work."

"I don't have to read a report to know what you're claiming isn't true."

In frustration, Layla blew out a breath and threw up her hands. "Why are you so stubborn?"

Instead of answering he gave her a careless shrug of his broad shoulders. "I'm not being stubborn. Just realistic."

He wasn't even trying to be reasonable. "So what do you want, Gavin? Since you believe that I've hoodwinked your grandmother and I'm a lunatic on the hunt for buried treasure, did you come here tonight to ask me to leave? To tell me to get off your property because you won't allow me and my team to dig?"

When he didn't say anything but continued to stare down at her with those dark, penetrating eyes of his, she knew what she'd just said was true. "Fine. I'll leave in the morning."

She moved with the intention of walking around him to show him the door. He surprised her when he reached out and grabbed her arm. The moment he touched her it seemed every hormone in her body sizzled. She couldn't move away from him. His hand skimmed down her arm in a sensual caress.

"What do you think you're doing?" She heard the tension in her voice and felt her heart rate quicken. Their gazes held and something hot in the depths of his eyes held her hostage. She wanted to break eye contact and couldn't. How could any one man have so much sex appeal? Create such primal attraction?

Layla became angry with herself because of her reaction to him. The man standing in front of her had destroyed her plans. He'd placed her in a difficult position with the administration at the university and with her team. She'd have to cancel excavation and lose her funding. She might never get another chance to prove her theories. Yet at that moment all she could think about was how fully aware of him she was.

"What I'm doing is touching you," he answered moments later, as if he'd needed time to give her question some thought.

Well, she had news for him. He should keep his hands to himself. So why wasn't she telling him that? And why was there a throb inside her? One that had started in her stomach but was now going lower to the juncture of her thighs? And why, when she saw his head lowering, did she just stand there? When his lips touched hers and he wrapped her in his arms, she sank into him. The same way he was sinking into her mouth.

The kiss was making her forget everything, even the fact that he wanted to throw her off his ranch. The only thing she could concentrate on was how his tongue was moving around in her mouth, sending shivers up her spine until she heard herself moan.

But he was moaning as well, and then he deepened the kiss. She recognized this for what it was. Lust. And that usually led to sex. If that was his plan, he could take it elsewhere. She had no intention of getting involved, no matter how fleetingly, with a man who refused to take her work seriously.

She pulled her mouth free and took a step back. "Like I said. I'll be off your property in the morning." She then walked around him to the door.

Before opening it, she glanced back at him. He stood in the same spot, staring at her as if she was a puzzle he was trying to figure out. Seriously? Did he think she was that complicated? As far as she was concerned, he was the problematic one.

He was the man who, with very little effort, it seemed, could tempt her to lower her guard, to surrender to this need he created inside of her. A need she hadn't realized even existed. And it appeared he was dealing with his own need if the huge bulge pressing against the zipper of his jeans was anything to go by. There were just some things an aroused man couldn't hide.

"We need to keep sex out of this, Gavin." She'd had to say it, considering the strong sexual chemistry flowing between them. Chemistry both of them were fully aware of.

He stared at her for a long moment, saying nothing, but she saw the tightening of his jaw. Had her words hit a nerve? Had they made him realize that she wasn't as gullible as he thought?

When he began walking toward her, her heartbeat quickened with every step he took. Never had she felt such a strong primal attraction to any man. Even his walk, his muscled thighs flexing erotically with every step, tripped her pulse. It had her drowning in the sexual vibes pouring off him.

When he came to a stop in front of her, he grabbed her hand to keep her from opening the door. Immediately, like before, they became attuned to each other. Why was there such a strong physical attraction between them? No man had ever made her forget about work. But she struggled to remember that work was the reason she was here. That and nothing else.

"Don't know about you, but I can't keep sex out of it, Layla. I think you know why. Whether we like it or not, there's a strong sensual pull between us. I felt it the moment I set eyes on you this morning, and if you say you didn't feel it as well, then you would be lying. You might pretend otherwise, but you want me as much as I want you."

No matter what he said, she would deny it. She hadn't come to the ranch for this. She had come to Cornerstone, Missouri, to do a job—to prove her theory and move up in her career—*not* to have an affair with a navy SEAL who could overtake her senses. A man who was proving, whether she wanted him to or not, that she had sexual needs she'd ignored for too long. But regardless of that proof, under no circumstances would she sleep with him. Doing so would be a very bad idea. It would be a mistake that could cost her all she'd worked for up to this point. Besides, hadn't he all but told her to get off his land?

Instead of a straight-out denial, she said, "What I want is to be allowed to do my job. I need to do that dig, Gavin."

His gaze hardened. "Why? To prove me wrong?"

"More than proving you wrong, I need to prove to myself and my peers that I am right. There's a difference, but I don't expect you to understand."

Yes, he understood the difference. Hadn't he felt the need to prove that he was his own man? To prove that being a SEAL hadn't been about his grandfather's and father's legacies but about establishing a legacy of his own? The first Gavin Blake had been handpicked to be part of the first special operations unit that became known as the SEALs. And Gavin's father, Gavin Blake Jr, had died a war hero after rescuing his team members and others who'd been held hostage during Desert Storm.

For years, he'd thought being Gavin Blake III was a curse more than a blessing. You couldn't share the name of bigger-than-life SEAL predecessors without some people believing you should be invincible. It had taken years to prove to others, as well as to himself, that he was his own man. Free to make his own mistakes. Now he cherished the memories of the heroes his grandfather and father had been and he was proud to carry their names and to continue the family legacy of being a SEAL. In the end, he'd realized becoming his own man hadn't been about proving anything to others but proving it to himself.

A part of him wanted to believe that Layla's issues were hers alone. They were her business to deal with and not his. But for some reason he couldn't let her go. His curiosity pushed him to say, "Don't leave the Silver Spurs just yet, Layla."

He saw that his words surprised her. Gave her pause. "Why? You ridiculed my years of research, accused me of manipulating your family and told me not to dig on your land. Why should I stay?"

"To convince me that you're right."

He could tell from her expression she thought what he'd said didn't make sense. "I can't do that unless you give me permission to excavate, Gavin. That's the only way I can prove anything."

Gavin was totally captivated by Layla Harris—by her passion for her work, and this passion between them. Why? He wasn't sure. She was beautiful, but he'd been around beautiful women before. She was built—with lush curves, a nice backside and very attractive features—but all those were just physical attributes. Deep down, he believed there was more to Layla Harris than just her beauty, more than her intelligence. There was something inside of her she refused to let surface. And it was something he wanted to uncover.

One thing for certain, he honestly wasn't ready for her to leave the Silver Spurs. But she was right. Why should she stay if he wouldn't allow her to dig on his property? He gritted his teeth at the thought of any woman making him feel so needy that he'd allow her to dig up the south pasture, his special place. But he quickly remembered he'd gone six months without sex, which had a way of crippling a man's senses.

"It's late," he heard himself say. "Let's talk more tomorrow."

"Will talking tomorrow change anything, Gavin?"

All he knew for certain was that he couldn't think straight being this close to her. But the last thing he wanted was to wake up tomorrow and find her gone. "It might," he said. "I'm not making any promises, Layla. All I can say is that right now I'm exhausted and can't think straight." He would let her think his muddled mind was due to exhaustion and not the degree of desire he had for her.

"Will you read my research?"

He wouldn't lie about that. "No. You can go over the important aspects of your work when we meet tomorrow."

She stared at him for a long moment as if weighing his words. Finally, she said, "Alright. I'll stay until we can talk."

Relief poured through his body, quickly followed by frustration and annoyance. No woman could tie him in knots like Layla seemed capable of doing. "I'll see you tomorrow."

When he'd first arrived, her hair had been neatly pulled back. Had he mussed up her hair when he'd kissed her? Maybe that was why the loose curls now teasing her forehead were a total turn-on.

"Good night, Gavin."

That was his cue to go. "Good night." He opened the door and stepped out into the cold Missouri night.

Three

Layla awakened the next morning wondering what she'd gotten herself into. Would remaining an additional day to meet with Gavin really change his mind?

There was always the possibility that it could, which was the reason her bags were not already packed. Besides, she was a fighter, a person who didn't give up easily. It had taken over a year to convince the university to give her funding for the dig, and another six months to get them to ease off some of their restrictions and ridiculous conditions. Even now, she wasn't sure the heads of the department believed in her 100 percent, but at least they were giving her a chance.

Now all of that forward momentum—the work that could change the history books and earn her a tenured position—could end because of Gavin. She drew in a deep breath. What was she going to do? Short of sleeping with him, she would do just about anything to convince him to reconsider.

She shifted in bed to look out the window. She'd thought she had a beautiful view in her high-rise apartment overlooking downtown Seattle—until now. The rolling plains, majestic hills and valleys of the Silver Spurs were awesome. The concrete jungle she saw each morning from her bedroom window couldn't compare.

She loved it here. She wouldn't mind returning to visit. But this time, she wasn't here for a vacation. She had a job to do and she hoped Gavin wouldn't stand in the way of her doing it.

Gavin.

He thought she'd been manipulative enough to use her musician grandfather's name to get in good with his grandmother. Although he had apologized, those accusations still bothered her. Yet in spite of them, she had allowed him to kiss her. And it was a kiss she couldn't stop thinking about. A kiss so deeply entrenched in her mind that she'd thought about it even while she'd slept. She was thinking about it now while wide-awake.

Layla realized that kissing, something she'd never enjoyed doing before, wasn't so bad after all. At least with Gavin it wasn't bad. Evidently other guys had lacked his expertise. Not only did he have a skillful tongue, but he knew how to use it. The feel of being in his strong arms had sent pleasure throughout her entire body.

She drew in a sharp breath as memories flooded her, filling her with a longing for them to kiss again. Yet how could she even contemplate repeating that kiss when she wasn't sure she even liked him? The one thing she did know was that she definitely desired him and he'd been arrogant enough to call her out on that.

In frustration, she rubbed a hand down her face. She needed to rid her mind of thoughts of Gavin. She'd never mixed business with pleasure and she had no intention of doing so now. The most important thing in her life had always been her work, and she deliberately avoided relationships to keep her focus where it should be. She wouldn't let her attraction to Gavin interfere with what she needed to do.

And the first thing she needed to do was get out of bed and start her day. Gavin said they would talk today and she could only hope for the best.

It was early evening when Gavin finally opened his eyes and he immediately thought about the woman staying in the party house. The woman he'd kissed last night.

Layla had mated her tongue to his with an intensity that made every muscle in his body throb. It was as if she had just as much passion bottled up inside as he did. And he'd unleashed it all with that kiss.

He would love to pick up where they'd left off last night. Take the passion to a whole new level. That made him think of other things…like making love to Layla. How it would feel to run his hands through her hair, lock his mouth and his body to hers. Become immersed in all that sexual energy they seemed to generate. He got hard just thinking about the possibilities.

Gavin glanced over at the clock. He had slept the day away, but he had needed the sleep. Images of Layla had sneaked into the deep recesses of his mind, whether he had wanted them to or not. She'd been in his dreams.

He wanted her.

There. He'd confirmed it in his mind without an ounce of regret. He was a man with needs and that kiss last night had totally obliterated any desire for the Mississippi vixen. He'd lost interest in heading south as planned. Nor did he want Layla to leave the ranch. But like she'd reminded him last night, unless he agreed to let her dig on the property, she had no reason to stay.

That meant he had to come up with a plan.

He rubbed sleep from his eyes, remembering that he had detected a few insecurities lurking within Layla last night. Something about her need to prove herself. What was that about? Did he really want to know? Did he even care?

Yes, he cared. He would go so far as to say that he even admired her spunk. Layla was tough and he had a feeling he hadn't even seen half the strength she possessed. She had to be resilient to have become a college professor at such a young age. He could see her holding her own when it mattered. He couldn't help but smile when he recalled her saying that he needed to keep sex out of this situation. Little did she know he had no intention of doing that. Their attraction was too strong and he intended to use it to his advantage.

As he stood to head for the bathroom, he halted upon hearing voices. They were his grandmother's and Layla's. His body immediately reacted to the sound of Layla's voice. They were in the kitchen. And he could tell his grandmother was enjoying the conversation.

He could understand why Gramma Mel was so taken with Layla. Although he never thought about it much, his grandmother probably got lonely around here whenever he was away. Even though she had Caldwell, there hadn't been another woman staying on the Silver Spurs since Gavin's mother had left.

He tried pushing thoughts of Jamie Blake from his mind like he'd always done. Why should he think about the woman who hadn't thought of him? One day she'd packed up and left, drove away leaving only a letter claiming she needed time away and would return. She never did. That's what had bothered Gavin the most, knowing a woman could just walk away from her husband and eight-year-old son without looking back.

Refusing to think about his mother anymore, Gavin

entered his bathroom to shower. He hoped Layla stayed in the kitchen with his grandmother for a while because he definitely needed to talk to her.

Layla's hand tightened on her glass of iced tea the moment Gavin entered the kitchen. She didn't have to glance behind her to know he was there. His presence filled the room and sent all kinds of sensations vibrating through her. She was a little irritated that she was so aware of him. The sexual chemistry she'd hoped was a fluke was back in full force.

"Gavin, I figured the smell of food would wake you sooner or later," Melody Blake said, smiling at her grandson.

When he moved into Layla's line of vision she had no choice but to glance over at him. "Yes, it definitely did," he said, answering his grandmother but staring straight at Layla.

Then he spoke to her. "Layla. How are you today?"

She wanted to tell him she'd been fine until he'd made an appearance. She couldn't stop her gaze from roaming all over him. He stood near the window and the fading afternoon light highlighted his features, his clothing, everything about him. Not for the first time, Layla thought he had to be the sexiest man alive.

When he lifted a brow, she realized she had yet to answer his question. "I'm fine, Gavin. Thanks for asking."

She quickly switched her gaze away from him and back to her plate. Why had she waited so long to answer? Doing so had made it obvious she'd been checking him out. Thoroughly.

"I left your food warming in the oven, Gavin," Ms. Melody said, breaking the tension.

"Thanks, Gramma Mel. All I've been able to think

about these last few days was getting back to your home-cooked meals." Gavin opened the oven to peek inside.

After getting his plate out of the oven, he smiled at Layla and crossed the kitchen to sit in the chair beside her, brushing his thigh against hers. He said grace and then lifted his head and looked over at Layla. He caught her staring at him again. She knew his touch had been no accident. Totally deliberate.

He pasted an innocent smile on his face and asked, "So, Layla, how was your day?"

Layla gritted her teeth. The nerve of him asking how her day had gone when she'd been waiting to meet with him. She hadn't mentioned anything about Gavin's visit last night to Ms. Melody. There was no way Layla could have mentioned it with a straight face, especially when she couldn't help thinking of the kiss they'd shared.

Knowing he was waiting for her response, she said, "My day has been going great."

"Gavin, I'm glad I got to say hello before I leave," his grandmother said, standing to her feet.

Gavin looked at his grandmother. "Where are you going?"

"The civic center. It's bingo night and Viola is picking me up. She should be here any minute."

It suddenly occurred to Layla that she would be left alone with Gavin. That shouldn't be a big deal since they still needed to talk, but it was. Already nerves stirred in the pit of her stomach.

"We'll take care of the kitchen," she heard Gavin say. "Layla and I need to talk anyway."

Ms. Melody looked back and forth at the two of them before directing her gaze to her grandson. "I think that's a good idea." At the sound of the car horn, a smile touched her lips. "That's Viola."

Before Layla and Gavin could tell her goodbye, Melody Blake had grabbed her purse and was out the door.

That's when Gavin turned his attention back to Layla.

When Gavin saw Layla loading her dishes into the sink, he said, "You don't have to help me with the dishes."

She shrugged her shoulders. "I don't mind."

Her back was to him and he couldn't stop his gaze from covering every inch of her backside, wrapped tight in her skirt. And before she'd left the table, more than once he'd checked out her pink blouse, noticing the deep V neck. There was nothing like seeing a little of a woman's cleavage every now and then. Made him wonder what her breasts looked like. How they would feel in his hands. Taste in his mouth.

"Your grandmother forgot to mention she made a dessert," Layla said, breaking into his thoughts and turning around to meet his gaze.

"What is it?"

"Peach cobbler. Do you want some?"

That question was not one she should be asking him. Not when he had an erection nearly hard enough to burst out of his jeans. Yes, he wanted some, but his thoughts weren't on the peach cobbler.

Why did the picture of her standing at his grandmother's sink make a pang of desire shoot through him? The hair she'd worn down and around her shoulders yesterday was now confined in a ponytail. It wouldn't take much to walk across the room and set it free. After doing that, he would proceed to do all kinds of naughty things to her. Gavin shifted in his seat to relieve the pressure against his zipper.

"Yeah, I'd love to have some," he said in a deep, husky voice. And he knew Layla had figured out they weren't talking about peach cobbler.

She didn't say anything, just stared at him. He wished she didn't look so damn sexy while she sized him up, trying to figure him out. There wasn't much to find out on that score. He was a horny bastard and would remain so until he'd taken care of his sexual needs. That meant they needed to talk, and the sooner the better.

"We can talk while eating peach cobbler," he said.

Layla seemed relieved to finally begin their discussion and returned to the table with two plates of peach cobbler. "Where do we start?" she asked, sliding one of the plates in front of him before sitting down.

He picked up his fork and looked over at her. "We can start by talking about us."

Her expression clearly said that wasn't what she thought they should be talking about. "We agreed to discuss the dig and not this thing between us."

Gavin wondered if Layla knew that "this thing" actually had a name. It was called physical desire. "I think we should talk about us before discussing the dig."

She gave him an annoyed look. "Why? I told you last night we needed to keep sex out of it."

Yes, she had said that, but did she actually think they could keep sex out of it when there was so much chemistry between them? So much that even now he would have no problem taking her right here on this damn table? "You're an intelligent woman, Layla. I'm sure you're well aware of how the human body operates. All of us have needs."

"Speak for yourself, Gavin."

He watched her nervously gnaw on her lower lip and heated lust danced up his spine. He was trying like hell to figure her out. Was she denying she had needs, as well? He knew from last night's kiss that that was a lie. Her denial made Gavin wonder about her experience level.

"Are you saying you don't want to have sex with me?"

As if the question shot her to full awareness, she leaned

over the table and glared at him. "I don't want to have sex with you, Gavin. I don't want to have sex with anybody. All I want is to do my job. A job you refuse to let me do."

They weren't getting anywhere. For some reason he didn't want to talk to her about the dig until he found out why she kept certain emotions in check. So he tried another approach.

"Tell me about yourself, Layla."

Layla lifted a brow. That was clearly not what she'd expected. "I graduated from high school at sixteen and immediately went to college. Graduated with my bachelor's degree in history, then went on to get a master's in archaeology. My doctorate is in both history and archaeology."

"And you're just twenty-six?"

"Yes. I went to college year-round. I've worked on dig sites as an undergrad and while working toward my PhD so this won't be my first excavation."

"But it will be the first one you've been in charge of, right?"

"Yes, that's true."

He leaned back in his chair, deciding to keep her talking about the dig for a while, after all. He doubted she realized that whenever she talked about her work she lowered her guard. "So you admit you're inexperienced."

Layla frowned. He could tell she wasn't sure if they were still talking about the dig. "I don't think of myself as inexperienced, Gavin, so you shouldn't think that, either."

"Then tell me what I should think."

After several moments, she said, "You should focus on the fact that my being here is the result of several years of research. I didn't just wake up one morning and decide to do this. I've tracked each and every one of James's bank robberies in this area. Mapped out every possible trail he could have taken, every single place he and the gang could have hidden out. Then I obtained records of this land and the surrounding properties. I had my team digitally re-create how this area would have looked back then.

"The Silver Spurs would have been the ideal place to stop over because of the low-hanging trees. And the lake between here and the Lotts' spread would have allowed the gang time to wash away their scent and stay hidden from the sheriff's posse. I could even see James's gang being smart enough to use a decoy to send the posse racing in another direction. One away from here to give them time to bury their loot and lighten their load."

Gavin was trying not to get caught up in the sound of her voice. He wanted to hear the words she was saying. She was excited about her work and discussing it energized her. He couldn't help noticing the glow in her eyes, the confidence in her voice, the smile on her lips. The same lips he had tasted last night.

She was trying like hell to convince him that she was onto something, that she had researched her findings and believed in everything she was telling him. He knew there had to be a number of doubters…like himself.

When she stopped talking, he shifted his gaze from her lips to her eyes. "I take it you've already surveyed the area, used ground penetrating radar on the location already."

She nodded. If she was surprised by his knowledge of her preliminary assessment, she didn't show it. "I've gone further. I was able to get an infrared spectrum."

He lifted a brow. "How?"

"One of my students is big into digital technology and created it for me. That's the advantage I have over others working on this subject, I'm bringing this excavation into the digital age."

The technological aspect was an area Gavin was somewhat familiar with. The military already used all sorts of futuristic developments. It was important whenever they were sent into enemy territory that they didn't step on booby traps or buried explosives.

She looked at him expectantly, as if he would question what she said. He merely nodded. "I'm familiar with the use of high-tech digital to detect buried items."

She smiled, obviously glad that he was following her. "All the equipment my team and I use is state-of-the-art, some have never before been used in an archaeological context and they were developed exclusively for this dig by students in my department," she said proudly.

Because she was young he couldn't imagine her getting others to rally behind her for the cause. Whether she knew it or not, that spoke volumes about her character as a leader. It would take a strong individual to coax others on board. He knew how that could be.

"It's too late today but tomorrow I want to check out the area you've targeted." What she would discover was that he also had a high-tech camera, one designed by Flipper for marine purposes. However, it had proven effective at detecting objects underground, as well.

"Alright."

He heard the hope in her voice and figured that was because he'd shown interest in the dig site. She probably thought he was almost on board. That wasn't the case. But he wouldn't tell her that yet.

When he didn't say anything else for a while, she lifted a brow and looked over at him. She even had a little smile on her face. That glow brightening her eyes almost undid him. "Any more questions, Gavin?"

There was something else; something he had to know. "Yes, but not about the dig. It's something about you that I want to know."

"What?" she asked, lifting an arched brow.

He held her gaze steadily. "When was the last time you made love with a man?"

Four

Layla gaped, certain Gavin hadn't asked her what she thought he'd asked her. What man would inquire that of a woman…especially one he'd known barely twenty-four hours? However, from the look on his face, he evidently saw nothing wrong with the question. He was sitting there waiting on an answer.

She lifted her chin and crossed her arms over her chest. When she saw his gaze shift from her eyes to her upraised breasts, she dropped her hands. "Do you actually expect me to answer that?" Somehow she managed to get the words past a constricted throat. The way he stared at her was making her head spin.

He shrugged massive broad shoulders. "Don't know why not. We're sexually attracted to each other. Just want to know what I'm dealing with when we decide to go for it and take the edge off."

Go for it? Take the edge off? Layla shook her head, clearly missing something. She knew they were attracted to each other; she got that. What she didn't get was him thinking that attraction meant they would eventually decide to "go for it." She had no intention of going anywhere. She was here to do a job and not indulge his fantasies… or her own, for that matter.

"I think you need to explain what exactly you're getting at. We agreed to keep sex out of this, Gavin."

"I didn't agree to any such thing. You suggested it but I didn't agree to it. Why would I?"

"Why wouldn't you?" she countered, not understanding his way of thinking.

He leaned back in his chair and her gaze watched his every movement. Restrained and controlled. She wondered if his actions were intentional, to put her off-kilter. When he picked up his glass of tea, her gaze automatically shifted to his hands. They were large and callous. They were the same hands that had sent shivers up her spine last night.

Memories of their kiss suddenly bombarded her and then her gaze shifted to his mouth as he took a swallow of iced tea. She was drawn to the way his mouth covered the rim of the glass and the way the liquid flowed down his throat. But what really got to her was the way he licked his lips afterward. When he caught her staring, those penetrating eyes darkened as they held hers.

"Want some?"

She snatched her gaze away. The lump in her throat thickened. She was glad to be sitting down; otherwise it would have been impossible to stand on both feet. The look he was giving her had her weak in the knees.

Somehow she managed to clear the lump in her throat and hold up her glass. "No thanks, I have my own."

His eyes blazed as they continued to hold hers. "I wasn't offering you any of my tea, Layla."

She sucked in a deep breath. He couldn't have set her

straight any plainer than that. There was no need to ask what he was offering. That was the moment she knew Gavin Blake intended to be a problem. One she needed to deal with here and now.

"You never did answer my earlier question. When was the last time you were with a man?"

She set her glass of tea back down on the table. "And you never answered mine about why you wouldn't agree to keep sex out of it." Feeling flustered, she added, "We need to talk."

A smile touched the corners of his lips. "I thought that's what we were doing."

There was no way he could have thought that. What he was doing was deliberately getting her all unglued. If he thought for one minute his arrogant behavior would make her run, then he didn't know her very well. "There seems to be some sort of misunderstanding here."

"Is there?"

"Undoubtedly. I'm here to do a job…that is, if you let me stay to do it. But under no circumstances am I here for your pleasure, Gavin. I don't play those kinds of games. Evidently just because we shared a kiss last night, you've gotten the wrong idea about me. I need to set the record straight now. So hear me and hear me good." She leaned part of the way over the table toward him. Although his face was void of any expression, she was certain she had his undivided attention.

"I am *not* here to engage in an affair with you, if that's why you want to know about my sex life." *Or lack thereof.* But that was something he didn't need to know.

Gavin didn't say anything. He knew she assumed his attention was on her words. In truth his attention was on the mouth delivering those words. Her lips were perfectly shaped with a little cute dip in the center. He liked the play of that mutinous tip whenever she frowned and how those same lips folded pensively when she appeared in deep thought. But more than anything, he couldn't forget how those lips felt beneath his. Their lushness. How delicious they'd tasted. How sweet.

When she got quiet after delivering her spiel, he figured she thought she had set him straight. Far from it and it was time to let her know where he stood. "Are you finished?"

She seemed surprised by his question, but nodded nonetheless and said, "Yes, I'm finished." She then straightened in her chair, her posture a lot more relaxed than it had been moments ago.

"Evidently, there's a lot you don't understand about sex, Layla."

Her body tensed again. And somehow those gorgeous lips looked even more sensual. "What's there to understand?" she asked.

Gavin continued to study her. He saw her nonchalant expression and noted her features had taken on a blasé look. Her apparent indifference to this discussion of sex could mean only one thing. She'd been cheated of something he considered as vital as breathing. Reaching her level of success in such a short period of time meant something had been sacrificed. An active sex life, perhaps?

"I want you and you want me," he said, deciding to point out the obvious.

"And?"

He forced himself not to smile, thinking she was pretending not to have a clue. Then it occurred to him that maybe she wasn't pretending. Maybe it was time to explain to her what it meant whenever a woman became the object of his personal fantasies.

"And..." he said, "we *will* sleep together."

She sat up in her chair, straightening her spine. Her

lips went from sensual to tense but turned him on even more just the same. "No, we will not," she said adamantly.

He smiled. "Yes, we will. It's inevitable."

She frowned. "No, it's not. Just who do you think you are?"

He figured it was time she knew the answer to that. "A man who wants you. A man who intends to have you. A man who will show you, Layla Harris, just what you've been missing."

Layla tried to keep her heart from pounding deep in her chest, while at the same time fighting off the heat stroking through her body. She knew she shouldn't ask but she couldn't hold back.

"And just what do you think I've missed?"

"Hot, raunchy, mind-blowing sex. Evidently over the years you've been too preoccupied with other things to indulge. Don't you know it's not good to deprive your body of meeting certain needs?"

Her frown deepened. "I haven't deprived my body of anything."

"Haven't you? Why do you think you're so attracted to me?"

Layla actually rolled her eyes. Really? Honestly? Had he looked in the mirror lately? When was the last time he'd studied all those photos Ms. Melody had plastered on the walls. Any woman would be attracted to him. Even now he sat there not doing anything and still looked sexy as hell with that well-toned body of his. And here she was sitting across the table from him. Right within kissing distance.

As far as she was concerned, Gavin Blake was eye candy of the richest kind. Passion personified. But she definitely wouldn't tell him that. She would deny everything he'd said with her last breath if she had to.

"I am not all that attracted to you." At least she hadn't completely lied and said she wasn't attracted to him at all.

"You want me to prove otherwise?"

What was it with men always wanting to prove things when it came to sex? "No, thanks. That's not necessary."

"I think that it is."

He'd said the words in a low, vibrating tone with a sexy rumble she wished she could ignore. But there was no way, what with all the shivers oozing down her spine. "Are you trying to scare me off, Gavin?"

He lifted a brow. "Scare you off?"

"Yes. Say all these things so I get angry enough to leave the ranch, sparing you the trouble of making a decision one way or the other about whether I can dig on your land or not."

"Is that what you think?"

To be honest, she didn't know what to think. She needed his land and all he had on his mind was sex. That made her wonder…

"Then are you trying to box me into a corner? Implying that I will have to sleep with you before you'll give me permission to dig?"

Gavin shook his head. "I would never put pressure on you to sleep with me. But be forewarned, Layla. If you hang around here doing that dig, we *will* sleep together. There's no way we won't. Your own body will betray you. When it does, I will be ready for the opportunity."

Seriously? If he thought her body would eventually weaken, he didn't know her. And that was the point, one she couldn't lose sight of. He *didn't* know her. He didn't know about her dedication when it came to her work. Nor did he know of her ability to be single-minded when it came to her career goals. She could put everything out of her mind except what was most important. She was driven to be successful in her field, and she wouldn't let Gavin—or any other man—stand in her way.

He was pretty sure of himself where women were concerned. A man couldn't look like him, be built like him, and not be in demand and get any woman he wanted. All Gavin had to do was snap his fingers and she figured the women came running. Being denied anything from a woman would be foreign to him.

"Think whatever you want, Gavin, but I'm not the kind of woman you're used to. I won't break."

He rubbed his hand over his chin as he studied her. "Would you want to bet on that?"

Layla frowned. She had no intention of betting on anything and she proceeded to tell him that. He only smiled, and it was one of those smiles she was getting to know too well. The one that made her body sizzle when it should make her angry. His smile all but said he had her where he wanted her.

"Would you be willing to bet on it to guarantee your dig on the Silver Spurs?"

That piqued her interest. "Depending on what you have in mind." She hoped she was not setting herself up for something she would regret.

Gavin held back his *gotcha* smile. Little did Layla know but his teammates didn't call him Viper for nothing. To some, a viper might be considered a spiteful or treacherous person, but for him the name meant he knew how to capture his prey using any means necessary. Striking when they least expected it. He wanted her in his bed willingly and he intended to do whatever it took to get her there. It was time to push his agenda.

"I'm willing to make a deal, Layla."

"What sort of a deal?" She held his gaze.

Did she know how beautiful her facial features were?

How striking her bone structure? He could sit for hours and stare, taking her in. But doing so would make him want her even more than he already did. Before he'd met her, he couldn't have imagined that degree of need for any woman. But he could imagine it for her.

He lifted his shoulder in a half shrug as if what he was about to say wasn't of grave importance. As if he really didn't care one way or the other if she took the deal or left it on the table.

"I'm not as convinced about this buried loot as you and my grandmother seem to be," he said. "And I doubt reading any report will make me change my mind. But wanting you in my bed will," he said bluntly, needing her to fully understand what he was saying.

"This is the deal," he continued. "I will let you dig, regardless of what I think. If you find something, great. You will have proven me wrong. I will be happy for you. Be the first to congratulate you on a job well done. However, if you come up with nothing then you admit you want me as much as I want you and we sleep together."

"You are counting on me failing? And plan to take advantage of me if I do?"

The thought was firing her up. He could tell. The flash of fire in her eyes told it all. "You shouldn't worry about failing. Unless you think you will. If there's some doubt in your mind regarding the accuracy of your research, then I understand if—"

"My research is on point. There's no doubt in my mind about anything."

His smile spread across his lips. "In that case, do we have a deal?"

Five

At that moment Layla realized just what was going on. Whether it was his intent or not, Gavin was forcing her to believe in herself, to prove that she was right in her belief that Jesse James had buried treasure on Gavin's land.

"Well?"

The determination was clear in his eyes. He intended to sleep with her. She was just as determined that he wouldn't. She didn't like the deal he'd offered. In all honesty, she should be appalled by it. Instead she saw it as her chance to prove she was above the desire he couldn't stop talking about. She would find Jesse James's loot. She had no doubts. There was no need getting irritated that he was a typical male who thought a good roll between the sheets was the answer to everything. She would never be able to convince him that when it came to sex, she had always been able to take it or leave it, no matter how tempting it was to indulge. He would find that out for himself.

She'd be free to run her dig and make the finding of not only her career but of a lifetime. She wouldn't think about the traitorous voice that said it might be nice to lose this bet and get the consolation prize…

"Fine."

He lifted his brow. "Does that mean you accept the deal?"

"As long as you give me your word you won't try to hinder me and my team in any way."

"I wouldn't do that."

Yeah. Right. There was no reason for her to trust he wouldn't do just about anything to make sure the result worked out in his favor. Another typical male trait. No man liked losing. "Whatever you say."

"You're going to have to trust me."

Layla rolled her eyes. "Sorry to disappoint you, but I don't know you enough to trust you."

"I can remedy that."

"Don't do me any favors." Layla eased out of her chair, feeling like she'd mentally run a marathon. "So will you give me your word as a SEAL that you won't try anything underhanded?"

"You think my word as a SEAL means something?"

"Yes. SEALs are a special team of men who take the job of protecting our country very seriously, and they live by a code of honor and integrity."

Gavin nodded. She was right. "And you know this how?"

"My father's cousin used to be a SEAL. He retired a few years ago, but he told us all about them. At least what he could share. A lot of the stuff he did was classified."

"The majority of our missions are," Gavin said.

"So, will you give me your word?"

"Yes, you have my word."

* * *

As far as Gavin was concerned, getting her into his bed before the dig began would not be interfering with the job she wanted to do.

"Good." She glanced at her watch. "It's getting late. I'm sure you need more sleep. However, if you need help with the dishes, then I—"

"No, I don't need help with the dishes. That's what dishwashers are for."

"Do you still want to see where we plan to dig?"

"Yes. I want to know what you have planned on my property and where."

"No problem."

"Then I'll come by the cottage in the morning," he said, standing, as well. "Come on. I'll walk you back."

She shook her head as she put on her sweater. "That's not necessary."

"It is for me, Layla. I'll walk you back."

She didn't deny him, maybe she didn't want to appear ungrateful. She headed for the door and when she reached out to open it, he moved his hand forward, as well. She didn't seem aware that he'd been standing so close behind her. His fingers closed over hers and his chest was flush against her back.

"I can open the door, Gavin," she said, glancing over her shoulder, obviously flustered at his nearness. He loomed over her five-foot-three-inch height. He stood so close he could smell her with every breath.

"Your choice." Releasing his hand from hers he eased back. She opened the door and inhaled the cool Missouri air.

"Nice night, isn't it?" he asked her. He walked beside her now.

"Yes, it is a nice night." She glanced over at him again. "Glad to be home?"

A smile touched his lips. "Yes. It's always good to be home. Time to go from SEAL to rancher."

"Is it that easy?"

"I'm used to it now. I have good men working for me who make the transition less difficult."

She nodded. "You love being a SEAL?"

"Yes."

"I understand your father and grandfather were SEALs."

Gavin wondered what else his grandmother had told her about their family. "Yes, they were SEALs. So I guess you can say it's in my blood. What about your folks? Are they college professors like you?"

"No. They're both neurosurgeons. I didn't follow in their footsteps. Medicine didn't interest me."

He hadn't asked her to explain, but the fact that she did led him to believe her choice of a career was a sore spot with someone. "You are your own person, Layla." She was definitely her own woman, he thought further to himself. "Just because following in my father's and grandfather's footsteps worked for me, doesn't mean following family tradition works for everybody."

She didn't say anything for a minute. "My parents wanted me to be a mini-them and go to medical school. But I couldn't. I'm not a healer. I'm a historian."

"Then you did the right thing by following your heart. When did you decide on archaeology?" Gavin wondered if she noted how in sync their steps were.

"In my junior year of high school." She paused as if she was remembering. "My history teacher had gone on an excavation in Egypt the summer before and told us about it. I found it fascinating how her team was able to dig up artifacts, how they found history buried beneath the earth's surface. It made me realize that's what I wanted to do."

"Why Jesse James?"

He heard her chuckle and the sound stimulated him in a way he wished it didn't. "Why *not* Jesse James?" He heard the amusement in her tone. "I used to watch Westerns with my grandfather whenever I visited him in New Orleans. He was a fan of the outlaw Jesse James. He read a lot of books about him. Watched movies and documentaries. I shared his love and interest. That's how my research began. And it's only grown over the years."

He heard the passion for her subject in her voice. It was there whenever she spoke about her work. She believed in it. If there had been any doubt in his mind before, there wasn't now. She would risk sleeping with him to prove her work.

She'd be disappointed not to find what she was searching for. But Gavin looked forward to helping her get over the disappointment. He didn't believe for one minute that James's loot was buried on this land. It wasn't. He recalled years ago when he'd been in high school, his father had given some outfit permission to check out the land because there was a chance of finding oil. They'd come up with nothing then, and he was certain Layla and her team would come up with nothing now.

"I guess this is where we need to say good-night."

They had reached the party house. Her words told him he wouldn't be invited inside. Maybe that was for the best. He doubted he could keep his hands off of her if they were behind closed doors. And regardless of what she thought, she wouldn't resist him. Last night's kiss had proven that. He wasn't worried about the outcome of the deal between them. Like he'd told her, eventually her body would betray her and she would break. What had happened in his grandmother's kitchen when their hands touched at the door was a prime example of the intensity of the desire between them.

"So what time do you want us to meet tomorrow?" she asked, reclaiming his attention.

"I need to ride out with Caldwell and my men at the crack of dawn to check on a few things. I'll be back around ten. Will that time work for you?"

"Yes."

"Good. We can ride in my truck."

"Alright. Good night."

She turned toward the door, intent on opening it quickly and going inside. He was just as determined not to let her get away that easily. Reaching out, he wrapped his arms around her waist and tugged her close to him.

"What do you think you're doing, Gavin?"

"This."

Lowering his head, he claimed her mouth in a long, passionate kiss. She didn't push him away. Instead, she pulled him closer. Emotions he hadn't expected pushed him to let her know with this kiss just how much he wanted her.

The kiss they'd shared last night had been a game changer. This one sealed their fate.

Gavin knew at that moment that kissing her would never be enough. What he really wanted to do was sweep her off her feet, open the damn door and head straight to the bedroom. But he couldn't do that.

He wanted her to admit how much she wanted him, too. He'd give her time; he'd remember their deal. The one he had initiated. The one he intended to end in his favor. There was no way she would leave the Silver Spurs without them making love.

He finally broke off the kiss. As he drew in a deep breath he watched her draw in one, as well. Studying her mouth, he saw her lips were wet and swollen, and he had to fight back the urge to kiss her again.

"Why did you kiss me?" she asked, touching her finger to her lips.

He smiled, tempted to replace her finger with the tip of his tongue. "For the same reason you let me kiss you. I want you and you want me."

From the look he saw in her eyes, he knew she was angry. Why? Because he'd stated facts when she preferred hiding behind denials?

"I'm going inside now."

"I'll see you in the morning around ten."

She nodded, then quickly opened the door and went inside. When the door closed behind her, Gavin shoved his hands into the pockets of his jeans and headed back toward the main house. He knew she was confused. Confusion came with the territory when you tried to deny the truth of your feelings. However, she was smart. He knew she would figure it out. Eventually she would see things the way he did.

He would make sure of it.

Six

Layla, feeling tousled from a restless night, stepped out on the porch with a cup of coffee in her hand. She took a sip. She needed the hot liquid as much as she needed more sleep. Kissing Gavin was hazardous to her health when the aftereffect was a frazzled mind.

What could she have been thinking to agree to the deal he'd put on the table? What woman in her right mind would agree to have sex with a man who counted on her to fail at the most important project of her life? She kept assuring herself that she had nothing to worry about because her research wasn't wrong.

But what if it was?

She shook her head, refusing to second-guess herself or allow something as insignificant as sex to undermine her confidence in years of research. She lifted the cup to her lips again, took another sip and smiled. She couldn't wait to show Gavin just how wrong he was. She would leave the Silver Spurs with Jesse James's loot *and* she'd keep Gavin out of her panties.

She glanced over at the main house and tried to ignore the heat that settled in her stomach. Ms. Melody had called to invite Layla to breakfast, but she'd declined saying she needed to read over a few reports. The last thing Layla wanted was to run into Gavin. She would see him at ten and that suited her just fine. The man had a way of making her distracted.

And then there was that kiss she couldn't stop thinking about. The one that still had her lips tingling this morning. While getting dressed she'd tried to convince herself not to worry about that kiss—not to worry about anything, especially not Gavin Blake. Agreeing to his deal meant nothing more than a reason to work harder to find James's stash. She hadn't lied to Ms. Melody. Layla had used this morning to review several documents. It was important to make sure she hadn't missed anything in her research.

Layla checked her watch. Gavin would be arriving in an hour. That wasn't a lot of time to prepare to see him again. But then she doubted she would ever be prepared for the likes of Gavin Blake.

"So what have you decided about the dig, Gavin?"

Gavin glanced up from his breakfast plate and met his grandmother's eyes. He'd been in bed when she'd returned last night, but there was no getting out of the conversation this morning. One thing was for certain, he would not tell her about the deal he'd struck with Layla.

"Layla is showing me the site this morning. I want to check it out for myself before I make a decision." He then resumed eating, hoping to end the conversation.

"So when are you leaving for Mississippi?"

He looked up at his grandmother again with a raised brow. "Who said anything about me going to Mississippi?"

She lifted her own brow. “Yesterday you mentioned you had important business to take care of there.”

Now he recalled mentioning it. “I changed my mind and won’t be leaving after all.” He resumed eating again, knowing his grandmother was eyeing him suspiciously.

“Why?”

He lifted his head again. “Why, what?”

“Why are you hanging around here?”

He held her inquisitive gaze. “Do you have a problem with me hanging around here, Gramma Mel?”

“Not as long as you don’t have some shenanigans brewing in that head of yours, Gavin.”

If only you knew, he thought. He pushed his plate away. “Breakfast was good as usual. I’m surprised you didn’t invite Layla to join us.”

“I did. But she made an excuse for not coming. I wonder why.”

He stood. His grandmother was fishing for information and he was determined not to get caught. “I have a call with Phil to go over the books. I’ll be in my office for an hour or so.”

“Alright. And you may have changed your mind about going to Mississippi, but I’m still scheduled to go to that library conference in Cincinnati. It lasts a week, and I booked it before I knew you were coming home.”

Gavin knew his grandmother enjoyed going to those conferences. “You should go,” he encouraged.

She looked at him as if he wasn’t trustworthy…of all things. “Is anything wrong?” he asked her.

“You tell me, Gavin. You’re not fooling me one bit. I know that look. You’re up to something and whatever it is, I hope you don’t get caught in your own trap.”

“What trap?”

“I’ll let you figure that one out. But keep something in mind.”

He lifted a brow. “What?”

“Layla is not Jamie.”

He frowned deeply. “What is that supposed to mean?”

“It means I think something good could develop between the two of you, if you let it. But you won’t. You’re afraid she will be like Jamie. Whether you choose to believe me or not, your mom loved you and your dad. I would sit and hear her crying for him at night when he was gone.”

“Then why did she leave?”

“Loneliness drove her away, Gavin. The Silver Spurs isn’t meant for everyone and she was miserable here. Not everyone can handle the isolation.”

“But that was no reason for her to desert me and Dad.”

Without saying anything else he turned and walked out of the kitchen toward his office.

A lump formed in Layla’s throat when she heard the knock at the door. She didn’t have to look out of the peephole to see who it was. Gavin had said he would arrive at ten and it was ten on the dot. She glanced down at herself and then wished she hadn’t. Why should she care what he thought about how she looked today? And why had she decided to wear her hair down instead of back in a ponytail?

She opened the door and Gavin stood leaning in the doorway. He filled the space, looking like he needed to be some woman’s breakfast, lunch and dinner. Why did the man have to be so over-the-top gorgeous? Why did she want to drool, drool, and then drool some more?

And why did she want to snatch him inside and have her way with him?

She had no right to think any of those things, no right to fantasize. She had to stay focused on her work. “Good morning. I’m ready,” she said, grabbing her jacket. He moved aside when she stepped out and closed the door behind herself.

"Good morning, Layla. I hope you slept well," Gavin said as they walked off the porch.

He slid his hand to her elbow to help her down the steps and she wished he hadn't. Immediately, a spike of desire shot through her and she was tempted to snatch her arm away.

"Nice day, isn't it?"

"Yes, it's nice." She glanced over at him as he kept his hand on her elbow while he led her to his truck and opened the door.

"And speaking of nice," he said, gripping her elbow a little tighter as he helped her up into the passenger seat. "You look good this morning. Real nice."

"Thank you."

He closed the truck door and as she watched him move around the front of the truck to the driver's side, she couldn't help thinking that he looked pretty good himself. Real nice. A pair of jeans hugged masculine thighs, a pullover sweater and a leather bomber jacket with the crest of a SEAL on the back graced broad shoulders. In her book there was something about a man who wore a leather bomber jacket, whether he was a biker, a model or a navy SEAL.

She kept her gaze trained on him. When he opened the door and slid onto the leather seat, she couldn't help but appreciate how the fit of his jeans tightened on his thighs.

"You went riding around your ranch dressed like that?"

"No. We finished early so I had time to change before joining my grandmother for breakfast. She missed your presence at breakfast by the way."

"I told her about the report I had to review this morning."

He didn't say anything and she wondered if he believed her.

"You okay?"

It was only then that she realized she was still staring. She snatched her gaze away from his thighs, regretting that he'd caught her ogling him. "I'm fine."

A smile curved his lips and her insides felt like they'd turned to mush. "Just checking," he said, snapping his seat belt in place. "I don't want you to start admitting you want me anytime soon."

Layla frowned, remembering what he'd said last night. "Trust me. That won't be happening." She spoke with a degree of confidence she wasn't feeling, especially when he shifted gears, causing those thighs to catch her attention again.

She forced her gaze out the window to view the pastures, valleys and hills they passed. Not for the first time, she thought the Silver Spurs was beautiful. Already they'd passed the new barn and several other smaller buildings. And there were several fenced rolling plains filled with cows. The sun peeked through a bevy of trees that layered the countryside and she knew it would be a beautiful day even with the chill in the air.

"Sleep well?"

She glanced over at him, wondering why he would ask. Did he assume that she hadn't? Well, she intended to crush that assumption right then and there. "Yes, like a baby, straight through the night." Maybe she'd laid it on too thick since most babies didn't sleep straight through the night.

"Glad to hear it. So did I. I slept so well that I almost overslept this morning." He didn't say anything for a minute. "Which way?"

She lifted a brow. "What?"

"Directions. Gramma Mel said the spot is just past the old barn. Which way do I go after that?"

The barn he was talking about was a big empty building painted red. According to Ms. Melody, it hadn't been used in years but the structure looked sound. More than once

Layla had been tempted to take a peek inside but the doors were bolted up. She wondered if Gavin would allow them to keep their excavation equipment stored there. Since he seemed in a pretty good mood this morning, it might be a good time to ask. “And about that old barn?”

“What about it?”

“I’m going to need a place to store my heavy equipment, like the loader backhoe and tractor, for the excavation. May I use the old barn?”

He glanced over at her and she could imagine what he was thinking. Why should he do anything to help her when he was counting on her to fail? He surprised her when he said, “Yes, you can use the old barn.”

She smiled. Since he was being so generous she decided to go for the gusto. “There’s also a smaller building next to the barn. I understand it used to be the old bunkhouse.”

“What about it?”

“May I use that, as well? I’ll need somewhere to test soil samples and such.”

He looked at her again. “Are you trying to take advantage of my kindness, Layla?”

“Yes, I guess I am, Gavin.”

A husky chuckle escaped his lips. “At least you’re honest. Yes, you can use that old shack, as well.”

“Thank you.”

“You’re welcome.”

She didn’t say anything for a minute as they drove. “Make a left turn at the next tree and drive another couple of miles,” she said. “You can park in the clearing next to the stumps. I’ve marked the exact spot where we’ll be digging.”

“Okay.”

The rest of the drive was done in silence. She was glad when he finally brought the truck to a stop a short while later.

* * *

Gavin drew in a deep breath. With his hands still gripping the steering wheel he stared straight ahead at the view out of the windshield. He needed to get his bearings. Everything about Layla was getting to him. The way she looked, her scent, the way she wore her hair. The way that same hair had blown in the wind when his truck whooshed across his property.

"I can tell you miss coming here."

Did she make that assumption because of the way he was still sitting here, trying to keep his mind and body under control? Yet, she was right. He had missed coming here.

"Yes. As a kid I used to come to this area a lot. There's a huge lake not far from here. It separates our land from the Lotts' property and it's on the Lotts' land. But that didn't mean anything to me. Not even the no-swimming-allowed sign Sherman Lott had posted. I used to sneak into the lake and go swimming as a teen every chance I got. On a good day I would swim for hours without getting caught."

"And on a bad day?"

He chuckled. "On a bad day Sherman Lott would call my grandmother and report me for trespassing."

She lifted a brow. "Honestly? He would actually call and tell on you?"

"All the time. He didn't like anyone swimming or fishing in that lake. But I had a lot of years of good fishing there, as well."

He smiled, remembering how defying Mr. Lott had pleased him immensely. "Time to look around. But before we get out there's something we need to do."

She lifted her brow. "What?"

"Kiss. More than anything, I want to kiss you, Layla."

* * *

Layla couldn't believe he'd said that. Kiss? Hadn't they done that enough already? Not that she was counting but he'd kissed her twice. Why was he going for three? Why was she hoping that he would?

"Kiss me?" she asked, softly, hoping he didn't pick up on the yearning in her voice.

"Yes, kiss you. It's either that or talk you into my truck's backseat."

She nibbled on her bottom lip. "And you think doing that will be easy?"

"No, but it will be worth all the effort I plan to put into it. So how about unbuckling that seat belt and leaning a little over here? I promise it will be painless."

Being painless, Layla thought, was the least of her worries. "Haven't you gotten enough? Of kissing me?" she asked, studying the look in his eyes.

"No, I haven't gotten enough, so lean over this way. Let's engage in something pleasurable."

The urgency in his voice was so intense, it sent shivers through her. She knew they shouldn't kiss again. Doing so would lead to assumptions on his part that she'd rather he not have. But she'd had a hard time forgetting how pleasurable their last two kisses had been. Both times his tongue had stroked hers to a feverish pitch, until she had greedily responded.

Frustration spilled from her lungs in a sigh and with very little control left, she unsnapped her seat belt and leaned closer to him. In spite of her misgivings, she was prepared to give him the kiss he wanted because it was a kiss she wanted, as well.

He leaned in to meet her and their lips touched. On her breathless sigh, he slid his tongue inside her mouth and began mating with her tongue. She felt his intensity all the way to her toes.

She wrapped her arms around his neck as he wrapped his arms around her waist. They were sitting in his truck, kissing like oversexed teenagers. Like they had nothing better to do and all day to do it. How crazy was that? But the insanity was lost as she tasted him. He tasted primitive, untamed and wild with lust. How could she detect such a thing in a kiss? Was this a warning that she should back off? That Gavin Blake would be the one man she couldn't ignore?

The latter gave her pause, but not enough to stop her tongue from mingling with his. Not enough to refrain from following his lead when he deepened the kiss. Not enough to stop the moan escaping her throat.

Layla knew then that she was a goner.

Seven

Gavin greedily devoured Layla's mouth. Never before had any woman escalated his arousal to such a state. And never had any woman made him want to kiss her each and every time he saw her.

Every bone and muscle in his body throbbed with a need for her that went beyond desire. Intense heat curled inside of him, threatening his control. And the one thing he was known for was control. So why were his brain cells faltering under the onslaught of such a delicious kiss? Why was his body making urgent demands for him to make love to her right here in his truck? Damn. What could he say?

Nothing. He was totally at a loss for words, which was a good thing since he didn't have time to indulge in any. He preferred using his mouth for this kiss. He intended to get his fill. But a part of him wasn't sure he could ever get his fill of Layla. He saw her and he wanted her. That wasn't good. He had to get control of his body and of the situation. And he needed to do so now.

Gavin reluctantly broke off the kiss. Drawing his mouth away from hers was one of the hardest things he'd had to do. He saw the look of denied need in her eyes before she leaned back, dropped her head against the headrest and closed her eyes. He figured she was as in awe of what just happened as he was.

What they'd shared wasn't just a kiss. It was an acknowledgment of deep sexual desires. He knew what was driving his and he thought he had figured out what was driving hers. She just refused to accept it. She was stubborn. It would take a lot more kisses like this one to bring her around. They'd felt an intense attraction to each other from the first, and from all appearances, things had gotten worse.

He continued to stare at her as heat curled inside of him. He wanted her. Bad. And that pushed him to say, "So tell me again why we can't sleep together."

Layla heard his words but she couldn't respond. Neither could she open her eyes to look at him. There was no point. She knew what she would see in the depths of his dark gaze. A sexual need so hot it was likely to sizzle her insides. It would make her fully aware of her own sexual need. A need he stirred to life inside her whether she wanted him to or not.

"Open your eyes, Layla. I'm not going anywhere."

At least not today. She suddenly remembered Ms. Melody mentioning he had to go to Mississippi on business. "When are you leaving?" she asked, opening her eyes.

Just as she'd expected. The eyes staring at her were dark and seductive.

He lifted a brow. "Leaving for where?"

"Mississippi. Your grandmother mentioned you had important business to take care of there."

"Trying to get rid of me, are you?"

"It wouldn't hurt," she said and saw his eyes get even darker when she moistened her bottom lip with the tip of her tongue. "So when are you leaving?"

He moved his gaze from her mouth to her eyes. "I changed my mind about Mississippi. I'm not leaving here any time soon." She couldn't stop the disappointment that flashed through her.

"But I thought you had important business to take care of."

"My plans have changed. Do you have a problem with that?"

"I just hope you don't plan to get underfoot."

"I'll try not to. Now show me the exact spot where you plan to dig," he said, opening the truck door to get out.

No matter what he said, Layla knew Gavin would try getting underfoot.

When Gavin pulled an odd-looking camera from his backseat, Layla lifted a brow. "What is that?"

He smiled. "A Vericon 12D. It's a high-tech camera that's mainly used underwater. Flipper messed around with it so we could use it on land, as well."

"Flipper?"

"Yes, Flipper. One of my team members. He's into technology and all that high-tech stuff," Gavin said as they walked side by side.

"Surely Flipper isn't his real name."

Gavin chuckled. "His real name is David Holloway. His code name is Flipper."

"Oh," she said, glancing up at him. "Do you have a code name?"

"Yes."

"What is it?"

He saw no reason not to tell her since his grandmother was well aware of it, too. His teammates called Gavin by his code name whenever they came to visit. "Viper."

Layla scrunched up her features. "Viper?"

"Yes, Viper."

"Why?"

"Why what?"

"Why do they call you Viper?"

He stopped walking to answer her, and when he stopped, she did, too. He hadn't noticed before how small she seemed, standing close to him. He figured he'd never noticed because usually when he faced her he was fixated on her mouth.

"The reason I'm called Viper is because when I set my sights on a target, I don't give up until I make a hit. I love taking the enemy down."

She tilted her head to look up at him. "Do you consider me an enemy?"

He didn't hesitate. "No." She wasn't the enemy, but he had every intention of taking her down…right into his bed.

Evidently satisfied with his response, she looked around him, back toward where the truck was parked. Then she turned around. She did it several times and each time he saw her confusion deepen.

"Is something wrong?" he finally asked.

She whipped around to look at him. "Yes, something is wrong."

He glanced around before returning his gaze to her. "What?"

"Someone moved my marker. It's gone."

He lifted a brow. "What do you mean your marker is gone?"

She frowned. "Just what I said. Someone moved my marker. It's not here."

Gavin released a deep sigh. "Why would anyone move your marker? Are you sure you put one down?"

"Of course I'm sure," she answered in an annoyed tone. "Someone moved it."

Gavin raised his gaze upward. "And who would do that?"

"I don't know, but someone did."

He shook his head. "Layla, the Silver Spurs is out in the middle of nowhere. And this particular spot is considered way outside our working area, almost six miles from the main house. No one would deliberately come on this land to remove your marker."

"Well, someone did, Gavin. I marked the digging site," she said with deep irritation in her voice.

Gavin stared down at her. "Are you sure? Maybe your mind is clouded right now. I can understand my kiss leaving you that way."

Her frown deepened. "I'm serious, Gavin."

"So am I, Layla."

Exasperation darkened her expression. "Will you get your mind off sex for a minute?"

A smile touched his lips. "My mind wasn't on sex," he said. "It was on that kiss we shared. But since you've pulled sex into the conversation…it's hard to think of anything other than getting you in my bed when you look so good."

Layla pushed to the back of her mind that she'd deliberately taken more time with her appearance just so he would think she looked good. That was before she'd come out here and discovered her marker *had* been removed.

"You moved it, didn't you?" she asked with an accusing glare.

"Now why would I want to do that?"

When she didn't say anything but continued to stare at him, his amusement was replaced with a deep frown.

"I have no reason to mess with any marker you claim to have put down. This is the first time I've been out this far from the house since returning home."

He rubbed a hand down his face in frustration. "If that marker has in fact been removed, then that means someone trespassed on this land to do it. Although for the life of me I can't imagine who would have cared enough to do such a thing. I just think you're confused as to where you placed the damn marker," he said, glancing around. "The south pasture is rather large. Maybe it's all the way on the other side."

"I am not confused and it's not on the other side. Not only did I map its coordinates, I recall parking near those tree stumps and walking twenty to thirty feet to my right. The marker was a wooden stake with a red flag on it, and I planted it exactly where we would dig."

"If you're sure of that, then you need to consider who knows you're here. And who would want to see you fail."

She lifted her chin. "And why wouldn't your name head the list? The deal we agreed on means I would have to sleep with you if I fail."

Gavin took a step closer to her. "Whether you fail or succeed means nothing to me because I have every intention of sleeping with you regardless of the outcome of this dig."

Layla was taken aback by Gavin's words. Of all the audacity. She placed her hands on her hips. Anger poured through her. "And how do you figure that?"

"Because, like I explained to you earlier, I'm Viper. I set my sights on a target. I don't give up until I make a hit. You are my target, Layla, and I plan to break down your resolve."

She all but stomped her foot in frustration. "And I've told you that won't happen. What part of that don't you understand?"

"This part," he said, brushing his finger across her cheek. She couldn't downplay her sharp intake of breath or the way her body shuddered beneath his touch. "You do something to me and I do something to you," he continued. "We do things to each other. We can only hold out for so long."

She tilted her lips stubbornly. "I will fight you on that with my last breath."

"And I suggest you save that breath for that explosive orgasm you're going to have."

Layla opened her mouth to blast out a resounding retort but then she closed it without responding. What was the use of arguing with him about something she knew for a fact wouldn't be happening, no matter what he thought? So what if his touch warmed her to the core? She would put him out of her mind. She had more important things to be concerned with. Like who'd removed her marker and why. No matter what Gavin might assume, she was not imagining things.

"My marker was removed, Gavin."

He rolled his eyes. "We're back to that again?"

"Yes. The dig is why I'm here. Why I crazily agreed to your deal. If you didn't remove the marker, then who did?"

Gavin drew in a deep breath, trying to hold his aggravation and frustration at bay. He knew for certain she was not incompetent. So someone had removed the marker like she claimed.

"Here, hold this," he said, handing Flipper's camera to her. He then began walking, studying the ground. He slowed when he saw footprints he knew weren't hers or his. He crouched down and pressed his finger to one, touching the indention in the earth. It was cold. The tracks looked fresh, as if they hadn't been made any more than forty-eight hours ago. Whose prints were they? One of his men? Possibly, but for some reason he doubted it. All his men had been working in the north and west pastures for the past few days. None had any reason to come to the south pasture.

It appeared more weight had been placed on the left leg as that impression was deeper. He also noted the sole of the right shoe appeared more worn than the left.

He stood and backtracked to where Layla said she'd parked her vehicle when she'd come out here. He walked, looking down and around the entire time. When he'd gone about thirty feet he stopped. Crouching down again he studied the earth and that's when he saw the small plug where the marker had been. He glanced to the right and the left, studying the ground. Again he saw footprints. The same ones.

He stood and slowly walked back to Layla. Without saying anything, he took the camera out of her hand. "Thanks."

She raised a brow. "Well?"

She hadn't asked what he'd been doing. She was smart enough to figure things out. He was using his skill as a SEAL to determine if there was proof that the marker had been removed.

He met her inquisitive expression. "I saw footprints. I also saw where the marker had been. You're right. The marker was removed."

"Why? By whom?"

"Don't know, Layla." He honestly didn't have a clue. The Silver Spurs was private property. And although there were numerous ways to get on the property, he couldn't imagine anyone having a reason to come to this particular area. The one thing he didn't see was tire tracks. But the person could have parked elsewhere and walked.

"I planned on using this camera to scan the area," he

said. “I suggest you make a list of anyone who might have a reason for wanting you not to succeed in your dig. And make sure you take me off the list. I told you my position and I’m sticking to it.”

And without saying anything else, he walked off.

Eight

I told you my position and I'm sticking to it.

Later that day, Layla paced the floor. Gavin Blake was bullheaded, stubborn and full of himself. He was crazy if he actually thought he could get her to bend to his will. No way. No how. So why was she pacing the floor, wearing out both herself and her shoes?

She had watched him use that high-tech camera, but she hadn't been impressed with his findings. Gavin agreed there was something buried in the area but he refused to consider it was Jesse James's loot. To his way of thinking, since that area used to be a popular hunting spot, the camera had picked up nothing more than buried bullet shells.

Layla refused to believe her research was wrong. There was buried treasure somewhere in the south pasture, she was sure of it. And as far as who would not want to see her succeed in this project, that could be a number of people, including her parents. But she didn't for one minute think they would go so far as to sabotage the dig site. They were hoping failing at this would make Layla realize she should pursue medical school, after all. Then there was her older colleague Dr. Clayburn and others at the university who felt she'd been too young and inexperienced for such an expensive project. Did the person who removed the marker actually think she wouldn't have kept the coordinates and just re-marked it? That she would give up so easily?

She stopped pacing when she heard a knock on the door. The tightening in her stomach told her who it was. Why was Gavin here? She had spoken to Ms. Melody an hour or so ago when she'd called to invite Layla to dinner. Layla had regretfully declined, knowing she would not have been the best of company this evening. Besides, she needed distance from Gavin. Evidently he hadn't taken the hint.

The knock on the door sounded again. There was no need to pretend she wasn't there when Gavin knew she was. Crossing the room, she opened the door to find Gavin with a tray of food in his hand.

"After you told Gramma Mel you weren't coming to dinner, she strongly suggested I bring you something. I believe she thinks I'm the reason you didn't come to breakfast or dinner."

Layla moved aside to let him in. Tray and all. Especially the tray. Everything was covered but the food smelled good. "I'll let her know that's not the case when I talk to her tomorrow." No need for him to know he *had* been a factor in her decision.

"She might not be here. Not sure when she's leaving, whether it's tomorrow or the day after."

Layla closed the door and followed him to the kitchen. "Leaving? Ms. Melody is going somewhere?"

"Yes, to a library convention in Cincinnati for a week. But I'm sure she won't leave without saying goodbye. And if you expect me to take her place and make sure you don't miss meals…that won't be happening."

She frowned. "I never asked your grandmother to cook for me, Gavin."

He put the tray on the kitchen table and turned to her. "Don't you think I know that?"

"Then why did you insinuate otherwise?"

"Did I?"

She crossed her arms over her chest. "Yes, you did."

"Then I apologize." She couldn't help noticing how his gaze roamed over her. "You changed clothes," he said.

Was that disappointment she heard in his voice? Seeing his gaze had moved to her chest, she dropped her hands to her sides. "I showered."

"I know. You smell good. And you look good in that dress. Nice legs."

She would have appreciated the compliment if she wasn't still so uptight about that marker being moved. "I want to go back out to the dig site tomorrow and look around, Gavin. This time I want to use my own detector."

"If you're still concerned about why the marker was moved, I might have a reason for that."

She came into the kitchen, trying to ignore the way he was checking out her legs and the way her nipples responded to his blatant appraisal. "What reason is that?"

"Clete. He's an older man we hired years ago to keep the grounds clear of trash and debris as well as repair anything that needs fixing. That way Caldwell and the men can concentrate mainly on the cattle. When I mentioned the marker to Gramma Mel, she reminded me that Clete has a tendency to move stuff when he's keeping the land cleared."

"But why would he remove the marker?"

Gavin shrugged. "He probably didn't know what it was and thought it was trash. He and his wife left a few days ago to visit their son who is in the navy and stationed in Hawaii. I'll talk to him when he gets back."

Layla drew in a deep breath, feeling somewhat relieved. The thought of someone tampering with the dig site had definitely bothered her.

"Sit down and eat. I promised Gramma Mel that I would make sure you did."

She raised a suspicious eye. "Why?"

"Why what?"

"Why would you care one way or the other if I eat?"

A slow, sexy smile touched his lips and her womb seemed to contract with the weight of that smile. And his dimples had bone-melting fire spreading through her blood. "The reason I care is because I don't want you to start losing weight."

She crossed her arms over her chest again, and then quickly dropped them by her sides when she saw his gaze shift back to her chest. Could the man think of anything other than sex for a minute? "And what does my weight have to do with you?"

"When I make love to you, I want to feel meat on your bones."

His statement answered her earlier question. No, he obviously couldn't think of anything other than sex. "We won't be making love, Gavin."

"Your food is getting cold."

He was blatantly ignoring what she'd said. "I'll eat after you leave."

He chuckled. "If that was a hint that you want me to go, forget it. I want to make sure you eat."

She frowned. "What do you plan to do? Stay here and watch me."

"Yes, that was my intent."

He was serious. "I don't need a babysitter, Gavin."

"No. What you need is a lover, Layla. And you never

did answer my question from last night. When was the last time you made love with a man?"

"And I don't intend to answer it because it's none of your business."

If he insisted on staying, she would ignore him. She moved to the table where he'd placed her food. Her mouth began watering the moment she uncovered it. Fried chicken, mashed potatoes, broccoli, candied yams and iced tea. And a slice of chocolate cake for dessert.

A smile lit her face. "Your grandmother is something else." Layla walked over to the sink to wash her hands. After grabbing utensils out of a drawer, she returned to the table and found Gavin sitting there. Did he plan to actually watch her eat? Didn't he have anything better to do?

Deciding nothing would stand between her and that food, she sat down, bowed her head and said grace, determined to ignore him. When she slid a forkful of mashed potatoes between her lips, she closed her eyes and groaned. Delicious.

"If you get off eating mashed potatoes, I can only imagine your reaction when we make love."

A part of her wanted to claim she wouldn't enjoy it. She quickly dismissed the idea when she glanced over at him. A woman could climax just from staring at him. Even so, she said, "In your dreams."

"My dreams will one day become your reality, Layla."

She decided not to argue with him anymore. But if he was intent on watching her, she might as well ask him a few questions. Get him talking, so she wouldn't think about how good he looked sitting there. How sexy.

She took a sip of her tea. "You mentioned your teammate named Flipper. Any others you're close to?"

"I'm close to all of them. We're a team."

"How many?"

"Enough."

She rolled her eyes. Had she asked about classified information or something? "I'm sure you're closer to some of the guys more than others."

He leaned back in the chair as if getting comfortable. She couldn't recall the last time she'd shared a private, intimate dinner with a man. And, whether she liked admitting it or not, this *was* intimate. They were alone, sitting at a table with the backdrop of a blazing fire roaring in the fireplace.

"In that case, I would say Flipper, Bane, Coop, Mac and Nick. The six of us went through all phases of training together. A couple of years ago, Nick took a job with Homeland Security. He needed a little more stability in his life when his wife gave birth to triplets."

As if he felt right at home, he stood and went to the refrigerator to get a beer and then returned to his chair. "Bane is a master sniper," he continued, popping the cap. "Coop is the mastermind behind most of our strategic moves. Mac is slightly older than the rest of us and likes to think he can keep us in line most of the time. He's been married for ages, has four kids and likes to impose his words of wisdom on us whether we want to hear them or not. And Flip can hold his breath under water longer than any human I know." He chuckled as he took a swig. "We're convinced Flipper has gills hidden somewhere."

Layla heard the fondness in his voice when he spoke of his teammates. "What's a master sniper?"

He looked at her. She thought he would say she was asking for classified information but then he said, "A master sniper is the best shot on the team. Bane is one badass. He can hit a target with one eye closed. He's covered all our backs more than once." He paused. "Bane and his wife, Crystal, are renewing their vows next month."

"Oh, were he and his wife separated for a while or something?"

"Yes, you could say that."

Layla knew he was being elusive but she was getting used to it. She didn't have to ask if his job was dangerous. Anyone who knew of the navy SEALs was aware of the types of missions they went on. She finished the rest of her meal in silence, with him watching her. She was tempted to ask if he wanted some but knew the trouble she'd gotten into when she'd asked him that question the last time.

She took a sip of her iced tea and looked over at him when she pushed her plate aside. "Satisfied, Gavin?"

He gave her a crooked smile. "Baby, my satisfaction will come when I get inside of you."

The glass nearly slipped from her hand. She recovered long enough to set it down by the plate. The impact of his words had her burning from the inside out. "Why do you say such things?"

"Just keeping it honest."

Gavin liked rattling Layla. Evidently she wasn't used to a man talking to her this way, telling her what he wanted and how he planned to make her feel. While watching her eat, his imagination had run wild. The conversation hadn't distracted him enough to demolish his desire. He doubted that was possible. He wanted her. He'd made that point pretty damn clear and he knew she wanted him as well, so what was the holdup?

"I've finished eating so you can leave now."

He held her gaze, felt the flare of response in their bodies when they looked at each other. Giving in to temptation, he lightly traced his fingertips along her arm. He felt her shiver beneath his touch. He heard her sharp intake of breath. "Why are you fighting this, Layla?"

"And why are you being so persistent?"

He could tell her that one of the reasons was because he hadn't been with a woman in six months, eight days, twelve hours and no telling how many minutes. Being around her was taking its toll. However, telling her such a thing would make him sound like a greedy jerk with only sex on his mind. That was only partly true. The other part was that he found her as fascinating as he found her beautiful.

"Being persistent is part of my nature."

When he saw her lips form a frown, his groin hardened and he couldn't help drawing in a ragged breath. Standing, he said, "I'll leave you alone now and report to Gramma Mel that you ate all your food."

He reached to remove the tray, but she blocked him. "Surely you don't think I'll let you return with dirty dishes."

"We've had a conversation about the purpose of a dishwasher before, Layla."

"That might be your way of doing things but it's not mine. I will wash the dishes and return them to Ms. Melody tomorrow," she said, standing.

Doing so brought her right smack in front of him. Gavin knew that if she inched closer, she would feel his erection. Even so, he intended to kiss her before he left.

"Walk me to the door, Layla."

From the look in her eyes, he knew she was aware of his plan. He watched her nibble her bottom lip. "Relax, baby. I won't bite."

She stopped nibbling her lips long enough to lift her chin and stare into his eyes. "You'll do something even worse, Gavin."

"What is that?"

"You will make me want you."

He eased closer, pressing his body to hers, wanting her to feel his erection. There was no way she could miss it. "Welcome to the club. And you already want me, Layla. Why are you having a hard time accepting that?"

Gavin could tell she was at a loss for words, which suited him just fine. He had other uses for her mouth. He leaned in to capture her lips.

Why was she having such a hard time accepting this? Layla asked herself when Gavin took her mouth. She didn't resist. She couldn't. In fact she felt herself practically melting into his arms. That was why, she reasoned, she wrapped her arms around his neck. Otherwise she would become a puddle on the floor.

He kissed her with an intensity she reciprocated in every part of her body. His mouth locked onto hers, not leaving any part of her mouth untouched. He tapped into areas she hadn't known existed. He was staking his claim on her mouth in a scandalous way. It was as if he was intentionally making her crazy for his kiss.

And then there was the feel of his erection, pressing hard against her middle. What man could get *that* aroused? To know she was the cause sent heated shivers through her body. The hard tips of her breasts pressed through the material of her dress as if eager to make contact with his chest.

Gavin broke off the kiss and when Layla drew in a deep breath, she was swept off her feet into his arms. He sat back down at the table with her firmly planted in his lap. Before she could ask just what he thought he was doing, his mouth was on hers. And just like before, this kiss robbed her of her senses, made her purr deep in her throat. It was a good thing his arm gripped her tightly otherwise she would topple to the floor. His hand was on her thigh, slowly caressing her skin underneath her dress.

Maybe she needed to ask herself why she was letting him do such a thing when she'd never let any man take such liberties before. Hadn't she kicked Sonny Paul in the groin when he thought he could reach into her blouse and touch her breast? Why did she believe this was different? Just because Gavin's mouth was driving her crazy with lust—could she accept this as okay?

And why was she still clutching him around the neck as if her life depended on their mouths being so intimately locked? Red-hot passion was making her dazed.

Somewhere in the haziness of her mind, she noted he had stood, without their mouths disconnecting. He was moving, headed somewhere rather quickly. It was only when he placed her on the bed that she regained her senses. Snatching her mouth from his, she scrambled away from him.

She blinked upon seeing he was about to take off his shirt. "What do you think you're doing?"

He stared down at her, panting like he'd run a marathon. His eyes, she saw, were glazed with heated lust to such a degree it made her heart pound. "About to make love to you, Layla." He then whipped his shirt over his head.

Seeing him bare chested caused goose bumps to ripple all over her skin. She scrambled farther away from him. "No you're not!"

He stared at her. "Can you look at me and say you don't want me to make love to you?"

She nervously licked her bottom lip and looked away. Yes, she could say it but she couldn't look at him while doing so. Mainly because she *did* want him to make love to her. There was no doubt in her mind that the sheets on the bed were calling their names.

"Layla. Look at me."

No, she wouldn't look at him. Nor would she tell him anything. Scrambling off the bed, she stood and began straightening her clothes before quickly walking out of the bedroom. "I'm showing you the door, Gavin," she called over her shoulder.

Once she reached the door, she waited. It took him a few minutes to follow her. He probably needed time to put his shirt back on and get his lusty mind under control.

When she saw him walking toward her he had an unreadable expression on his face. She drew in a deep breath. What thoughts were going through his mind? Did he think she was nothing more than a tease because she'd stoked his fire and then doused it with water? She would admit to having gotten caught up in the moment like he had. However, although he was ready to take things to the next level, she was not.

When he got closer, she saw the way he stared at her and figured he was angry to the point that he would walk out the door without saying anything to her.

She figured wrong. When Gavin stopped before opening the door, he turned dark, livid eyes on her. He then said in a furious voice, "The next time we kiss, Layla, will be when we make love. It's going to be a package deal."

He then opened the door and left.

Nine

Late afternoon the next day, Gavin walked out on the porch with a steaming cup of coffee. He couldn't believe he'd jogged around the ranch house twenty times last night. That would be equivalent to ten miles. When was the last time he'd done that?

On top of his workout last night, he'd gotten up at the crack of dawn to ride the range with Caldwell and his men. Sharing breakfast with them over an open fire had brought back memories. Most of the men who worked for Gavin had worked for his dad and had known Gavin when he'd been a kid. Although they called him boss, he knew they did it out of respect and not because he was involved in the day-to-day operations. Caldwell took care of the place. No matter how long Gavin was away from the ranch, he rested easy at night knowing the Silver Spurs was in good hands. Gavin also knew that whenever he returned Caldwell had no problem relinquishing that leadership role to him.

He took another sip of coffee as he eased down to sit on the steps. The cold weather was settling in. It was hard to believe Thanksgiving was next month. He'd gotten word that morning from his commanding officer that the team would be headed out again in late January. At least his teammates with families would get to spend the holidays with them. Gavin wondered if his grandmother would hang around the ranch this year. Because he was rarely home during the holidays, Gramma Mel usually flew to Saint Louis to spend time with her sister and her family.

"How did things go today with Caldwell and the men?"

Gavin glanced over his shoulder at the sound of his grandmother's voice. "Good, but that's no surprise. They know how to keep things going in my absence. And I covered just about everything with Phil yesterday. We talked again today and the books look good." The only thing he hadn't done that he'd wanted to do today was take another ride out to the dig site.

"When do you expect Mr. Clete back in town?" he asked.

"By the middle of next week," she said, taking a seat in the porch swing.

"Good." Although Gavin felt certain Clete was the one who'd moved the marker, he wanted to be absolutely sure. However, for the life of him, he couldn't imagine anyone else coming onto the property and tampering with Layla's markers. What purpose would it serve?

Flip's camera had picked up something underground, both in her marked spot as well as another spot close by. Like he'd told her, it was probably nothing more than bullet shells or branding irons. One section did have a relatively higher reading than others but he'd figured out a reason for that, as well. Buried Native American artifacts. Gavin's grandfather had claimed this had been Native American land generations ago. If Layla's research was as thorough as she claimed, she would already know that.

"I had a salad earlier, but if you're hungry I can fix dinner."

"No need. I plan to go into town in a few and I'll grab something at the café."

No way he would tell his grandmother that in addition to dinner he intended to make a booty call. Word was out that he was home and a ton of women had left voice mails. On the drive into town, he would decide which woman would be the recipient of his visit. Not having Layla was getting to him. He needed to get laid and then he could be more rational about her, take his time seducing her without losing his cool.

"Looks like you aren't the only one going into town, Gavin. Now, doesn't she look extra pretty?"

He followed his grandmother's gaze. Layla was crossing the yard and walking toward them. He had seen her in dresses before, but this was one with a skirt that was shorter in the front and longer in the back. Instead of boots she wore high heels and she had a knitted shawl around her shoulders.

Her hair was styled the way he liked best, flowing around her shoulders. And he could tell she was wearing makeup—not much…except for the ruby-red lip color. He frowned, refusing to let her get next to him the way she had last night. He'd been stupid enough to think their evening would end differently. Namely, in bed together.

"Good evening, Ms. Melody. Gavin."

He did the gentlemanly thing and stood. He couldn't help noticing she'd given his grandmother a huge smile. But the one she'd given him was forced. Not that it bothered him one iota.

"Layla," he said, letting his gaze roam all over her.

His grandmother moved forward and gave her a hug.

"Now, don't you look pretty. Have big plans for the evening?"

Layla shrugged her shoulders, keeping her focus on Ms. Melody and ignoring Gavin. "Not that big. The equipment arrives tomorrow and my team the day after. Then it's all work and no play. I decided to spend my last day of freedom doing something I enjoy doing but rarely have time for—going to a movie."

"By yourself?" Gramma Mel asked.

Layla chuckled. "Yes, by myself."

"What are you going to see?"

"That new romantic comedy with Julia Roberts."

"Now, isn't that a coincidence. I was going into town to see that one myself," Gavin said.

Both Layla and Gramma Mel turned to stare at Gavin with raised brows. He smiled at both women's expressions. He then directed his next statement to Layla. "Since we're going to see the same movie, is there any reason we can't go together?"

Gavin was certain there was but he knew Layla wouldn't call him out on it in front of his grandmother. When she didn't say anything he leaned closer to ask, "Well, is there?"

As if recovering from her initial shock, she opened her mouth, probably to say something that would blister his ear. Then she quickly closed it, seeming to remember that his grandmother was standing there, listening to their exchange.

"No, there's no reason," she said. "I'm just surprised you would want to see a *chick flick*. I took you for a blood-and-guts sort of guy."

He shook his head. "As a SEAL, I see too much of that in real life. A chick flick should be interesting. Besides, I like Julia Roberts."

"In that case, I see no reason why we can't go together," she said.

Although she'd tried to sound cheerful about it, he knew she wasn't. Was that her teeth he heard grinding? "Great. We can go in my truck. I just need to grab my Stetson and jacket."

"I enjoyed the movie, didn't you?"

Layla had pretty much given him the silent treatment since leaving the Silver Spurs earlier but he didn't seem to mind. In fact he seemed amused by it. "Yes, I enjoyed it."

She probably would have enjoyed it even more had he not been there to cloud her concentration. It had been hard to focus on the huge movie screen with a sexy man sitting beside her.

"When are you going to stop acting childish, Layla?"

She glanced over at him. "Childish? You think *I'm* acting childish when you told me last night that we won't kiss again unless sex is part of the mix?"

"Yes, that's what I said and I meant it."

"Well, sorry if you think I'm acting childish but I'm the one acting more adult than you. All you can think about is—"

"Making love to you."

She swallowed, seeing a picture of that very thing in her mind. "Yes."

"Can't help it. You do things to me, Layla."

When she was honest with herself, she could admit that he did things to her, as well. But she would never admit it to him. He was just like all the other men she'd known, which is why she'd sworn off relationships. All men wanted of a woman was a roll between the sheets. She wanted more from life; she had a career to build. Men and sex only got in the way of her goals.

She glanced over at him. "You were an only child, right?"

"Yes, as far as I know."

When she looked at him in surprise he added, "My mother deserted us when I was eight and never came back. For all I know, she could have married and had more kids by now."

Layla nodded. "She and your dad got a divorce?"

"No, but she might have changed her name and started over. Who knows?"

Layla didn't say anything for a moment. "You've never tried to find her?"

"No."

"Not even when your father was killed in the war?"

His jaw tightened. "Especially not then. If she didn't return to see him while he was living, I sure as hell didn't plan to give her the opportunity to see him dead," he said in a biting tone. "Dad always believed she would come back to us. Even said he understood her need to get away. After all, he'd talked her into coming to Cornerstone."

"Where was she from?"

"New York. Manhattan. They met while he was on military business at the United Nations. They'd only known each other a week when they married. They met one night at a restaurant, a month after her only family, an aunt, died."

"So when they met, she had no living family?"

"No."

He didn't say anything else for a long moment, and then he added, "According to Dad she lasted out here longer than he expected her to. She tried being a good wife, and I remember her being a good mom. Dad placed a lot of blame on himself since he had to carry out a lot of missions, leaving her here with Gramma Mel and Grampa

Gavin. And when I came along a year later, he thought she'd adjusted."

"But she hadn't?"

"Evidently not. One day she up and left. She told my grandparents she needed to get away for a while and asked them to watch me. She said she'd be back before Dad returned from his overseas tour. Then she got in her car—the one Dad bought for her—and drove off."

"And she never came back?"

He shook his head. "No, she never came back. Months later, when Dad returned home and found her gone, he was heartbroken. She left him a note saying she would come back. But she never did."

"And after all this time, you've never tried finding her?"

"No. She decided she didn't want me or Dad in her life."

Gavin inwardly admitted that more than once he had thought about locating his mother, if for no other reason than to ask her why she never came back. One of his former SEAL teammates, Nick Stover, worked for Homeland Security. All Gavin had to do was give Nick her name and there was no doubt in his mind that Nick would tell Gavin her whereabouts. A part of him knew the main reason he hadn't done so was his fear of what he would find out. What if his mother had never wanted him or loved his dad? At times it was easier to do what his father had done and believe the best…even if it was a fairy tale.

He drew in a deep breath. Why had he shared any of that with Layla when he'd never shared it with a woman before? For some reason, when she'd asked if he was an only child, the floodgates had opened. Emotions he usually kept locked inside had come pouring out.

"Any other family besides Ms. Melody? What about aunts, uncles or cousins?"

He figured she was asking for conversational purposes only, so he obliged her. "My grandmother has a younger sister living in Saint Louis. Her only grandson, Benjamin, and I are close. We're more like brothers than cousins. He spent a lot of his summers here. Ben's a year older and in the Marines. Right now he's stationed in Afghanistan, and we're hoping he'll be home for the holidays."

He glanced over at her. "What about you? Any cousins?"

She shook her head. "No. My grandparents didn't have any siblings and they had one child. I never knew my mother's parents. They died in a boating accident when she was in her teens."

He said nothing as he drove. They were ten minutes from his home and although there had been sexual chemistry between them as usual, they'd managed to keep it under control. That was a surprise since his plans for this evening had originally been to end up in some woman's bed. A part of him couldn't believe he'd given up the chance for sex just to spend time in Layla's company. And he had to grudgingly admit that although she'd tried to ignore him for most of the evening, he had enjoyed being with her.

Moments later, he pulled into the yard in front of the ranch house. His grandmother would be leaving tomorrow and he would have the house all to himself. Bringing the car to a stop, he cut the ignition and turned to Layla. "I'll see you inside."

"That's not necessary," she said, already opening her door to get out. "Thanks for driving me into town and joining me at the movies."

Although she'd said he didn't have to see her in, he

walked beside her anyway. "You're welcome, although I know you really didn't prefer my company."

When she didn't deny what he'd said, he chuckled. "No wonder you don't have a boyfriend."

She glanced over at him. "What makes you think I don't have a boyfriend?"

"I asked Gramma Mel if any man had visited you here and she said no."

Layla frowned. "That doesn't mean anything."

He chuckled again. "Yes, it does. If you had a boyfriend he would have come here, if for nothing else but to check on you. To see how you were doing. To feel out the competition. To stake his claim."

Even in the moonlight, he saw her roll her eyes. "Not all men are territorial, Gavin."

"Any man connected to you would be."

They had made it to the porch. When he offered her hand to assist her up the steps, she said, "No need." And then she walked up to the door without his help. He knew why. All it would have taken was one touch and they would have lit up like the Fourth of July and they both knew it.

"Thanks for seeing me home. At least my temporary home."

"No problem. What time does the equipment arrive tomorrow?"

"Sometime before noon. Thanks again for allowing me to store the equipment in that old barn."

He nodded. "When will your team get here?"

"Some will start arriving the day after tomorrow and will be staying at a hotel in town. We're hoping to finish the dig in a couple of weeks and then we'll be on our way."

A couple of weeks. He had every intention of making love to her before she left. In the meantime, he planned to stick to his resolve about not kissing her until she was ready to give in to their desire—even if it killed him.

"Good night, Layla."

When she just stared at him, he smiled. Evidently she'd expected him to kiss her good-night. "I'll stand here until you go inside."

She nodded. "Good night." And then she quickly opened the door and went in.

He didn't move until he heard the lock click in place. Then he tilted his Stetson back from his face as he moved down the steps. Not kissing her had been hard but he meant what he'd told her yesterday. The next time they kissed would be when they made love. Just thinking about how intense that kiss would be sent heat through his body, especially to his lower extremities.

If he hadn't needed to meet with Caldwell and his men first thing in the morning, he would have taken another ten-mile run around the ranch.

Ten

Three days later, while out riding Acer, Gavin came upon Layla and her excavation team in the south pasture. Most of them had arrived a couple of days ago but he hadn't been around to meet them. He and his men had driven the cows to the north pasture where they would be kept during the winter months.

Over the next few weeks, the cows would be fed to maintain their good heath during the cold spell. Unlike the south pasture, there was plenty of grazing land in the north and a small pond to help irrigate the area. The pregnant cows had to be separated and tagged and the process had taken a lot longer than expected.

Just as well, he thought, as he brought Acer to a slow trot and then a complete stop at the top of the hill. He'd needed distance from Layla. With his grandmother in Cincinnati and him being out on the range for the past three days he'd assured their paths didn't cross.

But now he was back and as he looked down at the activity going on below, he couldn't stop his gaze from seeking her out. At first he didn't see her, but when the crowd dispersed somewhat, there she was, looking as beautiful as he knew she would be.

He rubbed his hand down his face. Nothing about this seduction was working out like he'd figured it would. It seemed he would be the one to break before Layla. He just didn't get it. They wanted each other. That was definite. So how could she keep fighting the attraction? Desire had to be eating away at her as much as it was at him.

He hadn't seen her since that night they'd gone to a movie. Seeing her now made him realize that after all those hot and steamy kisses, and copping one good feel of her thighs, she had gotten into his system. That was crazy. Women didn't get into his system—ever. So how had she managed it?

He fixed his gaze on her as if three days could have changed her. They hadn't. Even from where he sat unobserved on Acer's back, he could still see her flawless skin. She looked just as young as the members of her team. Her students. Wearing her hair in a ponytail, jeans, a pullover sweater and boots should have made her fit in. Yet there was something about Layla that stood out. Something that made his stomach churn and his groin ache every time he saw her.

He never did make it into town just for that booty call. The only woman he wanted was Layla.

Bottom line—she had stirred something deep inside of him that wouldn't go away. At least not until he was inside of her, all the way to the hilt. It was only when his body connected with hers that he would be able to rid his mind of the belief that she was the only woman for him.

Watching her team work, he remembered something else. Namely that phone conversation he'd had with Clete yesterday. The old man recalled seeing the marker. He'd known why it was there, since he'd heard talk in town about someone digging on the property. But according to Clete, he hadn't moved it. That made Gavin wonder who had. Both he and Clete agreed the wind could not have blown it away nor could it have gotten washed away by the rain. Which meant someone had come on Gavin's property and pulled it out. Why?

Gavin hadn't been receptive to the idea of Layla digging on the Silver Spurs. But if someone was intentionally setting her up to fail, they would have to deal with him. Flip's camera had picked up something buried here. That made Gavin wonder if someone intended to unearth whatever was buried before Layla did so they could get the credit? His jaw tightened at the thought. Not on his property. And not on his watch. And not with his woman.

His woman…

How in the hell could he consider her his woman when he hadn't bedded her yet? Besides, Gavin Blake never claimed any woman. But as he fixed his gaze on Layla, he knew that she was his. Bedded or not.

Layla had been reading what looked like a report when suddenly, as if she felt him watching her, she tilted her head up and stared straight at him.

A lump formed in Layla's throat. Beneath the brightness of the noon sun sat a gorgeous man on a beautiful horse. She'd seen the horse before. One day after arriving on the Silver Spurs, she'd noticed when one of the men had taken it out of the stall to groom it. She had been admiring the animal when the man, Curtis, told her the horse's name was Acer and that he belonged to the boss. This was the first time she'd seen Gavin on the horse and the sight took her breath away.

It had been three long days since he'd taken her to the movies and later walked her to the guest cottage, leaving her there and blatantly ignoring her since. Honestly, what had she expected? For him to have kissed her good-night regardless of what he'd said the night before? What he'd done was to toss the ball in her court. He probably figured she didn't have the guts to play it.

But it wasn't that she didn't have the guts. She didn't have the time or the inclination… Oh, who was she fooling? Definitely not herself. If anything, not seeing him these past few days had made her realize that out of sight, out of mind didn't work when it came to Gavin.

"Who in the blazes is that?"

Layla didn't have to move her gaze from Gavin to know one of her students, Tammy Clemons, stood beside her looking at Gavin, as well. "That's Gavin Blake. He and his grandmother own the Silver Spurs. They were kind enough to let us dig here."

"Um, maybe I should thank him. Properly."

A sudden stab of jealousy ran through Layla, and as much as she tried pushing it back, she couldn't. *Properly?* She didn't have to wonder just what Tammy meant by that. It was rumored around campus that Tammy often bragged about sleeping with her professors to get better grades.

Layla knew not to believe everything she heard, but Tammy's behavior made Layla think there was some truth in that claim. Especially since Tammy was here on this dig. Some said her latest conquest was Dr. Clayburn. That wouldn't surprise Layla since the married man and father of two was known to have roving eyes. More than once she'd heard about his late night meetings with female students. Those meetings were something Layla was certain the college president had heard about but had chosen to ignore.

Tammy's grades should have made her ineligible for this team, but Dr. Clayburn had personally added her name above other more well-deserving students. When

Layla had brought it to Dr. Clayburn's attention, he'd gotten upset that she'd questioned him. He'd reminded her that he had the power to withdraw the school's funding for the excavation.

"That guy is what you would call a real cowboy. And I didn't have to travel to Texas to get one."

Layla saw the twenty-one-year-old lick her lips with her gaze trained on Gavin. It shouldn't matter to Layla. But it did. Why? She didn't want to be Gavin's bed partner so why should it bother her if someone else did?

"Need I remind you, Tammy, that you're here to work on this project?"

Tammy frowned. "No, Dr. Harris, you don't need to remind me of anything. Just like I'm sure I don't need to remind you that although we're dedicated to this dig during the day, the nighttime hours are ours to enjoy. And I intend to enjoy him."

The young woman stated the words so matter-of-factly that Layla had to take pause. Was Tammy the type of woman Gavin wanted? The kind who could handle both work and play without breaking a sweat? A woman who enjoyed the challenge of both?

Layla was about to reply when a huge smile covered Tammy's face. "He's seen me checking him out and is coming down for me."

The thought that Gavin might be showing some interest in Tammy made Layla's chest ache.

She turned her attention back to Gavin. He was sprinting down the hill on the huge horse and she recalled something he'd once said. When he saw a target he wanted he went after it. Was he now galloping down the hill because he wanted Tammy? The young woman evidently thought so.

He looked good on the horse, wearing a Stetson on his head. Tammy was right. He was the epitome of what a cowboy should be. Tough. Rugged. Fearless. But then she could probably use those same adjectives to describe him as a navy SEAL. Gavin slowed his horse to a trot when it hit level ground and then he headed in their direction.

"Didn't I tell you he was coming to check me out?" Tammy said, with a ton of confidence in her voice.

The young woman didn't lack any faith in herself as a woman who could draw a man's interest. Gavin reached them and brought the horse to a stop. A lump formed in Layla's throat when she saw his attention hadn't even flickered to Tammy. He was staring straight at Layla.

"Gavin."

"Layla."

"And I'm Tammy," the younger woman quickly said, not waiting for an introduction. She flashed Gavin a huge, flirty smile.

Gavin switched his gaze from Layla to Tammy. "Hello, Tammy."

"You look good on your horse. I would love for you to give me a ride."

Gavin released a smooth chuckle. "Sorry. Acer is temperamental. I'm the only one he lets on his back."

"Um, I'm sure there are other ways we can ride," Tammy purred suggestively. "Without your horse."

Layla cleared her throat. Did the young woman have no shame? Tammy had pretty much offered herself to Gavin. Talk about being over-the-top brazen. The smile, she noticed, didn't leave Gavin's features when he said, "Thanks. But no thanks." He then turned his full attention back to Layla. "Have dinner with me tonight."

Layla swallowed. "Dinner?"

"Yes. I figured we could grab a meal in town."

Before Layla could say whether she would go or not, Tammy spoke up in an irritated tone. "Dr. Harris is in charge of this project, and I'm sure she has a lot to do tonight since we start digging in a few days. There are preliminary reports she has to complete and soil samples that need to be reviewed. But I'll be glad to go out with you tonight."

An annoyed frown replaced the smile on Gavin's lips when he turned to Tammy. "Are you her spokesperson?"

It was obvious Tammy had been caught off guard by Gavin's question. "No."

"I didn't think so. As far as taking her place, I didn't ask you to, did I?"

He couldn't have been I'm-not-interested-in-you plainer than that, Layla thought. Rage appeared in Tammy's face, making it quite obvious she wasn't used to men rejecting her and she didn't appreciate Gavin doing so. Instead of answering his question, she turned and angrily strutted off.

Layla watched her go and then turned her attention back to Gavin. "You might have hurt her feelings."

He shrugged massive shoulders. "She'll get over it. Besides, someone needs to teach her some manners." He leaned back. "So what about it? Will you have dinner with me tonight? We can even take in another movie if you like?"

Layla nibbled at her bottom lip. Tammy had been right about her having a lot of work to do to prepare for the start of the dig. But then hadn't Tammy also reminded her that although they were dedicated to this dig during the day, the nighttime hours were theirs to enjoy? Besides, after witnessing Tammy come on to Gavin the way she had, Layla had realized something. He could have taken Tammy up on her bold offer but he hadn't. He had even made it crystal clear that Layla was the woman he wanted.

Though she had convinced herself that she could do without him even if she wanted him, she now knew she couldn't. And why should she? She'd spent her whole life proving she could accomplish what she set her mind to. Now, she was setting her mind to finishing this dig and having Gavin, too.

She had set her target and she was going after what she wanted. In other words, she was about to become Viper Jr.

She met Gavin's gaze. "Dinner and a movie sound nice. Yes, I'd love to go out with you tonight."

Eleven

The moment Layla walked up the porch steps her nerves tightened. Was she doing the right thing? Was following her desires rather than common sense the best move for her tonight?

Her gaze swept over at the man at her side. Gavin had been quiet since parking his truck. Now he was walking her to the door and she knew it would be her decision how tonight would end. He wouldn't even kiss her good-night unless he knew for certain more came with that kiss. Was she ready to give him more?

They had been careful not to touch all night. Holding hands would have led to heaven knows what. The sexual chemistry between them was that explosive. She had been aware of everything about him all evening. His breathing pattern, the sexual vibes that poured off him and the heavy-lidded eyes that stared at her.

Even now, there was this sensuous pull of desire between them. She was aware of it and she knew he had to be aware of it, as well. That consciousness was a slow roll of longing in her stomach and a throbbing intensity at the base of her throat. Never had she felt such primal awareness of a man before.

When they reached the door she turned to him. Although his Stetson shaded his eyes, she felt his stare. She inhaled his masculine scent. The man was a living, breathing sample of testosterone at its best.

Drawing in a deep breath, Layla tightened her hands on the shoulder straps of her purse. "Dinner was wonderful. So was the movie. It's been a long time since I've seen a musical." His taste in movies surprised her. Last time it had been a chick flick and tonight a musical.

"Glad you enjoyed both."

She smiled up at him. "I did. Thanks for asking me to go. To be with you."

He nodded. "I can't think of any other woman I'd rather have been with tonight, Layla."

His words sent profound happiness spiraling through her. He could have spent the evening with Tammy, who was almost six years younger, and to Layla's way of thinking, a lot prettier. But she was the one he'd asked out. "Thank you for saying that."

"It's the truth."

When she didn't respond, she heard Gavin draw in a deep breath before saying, "I know you have a lot of work to do so I'll let you get to it."

He was giving her an out. He wouldn't pressure her. He'd stated days ago where he stood. If things between them escalated it would be up to her.

Swallowing deeply, she asked, "Would you like to come in for a drink, Gavin?"

He held her gaze for a long moment before smiling. "Yes, that would be nice, Layla."

As she opened the door to let him in, Layla knew it would be a whole lot better than just nice.

Gavin followed Layla inside. Removing his Stetson, he placed it on the rack by the door. She walked ahead, toward the living room and his groin tightened with each sinfully erotic sway of her hips.

"Beer or wine cooler?" she asked over her shoulder.

"Beer." He closed the front door. He actually needed something a lot stronger. A straight shot of bourbon might do the trick, to stop his testosterone from overloading. But then he figured there wasn't a drink on earth that could deaden his desire for Layla. It went too deep. He could actually feel a throb in his veins. Drawing in a deep breath he inhaled her scent.

"Here you are," she said, reentering the living room.

He recalled the last time she'd offered him a beer and what had occurred when their hands touched. What he'd felt. Would she avoid touching him this time? There was only one way to find out.

When she handed him the bottle, he deliberately held her gaze. Intentionally, he rubbed his finger against her hand. Hearing her sharp intake of breath, he'd gotten the reaction he'd hoped for. Unlike the last time she didn't wipe her hands on her jeans.

Still holding her gaze, he opened the bottle and took a huge gulp. He then lowered the bottle, licked his lips and asked the same question he had asked that night. "Want a sip?"

He'd given her an opening. Instead of retreating like she had before, she covered the distance separating them. "Yes, I want a sip." But instead of taking it, she said, "I'd rather sip it from your lips."

He lifted the bottle to his mouth. Then she took the bottle from him and placed it on a nearby table before leaning up on tiptoes to place her mouth over his. With a boldness he hadn't expected from her, she wrapped her arms around his neck and began sipping the beer from his lips.

Gavin felt light-headed and hot at the same time. Never had a woman stirred such passion within him. Never had any woman made his erection throb to this point. Layla was full of surprises and she was driving him insane with need.

As their mouths mated, he wrapped his arms around her. He wasn't surprised by how fluidly her body aligned with his. Sensations swamped his body. He knew from the way she was tasting him that tonight would not end with this kiss. The mating of their mouths was just the beginning. Tonight they were on the same page.

He swept her into his arms. Breaking off the kiss, he whispered against her lips, "I'm taking you to bed, Layla. If you have a problem with it, you need to say so now."

A seductive smile touched her lips. "I don't have a problem with that, Gavin."

Sexual excitement rushed through his veins as he moved quickly toward the bedroom.

Twelve

When Gavin placed Layla on the bed she looked up at him and saw eyes filled with intense desire gazing down at her. She'd meant what she said about going to bed with him. But he might not feel the same way after she said what she had to say.

"We need to talk first, Gavin."

He pulled her sweater over her head. "Okay, I'm listening."

Was he really? Or was he concentrating on undressing her? "A while back you asked me when I last did this. Do you remember that conversation?"

Her sweater was off and his swift hands went to the front clasp of her bra. Within seconds he had her breasts tumbling free. She watched his eyes get smoky as he stared at her nipples, which hardened as he watched. When he brushed against one with a feathery stroke of his fingertips, she drew in a sharp breath.

"Yes, I remember that conversation," he said in a husky

voice, stroking her other breast as if fascinated with its size and shape. "What about it?"

Layla had to think a minute to remember the conversation. His hands were driving her insane. And when he began stroking her nipples in earnest, it created a throbbing ache in her center. She couldn't help but moan.

"Layla?"

"Um?"

"What about the conversation?"

What conversation? Her brain was turning to mush and she fought hard to recall what he was talking about. Then she remembered. "Are you ready for an answer to the question you asked?"

"Doesn't matter now."

And before she could draw in another breath, he lowered his head and eased a rigid nipple between his lips. He sucked hard, feasting in earnest. Greedily. Ravenously. At the same time, he eased the hem of her skirt toward her waist.

And then he pushed aside her panties to ease fingers inside of her. The moment she felt the intimate invasion, she shuddered in pleasure. How could his mere touch do that? Make her come so unglued? Make her feel like a woman?

And when those same fingers stroked her down there, with the same rhythm his tongue was using to suck on her nipples, she moaned aloud.

"That's it. Get all wet for me, baby. Your scent has been driving me mad for days now. I can't wait to taste you."

She wasn't sure what he meant. All she knew was Gavin Blake had fingers that should be considered illegal and a mouth that should be banned. Using both, and at the same time, should be forbidden.

Sensation gathered force in her stomach and when he sucked harder on her breasts, while at the same time inserting his fingers deeper inside of her, she could not bear the pleasure any longer. Her body began to shake with the need for release. A climax ripped through her body. On instinct, she threw her head back and screamed his name.

"Now for my taste."

Before she realized what Gavin was doing, he had pulled off her skirt and tossed it aside along with her panties. Before she could ask what he thought he was doing, he lifted her hips to his mouth and firmly settled his head between her legs.

Layla tried pushing him away—until the moment she felt his tongue ease between her womanly lips. He kissed her down there the same way he'd kissed her on the mouth. Deeply. Thoroughly.

She stopped pushing him away. Instead she grabbed his shoulders and held on. Held him. She needed him to stay right there and continue what he was so expertly doing. When she felt his tongue delve deeper inside, flicking back and forth, her body shattered into what felt like a million pieces.

"Gavin!"

He didn't let up. He continued using his mouth to drive her over the edge yet again. Never had she experienced anything so powerful. So utterly amazing. For a minute she thought she had passed out. Maybe she had. She was completely drained. Limp. Too weak to move. So she lay there, nearly convinced she had died and gone to heaven. Surely there was nothing on earth that could make her feel this good. This satisfied.

She didn't move. She couldn't find the strength to open her eyes. Not even when she heard him remove his clothes before he pulled her boots and socks from her feet. Not even when his hands stroked her thighs and eased them apart.

And not even when she heard the sound of a condom packet being ripped open.

Moments later she heard Gavin's deep voice directly above her. "Open your eyes, baby. Look at me."

Although her eyelids felt heavy, she somehow found the strength to force them open. Gavin's naked body was braced above hers and desire-filled eyes stared down at her. Was it her imagination or were his eyes getting even darker as she stared into them?

"I'm looking," she said softly. Not only was she looking but she was being held in some sort of hypnotic trance.

"I wanted you this way from the first moment I set eyes on you."

That was nice. And she was about to say something, she wasn't sure what, when she felt the hot tip of his erection press against the core of her womanhood.

Her gaze widened and she knew she needed to tell him. Now. "Gavin?"

He leaned in and kissed the words off her lips. Using that scandalizing tongue of his, he began driving her crazy. Instinctively her legs opened wider and she felt him pressing down gently, as he tried entering her body.

He broke off the kiss and stared down at her. She knew from his expression exactly when he realized the *something* she'd tried to tell him about. The *something* he'd said no longer mattered.

"You're a virgin," he whispered in shock.

"Yes." Would he change his mind? Would it matter? She swallowed and said quietly, "I'll understand if you no longer want me."

Something flickered in his dark gaze. "Why wouldn't I still want you? Because you're a twenty-six-year-old virgin?"

When she nodded, he smiled and said, "Doesn't bother me if it doesn't bother you."

That was the moment she knew she had fallen in love with Gavin. She had tried denying it, had even called herself several kinds of a fool for letting it happen. She'd never loved a man before, but she knew what her feelings were. For all the heartbreak it would cause when she left the ranch in a week or so, it didn't make much sense for her to love a man now. But her heart had declared Gavin was it and there was nothing she could do about it.

Making love with him seemed right in a way it had never been with any other man…which was the real reason why she had remained untouched all these years. Sex had never interested her. She had never been turned on by the mere thought of it. Things were different with Gavin. Even before she'd met him face-to-face, his pictures had done something to her. They had pretty much warned her of her fate but she'd refused to accept it until she'd welcomed him inside tonight.

"Layla?"

She held his gaze. "Doesn't bother me, either." *Please don't ask me why I chose you. At least not now.*

He didn't ask her anything. Instead he kissed her before using his knee to widen her legs. And then she felt him, easing inside of her, inch by inch. He was big and she sucked in as he filled her deeply, her body stretching for his invasion. Her muscles clamped down—not to stop his journey but to make it even more sensuous for the two of them. He continued to ease deeper until there was no place left for him to go. He was fully embedded in her in a fit so snug and tight she couldn't tell where her body ended and his began.

When her muscles tightened even more, she actually felt his erection throb inside of her. "If you keep that up do you know what's going to happen?" He leaned in close to ask her.

"No."

"It's going to make me want to do this."

Then he began thrusting, gently, in a sensuous rhythm

that drove her to lift her hips with his every downward stroke. When her inner muscles clenched him harder, he thrusted harder, with a steady fluid beat.

Too steady. Each stroke inside her body pushed her to a place she'd never been. He'd made her come using his mouth. But this was different. It was more intense. Insanely gratifying. And when he went faster, harder, deeper, she screamed his name as sensations washed over her. She clawed at his back, bucked upward to tighten her legs around him and lock their bodies together.

An intense explosion swept her away in an earth-shattering release. Although this might be the first time she'd made love with a man, she knew that this wouldn't be her last with Gavin.

That had been totally unreal, Gavin thought, a short while later as he lay flat on his back staring up at the ceiling. When had making love to a woman ever left him so physically sated and mentally drained? Hell, he was used to making out with women, sometimes all night long. And as a SEAL he was physically fit for all the rigors of combat. Yet, the woman sleeping beside him had practically drained him, made him weak as water with their first sexual encounter. How was that possible?

And she'd been a virgin. Gavin didn't have to wonder how that was possible, given her status in life. To accomplish what she'd accomplished at her age meant she'd made sacrifices. He'd suspected her experience with men had been limited, he just hadn't figured it to be nonexistent. Not that it bothered him. Normally, he preferred not to be any woman's first, but he was glad he'd been Layla's. The thought that no other man had been inside her body before him felt good, made him want to beat on his damn chest like a caveman. He'd branded Layla as his.

His?

Where in the hell had that thought come from? This was the second time he'd thought of her as being his woman. His. He needed to remind himself once again that he wasn't into possessiveness. He'd even participated in a ménage à trois a time or two during his college years. So the idea of laying claim to any woman didn't sit well with him. Sex was sex, no matter how good it was. No need to act crazy.

So why was he?

As he tilted his head to stare down at the woman sleeping peacefully beside him, he had to admit the sex had been better than good. Off the charts. He had studied her face when she'd come. Her expression had been utterly and incredibly spellbinding. Beautiful. Touching. She was such a passionate being it was hard to believe she'd held out for this long. Her presence on the Silver Spurs was the best luck he'd had in years. With sex that good she could dig up the entire damn ranch looking for whatever treasure she wanted. His treasure was right here with him in this bed.

Gavin frowned. He was thinking like a love-struck puppy, and he refused to go there. Isn't that what had happened to his father? He'd quickly fallen in love with a woman only to die of a broken heart in the end? Okay, it had been an enemy's bullet that had taken him out, but Gavin of all people knew of his father's heartache.

Layla shifted her weight. Her leg, which rested between his, touched his groin. Immediately, he got hard. His erection had no problem coming to life. He glanced over at the clock. It was almost two in the morning. He should leave but the thought of waking up beside her in the morning had an appeal he couldn't dismiss.

And then there was the temptation to wake her now and make love to her all over again. Move between her legs and slide inside of her. Go deep until he couldn't go anymore. Then he would thrust hard like he'd done before. Even harder since she was no longer a virgin. He even thought about how it would feel not to wear a condom. To blast off inside of her. Fill her with the very essence of him.

Now that was taking his imagination a little too far. He was a man who played it safe so he would never be sorry. Babies of any kind were not in his immediate future. So why did the thought of a daughter who would be a mini-Layla appeal to him? Make his erection even harder?

Gavin closed his eyes. He had to stop thinking with the wrong head. Doing so could get him in serious trouble. He couldn't let sexual feelings take control of his common sense no matter how wrapped up he wanted to get with the woman beside him. No matter how much inhaling her arousing scent was getting to him.

Shifting his body, he pulled Layla closer and let sleep overtake him.

Thirteen

The strong aroma of coffee woke Layla. She blinked, and then sluggishly realized where she was and what she'd done last night and with whom. If there had been any doubt in her mind about what had happened, all she had to do was tilt her head to gaze across the room to where a half-naked man lounged in the doorway holding a steaming cup of coffee.

Gavin.

She blinked. Okay, since he was wearing jeans, he wasn't half-naked but half-dressed. Still, that was all he was wearing. And those jeans were riding low on his hips, making it pretty obvious just what a well-built body he had. His pose was picture perfect. He was the epitome of a sexy cowboy. A wealthy rancher. A scrumptious navy SEAL. How could one man exemplify all three and do it so well?

Her gaze roamed over him, from the top of his head all the way down to his bare feet. She'd paused when she'd seen that his zipper was undone. He'd either dressed quickly and hadn't bothered to zip up, or he had plans that included her so he'd figured why bother.

Those tantalizing thoughts made her recall last night. Her first time. And she knew without a doubt it had been worth the wait. She couldn't help it. Her gaze traveled the full length of him all over again. This time when her gaze settled on his midsection, she saw something she hadn't seen before. A huge erection. She drew in a deep breath and swore that it got bigger as she stared at it.

"Want some?"

She snatched her gaze from his groin up to his face. The smile that touched his lips was priceless and way too sexy for words. "What are you offering?" she asked.

"Whatever you want."

Reluctantly, she broke eye contact with him to glance outside the bedroom window. It was still dark but she knew it would be daybreak soon. Her team would be arriving from town within an hour or so. Her gaze returned to his. "I should take the coffee, get up, shower and get dressed."

"But..."

How had he known there was a *but* in there? "But I much prefer taking the man holding the coffee."

His smile widened. "And the man holding the coffee doesn't have a problem with you taking him."

Layla was only beginning to fully understand what heated lust was all about. "Did I tell you that last night I thought of myself as Viper Jr?"

He lifted a brow. "Viper Jr?"

"Yes. I set my sights on my target and went after what I wanted, and you, Gavin Blake, were my target."

A wry grin split his lips. "Was I?"

She nodded. "I wanted you."

"And I wanted you."

Layla then saw a somewhat serious look appear in

his eyes as he said, "How do you feel? I wanted you so much…because of that you're probably sore. You sure you're up to another ride this soon?"

Ride? She inwardly chuckled. Yes, he'd definitely ridden her last night. And yes, she was sore from it. However, as far as she was concerned, he could ride the soreness away.

"I'm sure."

"In that case." Placing the coffee cup on a nearby table, he crossed the room to the bed. "But first I want to see something." Before she could blink, he threw the bedcovers aside to expose her naked body.

Surprised, she scrambled to get back under the covers but he tossed them aside again. "No. Don't cover yourself. I just had to make sure I hadn't imagined anything. That you were as beautiful and delectable as I remembered. My mind didn't play tricks on me last night."

His words touched her. Made her feel wonderful. Made her feel like a real woman who had sexual feminine powers over a man. And when she watched him lick his lips with the tip of his tongue, she couldn't help remembering just where that tongue had been and what it had done.

Recalling that part of their lovemaking sparked an ache between her legs. As if he knew what sensations were enthralling her and where, he slowly eased his jeans down his strong, muscular thighs. Just as she'd thought. The jeans were the only thing he'd been wearing. He hadn't bothered to put back on his briefs.

"Now for this."

His words grabbed her attention and she watched him slide a condom over his erection. And boy was it large. How had it gotten inside of her last night? But he'd managed it and she knew he would again. This was the first time she'd seen a man prepare himself for sex. From the way he was doing it, it was obvious he was used to doing it.

"Ready?"

"Yes." She drew in a deep breath. The ache between her legs had made her nipples harden like tight buds.

"We're going to try something different this morning. It will be easier on you and help with your soreness."

In a way, she felt embarrassed engaging in such a conversation with him…about her body. But she pushed her discomfort aside. After last night—and all he'd done to her and how he'd done it—there was no room left for shame. "What?"

He smiled as he moved back toward the bed. "I want you to ride me."

She swallowed. "Ride you?"

"Yes. Do you know how to ride?"

She nodded. "Yes. My parents own several horses." And she'd ridden them often enough.

"Good. So show me what you know," he said, lying back on the bed beside her, then lifting her over him. Just like that. As if she was weightless.

"I'll do my best," she said, sliding into position. The long, hard length of his erection was like a rod, standing straight up, ready for her to mount. So she did. Widening her legs, she took him into her body. The hot texture of his male organ seemed to blaze her insides as she took him fully inside of her.

She watched his face, the same way she'd known he'd watched hers last night. Their gazes held. No words were spoken. This was all about feeling. And she felt him in each and every part of her body. Her muscles clenched around him. Holding tight. And then as if of one accord they shivered with a need they both felt.

"Okay Viper Jr. Ride me, baby. Hard."

Gavin's words incited her to move up and down. She

felt him grip the sides of her hips—to hold on to her, to guide her. Then, as if something elemental had taken control, she threw her head back and rode him hard.

What was happening to her? It was as if she'd lost control of her mind and her body. Having sex with Gavin this way, with her on top, riding him, sent an exhilarated feeling through her, one she couldn't explain.

When he leaned up and whispered naughty words in her ear, sinfully erotic words, she went mad with lust. She heard the bedsprings as she continued to ride. Each time her body came down against him, his came up to meet her.

Suddenly her quivering became uncontrollable and she felt her body explode into a thousand pieces. It was then that Gavin caught the back of her head with his hands and brought her mouth down to his, kissing her with a hunger that made her climax all over again.

Once again he came with her. She felt it. As their tongues continued to mingle, she knew that she loved him with a passion she would never rid herself of, no matter the distance between them. While she was here on the Silver Spurs, she intended to make memories that would last her long after she returned to Seattle.

"Well, how did your dinner date with the handsome rancher go? Did the two of you do the nasty, Dr. Harris?"

Layla didn't immediately look up from studying the soil samples. Tammy was the last person she wanted to talk to, but to ignore her student would be rude. Yet no student had the right to inquire how their professor spent their evening. Layla had always maintained a distance between herself and her students. Because of her age, she took pains to ensure they never lost sight of the fact that she was their professor. As far as she was concerned, Tammy's question was out of line and lacked respect.

Layla raised her head from the microscope and met

Tammy's gaze. "I don't think that should be your concern, Tammy. Did you finish your report?" Layla knew she hadn't. Several students had brought it to her attention that Tammy was slacking. It seemed whenever there was hard work to do, Tammy had a tendency to disappear.

Tammy scrunched up her features. "No. And why do I have to be the one to do that report? Donnell has a lot of free time."

"Only because Donnell has finished all his assignments. You haven't."

A smile touched Tammy's lips. "Doesn't matter. I'll still ace this class."

Layla frowned. "Not if you don't do your share of the work. And if you're not going to be a team player, I will have to replace you. There are several students who would love to be here."

"Doesn't matter. They don't have the connections I have," Tammy bragged. "I'm on this team, Dr. Harris, whether you want me here or not. I thought you understood that."

Layla refused to get into a confrontation with a student. It was clear Tammy thought that being Dr. Clayburn's occasional bed partner meant she could do whatever she wanted. Wrong. Not on Layla's team. "The only thing I understand is that I expect you to carry your load. If you can't, then you're out of here."

Tammy tossed her hair as a smirk touched her lips. "Wrong. You'll be out of here before I will. I'll make sure Mark… I mean Dr. Clayburn knows I'm being harassed." She then turned and sulked as she walked out the door.

In frustration Layla rubbed her hand down her face. Tammy might be right. Layla wasn't one of Dr. Clayburn's favorite people and it was obvious the man was quite taken with Tammy. And Tammy knew it.

"She'll eventually hang herself and Dr. Clayburn. Don't waste your time worrying about her, Dr. Harris."

Layla turned to find another one of her students, Donnell McGuire, standing in the doorway. Had he overheard her conversation with Tammy? Did he and the other students suspect something was going on between Tammy and Dr. Clayburn? The one thing Layla wouldn't do was discuss one student with another, no matter how much she wanted to sound off to someone about Tammy's atrocious attitude.

Before she could say anything, Donnell added, "And don't worry about that report Tammy hasn't done. I'll take care of it. I do have some free time."

His words told Layla he *had* overheard her conversation with Tammy. "That assignment was given to Tammy, Donnell, and I expect her to do it. Besides, I have something else for you to do. I just got a call that the last of our supplies arrived at the post office in town. I need you to go pick them up. If everything looks good, we'll start digging by the end of the week."

A huge smile touched Donnell's face. "Alright! I can't wait." The young man rushed off to tell the others.

Layla chuckled at his enthusiasm. She would give anything for more students like Donnell who took being a team player seriously. He was a hard worker. Most of the students on this team were. Although being an archaeologist was Donnell's first love, she knew he was also good with a camera and had won a number of photo contests. At twenty-two he would be graduating in the spring with a major in archaeology and a minor in photography.

She refused to let Tammy put a damper on her day, especially when it had started off with the promise of being wonderful. She'd had such a wonderful night with Gavin. Then this morning, before the crack of dawn, she'd proven just what a great horsewoman she could be. Memories of what they'd shared still sent shivers down her spine. She couldn't help but blush. Being intimate with a man had never been anything she'd thought about until now…

She glanced at her watch. She had a full day planned here on-site and then Gavin had invited her to dinner again. This time he would be the one cooking. He claimed he wasn't bad in the kitchen. Tonight she intended to see if that was true.

Gavin had always prided himself on being a man in control. As a SEAL, he couldn't be any other way. The success of any mission called for it. There was no time to let your guard down. Weakness of any kind wasn't acceptable. Then why did he lose control every time he entered Layla's body? Why did overpowering weakness overtake him whenever they made love?

He had prepared dinner for her tonight at the party house. He'd fed her well. Surprised the hell out of her with his culinary skills. At the moment, he contemplated impressing her with another skill. One of seduction. When he'd arrived at the party house with his arms filled with groceries, Layla had opened the door wearing an outfit that only made him think of filling her.

She'd tempted him the entire time he was in the kitchen. There was no doubt in his mind that she'd known exactly what she was doing as she'd sat at the breakfast bar watching him. She had known each and every time she crossed and uncrossed her legs that she was showing him a portion of her thigh and exactly what that did to him. How he had managed to finish cooking and then sit across from her and eat was a testament to his control.

Now it was payback time.

"So how was your day, Gavin?"

He'd cleared off the table and was loading up the dishwasher as he fought to retain control. "It was the usual day in the life of a rancher. The cows are finally settled in for the winter, which is good since forecasters predict a cold wave coming through first of next week."

"I heard. I'm hoping bad weather won't delay the completion of the dig. Our goal is to start later this week."

He closed the dishwasher door, then turned around and watched her gaze shift from his face to his midsection. She saw the evidence of his desire for her. That couldn't be helped when she was sitting there looking as sexy as any woman had a right to look. "Did I tell you how much I like your outfit?"

She chuckled and the sound made his erection thicken even more. "Yes, you told me. I figured you would like it since I understand men like to see skin."

She understood right. Men liked touching and tasting skin as well, which was something he'd shown her last night. Her short dress showed a lot of her thighs since the hem barely covered them. And the top had a neckline that showed a lot of cleavage, reminding him of how much he enjoyed her breasts. He wanted her bad. He wanted her right here. Right now.

He slowly crossed the room toward her. Any other woman would have run after seeing the predatory look in his eyes. But Layla stood her ground. That was fine with him. When he reached her, he removed her dress with a flick of his wrist and a little muscle power, leaving her totally naked. Like he'd suspected, she hadn't had a stitch of clothing on underneath that dress. He knew he had surprised the hell out of her with how quickly he'd undressed her.

He smiled at her shocked look. "A SEAL pays attention to detail. While sitting across from you at dinner I studied the design of your dress and figured out the best way to take it off without ripping it to shreds. I like the dress too much to tear it."

He stepped back. "Now to remove my clothes."

Gavin undressed quickly. And then he picked her up and spread her across the same table he'd cleared just moments ago. "Open your legs for me, Layla."

He intended to bury himself inside of her as deeply as he could go. He was certain the hot and hungry look in his eyes said as much. But he knew all this was still new to her and he wanted her to be comfortable with everything they did together.

She lay there, on his table, with her legs spread. For a minute he just stood and looked at her. Remembering her taste, he couldn't help but lick his lips. Tasting her would have to come later. Right now he needed to *come*. Quickly putting on a condom, he settled his body between her thighs. She held his gaze when he entered her, filling her completely. Being inside her, feeling her muscles clench around him, felt so damn good. Her muscles were trying to pull everything out of him and the sensation was driving him insane.

Gavin held tight to her hips as he moved in and out. She wrapped her legs around his waist, locking him inside of her. He wanted her to feel every stroke, the same way he was feeling it. On and on, each thrust was hard and precise. Back and forth, he rocked inside of her. Steady, with meaningful precision. He thrust hard, creating pleasure that spread like molten heat throughout both of their bodies. The sound of Layla's moans only increased his desire to please her. When he felt her body explode, his explosion soon followed.

That's when he realized why things were so different with her. Why with her he so easily lost control.

As much as a part of him wished it wasn't true, he knew he had fallen head over heels in love with Layla Harris.

Fourteen

"So what are you going to do about Tammy?"

Layla lifted her head off Gavin's chest. It was two days after the night he'd prepared dinner for her. She had arrived at the guest cottage to find him sitting on the steps waiting for her. Her heart had pounded the minute she'd seen him sitting there. He'd stood when she got out of the car and her gaze had taken him in. With the Stetson on his head, his Western shirt, a pair of well-worn and scuffed boots, he looked like a quintessential cowboy. She wondered how he would look dressed as a SEAL. Too bad she would probably never see him that way. Gavin as a rancher would be the memory of him she would keep in her heart forever.

He had taken her hand into his and once they were locked inside the house, he had swept her into his arms and headed for the bedroom where they'd made love a number of times. Then he'd told her some troubling news. It seemed earlier that day he'd overheard one of his men bragging about sleeping with Tammy. The man had said she'd told him she was into group sex, so if he had any friends who were interested, she was available.

Gavin hadn't liked what he'd overheard and felt he needed to bring it to Layla's attention. She was glad he had. Unfortunately, she was battling her own issues with Tammy. The young woman's promiscuity wasn't Layla's number one concern. Tammy's entitled attitude was impairing the success of the dig. The report Layla had assigned to Tammy had yet to be done, and Tammy's slacking off on her duties had increased to the point where the other students were complaining. Low morale was the last thing Layla needed to deal with.

Layla had confided in Gavin, telling him of her own issues with Tammy including Tammy's ongoing affair with the head of Layla's department and how Tammy was blatantly using that affair to do whatever she wanted…as well as avoiding the things she didn't want to do.

Finally answering Gavin's question, Layla said, "There's only one thing I can do about Tammy and that is to release her from the team and brace myself for the backlash from Dr. Clayburn. She isn't a team player, she lacks respect for everyone and she isn't pulling her own weight. I refuse to give her more chances than I would give anyone else, no matter who she's sleeping with."

Gavin nodded. He thought Layla was making the right decision by releasing Tammy from her team. He'd known Tammy had been trouble from day one. "So you'll start digging on Friday?"

"Yes. We got delayed when one of the supply shipments was late. We haven't had any other problems, but I wanted to ask, did you ever talk to that guy to see if he was the one who moved my marker?"

"Yes, and Clete said he didn't move anything. So what happened to your marker is still a mystery."

"It doesn't matter since we're moving ahead. I'm excited."

He pulled her tighter into his arms. "So am I. I can't wait to see what you find."

She pulled back and stared up at him. "And now you think I will find something?"

"Yes. I told you I'd gotten a good reading from Flip's camera. I'm sure you'll find something, I'm just not certain it's the loot you're looking for."

She smiled up at him. "Well, I am certain, Mr. Blake." She then pulled his mouth down to hers.

Hours later, the ringing of his cell phone woke Gavin. He looked down at the woman plastered to his side. The phone had awakened her, as well. He glanced at the clock and saw it was three in the morning. Who would be calling him at this hour?

He reached for the phone on the nightstand before it could ring again. "Hello."

He heard the words his foreman said and was out of bed in a flash. "We're on our way."

Layla sat up. "What's wrong, Gavin?"

He glanced over at her as he reached for his clothes. "That was Caldwell. The old barn is going up in flames."

It didn't take long for them to both make their way to the south pasture.

"Arson?" Gavin asked, staring down Cornerstone's fire marshal. He knew Josh Timbales well since the man had been good friends with Gavin's dad.

"Yes, Gavin. Arson. And the person didn't even try covering their tracks. You could smell kerosene a mile away."

"But who would do such a thing?" Layla asked, staring at the building that was now burned to the ground as well as the charred remains of the equipment that had been stored inside.

"I don't know," Josh said to Layla. "My investigative team has been called in as well as the sheriff. Hopefully they will come up with some answers."

In the meantime… Layla turned to stare at her students who were huddled together a few feet away. They'd gotten word about the fire and had rushed from town. She could see the disappointed looks on their faces. They'd worked hard and now this. "I need to talk to my team," Layla said, and walked off.

Gavin watched her go. He could feel her anger and disappointment. He turned a livid gaze to Josh. "No matter what it takes, I intend to find the person responsible for this."

Layla approached the group. Before she could say anything, one of her students, Wendy Miller, spoke up. "Is it true what the firemen are saying? Did someone deliberately set fire to the barn?"

Layla drew in a deep breath. "Yes, the fire marshal has ruled it as arson. The sheriff is on his way."

"Looks like you have an enemy, Dr. Harris," Tammy said with a smirk. "Well, with no equipment for the dig, that means we're free to leave and return home, right? I didn't like this place anyway."

Layla had had enough. "Yes, you can leave, Tammy. I was going to release you from the team in the morning anyway. Have a safe trip back to Seattle."

Fury shone on Tammy's face. "You're dropping me from the team? You can't do that."

"I just did."

Tammy lifted her chin. "It really doesn't matter because there won't be a dig team. Once Dr. Clayburn calculates the cost of all the equipment that was destroyed in the fire, he will call off the dig."

"The college probably insured the equipment. It won't take long to get more in here," Donnell said angrily. He stared at Tammy suspiciously. "And just where were you tonight, Tammy? I was in the hotel's lobby and saw when you came in rather late. It wouldn't surprise me if you torched this place."

From the looks on the faces of her other students, Layla could see they were thinking the same thing. Evidently Tammy saw it, as well. She backed up, away from the others. "I was with someone, so I have a concrete alibi. But I plan on giving Dr. Clayburn a call to tell him everything."

"And how do you have his phone number?" another student asked, making it pretty obvious all of them had an idea.

"That's none of your business," Tammy snapped. And then she angrily walked off.

Layla turned back to her students. "I will call Dr. Clayburn in the morning myself. Regardless of what Tammy says, I doubt he will shut down the project."

Although Layla said the words, she truly wasn't so sure of that.

The next day, an angry Layla slammed down the phone. She could not believe the conversation she'd just had with Dr. Clayburn. She could not believe the audacity of the man.

"What's wrong, Layla?"

She turned and saw Gavin. She hadn't heard him enter the cottage. She saw the care and concern in his expression and she loved him even more than she already had. He had been so understanding and supportive. Incredibly, he'd been more concerned about the loss of her equipment than he had for the loss of his barn.

Last night they had both talked to the sheriff, whom she'd discovered was a high school friend of Gavin's. Sheriff Roy Wade was just as determined as Gavin to find the person responsible for the fire. And after checking for footprints, Gavin mentioned the ones around the burned barn were the same ones he'd seen when her marker had gone missing. It was obvious someone was trying to sabotage the dig. But who, and why?

She drew in a deep breath. "That was Dr. Clayburn."

"And?"

She blew out a frustrated and angry sigh. "Tammy got to him first. She probably called him last night like she threatened to do. He really didn't want to hear anything I had to say."

Gavin crossed his arms over his chest with a furious look on his face. "You mean to tell me he's taking a student's word over yours?"

Layla frowned. "Remember Tammy isn't just another student. She's also the man's side piece. I didn't want to believe it before, but I definitely believe it now. The influence she has over him! If I didn't know better I'd think there's more to it, that she's blackmailing him with something."

Gavin dropped his arms and came to stand in front of her. "Why? What did he say?"

"He wanted to let me know my students were notified this morning by email that the dig has been canceled and they are to return to campus." She paused. "He also wanted me to know that I've been terminated from my position at the university."

"He fired you?"

"Yes. He claims I botched things up. As far as he is concerned, the fire was my responsibility. I should have been more attentive to my work rather than indulging in an 'illicit affair with one of the cowboys.'" There was no doubt in Layla's mind Tammy had fed the man that BS and he'd believed it without question.

"Can't you go to the president of the university with your side of the story?"

"Yes, but Dr. Clayburn and President Connors are good friends. If I was terminated that means Dr. Connors approved the termination because he believed whatever Dr. Clayburn told him about me."

"Let them believe whatever they want. You came here to do a dig and that's what you'll do."

Layla dropped into a nearby wingback chair. "Gavin, didn't you hear what I said?"

He squatted down in front of her. "What I hear is the sound of you giving up. Letting them defeat you."

She touched his cheek. "What am I supposed to do? I don't have a job. Nor do I have a team. Did you not hear me say that Dr. Clayburn sent everyone an email telling them to return to Seattle?"

"You'll get another job. You're too smart and intelligent not to. As far as I'm concerned, losing you is the university's loss. Besides, I want to see what their reaction will be when you find James's loot. You don't have to be affiliated with any university to dig or publish your findings, right?"

Layla shook her head. "No, I can conduct an independent excavation, but I no longer have funding, or a team."

Gavin pulled her out of the chair. "I'll replace your equipment. And you might not have a team, but I do. They will come to help out if I call them."

Layla stared at him, not believing what he was saying, what he was offering. "B-but I can't let you do that. Like you, they just got back from their last operation. They need to spend time with their families and—"

Gavin lowered his mouth and kissed the words off her lips. He then deepened the kiss. By the time he released her mouth, she was panting. "Trust me on this, will you?" he said. "I don't want to brag or anything, but we will do it in half the time your team would have."

"But it will take time to get more equipment."

"We will get the equipment we need without any delays."

Layla knew he had money and influence. She just hadn't realized how much. Then she thought of something crucial. "What about the person sabotaging the dig? Things could get dangerous."

A sinister grin touched Gavin's lips. "If he or she is crazy enough to try something with a team of SEALs around, then let them go for it. We will be ready."

He quickly kissed her again, silencing any more questions. When he released her lips, he said, "Trust me. We've got this. We'll have your back."

There was a knock at the door. Gavin lifted a brow. "Gramma Mel isn't due back until tonight, so it might be Roy. Maybe he's found something."

Gavin crossed the room with her following beside him. Opening the door they found three of her students standing there. "Donnell? Wendy? Marsha? What are you doing here?" Layla asked them. "Why aren't you on your way back to Seattle? Didn't you get Dr. Clayburn's email?"

"Yes, we got it," Donnell said, frowning. "But we didn't want to leave until we talked to you. Until you say there won't be a dig, we are staying put."

"You could get into trouble if you defy Dr. Clayburn," she warned them.

The three students looked at each other and shared what looked like conspiratorial smiles before Donnell said, "We aren't worried about that. They'll be faced with their own troubles soon. So, are you still planning to dig?"

Layla wondered what they meant by "troubles," but before she could ask, Gavin said, "Yes, the dig is still on."

She could tell from the look of respect in his eyes that he admired the stance these three students had taken. Like his team had his back, these members of her team had hers.

Donnell, Marsha and Wendy let out loud cheers and gave each other high fives. Then Donnell said, "When we find James's loot, the university's going to regret letting you go."

Fifteen

"So…you're the fast-talking college professor, huh?"

Layla swallowed as she watched the four men standing in front of her. Gavin had introduced them as Flipper, Bane, Coop and Mac. It was Flipper who'd asked the question, the depths of his blue eyes dancing with amusement.

All four were big men. Muscular. Well built. Extremely handsome. Two wore wedding rings and two did not. Gavin had told her that Brisbane Westmoreland and Thurston McRoy were happily married and that Flipper and Coop were happily single.

"I don't know. Am I?" she asked, switching her gaze from them to Gavin, who stood by her side with his arms around her waist. It was as if he was intentionally making a statement regarding the nature of their relationship. If that was the case, then she wished someone would tell her where they stood. All she knew for certain was that they enjoyed spending time together and they shared a bed every night. She definitely didn't have any complaints about that.

Gavin muttered the words, "Smart-ass," to Flipper, then leaned down and placed a kiss on Layla's lips. He then turned to his friends. "She's more than a professor."

He knew his friends were checking out Layla and with good reason. The four men knew about his don't-get-attached policy when it came to women. But it was obvious that with this particular woman, he'd gotten attached. They would be shocked to discover just how attached he was.

Like he'd known they would, his friends had answered his summons for help. No questions asked. But now that they were here and had been briefed on the situation, they were also eyewitnesses to his possessiveness of Layla. They would have questions about that later. Fair enough. He would address them then. He would admit he'd fallen in love. Bane and Mac would understand. Flipper and Coop would suggest Gavin have his head examined.

"Did you get the equipment I asked you to bring?" he asked them.

"Yes. Two of my brothers will be towing the backhoe loader and tractor in this evening," Flipper said.

"And I've got the rest of the stuff in my truck," Mac added.

"Good," Gavin said. Flip had four brothers. All SEALs. And Flip's dad had retired as a SEAL commanding officer. Gavin had thought he'd had it bad living in his father's and grandfather's shadows—until he'd met Flipper. His friend had five legacies to compete with since all the male Holloways before Flip had stellar reputations as SEALs.

"So where are we staying, Viper? The party house?" Coop asked.

Gavin shook his head. "No. Layla's at the party house."

Flipper chuckled. "So? It's big enough. You don't mind if we crash, do you?" he asked Layla.

Before she could answer, Gavin said, "But I mind."

All four men laughed. Gavin scowled.

"Easy, Viper, let's not get territorial," Flipper said, grinning.

But he did feel territorial, Gavin thought. He figured it was all a part of being in love. He still wasn't sure what to do with his feelings. He didn't want to get caught up in a woman like his dad had done. He didn't want to ask her to give up her career to wait out here on the ranch through all his missions. He didn't want a repeat of what had happened with his mom.

Pushing all that aside, he said, "Gramma Mel got back from her trip a few days ago and she prepared rooms for you guys at the main house."

"Yes!" Bane said, pumping his fist in the air. "We'll get to eat her mouthwatering biscuits for breakfast."

Gavin shook his head. He had to admit he'd missed these guys.

"So, are you going to tell Layla how you feel about her, Viper?"

Instead of answering Bane's question Gavin stared into his beer bottle and shook his head. "Won't do any good. She doesn't feel the same way."

"How do you know?" Mac asked, taking a sip of his own beer. "Women like to hear stuff like that. And often."

Coop and Flipper, Gavin noticed, were keeping their mouths shut. His admission that he'd fallen in love had shocked them into silence. The five of them were sprawled in the living room of the party house. Layla was at the main house assisting Gramma Mel with dinner. Gavin figured his grandmother would go all out and prepare a feast. She'd been happy to see his friends and they'd been happy to see her. Of course Bane would be getting those biscuits for breakfast in the morning. Mac had put in his order for an apple pie and both Coop and Flipper requested peach cobbler.

"So who do you think is trying to sabotage the dig?" Flipper asked, obviously trying to change the subject to one he and Coop could take part in. Gavin was glad to leave the topic of his love life behind.

"Don't have a clue but I intend to find out," Gavin said. "I thought it was someone connected to the university, but now I'm not sure."

"Sounds like someone doesn't want anyone digging in the south pasture, Viper," Coop said, standing, stretching out his limbs. "You all know I'm a suspicious bastard by nature. I can smell a cover-up a mile away."

Mac leaned forward in his chair. "You think someone is covering up something?"

"Possibly," Coop said. He glanced over at Gavin. "Other than Caldwell, how well do you know the men who work for you?"

Gavin shrugged. "Most have worked here for years, some even during my dad's time. There are two new guys we brought on last year." He recalled both were single, and he specifically remembered that one of them had shared Tammy's bed.

"What if someone knows for certain the loot is buried around here, heard about the dig and doesn't want anyone else to find it before they do?" Flipper suggested.

Gavin nodded. That possibility had crossed his mind, as well. He knew these four men. In addition to helping with the dig, they intended to solve the mystery of who'd removed the marker and burned down the barn. So far, the sheriff hadn't found anything other than those footprints.

Gavin had mentioned the prints to his friends. "Um, that gives us something to go on," Mac said pensively.

"We start digging in the morning," Gavin said, leaning back in his chair. "Whoever doesn't want us to will either try to stop us or will hope whatever they don't want us to find is kept hidden."

Later that night, after making love to Layla, Gavin pulled her tighter into his arms as he tried to bring his breathing under control. She had ridden him again. She was getting too good at it. He was convinced the woman was trying to kill him.

"I like your friends, Gavin."

He decided not to tell her that they liked her, as well. They had joked with her at dinner and Bane had even told her about his wife, Crystal, who, like Layla, had gotten her PhD at an early age.

"I'm glad you like them."

Dinner had been a grand affair. Not only had his grandmother cooked enough food for his friends and Layla's students, she'd invited Caldwell and his men to stop by for a plate. Several of their neighbors who'd heard about the fire stopped by to make sure all was well. Gramma Mel had sent them home with boxed dinners.

"Are you worried about the dig tomorrow?" he asked Layla.

She snuggled closer to him. "Sort of. I want to make sure my students stay safe."

"They will. I'm glad Gramma Mel insisted everyone stay at the main house. She has plenty of room and loves all the company."

"I'm glad she made the offer. Without the university footing the bill, my students couldn't afford to stay at the hotel any longer. But there's plenty of room here," she said, smiling.

"No way anyone is staying at the party house but us. This is our special place. I like coming here every night." No matter how late he worked out on the ranch, he liked coming back here to Layla. Before he parked his truck he would hear her playing her harmonica and the sound would lure him to her. He didn't want to think about how involved they were getting.

Layla lifted her head and looked up at him. "Has your grandmother asked you anything about us?"

He smiled. "She didn't have to. I think it's pretty obvious we have something going on. She's fine with it. We're adults."

What Gavin decided not to say was that his grandmother hadn't needed to ask anything because he'd told her his true feelings for Layla—and about his doubts that it would go anywhere long-term. Needless to say Gramma Mel hadn't been surprised.

"Besides, she has her hands full with Caldwell now that she's back. They've been apart for a week."

Layla lifted an arched brow. "Caldwell?"

Gavin smiled. "Yes, Caldwell. Don't tell me you haven't picked up on what's between them."

Layla shook her head. "No, I hadn't. But you have?"

"Yes, for years. He's a widower and she's a widow. Never understood why they preferred being so discreet. I guess they like their privacy.

"Since the dig starts early in the morning I guess we need to get to sleep," Gavin said, but he wasn't very convincing, even to his own ears.

"Um, I have other ideas," she said, moving on top of him again. "I like riding you."

Gavin grinned. He definitely liked Layla riding him. More than ever, he was convinced the woman was trying to kill him. But he would enjoy every minute until the end.

* * *

Hours later, the ringing of his cell phone woke Gavin. He immediately grabbed it when he recognized the ring tone. "Coop?"

"Yeah, Viper, it's me. We couldn't sleep so we thought we'd set a trap."

Gavin sat up in bed as knots tightened in his stomach. Layla had awakened as well and quickly sat up beside him. Drawing in a deep breath, he asked, "And?"

"And I think you need to get here. I've already called the sheriff. We're here at the shack and we got our man."

Sixteen

Gavin made it to the shack in record time, but he wasn't surprised to see several vehicles already there, including the sheriff's. Roy must have been in the area.

With Layla walking quickly by his side, he moved toward the shack but stopped when the door opened and his grandmother stepped out. Her crestfallen features and the tears in her eyes made him pause. *What the hell…*?

He looked past her to Caldwell, who had his grandmother's hand tucked securely in his. The older man shook his head sadly. Gavin felt Layla move closer to his side and he placed his hand in hers.

"I'm taking your grandmother to my place," Caldwell said. "That's where she'll be. You need to go on in now. He's already confessed."

Gavin frowned. *He who? And why was his grandmother crying*? Tightening his grip on Layla's hand, he entered the shack.

Everyone looked up when he and Layla walked in. Roy

and Gavin's four SEAL friends. Was he imagining things or were the five looking at him strangely? A funny feeling settled in his gut. Stepping into the room, he glanced around. "Okay, guys. What's going on? Where is he?"

The group shifted and he saw the man seated in a chair with his hands handcuffed behind his back. Gavin shook his head as if to clear his brain. "Mr. Lott?" he said in shock.

Sherman Lott couldn't even look at him. Gavin shook his head again and looked over at his friends. "There must be some mistake. Mr. Lott has been our neighbor for years. He was a friend of Dad's. He—"

"I was never a friend of your father's!" Lott all but screamed. "Gavin Jr. always got anything he wanted. He was the town's hero in high school. I could never compete. Then he became a SEAL and was a war hero, and I couldn't compete there, either. He got all the girls. After my leg got banged up that time when a horse threw me, the women around here wouldn't give me the time of day."

Gavin stared at the man who was now glaring back at him with cold and hate-filled eyes. Gavin let go of Layla's hand. Evidently he had misunderstood this man's relationship with his father all these years. "Okay, so there was a rivalry between you and Dad, and he wasn't your friend. What does that have to do with you sabotaging a dig on my property?"

Instead of answering, Lott shifted his gaze from Gavin to Layla. "I removed that marker so you'd forget where you were supposed to dig, but that didn't stop you. I burned that damn barn down and that didn't stop you, either. You were determined to dig anyway."

"Why didn't you want her to dig, Mr. Lott?" Gavin asked.

The man didn't answer. He looked away as if ignoring the question.

Gavin looked over at his friends. "Would any of you care to explain just what the hell is going on? Why didn't Lott want Layla's team to dig up buried treasure?"

Roy cleared his throat and said in a somber voice, "It wasn't the buried treasure he was concerned with anyone finding, Gavin."

Gavin frowned. Now he was even more confused. "Then what was it?"

The room quieted and he felt Layla pressing her body closer to his. Then she again placed her hand in his. When no one answered, Lott hollered out, "Your mother! I didn't want you to find your mother's body."

Layla felt weak in the knees and wondered how Gavin could still be standing. His friends evidently wondered the same thing as Bane and Coop crossed the room to flank Gavin's other side. Suddenly, she realized they hadn't done so to keep Gavin steady on his feet. They'd moved to intercede if Gavin took a mind to kill Sherman Lott.

"You refused an attorney, Mr. Lott," Roy said angrily. "Like I told you before, any confession you make will hold up in court."

Layla saw Flipper hold up his phone, letting everyone know he was recording everything. Gavin moved forward, and she, Bane and Coop fell in step. It was apparent the shock of what Lott had said had worn off.

"What do you mean 'my mother's body'?" Gavin asked, standing less than five feet from Lott.

Layla thought she actually saw regret fill Mr. Lott's eyes when he said, "I didn't mean to kill her. Honest. It was an accident."

Gavin drew in a breath so deep, it seemed the room rattled from the effect. She felt it. She thought everybody in the room felt it. "You killed my mother?" he asked in an incredulous voice. "But how? She left here."

The man shook his head. "No, she didn't. She never left. I came across her one day with a flat tire. Said she'd planned on going away for a while but changed her mind and turned around before even making it to town. She missed you and your dad too much to go anywhere. She was on her way back home. Had made it to the main road to the Silver Spurs when her tire went flat. I offered to help. She was pretty. She smelled good. I thought she was too good for your dad. He didn't deserve her. What man would leave a young wife who looked like her all alone to go play soldier?"

The man paused. "I told her as much. I must have made her nervous by what I said. By the way I was looking at her and all. And then I don't know what happened but I tried to touch her. She slapped me and I got mad. I slapped her back. I admit to hitting her several more times. She managed to get away and she ran from me. That made me angry. I ran after her and she fell and hit her head."

"And you didn't go get help?" Gavin asked in a voice that was as hard as steel.

"No!" Lott snapped. "Too late. Blood was everywhere. I knew she was dead. Besides, had she lived she would have told everyone what I tried to do. So I dug a hole and buried her."

Layla could almost see steam coming out of Gavin's ears. He was breathing deeply. The hand holding hers tightened in fury.

"What about the car?" Roy asked. Maybe the sheriff figured the best thing to do was keep the conversation going. Otherwise the deathly silence might put crazy ideas into Gavin's head. Like crossing the room and breaking Sherman Lott's neck with his bare hands.

"I drove the car into my lake," Lott said.

"You bastard!" Gavin roared. He would have moved closer but Bane and Coop blocked him. "You buried my mother in a hole not knowing if she was alive or dead? And then you drove her car into the lake?"

Lott had the nerve to glare at Gavin. "Why do you think I wouldn't let anyone swim or fish in my lake? Why I kept it off-limits to you or anyone? Especially to you. I knew how well you could swim and figured one day you might dive too far down and see the car."

Layla saw fierce rage on Gavin's face and she felt it in his entire body. The thought of him being *that* enraged scared her. She glanced over at Bane and Coop. They looked just as enraged as Gavin.

Coop then said in a menacingly calm voice, speaking directly to Gavin but not taking his eyes off Lott. "Now you know why he tried keeping anyone from digging in the south pasture, Viper. Let Roy take him in."

"No!" Gavin roared. "That bastard killed my mother."

"We know," Bane said in a chilling tone, giving Lott one hell of a lethal stare. "We all heard. And although we want to get a damn machete and chop his ass into little pieces, we won't. Let the law take care of him, Viper. In the end he's going to get exactly what he deserves."

The room got quiet and all eyes shifted to Gavin. Even Lott looked petrified upon seeing the deadly glint in Gavin's eyes. There was no doubt in Layla's mind that everyone in that room remembered that, when he needed to be, Gavin Blake could become a killing machine.

Then suddenly Gavin pulled his hand free of hers, shoved both of his hands into the pockets of his jeans and began slowly backing up, not taking his eyes off Lott. It was as if he was trying to pull himself together. As if he knew that staying in that room with Lott one more second meant he would lose control and do the man bodily harm. Gavin kept backing up until his back touched the door. He turned to open it and then stopped. He paused before turning back around.

Layla held her breath, not knowing what Gavin intended to do next. From the tension in the room, she knew his SEAL friends were poised, anticipating his next move. Then his gaze shifted from Lott to her. She saw both pain and anger in his features and her heart hurt for him. The man she loved. She wanted to think he needed her, but would he shut her out of the emotions he was feeling?

The room was deathly still as he continued to stare at her. Then he moved forward…toward her. When he stood right in front of her, he took her hand in his again. Then, without saying a single word, he led her out the door.

Seventeen

Gavin wanted to pull his truck to the side of the road and catch his breath. But he couldn't. Something propelled him to keep driving until he reached the party house. He needed Layla as much as he needed to breathe. She wasn't saying anything. Just sitting in the bench seat beside him and staring straight ahead. It was as if she knew he needed complete silence. His mind was in a state of shock and he was fighting to keep control. Fearful that at any moment he might lose it.

Every time he thought about what Lott had confessed to doing, his mind would spin. Become filled with deadly thoughts and tempt him to turn the truck around and go back to the shack and beat the hell out of the man. How could anyone do what Lott had done and live with himself all these years? And to think no one had suspected a thing until Layla had shown up wanting to dig on their property.

Gavin released a deep breath when he turned into the

driveway. Moments later he brought the truck to a stop beside Layla's rental car. Then he was out of the vehicle and moving to the passenger side of the truck. He was there when she opened the door.

Sweeping her into his arms, he headed for the porch, taking the steps two at a time. Grateful that in their rush to leave they'd left the door unlocked, he pushed it open and went inside. Barely taking time to close it behind him, he put Layla on her feet and began ripping off his clothes. She followed his lead and quickly removed hers.

He needed to be inside her. Now.

Taking hold of her waist, he lifted her up and released a throaty growl while pressing her body against the door, spreading her legs wide in the process. Then he was at her entrance, filled with an adrenaline high so potent he could feel blood rushing through his veins, especially the thick ones at the head of his shaft. Desire, as intense as it could get, became a throbbing need pulsating within him.

He thrust hard into her. Over and over again. Needing the release that only her body could give him. Leaning in, he captured her lips with his as sensations, too overpowering to be controlled, rammed through him. When she wrapped her legs around him, she propelled him to make his strokes harder and longer.

Their kiss was so sexually charged he wasn't sure how much longer he could last. He was being robbed of any logical thought except becoming a part of this woman's body. This woman, who had come to mean so much to him. This woman, who made him feel things he'd never felt before with anyone else.

And when she tore her mouth away from his just seconds before her body detonated, her spiraling climax triggered his own and he stroked her with hard and steady thrusts. He hollered her name, drowning in emotions so powerful they seemed to rock his world. A world that a short while ago had been torn apart. He couldn't stop his heart from racing at the magnitude of what he felt. At the magnitude of all he desired.

He knew then that if he'd had any doubt before regarding what Layla had come to mean to him, there was none now.

"Sorry. I should not have taken you that way. But I needed you so damn much, Layla."

They lay together in bed. After making love against the door, Gavin had picked her up and carried her into the bedroom. Then they'd slid beneath the covers and he had held her. She had held him. Layla knew that sleep wasn't an option.

She snuggled closer, needing his heat. Needing a reminder of how much she had been desired. "No apology needed. I liked it."

"I was rough."

"You were good as usual." He had needed her, just like he'd said. Layla had felt that need with every stroke.

"I lost control," he admitted in a low voice. "That's never happened to me before. Hell, Layla, I didn't even take time to put on a condom."

She'd noticed. Had exhilarated in the feeling of being skin to skin with him. Had loved the moment he had blasted off inside of her. The feel of his hot release had felt so right. How could she tell him that? But she knew she had to.

She lifted her face from his chest, met the dark eyes staring down at her. "I liked the feel of you inside me without a condom, Gavin. And don't worry about me getting pregnant. Although I was never sexually active, I decided to get the birth control implant anyway. Better to be safe than sorry. I didn't have to think about it, not like the pill where you have to remember to take one every day." She paused. "And I'm healthy so you don't have to worry about me giving you anything."

He shifted their positions in bed, slipping his arms around her and holding her close. "I'm healthy, too, and you don't have to worry about me giving you anything, either."

He then cupped her chin. "Although I didn't like being rough with you, I enjoyed making love to you without a condom, too."

And then he didn't say anything and she didn't, either. She figured he needed the silence. But when it stretched for what she thought was too long, she moved to lie on top of him and stared into the face she loved so much.

"Talk to me, Gavin. Tell me what you're feeling."

A part of her wondered what right she had to stick her nose into his business, to assume he wanted to tell her anything. But another part of her knew she couldn't let him withdraw. Just like he'd needed her physically, she wanted him to need her emotionally, as well.

She knew his eyes well. Just as well as she knew the shape of his mouth and the fullness of those lips that had kissed her earlier. He would try to fight her on this but she wouldn't let him. He'd been by himself this way for so long she figured it was hard for him to allow another person into his space. Especially a woman. But she had news for him. She wasn't just any woman. She was the woman who loved him.

And for some reason, although he'd never given her reason to say the words, a part of her believed he knew how she felt. A part of her wanted to believe that he knew she wouldn't share her body with just anyone. This wasn't just an excavation fling for her. It was more. But maybe he didn't know. Men had a tendency to be dense when it came to the I-love-you stuff.

"For a minute I felt like a loose cannon, Layla," he

said, interrupting her thoughts. "So out of control. I could have snapped and killed Lott with my bare hands. It would have given me pleasure to hear the sound of his neck breaking."

His words, spoken with deep emotion, invaded her mind. She had felt his anger and she'd seen how he'd managed to hold it in check after hearing everything the man had said. Of course the sheriff had been there to stop Gavin from taking matters into his own hands. And his SEAL teammates had been there, too, although she wasn't sure if they would have stopped him or helped him.

"But now you know the truth, Gavin. Your mother never left you and your dad, after all. She's been here all this time. Here on the Silver Spurs."

She watched his eyes flash with confusion. She explained further. "You remember when you told me how the south pasture was your favorite area and your father's, as well. How the two of you would often camp out there. How you loved the feel of sleeping under the stars?"

"Yes."

"I want to think that although the two of you didn't know it, the reason that area meant so much was because your mom was there. She was *there*, Gavin, and when you were there, without knowing it, you were close to her."

She saw the moment when her words sank in. Something broke within him. His eyes might not have been expressive to others but they were expressive to her. Without saying anything, he cupped the back of her neck and brought her mouth down to his. Their tongues tangled in a mating so intense that when he finally released her mouth, she felt light-headed and breathless.

Layla was glad she had given him something to think about. But she knew he must still feel guilty over what he'd believed all these years—that his mother had deserted him and his father. His next words proved her right.

"But I didn't know, Layla. I thought she had gone. I thought she was living another life somewhere without us. I thought—"

She placed a finger to his lips. "What you thought was understandable. You were only a child when she disappeared. But your dad knew his wife. He knew their love. He always believed she would come back. And she did. In fact, she never left. She's been here for the two of you the entire time. And I know she was proud of your dad and was just as proud of you. The man you've become."

He pulled her close, buried his face in her neck. And she held him. Held him tight and near her heart. A part of her wanted to tell him now how much she loved him, but she knew it wasn't the time. That admission would come later. For now this was what he needed. To know she was here and that he wasn't alone.

Bane's ringtone woke Gavin and he glanced out the window as he sat up. It was daybreak. "Yes, Bane?" He nodded. "We're on our way."

When he clicked off the phone, he said, "Let's get dressed. Both your team and mine are ready. Now they have two treasures to find."

A short while later, Gavin pulled his truck to a stop in front of what Layla knew should have been the excavation site. Instead it resembled a crime scene with yellow tape marking the area. Upon hearing the sound of the truck, everyone turned their way. A blanket of snow covered the hillside and forecasters predicted even heavier snow by the weekend. They would need to work quickly.

Layla saw her students standing in a huddle. They'd probably heard what was going on and were trying to figure out how they'd slept through it all. She also saw Ms. Melody standing close to Caldwell, the man's arms wrapped protectively around her. Nothing discreet there.

If anyone hadn't realized they were a couple before, they sure knew it now.

Roy was talking on the phone and Gavin's teammates stood next to the digging equipment. She wondered if they'd gotten any sleep, although they looked wide-awake and ready for any action that might come their way.

She'd been so busy observing everyone that she'd failed to notice that Gavin had gotten out of the truck until he was opening the passenger door. He leaned over her to unsnap her seat belt and then effortlessly lifted her out of her seat. "Thanks," she said, when he'd placed her on her feet.

"Don't mention it."

Taking her hand, he walked to where the others were standing. His grandmother left her place by Caldwell's side and walked over to Gavin. He released his hold on Layla's hand and pulled Ms. Melody into a big hug. Giving the two some privacy, Layla joined her students. She figured they would have a lot of questions.

After talking to her team, she returned to Gavin and his teammates. Coop explained how they'd fingered Sherman Lott as the bad guy. "After you told us about the footprint and how it was apparent more pressure was being placed on one foot than the other, we knew we were looking for someone with a leg injury or some kind of impairment and who was wearing worn shoes. When we saw Lott's shoes and saw him rubbing his leg more than once, I got suspicious. I offered him my chair so he wouldn't have to stand. I told him that I noticed his leg seemed to be bothering him. That's when he said it occasionally did and was the result of a horse riding accident years ago."

Coop then nodded for Bane to continue.

"Last night after everyone had gone to bed," Bane said, taking up the tale. "Mac and I decided to go to Lott's ranch and snoop around, to see if we could find the kerosene can. Imagine our surprise when we got there and saw him loading up a kerosene can onto his truck, with plans to head back over to your place to burn down the shack. We called Coop and told him to contact you and to call the sheriff. Lott was caught red-handed about to pour kerosene around the shack to torch it."

Roy approached with an angry look on his face. "What's wrong, Roy?" Gavin asked.

"One of the disadvantages of a small town is not having manpower when you need it," Roy said, drawing in a deep breath. "I talked to the sheriff in Palmdale and he said it would be four to five days before their dive team could get here."

Gavin nodded as if he wasn't concerned with that news. "Is there any reason we can't start digging?" he asked.

Roy frowned. "Yes, there's a reason. This is a crime scene."

Gavin shook his head. "Technically it's not. Although I believe everything Lott said, until I find my mother's body there's no proof a crime has been committed. Besides, I'd rather be the one to find her, Roy. And those students over there are entitled to their treasure hunt."

Roy didn't say anything for a minute and then nodded. "Okay, but I will stay here to help and step in if any evidence is found."

"Absolutely," Gavin assured him.

Roy drew in a deep breath and ordered one of his deputies to remove the yellow crime scene tape.

Less than an hour later, the remains of Jamie Blake were found. And within twenty feet of where she'd been buried, a strongbox filled with gold pieces—Jesse James's loot—was also recovered.

Deciding not to wait on the dive team from Palmdale, Flipper had jumped into Lott's lake without any diving gear. When he hadn't resurfaced in five minutes, Roy became worried. Gavin and his other teammates had not. They explained that although the water was icy cold and Flipper had been under longer than normal, Flipper was far from ordinary. They were proven right when a short while later Flipper resurfaced with the license plate he had removed from the car. The license plate was identified as that registered to Gavin and Jamie Blake.

The charges against Sherman Lott were changed from suspicion of murder to murder.

Eighteen

Layla stood at the window. It was snowing and what had begun that morning as small flakes was now huge and covering the earth in a white blanket. Four days had passed since the dig, and activities on the Silver Spurs were returning to normal. Once Gavin's mother's remains had been unearthed, the town's coroner had been called and the yellow tape had been reerected. But not before Jesse James's strongbox filled with gold bars had been uncovered.

The Silver Spurs became the focus of two big news stories—a decades-old murder and the first recorded discovery of Jesse James's loot in the state of Missouri. No-trespassing signs had been posted when the media had converged on the ranch.

Gavin had given his one and only statement regarding the recovery of his mother's remains. "I am glad the truth about my mother's disappearance was discovered and I hope Sherman Lott rots in hell."

A news conference had been held regarding the discovery of Jesse James's loot, which was making international news. Dr. Clayburn arrived in town and tried to claim the university was associated with the dig. Layla refuted his statement since she had documentation in the form of an email from both Dr. Clayburn and the president of the university advising of her termination prior to the dig. The following day, the two men were in even more hot water when photographs surfaced of the two of them involved in illicit affairs with female students. Not surprisingly, Tammy was in many of the photographs, arriving and leaving various hotels with both men.

Layla didn't have to guess where the photographs had come from. Apparently Donnell and some of the other students had exposed the sordid activities. Within twenty-four hours of the photographs being splashed across the front page of the *Seattle Times* and making the national news, the two men, along with a few other faculty members, had turned in their resignations.

Donnell, Wendy and Marsha had joined Layla at the news conference and were acknowledged for their participation on the dig. The Missouri Archaeological Society had authenticated the loot as that stolen by Jesse James from the Tinsel Bank.

Already offers of employment from numerous universities had arrived for Layla, in addition to offers of book deals and television interviews. Yesterday she'd received a call from her grandmother and one from her parents. She had been surprised when her parents told her how proud they were of her. They'd even said she'd done the right thing by following her own dream and not theirs. They invited her to spend the holidays with them in DC.

She drew in a deep breath and moved away from the window to sit on the bed she'd just left a few moments earlier. She had awakened to find Gavin gone. He must have left to check on the ranch with his men. Even with the no-trespassing signs clearly posted, a couple of reporters and their camera crews had encroached on the property only to have Gavin's men run them off again.

The coroner had released his mother's remains and yesterday morning a private memorial service had been held. Jamie Blake had been reburied beside her husband in the family cemetery. Layla had stood beside Gavin along with his grandmother, Caldwell and Gavin's teammates. Even his commanding officer had flown in to attend the service.

After dinner, Gavin's teammates left to return to their various homes, but not before each one had given her a huge hug and told her how glad they'd been to meet her. She had gotten to know the four well and could see why they and Gavin shared such close relationships. Bane, Coop, Flipper and Mac were swell guys who were fiercely loyal to each other. She couldn't thank them enough for their part in recovering Jesse James's loot.

Now that the dig was over, Layla could feel Gavin withdrawing from her. She had tried ignoring it but she knew something was bothering him. She thought it was related to his mother but, to be totally honest, she wasn't sure.

There was no reason for her to remain on the ranch any longer and she had mentioned that she would be leaving in a couple of days to return to Seattle. She had hoped he would ask her to stay but he hadn't. Instead he'd merely nodded and hadn't said anything else about it. Was that his way of letting her know she had outstayed her welcome?

The thought that he wanted her to leave his ranch had tears welling up in her eyes. She'd known when she fell in love with him that there was a big chance he wouldn't love her back. So why was the thought that he didn't breaking her heart?

The time they had spent together on the Silver Spurs had been special but now she had to move on.

Gavin placed his coffee cup on the table, stared at his grandmother and then asked, "What did you just say?"

Melody Blake smiled brightly. "You heard me right, Gavin. Caldwell asked me to marry him. This was his third time asking and I finally said yes. We don't want to make a big fuss about it and Reverend Pollock agreed to perform the ceremony next weekend. I'll be moving into Caldwell's place afterward."

Gavin didn't say anything for a long moment. He was happy for his grandmother and Caldwell. It was about time. "Congratulations. I'm happy for you, Gramma Mel. Caldwell is a good man and I believe the two of you will be happy together."

"Thank you. What about you? What are your plans regarding Layla?"

He lifted his coffee cup and took a sip before saying, "What makes you think I have any?"

His grandmother frowned. "Don't try pretending with me, Gavin Timothy Blake III. You love Layla. You've admitted as much. I would think you'd want to take the next step."

Yes, he had admitted it to her and he didn't regret doing so. "Sometimes taking the next step isn't always possible."

"Why not? I'd think you'd want something permanent between the two of you."

He shook his head. "Layla and I are very different. Dad took Mom out of a big city and brought her here and she was miserable. Layla is from Seattle. She'd be just as unhappy and miserable here as Mom was."

"Have you talked to Layla about it? Have you asked her how she feels?"

"No."

"Then maybe you should. You're basing your opinions on assumptions. I know for a fact Layla loves the Silver Spurs. She said as much."

"But that doesn't mean she loves me. If she doesn't love me, then there's nothing to hold her here. She's gotten a lot of job offers from a number of big universities, including Harvard. All we have in Cornerstone is a small college. Why would she settle for that?"

"Well, I think you'll be making a big mistake if you don't talk to her about it, tell her how you feel. Let her decide what she wants to do. You might discover that she loves you as much as you love her."

An hour or so later, Gavin entered the party house. He removed his hat and shook off the snow from his jacket before hanging both items on the rack.

The first thing he noticed as he headed for the kitchen was that the curtains were still closed. Everything was just as he'd left it at daybreak, which meant Layla hadn't gotten up yet. Placing the box containing the breakfast his grandmother had prepared on the table, he moved down the hallway to the bedroom. Opening the door, he stuck his head inside and saw Layla curled up in bed still sleeping.

The bad weather had pretty much dictated that everyone stay inside. He knew his men had a card game going and he could certainly join them. But he much preferred staying here and joining Layla, right in that bed. What if Gramma Mel was right? What if Layla wanted to stay on the Silver Spurs with him? Would it be fair to ask her to stay when a call from his commanding officer meant he would drop everything for a covert operation? Would she want that?

He sat in a chair and removed his shoes and socks before standing to take off the rest of his clothes. No matter the temperature, he preferred sleeping in the nude, something he couldn't do while away on missions.

Crossing the room, Gavin slid into bed with Layla and pulled her into his arms, to warm his body as well as his heart.

Layla thought she was dreaming when she felt a hot and husky whisper against her ear. It took a moment to open her eyes and gaze into a pair of sexy dark ones staring back at her. Gavin's body was pressed close to hers. It was warm, even hot in certain places, and she knew without a doubt that he was naked.

"We need to talk, Layla."

She heard the seriousness in his voice. Why did they need to talk? He was ready for her to leave. She got that. But why was he rushing her away? Did he already have another woman lined up to share his bed? The thought made her mad and she buried her face in the pillow, but not before saying, "I don't want to talk. I have nothing to say to you."

He pulled the pillow away from her, frowning. "What the hell did I do?"

"Just being a typical man. You share a bed with a woman, and then you tire of her and want her gone so you can replace her with another."

He stared at her. "You think I would do that?"

"Why wouldn't you? You're a man, aren't you? You're not tied to any woman, especially not to me. It's not like I didn't notice that reporter flirting with you."

He frowned. "What reporter?"

Layla rolled her eyes. "The one that kept putting that microphone all in your face and kept touching your shoulders every chance she got, even when she didn't have to." Layla hated that she'd said something about that. Now she sounded like a jealous hag. Just because they'd slept together a few times didn't mean she had dibs on him.

Before she could catch her next breath, he had flipped her on her back. He loomed over her and held her hands in a tight grip above her head.

"Why would I want another woman, Layla?"

That was really a silly question. "Why wouldn't you want another one?"

He stared down at her with an intensity that made a rush of desire claw through her insides. "Because you are all the woman I need. Hell, I can barely keep up with you, Layla."

Lord knows that's the truth, Gavin thought, as he felt familiar need hammer through him. Only Layla could do this to him. Make him feel so consumed with desire for her, he would go up in flames. More than once his teammates had told him to take a cold shower when just looking at Layla heated an entire room.

Gavin just stared down at her. She was wearing a nightgown, but barely. It was made of flimsy material and part of it was bunched up around her waist, leaving her bare below. Her hair was loose and tousled around her shoulders. Because of the way he was holding her hands, her breasts jutted up, firm and hard. He could see the impression of rigid nipples through the thin material of her gown.

Just that quickly, her breathing changed. He heard it and then he felt the sinfully erotic movement of her hips against him. After all the times they'd made love right here in this bed, not to mention the times they hadn't made it to the bed, didn't she know how much he wanted her? Her and no other woman? She actually thought she had a reason to be jealous of some damn reporter who couldn't keep her hands to herself?

He knew from the eyes staring back at him that his grandmother was right. Layla had no idea how he felt about her. The woman hadn't a clue. He had told her they needed to talk, and then she'd gone on the offensive. Why? Had his grandmother been right on both accounts, that Layla cared for him as much as he cared for her?

There was only one way to find out.

"Let's backtrack for a minute, Layla. Earlier I asked you why I would want another woman, and you asked why I wouldn't want one. I don't think I made myself clear enough. The main reason I don't want another woman is because I love you. I've fallen in love with you, Layla, and when a man falls in love with one woman she takes away his desire for other women. She becomes the one and only woman he wants in his life, his bed, his home, his mind and his heart. You are that woman for me."

She stared at him for a long time without saying anything. And then he saw it, the tears forming in her eyes. "But if you love me, why were you sending me away?"

He frowned. "I wasn't sending you away. The other night you told me you were going. What was I supposed to do, tell you that you couldn't go?"

She frowned back at him. "You could have told me you loved me."

"Why would I tell you that when I didn't know how you felt? Hell, I still don't know. With your credentials, you can teach anywhere. I know about all those job offers that have come in. Why would you want to stay here? My mother hated it here."

"I love you, too, Gavin, and I love it here. I fell in love with the Silver Spurs the minute I drove onto the land. There are times when I will leave to do speaking engagements and interviews. Maybe even teach a class or two for a semester. However, I will come back. You leave, don't you? To go on your covert operations. Yet you come back.

You return and step into your role of a rancher. Why can't I return and step into a similar role."

"As a rancher's wife?"

She lifted her brow. "Wife?"

He smiled down at her. "Yes, wife. You don't think you'll hang around as my live-in lover, do you? I want to marry you. I want you to one day have my children. I want you to live here on this ranch with me."

"And be here whenever the rancher returns?"

He chuckled. "That would be nice."

A smile touched her lips. "That can be arranged." She didn't say anything for a minute. "About all those offers. I don't want to decide on anything just yet. After dealing with the likes of Clayburn and Connors, I just want to chill for a minute. Possibly write a book. I'd love to take my time and do it here."

He nodded. He needed to let her know something.

Layla waited for him to speak.

"Gramma Mel told me this morning that she and Caldwell are getting married. She's moving to his place. That means you'll be here by yourself whenever I'm away. I'm supposed to report back for duty at the end of January."

"I'll be okay. I will have enough to keep me busy."

Layla wouldn't tell him yet that she wanted lots of children. She'd always wished for siblings and would make sure she had more than one child. And she didn't want to wait a long time before she began having them.

Before Gavin, she'd never thought beyond her career goals. But now she'd achieved those. With him by her side, she could have everything—success and a family and the man she loved.

"So, will you marry me?"

That question, as far as she was concerned, was a no-brainer. "Yes, Gavin, I will marry you."

Epilogue

Layla couldn't help but dab at her eyes. The vow renewal ceremony for Bane and his wife, Crystal, was simply beautiful. The words they spoke to each other in the presence of family and friends were filled with so much love that Layla couldn't help but shed tears.

Gavin had told her how Bane and Crystal had eloped as teens, and then had been separated for five years when her family had sent her away. But what Layla found so precious was how their love had survived. They had reunited a year ago and since no family members had been present for their first wedding, they'd decided to renew their vows in front of everyone.

What was doubly special was that Crystal and Bane had announced to everyone earlier that day that they were expecting a baby. Everyone could tell from the smiles on the couple's faces that a baby was something they both wanted. Gavin and the guys couldn't wait to tease Bane about impending fatherhood. Mac, who had a number

He released her hands as he lowered his mouth to hers. She wrapped her arms around his muscled back.

She loved her SEAL, her rancher. For them, the best was yet to come.

of kids of his own, said he would give Bane pointers on changing diapers.

Today was officially the couple's sixth wedding anniversary and Crystal's twenty-fourth birthday. Layla thought it refreshing to find someone even younger than her with a PhD; they had a lot in common. Crystal was beautiful and Layla thought she was just the woman for Bane.

It was a lovely November day in the city of Denver. And since one of Bane's brother's had married an event planner, the home belonging to Bane's older brother Dillon, where the ceremony took place, had been decorated beautifully in colors of blue and gold. Layla had already talked to Alpha Westmoreland about planning Layla's dream wedding, which would take place in June.

"You okay, baby?" Gavin whispered before boldly using his tongue to lick away one of her tears.

"Behave, Gavin," she whispered back in a warning tone, knowing when it came to her he wouldn't behave.

She glanced around to see if anyone had noticed what he'd done. Bane certainly had a big family. There were Westmorelands everywhere. Gavin had warned her but she hadn't believed him. No wonder the locals referred to this section of Denver as Westmoreland Country. There were also some Westmorelands who lived in Atlanta, Montana and Texas. She'd even discovered Bane's cousin was married to a king in a country in the Middle East. All the Westmorelands she'd met were friendly and made her feel so welcome.

Another couple she'd met and liked right away was Bane's cousin Bailey and her husband, Walker Rafferty. They lived in Alaska. Layla hadn't wanted to keep staring at Walker but she remembered when he'd been a movie star years ago. He'd been a heartthrob then and he was definitely one today. She recalled seeing his picture on the cover of a recent issue of *Simply Irresistible* magazine. When she'd mentioned it to Bailey, the woman had chuckled and looked up at her husband adoringly before saying, "There's a story behind that. One day I will have to tell you about it."

It was good seeing Gavin's teammates again. Layla was glad to meet Mac's wife, Teri. The mother of four was simply gorgeous. Everyone planned to visit the Silver Spurs in June for Gavin and Layla's wedding. They'd agreed to spend Thanksgiving at the ranch and Christmas with her family. Ms. Melody and Caldwell had married and seemed to be very happy together.

Layla looked down at her engagement ring. It was beautiful. They had talked about Gavin giving Layla his mother's wedding set. Jamie had still been wearing the rings when her body had been unearthed. But Gavin had said he wanted Layla to have her own special rings and he would keep the rings his father had given his mother to pass on to their first son… Gavin Blake IV. She smiled at the audacity of Gavin thinking he would one day have a son to carry on the Blake name.

When the minister told Bane he could kiss his wife, everyone cheered. Bane pulled Crystal into his arms and gave her one hell of a kiss. What the couple shared was definitely special. Just as special as what Layla and Gavin shared.

Bane then leaned over and whispered something in Crystal's ear, which made her blush. Layla leaned over to Gavin. "I guess you heard that." He had told her about what his teammates dubbed as his sonic ears.

Gavin smiled. "Yes, I heard. Every single naughty word."

"The ceremony was beautiful," Layla said, fighting back more tears.

Gavin took her hand, brought it to his lips and kissed

her knuckles. "And so are you. I can't wait until the day you will officially have my name."

Layla couldn't wait, either. He'd been trying to talk her into eloping in January and having a huge wedding reception in June. He wanted them to be married before he left for this next covert operation. She was giving his suggestion some serious thought.

"And I can't wait until later, when I get you back to our hotel room," he added, whispering close to her ear.

Layla smiled as they linked hands and walked out of the church. She knew her life with her SEAL/rancher would never be boring.

* * * * *

HIS SECRET SON

BRENDA JACKSON

To the man who will always and forever have my heart,
Gerald Jackson Sr.

To Cozett Mazelin and Tamira K. Butler-Likely.
Thanks for your assistance in my research of
two-year-olds. Your information was invaluable and
I hope I did the character of "Little Laramie" justice!
I could tell from your responses
that you are great moms!!

To my readers who continue to love my
Westmorelands, this book is for you.

For none of us lives for ourselves alone,
and none of us dies for ourselves alone.
—*Romans* 14:7, NIV

Prologue

Bristol Lockett hurriedly moved toward her front door, wondering who would be visiting this late in the afternoon. Although it was still light outside, this particular Paris community was on the other side of town from the famous city center, where most people hung out on Friday nights and weekends. Normally, she would be there herself, but her habits had changed in the last couple of months.

She was one of those pregnant women who experienced morning sickness in the morning and at night. Smells alone would send her running to the nearest bathroom. Most morning sickness lasted until the twelfth week of pregnancy. She was in her sixteenth week and there didn't seem to be an end in sight. Her doctor had even placed her on a special diet to make sure she was getting sufficient nutrients into her body for her baby.

A glance out the peephole indicated her visitor was her best friend, Dionne Burcet. She and Dionne had met when Bristol first arrived in Paris four years ago to attend Académie des Beaux-Arts, which was considered one of the most prestigious and influential art schools in all of France.

Dionne also attended the art academy and with so much in common, they'd hit it off immediately.

Dionne, who'd been born in Paris, had introduced Bristol to French culture, and Bristol had taken Dionne home with her to America last Christmas to meet her aunt Dolly and to experience New Year's Eve in New York. A feeling of sadness fell over Bristol whenever she remembered that was the last holiday she and her aunt had spent together. Her aunt, her only relative, had died a few days later in her sleep.

Bristol opened the door smiling. "Dionne! This is a surprise. I thought you were leaving for—"

"I have something to tell you, Bristol."

Bristol heard the urgency in Dionne's voice, which resonated in her eyes, as well. "Okay, come on in. Would you like a cup of tea? I was just about to make a pot."

"Yes, thanks."

Bristol wondered about Dionne's strange demeanor as she led her friend to the kitchen, which wasn't far from the front door. She loved her studio apartment. It was small but just the right size for her. And it held a lot of memories. Her baby was conceived here, in her bed. She would miss this place when she moved back to the United States next month after graduation.

"Sit and tell me what's wrong. Did you and Mark have a fight?"

Dionne shook her head as she sat down at the table. "No. It's not about me, it's about you."

"Me?" Bristol said in surprise.

"Yes. You remember what you shared with me last month?"

"Yes. I told you I was pregnant." Telling Dionne hadn't been easy but she'd felt the need to confide in someone. The baby's father was a man she'd met one day at a café. He had been a US navy SEAL out with a few of his friends and he'd flirted with her outrageously. She'd done something she had never done before and flirted back. There had been something about Laramie Cooper that had made her behave like a different person and for the next three days, over the Christmas holidays, they had enjoyed a holiday fling. It was a period in her life she would never forget. Her pregnancy made certain of that.

"Yes, from that guy. The American soldier."

"Not just a soldier, Dionne. Laramie was a navy SEAL," Bristol said, smiling proudly.

"Yes, the navy SEAL Laramie Cooper," Dionne said.

From the time they'd been introduced, Bristol had liked his name and he'd said he liked hers. Laramie had told her very little about his work or even about himself. She knew he was an only child and his parents were still living in the US. He hadn't said where.

Bristol regretted that Dionne had been away visiting her grandparents in Marseille for the holidays and hadn't been around to meet Laramie. She believed her friend would have liked him. "What about him?"

"You told me how the two of you spent time together over the holidays and since finding out you were pregnant, you've been trying to locate him to let him know."

Since she'd known very little about Laramie, other than his name and age, she had mailed a letter to him in care of the US Navy. The letter had been returned weeks ago stamped UNABLE TO LOCATE.

"Yes, and like I told you, it doesn't matter to me that our time together was a no-strings affair, I believe he has a right to know about his child. I refused to do to him what my mother did to my father."

For years, Bristol never knew her father and, according to her mother, she never told her father about Bristol. It was information her mother had taken with her to the grave. It was only after her mother's death that Bristol's aunt Dolly had given her the man's name. She had met Randall Lockett at sixteen. He had been surprised to find out about her and had welcomed her into his life.

"Yes, I know. That's why I decided to help you."

Bristol raised a brow. "Help me?"

"Yes."

"How?"

"Remember I told you about that guy—an American—I dated years ago? The one who worked at your embassy?"

"Yes, I remember."

"Well, he was recently reassigned back to the embassy here and I ran into him. I gave him your SEAL's name and asked if he would try locating him and forwarding him a message to contact you."

Happiness eased into Bristol and spread to all parts of her body. Although it might have been nothing more than a holiday fling for Laramie Cooper, it had been a lot more for her. She had fallen in love with him. "Was your friend able to find him?"

Dionne slowly nodded her head. "Yes."

Bristol stared at her friend, knowing there was more. The happiness she felt earlier began dissipating at the sadness she saw in Dionne's eyes. "What is it, Dionne? What did you find out?"

All sorts of things began rushing through her mind. What if Laramie hadn't been the single man he'd claimed to be and had a wife and children somewhere? When Dionne didn't say anything, but looked down at the cup of tea Bristol had placed in front of her, Bristol slouched her shoulders in disappointment. "I think I know why you're hesitating in telling me."

Dionne looked back at her. "Do you?"

"Yes. He's married. Although he told me he wasn't, you found out differently, didn't you?"

"Bristol."

"It doesn't matter. He has a right to know about his child

anyway. If he decides never to be a part of my baby's life, it will be his decision and—"

"That's not it, Bristol," Dionne cut in to say.

Bristol frowned. "Then what is it?"

Dionne took a sip of her tea, hesitating. The dawdling was driving Bristol crazy. "For Pete's sake, Dionne, will you just get it out and tell me what you found out about Laramie?"

Dionne held her gaze and drew in a deep breath. "Some mission he was on went bad and he was killed. He's dead, Bristol."

One

The Naval Amphibious Base Coronado,
San Diego, California, three years later

"Let me get this straight, Lieutenant Cooper. You actually want to give up your holiday leave and remain here and work on base?"

Laramie "Coop" Cooper forced his smile to stay in place while answering his commanding officer's question. "Yes, sir. I actually want to do that."

He wouldn't tell anyone that he'd looked forward to going home for the holidays, because honestly, he hadn't. The phone call he'd gotten from his parents that they would be jet-setting to London again this year was expected. They'd done so every holiday for as long as he could remember. He doubted they'd even canceled those plans that Christmas three years ago when they'd thought him dead.

At thirty-two, he had stopped letting his parents' actions affect him. As far as Ryan and Cassandra Cooper were concerned, the universe revolved around them and nobody else. Especially not a son who, at times, they seemed to forget existed. It wasn't that he thought his parents didn't love him; he knew they did. They just loved each other more. He had long ago accepted that his parents believed there were different degrees of love, and that the love they shared for each other outweighed the love for their child.

In a way, he should be glad that after thirty-five years of marriage his parents were still that into each other. They shared something special, had this unbreakable bond, and some would even say it was the love of a lifetime. But on the other hand, that love never extended to him in the same degree. He knew their lack of affection had nothing to do with his deciding to become a navy SEAL instead of joining his parents' multimillion-dollar manufacturing company. His father had understood Laramie's desire to make his decisions based on what he wanted to do with his life, and he appreciated his dad for accepting that.

More holidays than not, for as far back as Laramie could remember, he'd been packed up and shipped off to his paternal grandparents' ranch in Laredo. Not that he was complaining. His grandparents had been the best and hadn't hesitated to show him the degree of love he'd lacked at home. In fact, he would admit to resenting his parents when they did show up at his grandparents' ranch to get him.

So, here he was volunteering to give up his holiday leave. It wasn't as if he hadn't received invitations from his SEAL teammates to join them and their families for the holidays, because he had. Bane Westmoreland—code name Bane—had been the first to invite Laramie to spend the holidays with his family in Denver. But given the fact that Bane's wife, Crystal, had given birth to triplets six months ago, Laramie didn't want to get underfoot.

Same thing with Thurston McRoy—code name Mac—with his wife, Teri, and their four kids. Gavin Blake—code name Viper—would be celebrating his first Christmas as a married man so Laramie didn't want to intrude there, either. The only other single guy in the group was David

Holloway—code name Flipper. Flipper came from a huge family of four brothers, who were all SEALs, and a father who'd retired as a SEAL commanding officer. Laramie had spent the holidays with Flipper's family last year and didn't want to wear out his welcome.

"I'm denying your request, Lieutenant."

His commanding officer's words recaptured Laramie's attention. He met the man's gaze and tried to keep a frown off his face. "May I ask why, sir?"

"I think you know the reason. SEAL Team Six, of which you are a vital member, has been pretty damn busy this year. I don't have to list all the covert operations successfully accomplished with very few casualties. You deserve your holiday leave."

"Even if I don't want to take it?"

His commanding officer held his gaze. "Yes, even if you don't want to take it. Military leave is necessary, especially for a SEAL, to recoup both mentally and physically. Don't think I haven't noticed how much you've been pushing yourself. It's like you're trying to make up for the time you were a captive in Syria."

Laramie remembered all eleven months of being held prisoner in that guerilla hellhole. He hadn't known from one day to the next if he'd survive that day. The bastards had done everything in their power to make him think every day would be his last. They'd even played Russian roulette with him a couple of times.

It was on one of those particular days when he'd been rescued. Leave it to Bane, who was a master sniper, to bring down the four men from a distance of over a hundred feet. Laramie was convinced there was no way he would have survived if his SEAL team hadn't shown up.

During those eleven months he'd fought hard to stay sane and the one memory that had sustained him was the face of the woman he'd met in Paris just weeks before the mission.

Bristol Lockett.

It had been a three-day holiday affair. Sadly, there was little he knew about her other than sharing her bed had been the best sexual experience of his life.

"However, since I know you're going to insist," his commanding officer said, reclaiming Laramie's thoughts again, "I've got an important job that I want you to do. However, it means traveling to New York."

Laramie raised a brow. "New York?"

"Yes. An important delivery needs to be made to a member of the United Nations Security Council."

Laramie wondered what kind of delivery. Classified documents no doubt.

He'd heard how beautiful Manhattan was when it was decorated for this time of year. He'd been to the Big Apple a number of times, but never around the holidays. "Once I make the delivery, sir. Then what?"

"That, Lieutenant, is up to you. If you decide to take your holiday leave, then you won't have to report back here until the end of January as scheduled. However, if you still want to give up your leave, then you're free to come back here and I'll find more work for you to do."

Laramie nodded. He might take a week off to enjoy the sights and sounds of New York, but there was no doubt in his mind that he would be returning to San Diego for more work.

Bristol glanced around the art gallery. She always felt a sense of pride and accomplishment whenever she saw one of her paintings on display. Especially here at the Jazlyn Art Gallery of New York. She wanted to pinch herself to make sure she wasn't dreaming.

She had worked so hard for this moment.

"Looks good, doesn't it?"

She glanced up at her manager, Margie Townsend. "Yes, I have to admit that it does."

Margie's tenacious pit bull–like skills had landed Bristol a showing at this gallery, one of the most well-known and highly respected galleries in New York. She and Margie had met last year on the subway and struck up a conversation. When Bristol discovered what Margie did for a living, she felt their chance encounter must have been an omen. She'd invited Margie to her home to see her work, and the excitement reflected in the woman's eyes had been incredible. Margie promised to change Bristol's life. She promised that Bristol would get to the point where she could quit her job as an assistant magazine editor and make her living as the artist she was born to be.

Less than eight months later, Margie had sold one of Bristol's paintings. The buyer had been so taken with her work that he'd also purchased several others. The money had been enough to bring about the change in Bristol's life Margie had guaranteed. She had turned in her resignation and now painted full-time in her home.

Bristol was happy with the direction of her career. She got to spend more time with her son since she kept him with her every day instead of taking him to day care like she used to do.

Her son.

She smiled when she thought about her rambunctious two-year old—the most important person in her life. He was her life. Every decision she made was done with him in mind. She'd already started a college fund for him and couldn't wait to share the holidays with him. Last night they had put up their Christmas tree. Correction, she thought, widening her smile. She had put up the tree. Laramie had gotten in the way with his anxiousness to help.

Laramie…

It was hard not to think of Laramie's father whenever she

thought of her son. She had named him after his biological father, Laramie Cooper, who had died way too young, and without knowing about the child they'd created together. Sometimes she wondered what he would have done had he lived and gotten the letter she'd tried to send him.

Would he have been just as happy as she'd been? Or would he have claimed the child wasn't his? She might not have known Laramie Cooper long, but she wanted to believe he was a man who would have wanted to be a part of his child's life. The way her father had wanted to be a part of hers. The two years she'd shared with the man who'd fathered her had not been enough.

"Are you ready to go? You have a big day tomorrow and I want you well rested."

She chuckled as she tightened her coat around her. "And I will be."

Margie rolled her eyes. "I guess as much as you can be with a two-year-old running around the place."

She knew what Margie was hinting at. Bristol was spending less and less time painting now that Laramie was in the terrible twos. It was also the get-into-everything twos. The only time she really got to paint was during his nap time or while he slept at night.

"Did you give any more thought to what I said?"

Margie had suggested that she send Laramie to day care two to three days a week. "Yes, but I'm thinking of hiring someone to come to my home instead of me having to take him somewhere."

"That might work, but he has to start learning to interact with other kids, Bristol." As they walked toward the waiting private car that was compliments of the gallery, Margie changed the subject. "Have you decided to go out with Steven?"

Bristol shrugged. Steven Culpepper was nice enough, and good-looking, too. However, he was moving too fast.

At least, faster than she liked. They'd met a few weeks ago when she'd closed a huge deal for a commissioned piece. He was the corporation's attorney. He'd asked for her number and, without thinking much about it, she'd given it to him. Since then he'd called constantly, trying to get her to go out with him. So far, she hadn't. She hated pushy men and Steven, she thought, was one of the pushiest.

"No."

"I like him."

Bristol grinned. "You would. You have a thing for wealthy businessmen." She knew Margie had been married to one. Or two. She was on her third marriage and not even fifty yet. But the one thing all three men had in common was the size of their bank accounts.

"Well, I know you still have a thing for Laramie's father and—"

"What makes you think that?"

"Bristol, you make it quite obvious that you haven't gotten over him."

Did she? The only thing she'd told Margie about Laramie's father was that he'd been in the military and had died in the line of duty without knowing he'd fathered a son. She'd even fabricated a tale that Laramie had been her deceased husband and not just her lover.

It had been pretty easy. Dionne's fiancé, Mark, had helped. Mark worked for a judge in Paris and had falsified the papers before Bristol left France. It was a way to make sure her son had his father's last name without people wondering why her last name was different. It wasn't as if she was trying to cash in on her son's father's military benefits or anything.

"If you ask me, I think you should finally move on… with Steven," Margie said, interrupting Bristol's thoughts.

Bristol wanted to say that nobody had asked Margie. But deep down, a part of her knew Margie was right. It was time for Bristol to move on. However, she doubted very seriously that it would be with Steven.

A short while later she was entering her home, a beautiful brownstone in Brooklyn that she'd inherited from her aunt Dolly. She loved the place and knew the neighborhood well. She'd come to live here with her aunt ten years ago, when she was fifteen. That had been the year her mother died.

She didn't want to think sad thoughts, especially after her positive meeting with Maurice Jazlyn, the owner of the gallery. The man was excited about tomorrow night's showing and expected a huge crowd. He loved all the artworks she would be exhibiting.

"How did things go tonight?"

She turned toward the older woman coming down the stairs to the main floor. Charlotte Kramer lived next door and had been a close friend of her aunt Dolly. With her four kids grown and living in other parts of New York, Ms. Charlotte had thought about moving to a condo not far away, but had decided she'd rather stay put since she'd lived in the area close to forty years and loved her neighbors. Ms. Charlotte said there were a lot of memories of Mr. Kramer stored in that house. He'd passed away eight years ago, a couple of years after Bristol had come to live with her aunt.

Bristol appreciated that Ms. Charlotte loved watching Laramie for her whenever she had meetings to attend. And Ms. Charlotte had offered to watch him again tomorrow night when Bristol attended the exhibition.

"Everything went well. Everyone is excited about tomorrow. Mr. Jazlyn thinks he'll be able to sell all my paintings."

A huge smile touched Ms. Charlotte's lips. "That's good news. Dolly would be proud. Candace would be, too."

She doubted the latter. Her mother had never approved

of Bristol becoming an artist. It was only after she died that Bristol learned why. Her father had been an artist who'd broken things off with her mother to study in Paris. It was only after he'd left the country that her mother discovered her pregnancy. She'd known how to reach him but refused to let him know about his child. She had resented him for ending things with her to pursue his dream.

Bristol had been sixteen when she'd met her father for the first time. She would not have met him then if it hadn't been for her aunt's decision to break the promise she'd made to Bristol's mother years ago. Aunt Dolly wanted Bristol to know her father and vice versa. When Bristol was given the man's name, she had been shocked to find that the person whose art she'd admired for years was really her father.

She'd finally gotten the courage to contact him on her sixteenth birthday. Randall Lockett was married with a family when they'd finally met. He had two young sons—ages ten and twelve—with his wife Krista. Bristol was his only daughter and she favored him so much it was uncanny. She was also his only offspring who'd inherited his artistic gift.

When he'd died, he had bequeathed to her full tuition to the school he himself had attended in Paris as well as the vast majority of his paintings. He'd felt she would appreciate them more than anyone, and she had. She'd heard that Krista had remarried and sold off all the artworks that had been left to her and their sons.

Paintings by Randall Lockett were valued in the millions. Art collectors had contacted Bristol on numerous occasions, but she had refused to sell. Instead her father's paintings were on display at the two largest art museums in the world, New York's Metropolitan Museum of Art and the Orsay Museum in Paris.

A few months before her father had died, they had completed a painting together, which was her most cherished possession. It was so uncanny that when it came to art she and her father had possessed identical preferences. They even held their brushes the same way. On those days when she felt down and out, she would look at the portrait over her fireplace and remember the six weeks they'd spent together on his boat while painting it. That was when they'd noticed all the similarities they shared as artists. She hadn't known he was dying of cancer until his final days. He hadn't wanted her to know. He was determined to share every moment he could with her without seeing pity and regret in her eyes.

Forcing those sad thoughts from her mind, she glanced back over at Ms. Charlotte. "Did Laramie behave himself tonight?" she asked, placing her purse on the table.

The older woman chuckled. "Doesn't he always?"

Bristol smiled. "No, but I know you wouldn't tell me even if he was a handful."

"You're right, I wouldn't. Boys will be boys. I know. I raised four of them."

Yes, she had, and to this day Ms. Charlotte's sons looked out for her, making sure she had everything she needed and then some.

After Ms. Charlotte left, Bristol climbed the stairs to her son's room. He was in his bed, sound asleep. Crossing the bedroom floor, she saw he had put away all his toys. That was a good sign that he was learning to follow instructions.

Approaching the bed, she sat on the edge and gently ran her fingers through the curls on his head. He favored his father. Laramie Cooper's features were etched in her memory. Whenever Laramie smiled, he displayed his father's dimples in both cheeks. Then there was the shape of his mouth and the slant of his eyes. Like father, like son. There was no doubt in her mind that one day Laramie would grow up and capture some woman's heart just as quickly and easily as his father had claimed hers.

As she sat there watching her son sleep, she couldn't stop her mind from going back to that time in Paris when she'd met US Navy SEAL Laramie Cooper…

Two

Paris, France, three years ago

Bristol glanced up from her sketch pad when she heard the male voices entering the café. Military men. All five of them. That was easy to deduce, even though they weren't wearing military attire. They were wearing jeans, shirts and dark leather jackets. The five walked confidently and were in perfect physical condition. Boy, were they ever! She wondered what branch of service they represented. It really didn't matter. Whichever one branch it was, they were representing it well.

The group took the table not far away from where she sat and one of the men, as if he felt someone staring at him, glanced over at her. Bam! She'd been caught. She hadn't averted her gaze back to her sketch pad quickly enough. For some reason, she knew without glancing back up that he was still looking at her. She could feel his gaze, just as if it was a physical caress. It made her heart beat faster. It seemed that every single hormone in her body had begun to sizzle. Nothing like that had ever happened to her before.

Okay, Bristol, concentrate on your sketch, she inwardly

admonished herself. Her father hadn't paid her tuition at one of the most prestigious art schools in France for her to get all hot and bothered by a bunch of military men. Although the five were extremely handsome, it was only one of the men who had caught her eye. The one who'd stared back at her.

"Excuse me, miss."

She glanced up and the man was now standing at her table. Up close he was even more gorgeous. Definitely eye candy of the most delectable kind. Hot. Sexy. You name it and this man could definitely claim it. That had to be the reason intense heat was plowing up her spine.

Bristol swallowed deeply before saying, "Yes?"

"I was wondering if…"

When he didn't finish but kept looking at her, she asked. "Wondering what?"

"If I could join you?"

She wished he could but unfortunately, he couldn't. She glanced at her watch then back at him. "Sorry, but I work here and happen to be on my lunch break, which will end in less than five minutes."

"What time do you get off today?"

She tilted her head to look at him. "Excuse me?"

"I asked what time you get off today. I'll wait."

She figured that he had to be kidding, but the look in his eyes showed that he wasn't. "I get off in four hours."

"I'll wait. What's your name?"

This guy was definitely moving fast. But she couldn't ignore the scorching hot attraction between them, even if she wanted to. And for some reason, she didn't want to. She liked it.

"My name is Bristol Lockett."

"The name Bristol is unusual. It suits you well. I like it."

And she liked his voice. It was deep and husky. The sound made heat curl inside her. OMG! What on earth was wrong with her? She'd never thought such outlandish things in her life. She might not have always been prim and proper but she'd been pretty close to it. She'd been in Paris close to four years and although she'd dated, most of the time she did not. She preferred curling up with her sketch pad and working on her watercolors than going out with any man. But now this ultrafine specimen was making her rethink that decision.

"Are you American or French?"

She blinked at his question. "I'm American."

"So am I."

She smiled. And what a good-looking American he was, with a body to die for. She felt as if she could draw her last breath just from looking at him. This guy was tall, at least six foot two or three. And his skin was the color of lightly roasted almonds. His dark eyes appeared somewhat slanted, and as far as she was concerned his lips were perfectly shaped. His hair was cut low on his head and his ears were just the right size for his face. But what captured her attention more than anything were those dimples in his cheeks. Doing absolutely nothing but standing there, he was arousing something within her that no other man ever had.

"And who are you?" she asked, deciding not to let him ask all the questions.

"I'm Laramie," he said, stretching out his hand to her.

She took it and immediately a spike of heat seemed to burst from his fingers and hit her dead center between the thighs. And when she stared into his eyes and saw the dark heat in his pupils, she knew he'd felt something, as well.

"Are you married, Laramie?"

"No. I've never been married. What about you? I approached you because I didn't see a ring on your finger."

At least he didn't hit on married women. Some men didn't care. "No, I'm not married, either, and never have been."

"So, Bristol Lockett, do I have your permission?"

She licked her lips. "For what?"

That sexy smile widened. "To be here when you get off."

Then what? she wondered but decided not to ask. "Sure, if that's what you want."

His chuckle made desire claw at her but it was his next words that sealed her fate. "There are a lot of things I want when it comes to you, Bristol."

Jeez. If he wasn't standing there she would close her eyes and moan. This man presented a temptation she shouldn't even think about yielding to. Too bad her best friend, Dionne, was out of town for the holidays and not around to talk some sense into her.

"What about if we share a drink at one of the pubs first?" she asked, and then frowned. Why had she made it sound as if she would be willing to move to the next stage once they shared a drink?

"That's fine. I'll be back in four hours."

When he walked off she glanced at her watch. Her break was officially over but she knew her encounter with this military man was just beginning.

She hurried behind the counter to put on her apron while watching Mary-Ann, another waitress, head over to the table to serve the five guys. More people entered the café, and Bristol was about to cross the room to serve a couple with a little girl when Mary-Ann stopped her.

"They asked for you," Mary-Ann said, smiling.

"Who?"

"Those soldiers. I've given them menus but they want you to serve their table. That's fine with me. Then I don't have to commit a sin by forgetting I've been married to Joel almost twenty years. Those five are too much temptation," she said, fanning herself. "I hope you can handle it."

Bristol hoped she could handle it as well, as she made her way to the table where all five men sat. Hot and heavy testosterone was thick in the air surrounding them. Drawing in a deep breath she approached them with her notepad in hand. "Have you guys decided what you're having?"

"Apparently, Coop has," one of the men said, grinning at her. "We're still deciding."

She nodded. "Okay, and who is Coop?"

"I am," the guy who had introduced himself to her earlier said.

She met his gaze. "I thought your name was Laramie."

He smiled again and she tried not to feel weak in the knees. "It is. My real name is Laramie Cooper. They call me Coop."

"Oh."

"Let me introduce everyone," Laramie said. "First off, guys, this is Bristol," he said to his friends.

"Hello, Bristol," they all said simultaneously as they stood to their feet, showing they had manners.

"Hello."

"I'm Bane," one of the men said, extending his hand to her.

She smiled at the very handsome military man as she shook his hand. "Hi, Bane."

"Is that a New York accent?" Bane asked.

"Yes, you would think after being in France for almost four years it would not be so easily detected."

Bane's smile widened. "Some things you can't get rid of."

"Apparently," she said, chuckling.

"I'm Flipper," another one of the guys said, offering his hand. He was definitely a hottie, with blond hair and the bluest eyes she'd ever seen. The color reminded her of the ocean and she wondered if that was why his nickname was Flipper.

"Nice meeting you, Flipper," she said, shaking his hand, as well.

"Same here, Bristol."

"I'm Mac," another one of the men said, leaning across to take her hand. This man appeared older than the others by at least three or four years.

"Hi, Mac."

"And I'm Viper."

She glanced at the man who introduced himself as Viper. He was taller than the others and just as handsome. His eyes seemed sharp and penetrating. "Hi, Viper," she said, shaking his hand.

"Hi, Bristol," Viper returned, smiling.

"And you know me," Laramie said, taking her hand.

And just like before, a spike of heat hit her. "Yes, I know you." She quickly pulled her hand away. "It's nice meeting all of you and I like all your nicknames," she said as the men all sat back down.

Bane chuckled. "They aren't nicknames. They're our military code names."

"Oh. And what branch of the military?"

"We're navy SEALs," the one named Flipper said, grinning proudly.

He had every right to feel that way. She'd heard about navy SEALs. Some considered them the American government's secret weapon against any enemy force.

"So, Laramie, I'll start with you. What will you have?" she asked, getting ready to write on her notepad.

"For now I'll take a juicy hamburger, a large order of French fries and a huge malted strawberry shake."

For now? She wondered what he planned to have later. From the way he was looking at her, she had an idea. And why didn't realizing this guy evidently thought she was on his menu bother her?

Bristol went around the table and took everyone's order. Apparently all five were big eaters and she wondered where they would put all that food and how they stayed in such great physical shape. After turning their orders in to the cook, she began waiting on other tables, but felt the heat of Laramie's gaze on her the entire time. Every time she glanced over in his direction, he was staring at her. Blatantly so.

Maybe it hadn't been a good idea for her to agree to have a drink with him when she got off work. She knew nothing about him, other than his name was Laramie Cooper, his military code name was Coop, he loved juicy hamburgers and he was a navy SEAL.

She delivered their food a short while later and watched them eat all of it. She could tell that the five were more than just members of the same military team. They shared a close friendship. That much was obvious from the way they joked around with each other.

Mac was married and had no problem showing her pictures of his wife and kids. It was evident he was proud of them. Bane, she'd discovered, was also married, but from the way the others teased him she could only assume he hadn't seen his wife in a while, which meant the two were separated. Like Laramie, Viper and Flipper were single and from the sound of things they intended to stay that way.

At the end of the meal when they paid their bill, she was shocked at the tip they left her. She would not normally have earned that much tip money in a week. "Thanks, guys."

"No, we want to thank you," Flipper said standing, like the others. "It was nice meeting you, Bristol, and the food was great."

The others shared the same sentiments as they moved to leave the café. Laramie hung back. "I'll be here when you get off work."

She knew now was a good time to tell him that she'd changed her mind about that. However, there was something about Laramie Cooper that made her hold back from doing so. It might have been his smile, or the way he was making her feel, or just the fact that she deserved to have some fun for a change.

For four years she had worked hard at the art academy and come spring she would be graduating. The café would be closing for the holidays and she had the next ten days off work. As far as she was concerned, there was nothing wrong with Laramie being there when she got off. They would just grab drinks at one of the pubs nearby. Besides, after today, she probably wouldn't see him again.

"I'll be waiting," she heard herself say.

She didn't have to wait. Laramie arrived a half hour before she was due to leave work. He ordered a croissant and coffee while he waited for her. She hung up her apron, wished everyone a Merry Christmas and then headed toward the table where he sat. He stood, smiling down at her.

"Ready?" he asked her.

"Yes" was her reply, although she wasn't sure what he had in mind and if she should be ready or not.

He surprised her by taking her hand, as if they both needed to feel the sexual chemistry between them. He led her through the doors and onto the sidewalk. Holiday decorations were everywhere. It was hard to believe tomorrow was Christmas Eve. Last year she had gone home for Christmas and had taken her best friend, Dionne, with her. But not this year. Her aunt Dolly had died in her sleep four days into the New Year.

She needed to stop thinking that she didn't have any living relatives when she had two brothers and a stepmother. She knew they'd only tolerated her while her father was alive and now, with him gone, they had let her know—by not returning her calls or letters—that they didn't have to put up with her anymore. That was fine. She'd adjusted to being a loner. At least she had Dionne and Dionne's family. The thought had even crossed Bristol's mind that she should not return to the United States after graduation and make Paris her home.

"Which pub are we going to?" she asked the man who was walking beside her and still holding her hand.

He smiled down at her. "Which one do you suggest?"

"Charlie's is a good one. It's right around the corner."

They didn't say much as they walked to the pub. They talked about the holidays. He told her that he and his team would be headed out in four days and they were in Paris for a little R and R.

"Your friends are nice," she said.

He smiled down at her as they continued walking. "They said the same thing about you."

She smiled at that, while trying to ignore all that desire she saw in his eyes. She figured if they kept talking it would go away. "The five of you seem close."

"We are. In fact, we're like brothers. Viper, Flipper, Bane and I attended the naval academy together and immediately became the best of friends. Mac is four years older and finished the academy ahead of us. He's been a SEAL longer and likes to think he's looking out for us."

They reached the pub and saw it was crowded with no tables available. It seemed everyone had decided to begin celebrating the holidays early. "I have an idea," Laramie said, tightening his hand on hers.

"What?"

"Let's go someplace private."

An uneasy feeling crept over her, but it was overpowered by exciting sensations that settled in her stomach. Their hands were still joined and his fingers felt warm and reassuring.

"I want to be honest with you about something."

She swallowed. "About what?"

"Usually I spend the holidays alone, but I want to spend them with you."

She held his gaze a minute and then asked, "What about your friends?"

"They'll be in touch with their families."

"But you won't?"

He didn't say anything for a moment and then he said, "My parents are still alive. I'm their only child. But we've never spent the holidays together."

She found that odd. Christmas was the one holiday she never had to worry about being alone. Her mother had always made it special and after her mother's death, her aunt Dolly had been there for her. She'd even spent one Christmas with her father. It had been the first and last holiday they'd spent together. This would be the first Christmas that she had no one. She thought it sad that Laramie had never really spent his holidays with family.

She saw the sincerity in his eyes, in what he'd told her. He wasn't trying to feed her a pity line but was telling her the truth. She felt it in her heart.

"I can think of a place we can go," she suggested.

"Where?"

She knew it would be crazy to invite him, a perfect stranger to her home, but she was about to issue the invitation. "My place. It's not far from here. Just so happens I was going to be alone for the holidays as well and would love some company."

His hand tightened on hers. "You sure?"

Was she? She had never done anything so daring in her life.

She wasn't a child. She knew the obvious signs. Desire was thick between them. Spontaneous combustion as volatile as it could get. She dated infrequently and most guys who'd hit on her had tried to work her. But she would say that Laramie was the first guy who'd tried and managed to elicit her interest. He was also the first guy she was trusting to this degree. She had never invited a man to her home before. There had to be a reason for her doing so now.

"Yes. I'm sure," she said.

From the way his lips spread into a smile, she knew her response had pleased him. "All right then. Lead the way."

That smile made her heart miss a beat as they continued to walk along the sidewalk. Like she'd told him, she didn't live far and they arrived at her studio apartment in no time. "It's small," she said, opening the door. "But it's the right size for me."

She stepped aside and he entered. She immediately thought her apartment might be just the right size for her, but with him inside it, it suddenly appeared small.

"Nice place," he said, glancing around.

Bristol was glad she was a neat freak. There was nothing out of place. "There's a bottle of wine over there if you want to pour us a glass," she said, removing her coat and hanging it in one of the closets.

"Okay," he said, removing his jacket. She took it and hung it in the closet, as well. She tried not to notice how perfect his abs were and what a broad chest he had. She also tried not to notice the sexual chemistry between them, which had increased now that they were alone and behind closed doors.

"Do you need to let your friends know where you are? Won't they be worried when you don't return to your hotel?" she asked him.

He shook his head as he grabbed the wine bottle and glasses off the rack. "No. They'll figure things out."

"Okay." She sat down at the table while he poured the wine into their glasses. And then he joined her there. "I know this isn't champagne but let's make a toast."

"To what?"

"To what I believe will be the best holiday I've ever had."

Deep down she believed it would be the best she ever

had, too. Their glasses clinked and then they took a sip. She met his gaze over the rim and immediately, a deep sexual hunger flared to life in her midsection. From the hot, penetrating look in his eyes, the same hunger hit him, as well.

Bristol placed her glass down the same moment he did. And then he stood and reached out to her. She went into his arms willingly and he lowered his head and captured her mouth in his. The moment she felt his lips on hers, a deep, drugging rush of desire filled her to the core.

He was using his tongue in the most provocative way, making shivers of need course through every part of her. She had never been kissed like this before and he was an expert.

He deepened the kiss and her mouth became locked to his. She couldn't hold back the moan that erupted from deep within her throat. Nor could she hold back the sensations overtaking her. She had been kissed before, but never like this. Never with this much possession, this much overwhelming power.

Moments later he ended the kiss and pulled back slightly to look down at her. A sexy smile touched the corners of his lips and the arms around her tightened, bringing her closer to him. "I wanted to kiss you from the moment I saw you. I had a deep yearning to know how you tasted."

Wow! She wasn't used to having such carnal conversations with a man. "Is that why you kissed me the way you did just now?"

"Partly."

"And the other reason?"

"I just wanted the feel of my tongue in your mouth."

And then as if he hadn't gotten enough of doing that the last time, he lowered his head and captured her mouth again. On a breathless moan she parted her lips, giving him the opening he needed. He slid his tongue inside, mating it with hers, over and over again.

When he finally released her mouth, [illegible]
him with glazed eyes. "What are you doin[illegible]
barely able to get the words out. Never had a [illegible]
so off balance.

"Starting our celebration of the holidays."

She could feel blood rushing through her veins with his words. She hadn't expected this so soon. She figured they would share a drink today and then tomorrow he could come back for lunch. But it seemed he had other plans, plans she was giving in to. She couldn't help it. So many sexual sensations were taking over her mind and body just from his kiss. She knew there was no way she could stop from wanting him. He sealed her fate when he began kissing her again and she felt herself being lifted into his arms.

He was carrying her someplace and she knew where when he placed her on the bed. What happened next was amazing. In record time he had removed both of their clothes, as if needing to be skin to skin with her was paramount. As if needing to see her naked body was essential.

In a way she understood, since seeing him standing there without a stitch of clothing was doing something to her, as well. He represented such virility and masculinity, and coiling arousal was throbbing deep in her core. Never had she wanted to make love to someone so badly. Never had she felt this filled with need. And she could tell from his huge erection that he wanted her. His desire for her was obvious.

She watched as he put on a condom before heading back to the bed. She reached out and glided her hands up his tight, sculpted abdomen and chest, loving the feel of his skin. Heat curled inside her with the contact.

"You touch me and I will touch you," he warned, grazing his jaw against her ear, while growling low in his throat. It amazed her that he would respond to her touch this way.

"I want you to touch me, Laramie."

he couldn't believe she'd said that. But there was something about Laramie Cooper that she didn't understand. Namely, how he could make her lose her common sense. How he could make her nerves dance and her brain race. How he had the ability to make her want to have things she'd done without in the past. And how he made her want him with a passion.

She needed to make him aware of something. Make him understand and she heard herself saying, "I've never brought a man here before."

She felt the intensity of his gaze all over her body.

"There's a first time for everything, don't you think?" he replied, slowly moving back toward the bed.

With each step he took, she felt her womb contract. He was staring at her with dark, penetrating eyes and her body heated under his intense regard. She'd never had a one-night stand in her life. Always thought she was above that. But at that moment the only thing she wanted was this man, who had the ability to mess with her mind and senses.

There was something else she needed to tell him and it was best if she did it now. "Laramie?"

"Yes?"

"I'm not on any type of birth control."

If she thought that revelation would stop him dead in his tracks, she'd been wrong. He kept moving toward her. "I have condoms. Plenty of them. Around a dozen or so. And if we need more we'll get them," he told her.

Get more? Did he honestly think they would use more than a dozen? Her heart began beating way too fast as she wondered just what kind of stamina he had. Would she be able to keep up?

She was about to find out.

He joined her on the bed and began kissing her again while touching her all over. Sexual excitement churned inside her, sending an intense throb through her veins. She slipped her arms around his muscled back, loving the manly feel of him.

"I'm dying to taste you," he whispered, just moments before shifting his body to place his head between her legs.

She gripped tight to his shoulders as she felt his hot tongue inside her, stroking and licking. He was unwavering in his determination to taste her like he wanted. Sensations she'd never experienced before rushed through her and instinctively, she made sinfully erotic movements with her hips against his mouth.

Over and over he laved her womanly core with greedy intent, making her whisper his name over and over. Suddenly, her body exploded like a volcano erupting and she surrendered to the pleasure he'd given her.

Before the last spasm left her body, he had shifted to position his body over hers, and then she felt him enter her, stretching her to accommodate his size. She inhaled the scent of him—the scent of them—and then used her tongue to lick his shoulder, needing to taste the texture of his skin.

He pushed his shaft as deep inside her as he could go and then he locked their legs together. He began moving, thrusting back and forth, in and out. He established a rhythm that sent sexual undercurrents all through her body.

He looked down at her, held her gaze as he made love to her. She clung to him, holding tight to his shoulders as if they were a lifeline. His languid, deep, hard thrusts were driving her over the edge and making every nerve ending in her body zing brutally to life.

He threw his head back and growled her name as he continued to make love to her, indulging her with his words. Her skin sizzled where their bodies connected and the more he stroked inside her, the more her body awakened to the aching hunger he was feeding.

And then he called her name again. Together they were slammed with another orgasm. He gathered her in his arms, touched the side of her face with his fingers as they rode the tidal waves of ecstasy together.

The next morning it had felt odd waking up with a man in her bed. They had made love practically all evening, only to get up around eight and eat some of the soup she'd made the day before with French bread. Then they had gotten back in bed and made love all over again. All through the night.

No personal information was exchanged. None was needed. She knew the next three days would be considered one and done. Chances were, they would never see each other again. They were taking advantage of the now.

"You're awake?"

She glanced over at him and saw desire in the depths of his dark eyes. "Yes, I'm awake."

"Good."

He got out of bed to put on a condom then returned to her. "And what if I wanted breakfast first?" she asked, grinning.

He grinned back. "And do you want breakfast first?"

She shook her head. "No. I want you, Laramie."

And she did want him. She had to keep telling herself this was just sex and nothing more. When he left here the day after Christmas he wouldn't be coming back, nor would they stay in touch. The only thing she would have were her memories. Regardless, she could not and would not ever regret any time spent with him.

After making love that morning they dressed and went out to grab breakfast. He surprised her with his suggestion that they get a Christmas tree. That meant they had to purchase ornaments, as well. He refused to let her pay for anything. Like kids, they rushed back to the house and decorated the tree. Their tree.

Since most restaurants were closed for the holidays, she decided to prepare Christmas dinner for them. That meant grocery shopping, which she told him she wanted to do alone. She knew from their earlier shopping trip how he liked to spend money and she wanted Christmas dinner to be her treat.

When she returned to her apartment he was waiting for her. The minute she opened the door and glanced over at him, heated sexual attraction consumed them. She couldn't put her grocery bags down fast enough before he was ripping off her clothes, making love to her against the refrigerator.

He surprised her on Christmas Day with a gift, a beautiful scarf and a pair of earrings. The gift touched her deeply. He'd apparently gone shopping when she left to get groceries.

She surprised him with a gift, as well. A pair of gloves, since she'd noticed his were well-worn. He said he enjoyed Christmas dinner, but most of Christmas was spent in bed making love rather than eating.

The next morning, the day after Christmas, she awoke to find him dressed and ready to go. Ready to walk out of her life. She hadn't expected it to be so hard, but it was. She knew she had fallen in love with him. Not with the sex but with the man.

He kissed her deeply, wished her the best in her artistic dreams and thanked her for making this one of the best holidays for him, ever. And then he turned and walked out the door…without looking back.

She'd quickly gotten up and stood at the window to watch him leave. He'd called a cab and, as if he'd known she would be there at the window, before getting into the cab he looked over his shoulder, saw her, blew her a kiss and then waved goodbye.

She blew him a kiss and waved back. And as the cab drove away she knew at that moment that Laramie Cooper had taken a piece of her heart with him.

Three

New York, present day

"I'm glad you guys are finding this entire thing amusing," Laramie said as he moved around the hotel room to dress. He had placed the mobile call on speaker while engaging in a five-way conversation with his teammates.

"Hey, Coop, we can't help but think it's pretty damn funny," Bane Westmoreland said. "I can just imagine the look on your face when you discovered what you were delivering to that member of the Security Council wasn't top secret documents like you thought, but her pet cockatiel."

Laramie couldn't help but smile as he slid on a T-shirt. "No, Bane, you can't imagine."

"Well, just think positive," David Holloway said. "You got a free trip to New York."

"Damn, Flipper, it's cold as the dickens here. I prefer California weather," Laramie said.

"Stop whining, Coop," Gavin Blake said, laughing.

"Kiss it, Viper."

And then he said, "Hey, Mac? You still with us? You're kind of quiet."

"I'm still here," Thurston McRoy said. "I'm trying to keep up with you guys and watch the game, too. In case none of you realized, it's Thursday night football."

That led to a conversation about their predictions for what team would make it to the Super Bowl. By the time Laramie had ended the call, he was completely dressed and ready to leave.

And go where? He figured that since he had a taste for a juicy hamburger, he would grab a meal at Xavier's. Flipper had recommended he dine there and said he wouldn't be disappointed.

A short while later, Laramie entered the restaurant and was shown to a table. It was busy and there had been a fifteen-minute wait but he didn't mind. This wasn't his first visit to Times Square, but he did note a lot of changes since he was here last.

"What would you like tonight?"

He glanced up at the waitress. No one could credit him with being slow and he immediately knew the double meaning behind her question. "A menu would be nice," he said, hoping that would defuse any ideas she had.

Maybe another time, but not tonight. He just wasn't feeling it. He chuckled and wondered if he was running a fever. There hadn't been too many times when he'd turned down sex. And there was no doubt in his mind the woman was offering.

"I'll make sure you get a menu…as well as anything else you might want," she said, smiling.

He smiled back. "Thanks. The menu will do for now and a beer."

She walked off and returned with the menu and his beer. "Thanks."

"You can thank me later." Then she sashayed off.

He wondered why he wasn't taking advantage of those

curves and long gorgeous legs. His excuse had to be that this place sort of reminded him of that café in Paris. The one where Bristol worked.

Bristol.

He'd been thinking about her a lot lately. Maybe because it was around this time—during the holiday season three years ago when they'd met. Whatever the reason, Bristol Lockett was on his mind.

After his rescue from Syria, one of the first places he'd gone had been to Paris to see her, a woman he hadn't meant to ever see again. But something had compelled him to seek her out, only to be told by the manager of the apartment complex where she'd lived that she had returned to the United States a couple of years ago and had not left a forwarding address.

When he noticed the waitress looking over at him, he decided to place his order, eat and then leave. He wasn't up for any female company tonight and didn't want the woman to get any ideas.

An hour or so later, he left the restaurant a pretty satisfied man. The food had been delicious but he'd had a hard time deflating the waitress's flirtation. By the end of his meal, she'd all but placed her apartment key in his hand.

Instead of catching a cab back to his hotel room, he decided to walk off the hamburger and fries he'd eaten. Although he'd complained earlier about the cold weather, it really wasn't too bad. He'd endured worse. Like that time his team had that mission in the Artic.

He was about to cross the street when a sign ahead stopped him. It was an art gallery and the poster said:

TONIGHT
SPECIAL SHOWING OF ART BY BRISTOL

Bristol…

He shook his head. He was losing it. He hadn't thought Bristol was a common name. Was it?

What if it wasn't? Could it be his Bristol?

He dismissed the idea that Bristol was his. She was merely a woman he'd had a three-day fling with while relaxing in Paris before a mission.

Merely a woman he hadn't been able to forget in three years.

The name was unusual. He'd told her so when they'd met. He knew she was an artist. She'd shown him some of her art.

There was no way she could be here.

But then, why not? She was a New Yorker. He'd gathered that much from a conversation she'd had with Bane. Laramie hadn't asked her anything. His main focus had been sleeping with her.

What if the Bristol on the sign was the same Bristol from Paris?

His chest pounded at the possibility. He watched all the well-dressed people getting out of their limos and private cars to enter the gallery. He glanced down at himself. Jeans, pullover shirt, leather jacket, Stetson and boots. Definitely not dressed to mingle with the likes of the high-class crowd entering the gallery. But at that moment, he didn't give a royal damn.

He had to find out if this Bristol was the same woman he hadn't been able to forget.

"Would you like some more wine, Bristol?"

Bristol glanced up at Steven Culpepper, forced a smile and said, "No, thanks. I'm fine."

He nodded. Looking over her shoulder, he said, "Excuse me for a minute. A few of my clients just arrived."

"Sure."

She let out a deep sigh when he walked off. Why was he hanging around as if they were together when they weren't?

She glanced around. There was a huge crowd and she appreciated that. A great number of her paintings had been sold already.

"I see Steven is quite taken with you tonight, Bristol."

She turned to Margie. "I wish he wouldn't be. He's barely left my side."

Margie lifted a brow. "And you see that as a bad thing?"

Bristol shrugged. "I just don't want him getting the wrong idea."

"Oh, I see,"

Bristol doubted it. Margie was determined to play matchmaker.

"A lot of the people here tonight are ones he invited. People with money. Need I say more?" Margie then walked off.

No, in all honesty, Margie didn't have to say anything. Steven had told her several times tonight just how many people were here because of him. It was as if he'd assumed Bristol would not have gotten anyone here on her own. Although he was probably right about that, he didn't have to remind her of it every chance he got.

"Hello, Bristol."

She turned to an older gentleman. His face seemed familiar and after a quick study of his features, she remembered him. "You're Colin Kusac, a close friend of my father's."

He smiled. "Yes, that's right. I haven't seen you since the funeral and the reading of the will."

That was true. Her father had named Colin as executor, and the scene hadn't been nice that day, especially when all her father had left her was revealed. Krista had accused Bristol of looking for her father only to get his money. Her stepmother had been wrong about that.

Her father had told her that he and Colin had attended high school together and over the years had remained the best of friends. Before Randall died, he'd also told her to contact Mr. Kusac if she ever needed anything. Since there was nothing she'd needed, there had been no reason to call him.

"How have you been?" she asked him.

"Fine. And you? I understand you have a son."

She wondered how he'd known that. She lived a quiet life and it hadn't been highly publicized that she was Randall Lockett's daughter. Although, at her father's request, she had taken his last name. At sixteen it had taken a lot of getting used to, going from Bristol Washington to Bristol Lockett.

Although she'd taken her father's name, she'd never flaunted it to influence her own career. And in the art community her father had used the pseudonym Rand, so very few people had made the connection anyway. However, over the years, people had mentioned how much her paintings resembled those of the renowned artist Rand. Although Margie was aware of her father's identity, Bristol had sworn her manager to secrecy. Bristol wanted to make it on her own and not use her father as leverage.

And now she was Bristol Cooper…

"Yes, I have a beautiful two-year-old son. His first name is Laramie, after his father. His middle name is Randall, after my father. He has the names of two good men."

"Randall would have liked that. He would have been proud of his first grandchild." Colin didn't say anything for a minute and then added, "I miss my good friend. He was there for me more times than not. When I first saw your work, I was taken back by just how much you and he painted alike."

She smiled, thinking how wonderful it was that on this very important night, although her father wasn't here, a man she knew to be his closest friend was. “Yes, we discovered that before he died.”

“Randall was a gifted artist and so are you.”

“Thank you.”

“There’s a beautiful landscape over there that I’m thinking about buying. I wonder if you can tell me what inspired you.”

She knew exactly which one he was talking about. It was the first painting she’d done after her father died and a lot of her pent-up emotions had been poured into it. “Certainly.”

And then she and Colin moved toward the huge painting on the wall.

“May I help you, sir?”

Laramie wasn’t surprised someone had approached him the minute he walked into the gallery. All he had to do was look around the room to see he seemed obviously out of place. He really wouldn’t have to stay a minute longer if the man could answer one question. “The artist on the sign. Bristol. What’s her last name?”

When the older man, who he suspected to be someone in charge, gave him a strange look, Laramie added, “I once knew someone by that name.”

The man nodded his understanding. “Oh, I see. Her last name is—”

“I will handle this gentleman, Jazlyn,” an authoritative voice said behind him.

Laramie didn’t turn around. He figured whoever had spoken would make himself known soon enough. Besides, he hadn’t liked the emphasis the man had placed on the word *gentleman.* As if he thought Laramie was anything but a gentleman. And what had he meant by “handle him”?

Laramie inwardly smiled. He would like to see that happen.

"Yes, of course, Mr. Culpepper." And then the older man walked off.

The guy who'd spoken came around to stand in front of Laramie and quickly sized him up. Laramie didn't have a problem with that since he was sizing up the other man, as well. And Laramie didn't like the arrogant glint in the man's eyes, like he assumed he was better than Laramie just because he was dressed in a designer suit.

A quick assessment told Laramie what he needed to know. The man was in his upper thirties, probably a Harvard or Yale graduate, a Wall Street type, most likely CEO of his own corporation.

"May I help you, Mr...?"

Evidently no one had explained to this man the proper way to introduce oneself. It wasn't by asking a question. Therefore, Laramie didn't intend to give his name unless this ass gave his. Besides, his name was irrelevant to what he wanted to know. "Like I was saying to the older man a moment ago, before we were interrupted—I once knew a woman name Bristol and was wondering, what is the artist's last name?"

The man's smile didn't quite reach his eyes. Who was this man and what business was it of his that Laramie was inquiring about the artist?

"I'm sure it's not the same person."

How the hell would you know? he wanted to say. Instead he said, "Let me decide that."

He could tell his response hadn't gone over well. The man's eyes darkened in irritation. Evidently, he wasn't used to being put in his place. "I won't let you decide anything. In fact, I'm almost certain Bristol doesn't know you."

Laramie was beginning to read the signs. This man was territorial. Evidently, there was something going on between him and the artist. "You sound sure of that, Mr..."

The man smiled. "Culpepper. Steven Culpepper. And

the reason I sound certain is because I know Bristol. We are well acquainted."

"Obviously. So what's her last name?" He tilted his Stetson back to stare down at the man, wondering why Steven was giving him a hard time.

"What's the name of the woman you're looking for? Just in case you haven't noticed, you're drawing attention."

And he was supposed to give a damn? Laramie drew in a deep breath, tired of playing this cat-and-mouse game. The man was probably right, it wasn't the same Bristol, but there was something about this man's attitude that rubbed Laramie the wrong way. "Lockett. Her name is Bristol Lockett."

The man smiled. "Lockett? Then I was right all along. Her last name isn't Lockett."

"So what is it?"

Evidently tired of this conversation as well, the man said, "It's Cooper. Bristol Cooper."

Laramie frowned. He and the woman had the same last name? What a coincidence. But then there were a lot of Coopers out there. "You're right. It's not the same woman. Sorry I took up so much of your time."

"No problem. Let me see you out."

"No need. I know my way." Laramie had made it to the door when he heard it. That laugh.

It was a distinctive sound that could only come from one woman. He turned and glanced around the room. He didn't see her. Had he only imagined hearing her laughter?

"Is anything wrong?"

That Culpepper guy was back. Laramie looked at him. "Not sure. However, I'd like to meet the artist, Bristol Cooper, after all."

"That's not possible."

Laramie was about to tell the man that with him anything was possible, when he heard the sound again. His gaze sharpened as he looked around the room. The sound had come from another part of the gallery. He was certain he hadn't imagined it twice.

He began moving toward the sound, not caring that people were staring at him.

"Wait a minute! You need to leave now."

When Laramie kept walking, he heard the Culpepper guy call out, "Mr. Jazlyn, I suggest you call for security."

They could call for security all they wanted. He wasn't leaving until he made sure…

He entered another area of the gallery and immediately felt it…that undisguised pang of longing and desire he hadn't felt in three years. He swallowed hard against the deep yearning in his throat as his gaze swept around the room.

And then he saw her.

Her back was to him. She stood beside an older gentleman as the two of them studied a landscape. Laramie knew without even seeing her face that the woman was his Bristol.

He'd only spent three days with her, but he knew that body, even if it was now draped in a beautiful gown. There were a few curves that hadn't been there before, but he was certain everything else belonged to Bristol Lockett, right, front and center. Especially that shapely backside.

He remembered the feel of his hand on that backside as well as the brush of his fingers along her inner thighs. He felt an immediate tightening in his gut at the memory.

Every muscle in his body tensed as he quickly moved in her direction. When he came within a few feet of her, he inhaled her scent. It was the one he remembered from Paris. Hurried footsteps were headed in his direction. Security was coming. Let them come. But not before he made his presence known.

"Bristol?"

She must have heard her name but she seemed almost afraid to face him. And when she slowly turned, she looked as if she was staring at the face of…a ghost?

She took a step forward. She whispered his name. And then she crumpled.

Four

Laramie managed to grab her before she passed out on the floor, sweeping her into his arms. People were staring, some had begun moving in their direction, no doubt wondering what the hell was going on.

"Put her down!"

He recognized Culpepper's voice. Laramie turned to see Culpepper flanked by several security guards and the owner of the gallery. Then suddenly a woman pushed through the crowd. "What happened?"

Laramie thought it was obvious but answered anyway. "She fainted."

"Fainted? How? Why?" She then narrowed her gaze at him. "Who are you?"

"Laramie Cooper."

"Laramie Cooper?" The woman gasped.

He wondered why hearing his name had such an effect on the woman. "Yes, Laramie Cooper. I need to take Bristol somewhere to lie down. And I need someone to get a wet cloth."

"Wait a damn minute," Culpepper was saying. "He has no right to be here. Who is he supposed to be?"

He heard the woman whisper something to the bastard that sounded like "He's her husband."

Laramie wondered why the woman would make such an outlandish claim. He wasn't anyone's husband. Then he recalled what Culpepper had told him earlier. Bristol's last name was Cooper. Now he was more confused than ever and confusion was something he didn't deal with very well.

Suddenly, the older gentleman Bristol had been talking to said, "Will someone do as this man asks and get a wet cloth? Jazlyn, where is your office?"

"Right this way, Mr. Kusac."

"Kusac?"

Laramie ignored the flutter of whispered voices repeating the man's name as if it meant something. Even the woman who was moving ahead of them stopped to look at the man in awe. Who was this guy Kusac? Was he a celebrity or something?

Laramie moved quickly toward the back of the gallery while carrying Bristol in his arms. He recalled the last time he'd carried her, from her kitchen to her bed.

Entering the gallery owner's office, Laramie laid Bristol on the sofa. The man who'd been identified as Kusac closed the office door, only admitting the three of them along with the woman. Laramie couldn't determine who she was studying more, him or Kusac. There was a knock on the door and Kusac opened it. Wet cloths were handed to him and he passed them over to Laramie.

"Is she all right?" the woman asked nervously.

"Yes" was Laramie's response as he began wiping Bristol's face with a cloth.

"By the way, Mr. Kusac, I'm Margie Townsend, Bristol's manager. I appreciate you coming out tonight and giving your support. You and Bristol seem to know each other."

"We do. I was a close friend of her father's."

"Oh." And then out the corner of his eye, Laramie noted

the woman moving closer to him. "And are you really Laramie Cooper?" she asked.

He didn't take his gaze off Bristol as he continued to wipe her face. She was even more beautiful than he'd remembered. Her chocolate brown skin was smooth and soft. He'd always liked the shape of her lips. They had the perfect bow. He recalled kissing them. How he'd licked them with his tongue.

Bristol was three years older now. Twenty-five. But you couldn't tell it by her features. It was as if she hadn't aged at all.

She still was the most beautiful woman he had yet to meet.

He switched his gaze to the woman who'd introduced herself as Bristol's manager and who'd asked him a strange question. "Yes, I'm Laramie Cooper."

"B-but you're supposed to be dead."

Laramie frowned. Bristol must have told her that. But then, how had Bristol known?

Deciding he would get all the answers he wanted from Bristol when she came to, he said, "Yes, I'd been captured, and they presumed I was dead."

"And you decided to show up after all this time?" the woman snapped. "Fine husband you are!"

Before he could ask her what in the hell was she talking about, Bristol made a sound. She whispered his name just moments before her eyes fluttered open.

And then she stared up at him. Tentatively, she reached up and touched his face, as if to make certain he was flesh and blood. Tears fell from her eyes when she whispered, "You're alive."

He nodded. "Yes, I'm alive."

"But they told me you were dead."

He nodded. "They thought so for a while, before I was rescued."

"Rescued?"

"Yes. Almost a year later."

From the look in her eyes, he saw something was bothering her. Maybe it was the fact that she was using his last name and claiming they were married.

"We need to talk privately, Laramie," she said, barely above a whisper.

She was right. They needed to talk. He nodded and then glanced at the other two people in the room. Before he could say anything, Kusac said, "We heard." He opened the door. When Margie Townsend hesitated, Kusac said, "They need time alone."

Margie nodded. "Yes, of course." She then said to Bristol, "If you need me I'll be right outside the door."

When the door closed behind them, Laramie helped Bristol sit up. She drew in a deep breath and stared at him. "I can't believe you are alive."

Laramie didn't say anything. He was trying to make sense of what he'd learned and was failing miserably. He needed answers to help him understand. "How did you know I was supposedly dead?" he asked, sitting beside her on the sofa.

She nervously licked her lips. "I tried to find you. I sent you a letter, through the navy, and it was returned. A friend of mine knew someone who worked in the State Department. They checked into it and that's what I was told."

"When was this?"

"A few months after I last saw you."

He nodded. "I was presumed dead, so the person was right. I was rescued just days before Christmas the following year."

"That was a long time."

"Yes, it was." Only his close friends knew about the nightmares he'd had for months following his rescue. Nightmares he still had at times. His enemies had tried to break him and he'd refused to be broken. But their attempts had become lasting scars.

"Why were you trying to reach me, Bristol?"

Bristol drew in a deep breath, not believing that Laramie was alive, not believing that he'd shown up here tonight. How had he known where she was? Had he been looking for her? If he had, that would make what she was about to tell him easier. But what if he hadn't been looking for her? What if he had forgotten all about her and moved on? For all she knew he could be married, although there was no ring on his finger.

She studied his features. He was even more handsome than she remembered. He looked slightly older and there was a hardness in the lines of his face that hadn't been there before. Instead of taking away from his striking features, the hardness defined them even more. And the look in his eyes reflected experiences she couldn't come close to imagining.

Even if those experiences had changed him, it didn't matter. He still had a right to know about her son. His son. Their son.

He could accept it or question whether Laramie was truly his, but he had a right to know. How he handled the news was up to him.

Drawing in another deep breath, she met his gaze and said, "The reason I tried reaching you was because I wanted to let you know I was pregnant."

Five

Laramie froze. He stared at Bristol. He'd heard what she'd said but he needed to verify it. "You were pregnant?"

"Yes," she said in a soft voice. "And you're free to order a paternity test if you need to confirm that my son is yours."

He had a son?

It took less than a second to go from shock to disbelief. "How?"

She lifted a brow, indicating she'd found his question as stupid as he had, but she answered nonetheless. "Probably from making love almost nonstop for three solid days."

They had definitely done that. Although he'd used a condom each and every time, he knew there was always the possibility something could go wrong. "And, where is he?" he asked, still trying to wrap his mind around the fact that he had a son.

"At home."

Where the hell was that?

It bothered him how little he knew about the woman who'd given birth to his child. At least she'd tried contacting him to let him know. Some women wouldn't have.

If his child had been born nine months after their holiday

fling, that meant he would have turned two in September. Laramie recalled that September. Although it had been hard keeping up with the days while being held hostage, somehow he'd managed, by counting each sunrise. He'd been lucky to be held in a cell with a tiny window.

He hadn't known that while being a pawn in his enemies' game of life and death that somewhere in the world Bristol was giving life.

To his child.

Emotions bombarded him with the impact of a Tomahawk missile. He'd been happy whenever Mac became a father again and had been overjoyed for Bane at the birth of his triplets. And now Laramie was a parent, which meant he had to think about someone other than himself. But then, wasn't he used to looking out for others as a member of his SEAL team?

"Have you gotten married, Laramie?"

He frowned at her question. Marriage was the very last thing on his mind. "No, I'm still single."

She nodded and then said, "I'm not asking you for anything, if that's what you're thinking. I just felt you had a right to know about the baby."

He stared at her while conflicting emotions warred inside him. She wasn't asking him for anything? Did she not know that her bold declaration that he'd fathered her child demanded everything?

"I want to see him."

"And you will. I would never keep Laramie from you."

"You named him Laramie?" Even more emotions swamped him. Her son, their son, had his name?

She hesitated, as if she wasn't sure how he would like her response. "Yes. His first name is Laramie and his middle name is Randall, after my father. I thought you were dead and I wanted him to have your name. So I named him Laramie Randall Cooper."

He didn't say anything for a full minute. Then he asked, "So, what's your reason for giving yourself my name, as well?"

Oh, boy. Bristol wondered why so much was happening to her tonight of all nights. When she'd left home she'd hoped for a great night for the showing of her work at the gallery. She hadn't counted on a lover—specifically, her son's father—coming back from the dead.

And now he wanted answers.

Although she knew he deserved to have them, she wasn't ready to tell him any more than she had already. She just wanted to go home and hug her son. Tomorrow, she would tell her son that the father he thought had become an angel was now a mortal.

She was about to tell him she was tired of talking for now when there was a knock on the door. "I'll get that," he said, standing.

She still appreciated the way he walked. Spine ramrod straight, steps taken in perfect precision with the best-looking tush she'd seen on a man.

When Laramie opened the door he practically blocked the doorway, but she heard Margie's voice. "How is Bristol?"

"I'm fine, Margie," she said. Thankfully, Laramie shifted aside so Margie could see for herself.

"Do you need anything?"

"No, I'll be out in a minute."

"No rush. Most of the people have left anyway. But the good thing is that all your paintings were sold. Tonight was a huge success."

Was it? As far as her manager was concerned, it had been a successful night. But Bristol saw beyond the money her paintings had earned. She saw the man standing by the door. Her heart slammed against her ribs. Already she was wondering what changes were about to be made in her life.

"And Steven is worried about you."

Bristol saw Laramie's body stiffen at the mention of Steven's name and wondered why. She became even more curious when he said, "Tell Culpepper she's fine and is in good hands. Now if you will excuse us, Bristol and I need to finish talking." He then closed the door.

How had Laramie known Steven's last name? Had the two of them met? If so, when?

Laramie slowly turned away from the door to stare at her. It was a good thing she was sitting down because her knees began shaking. The intensity of his gaze sent sensuous chills through her body. How was that possible when she hadn't seen him in three years?

The sexual chemistry that had drawn them to each other from the first was still there. She wanted to deny its existence, but she couldn't. She wanted to break eye contact with him and look away, but she couldn't do that, either. She sat there and endured the moment, hoping it would quickly pass. It didn't. It seemed to extend longer than necessary.

She decided to use it to her advantage; checking him out wasn't a hard thing to do. He wore a pair of jeans, a dark blue pullover shirt, a dark leather jacket, a Stetson and boots. He looked like a cowboy, ready to ride off into the sunset. He seemed to have gotten taller and his body appeared even more fit. Was he still a navy SEAL or had he given it up after that mission that had obviously gone all wrong?

Her gaze moved to his shoulders. She remembered them well. She could easily recall how she clutched tight to them when they made love. How she would cling to them while he thrust inside her. What she remembered the most was that Laramie Cooper was a very physical man, filled with an abundance of strength and virility.

She sighed as her gaze returned to his too-handsome face and stared into his eyes. And she saw it again, that hardness. Pain he refused to show. Ravaged secrets. A wounded heart. A damaged soul.

He probably didn't want her to see any of those things, but for a quick moment, she'd seen them anyway. She wondered what he'd endured during those months when everyone thought he was dead. Would he share the details of that time with her if she were to ask? Was it any of her business?

He didn't say anything as he continued to study her as intensely as she was studying him. What was he seeing? Besides a few extra pounds she hadn't shed after her pregnancy. Some men would think of them as curves. She thought of them as a nuisance that wouldn't go away no matter how much she exercised.

"Are you ready to answer my question?" he asked in a deep, husky voice that seemed to resonate inside her. "Because I have even more."

She'd been afraid of that. She also knew they couldn't stay holed up in Mr. Jazlyn's office forever. She understood she needed to fill Laramie in on so much that had happened but now was not a good time. "I suggest we meet tomorrow and—"

"No. I need to know tonight."

Tonight? "That's not possible," she said, glancing at her watch because she needed to stop looking into his eyes. His dark gaze wasn't just directed at her, it was assessing her in a way she knew too well. During those three days in Paris, she had been able to—most of the time—interpret what he was thinking from his eyes. Namely, she knew when he was ready to make love again by the desire she would see in them.

"Why tonight?" she asked.

"Why not tonight?" he countered.

Drawing in a deep breath, she said, "My neighbor, Ms.

Charlotte, is keeping Laramie and I don't want to get home too late."

He nodded. "And where is home?"

"Brooklyn."

He nodded again as he continued to stare at her. She couldn't help wondering what he was thinking. She found out when he said, "I want to see my son tonight, Bristol."

Why did him saying her name, no matter the tone, make an unexplainable warmth spread through her? "It's past his bedtime and he'll be asleep."

"Doesn't matter. I want to see him."

She eased up off the sofa. "Why?" she asked, not sure she was ready for him to come to her home, invade her space and meet Ms. Charlotte, who was the closest thing to a family she had now. "Don't you believe me?"

"Yes, I do. I just want to see him."

It was similar to her father's wish when she'd first made contact with him. She hadn't known what to expect when she'd first spoken with him. To break the ice, her aunt Dolly had spoken with him first. By the time Bristol had gotten on the phone, he had been eager to talk to her. Nervously, she'd blundered out the words, "I'm your daughter." And he'd said, "I believe you and I want to see you." He'd flown out that same day from Los Angeles and in less than eight hours was knocking on her aunt's door.

Bristol studied Laramie. Noticed his stiff posture. Was he expecting a fight? Hadn't she told him that she wanted him to know about their child? "Fine, you can see him tonight. A private car is taking me home."

She nervously nibbled her bottom lip. There was something she had to tell him before they left the office. It was the answer to the question he'd asked regarding her use of his name. "And to answer your question about me taking your name."

"Yes?"

"Before leaving Paris, I had already made up my mind to name my son after you, first name and last. But I didn't want people asking questions about why we had different last names. My friend Dionne came up with the idea. She had a friend who was an assistant to a judge in Paris who was willing to help with our plan. We did a fake marriage license where I listed you as my husband. It was then filed with the courts in Paris."

He didn't say anything for a minute before he asked, "Giving birth to a child without the benefit of a husband drove you to do that?"

She looked away for a second to figure out how to make him understand. "Yes. More so for Laramie than for me." She paused. "My mom was a single parent and I never knew my father. All my life the stigma of being born illegitimate bothered me because there were those who never let me forget. I got teased a lot about not having a father. I know having kids out of wedlock is more acceptable these days, but still, I didn't want to take a chance and put my child through that."

Although her mother had never said so, Bristol believed it bothered her mother as well, not only for her daughter but for herself. While growing up, there had been organizations Bristol's mother had tried to sign up for that had rejected their application because they hadn't met what was considered normal family dynamics. In other words, she didn't have a father and her mother didn't have a husband.

"I assume your manager believes we're married. She practically accused me of deserting you and my child."

Bristol rubbed her hands down her face, feeling bad about that. "I'm sorry. I'll tell her the truth."

"Don't bother doing that. At least I know why she's been acting like I'm scum. And I also now know why that Culpepper guy was acting like an ass when I asked about you."

"Steven?"

"Yes, I take it he's your boyfriend."

Where would he get an idea like that? "No, he's not my boyfriend. Steven and I have never even gone out on a date."

Laramie held her gaze, apparently finding it odd that the man would act so territorial under those circumstances. "But he has asked you out though, right?"

"Yes, but I've always declined. He's not my type." She checked her watch again and then looked up at him. "Are you going to deny you're my husband? People might question you about it."

"Don't worry. I won't give your secret away."

Six

When they walked out of the office, the first person Laramie noticed was Steven Culpepper and how the man's eyes narrowed when they got closer. If the guy had gotten word that Bristol's supposedly dead husband wasn't dead after all, then what the hell was he still hanging around for?

Laramie detected Bristol's nervousness. Did she think he would rat her out, expose her for lying about their marriage when he'd told her he wouldn't? He slowed his pace and she slowed hers. He glanced down at her. "You okay?"

"Yes. I'm just surprised to see Steven still here."

That made two of them. "You want me to ask him to leave?"

"No. I guess he was concerned. I see Mr. Kusac is still here, too. I can understand his concern since he was a good friend of my father's."

Laramie didn't say anything. He recalled how people had jumped into motion when the man named Kusac had barked out orders earlier. Even the owner of the gallery was quick to do the man's bidding.

Margie left the group to walk toward them, a smile on

her lips. "Well, did the two of you get things straightened out?" she asked.

Laramie answered before Bristol did. "Yes, and we're leaving."

The woman lifted a brow. "Leaving? To go where?"

Laramie was tempted to tell the woman that he didn't think it was any of her business, but Bristol answered, "I'm going home, Margie. Is the car ready to take me there?"

"Yes."

"Good." She then turned to Laramie and said, "I need to say good-night to everyone."

"Okay, let's do that."

Her eyes widened, probably in surprise that he'd included himself in the goodbyes, but she didn't say anything as he walked with her over to the three men. "I would like you to meet Laramie Cooper."

Laramie was sure it didn't go unnoticed how Bristol had introduced him. She hadn't referred to him as her husband. He figured these people assumed he was her back-from-the-dead husband, but she wasn't allowing anyone to presume anything about the nature of their relationship.

She thanked the owner of the gallery for hosting the event and apologized for all the commotion she'd caused by fainting.

Maurice Jazlyn waved off her words and said, "I would have passed out, too, had I thought my husband was dead and then he suddenly appeared out of nowhere."

Laramie didn't speak. If they were waiting for him to explain his absence for the past three years, they could wait on.

Then Jazlyn's face broke into a smile. "But then, I certainly can't complain since every last one of your paintings sold and you being here brought Kusac out tonight. It's been years since I've seen him."

"And I was glad to see him, as well," Bristol said, smiling at the man. "Thanks for coming."

Colin Kusac smiled. "Your first art show in New York—I would not have missed it for the world."

Then Bristol's attention went to Steven Culpepper. Laramie didn't like the vibes he was picking up off the man. He hadn't liked them from the first. "Steven," he heard Bristol say. "Thanks for inviting all those people here tonight. It was a nice turnout thanks to you."

"No need to thank me, but I'd like for us to meet sometime this week. Several of my clients here tonight were impressed with your work and want to see more. A few are willing to commission some of your future projects."

"That's wonderful! I'm sure we can arrange a meeting," Margie said excitedly behind them. "Just give me a call, Steven. I'll work out a date and time when Bristol is available."

A tight smile touched Culpepper's lips. "Yes, of course, Margie." Laramie had a feeling Culpepper had wanted a private meeting with Bristol and her manager had ruined those plans.

"I'll call you tomorrow to discuss your availability, Bristol," Margie said.

"That's fine," Bristol said, smiling. She then turned to him. "I'm ready to go, Laramie."

He nodded and took her hand, leading her toward the door.

"I don't bite, you know."

Bristol glanced across the back seat at Laramie and had to admit there was a lot of space between them. He might not bite but she could vividly recall a lot of other naughty things he could do with his mouth.

Jeez. Why was she remembering that now?

"I know you don't bite, but I figured you would want your space."

She thought the chuckle that ensued from his throat sounded way too sexy for her ears. "Is that a way of letting me know you like yours?"

She shrugged. "I guess I've gotten used to it." No need to tell him that she hadn't had another man in her life since him, serious or otherwise. After her son was born, he had become her whole world and there hadn't been room for anyone else. Some women needed a man to feel like a female; she didn't.

He didn't say anything for a minute and that was fine with her as the private car carried them through the streets of Manhattan and toward the Brooklyn Bridge. When they'd left the gallery she'd noticed the temperature had dropped. Forecasters had predicted a heavy snowfall before Christmas and with this cold snap being less than two weeks before Christmas, she could see it happening.

"Tell me about him. My son."

Laramie's words intruded into her reverie and she glanced over at him. The bright lights from the tall buildings they passed illuminated his features and she could see why she'd been taken with him from the first. Any woman would have been.

In Paris, Laramie Cooper had been handsome and charismatic all rolled into one. He was still handsome, she would give him that, but he had yet to unleash any of the charm that had swept her off her feet and into the nearest bed. But then she figured when a man was told he was the father of a child he hadn't known he had, his secret son, shock might put a damper on the charm.

Bristol settled her body against the leather seat. Talking about her son was one of her favorite subjects. "He's perfect."

There was that sexy chuckle again from him. "Besides

that. How about starting off telling me about your pregnancy. Was it a hard one?"

She could vividly recall all nine months of it. "Not after my sixth month. I was one of those unusual women who had morning sickness in the morning and at night. I could barely keep anything in my stomach, and the smell of some foods would send me rushing for the nearest bathroom."

"Sounds pretty bad."

"I thought so at the time. I had planned to leave Paris in my fifth month but my doctor restricted air travel until I was better. I'd lost a lot of weight. I wasn't eating much and what I was eating my baby was getting. That's why it doesn't surprise me now that Laramie is a big eater."

"When did you leave Paris?"

"In my sixth month. I wanted my baby to be born in the United States. Thank God for online shopping and for Ms. Charlotte, who lives next door to my aunt. The house was cleaned out and baby furniture delivered, which made things easy for me when I finally arrived back in New York. Once the morning sickness stopped and I could retain food, I blew up overnight but the weight gain was mostly all baby. Laramie was born weighing close to nine pounds."

"And during all that time you thought I was dead."

He'd said it not as a question but as a statement. "Yes. I had no reason not to believe what the State Department had reported. A part of me wished I'd known more about you so I could reach out to your parents. I recall you'd mentioned they were alive but you never gave me any personal information about yourself."

"And you never gave me any personal information about yourself, either," he said. "Though I do remember you telling Bane you were from New York."

No, they hadn't exchanged any of those details. She doubted if it would have mattered anyway. It was not like he'd intended to one day pick up where they'd left off.

There was no doubt in her mind that after he'd been rescued he'd gotten on with his life and hadn't given her a second thought.

"How did you stumble across me tonight?" She was certain now that he hadn't been looking for her.

"I came to New York on military business. After dinner I was headed back to my hotel room when I saw the sign at the gallery with your name. I figured there couldn't be too many artists with that name."

"So you came into the gallery on a hunch?"

"Yes, although I knew from the way I was dressed I would stand out like a sore thumb. And then I encountered your Steven Culpepper, who—"

"He's not my Steven."

"He tried to paint the picture that he was. Appeared pretty damn possessive, too. He'd convinced me you weren't the Bristol I was looking for, but then I heard your laugh."

"My laugh?"

"Yes. I was less than a foot from the door when I heard you laugh. Twice."

She nodded. "Colin Kusac was sharing something with me about how he and my father used to get in trouble in high school."

"Your laugh is what let me know you were the same Bristol. I remembered it."

Those three days they'd spent together had been memorable in so many ways. And it hadn't been all about the sex. They'd had fun sharing breakfast in bed, sharing jokes. They'd even watched movies together. She had enjoyed waking up in his arms and going to sleep the same way.

Those memories were what had held her sanity together while she carried his child and believed he'd been lost to her forever. Those memories were what she'd remembered when the labor pains had hit. She'd drawn comfort from them.

The car came to a stop and she glanced out the window. She was home. The place she'd escaped to when she needed to heal from the grief she'd endured when she thought Laramie had died. It was the place where, months later, she had brought her son. Because her baby had been so large, at the last minute she'd had to deliver by C-section. Luckily, Dionne had made plans to be with Bristol as her delivery coach and ended up being a lot more. Her best friend was a godsend during the weeks following the delivery.

The first time Bristol had seen her son she'd been filled with so much love. She'd been given a special gift. She'd immediately noticed how much he looked like his father. It was uncanny. Her son's coloring, the shape of his eyes, the tilt of his mouth, had all come from the older Laramie. And the older her son got the more he looked like his father. Would Laramie notice? There was no way he couldn't.

"Are you okay, Bristol?"

She looked over at him. "Yes, I'm fine." A part of her wondered if that was true.

The driver came around and opened the door. Laramie slid out, and she couldn't help noticing how his masculine jeans-clad thighs slid with ease across the leather. Then he stood by the door and extended his hand out to her, to help her out.

The moment she placed her hand in his, she felt it. That spark, that tingling sensation she'd felt the first time they'd touched. She glanced up at him and met the darkness of his eyes and knew he'd felt it, too. Knew he was remembering.

Then she decided she wasn't fine after all.

Seven

Laramie considered what had passed between him and Bristol a few moments ago. He was fully aware of the strong sexual chemistry that was still between them. Even when they weren't trying, they pushed each other's buttons. No surprise there. But what he found surprising was the intensity of what he'd felt from her touch.

Shoving his hands in his pockets, he turned to look at the line of brownstones, especially the one in front of them. The SEAL in him quickly surveyed his surroundings, took in every nook and cranny. It was a nice neighborhood of older well-kept homes on a tree-lined street with sufficient lighting. Even the sidewalks in front of the homes looked as if they'd been scrubbed clean. It was easy to see this was a block that took pride in their neighborhood.

He followed as Bristol walked ahead of him. Several live plants lined the steps to her front door. Had he told her how nice she looked tonight in that long, flowing black gown with a split on the side? The male in him couldn't help but appreciate how those curves filled out the gown. She was a beautiful woman and he could understand Culpepper's interest. What man wouldn't be interested?

She took the key out of her purse and looked at him. Had she sensed he'd been staring at her backside? "Nice neighborhood," he said, in case she had.

"Yes, it is." She paused. "I will have to tell Ms. Charlotte who you are, as well. She will be shocked."

He nodded. "She also assumes we're married?"

"Yes. The only person who knows the truth is my best friend in Paris. Dionne."

Laramie didn't say anything as she unlocked the door and opened it. Then she stepped aside. "No, after you," he told her. "I'm used to bringing up the rear."

She nodded and entered her home. He followed, closing the door behind him. Her place had a cozy air. It felt small and intimate compared to the monstrosity of a house his parents owned, where he'd grown up as a child.

He stood in a foyer with stairs on one side and a living room on the other. The lit fireplace reminded him of how cold it was outside. The heat in here felt good. She had decorated for the holidays. A Christmas tree sat in front of the windows and he couldn't help noticing that several of the ornaments were the ones he had bought for her in Paris. It made him feel good to know she had kept them.

"Nice place," he said, glancing over at Bristol as he removed his Stetson and placed it on a nearby hat rack.

"Thanks."

"I thought I heard voices. You're home."

An older woman came down the stairs and he figured her to be Ms. Charlotte. She smiled when she saw them. Then suddenly, the smile seemed to freeze on her face and she stopped walking to stare at him.

"Sorry I'm late, Ms. Charlotte. How was Laramie tonight?"

The older woman answered Bristol, without taking her eyes off him. "He was fine as usual."

It was then that Bristol said, “Ms. Charlotte, I’d like to introduce—”

“I know who he is,” the older woman said, still staring at him.

The woman’s words gave Laramie pause. “How can you know?” he asked, lifting a brow.

“Your son looks just like you.”

His son looked like him? “Does he?” he heard himself asking.

“Yes, your spitting image,” the older woman said.

“That’s one of the first things I noticed after he was born,” Bristol added.

The woman finally continued down the stairs. When she reached the bottom step, she said, “I know you’re not a ghost, so I can only assume you weren’t dead as Bristol thought.”

Laramie stared into the older woman’s eyes. He admired their sharpness. He had a feeling you couldn’t hide much from those eyes. “No, I wasn’t dead, although the government thought I was. I was missing in action for almost a year before being recused.”

For some reason he felt he should provide her an explanation. She nodded and her lips creased into a smile. “I’m glad you came back alive. You’re going to love that little boy up there. He’s a sweetheart.”

Bristol groaned. “You shouldn’t say things that aren’t true, Ms. Charlotte. You and I both know he’s just gotten the hang of the terrible twos.”

“Like I’ve always said, boys will be boys. I should know after raising four of my own.” She then glanced at her watch. “Time for me to leave. I’m sure the two of you have a lot to talk about,” she said, heading for the door.

She glanced back at them, specifically at Laramie, and said, “I’m glad you’re here.” The older woman then opened the door and closed it behind her.

Laramie saw Bristol was focused on the painting that hung over her fireplace. He'd seen it before. In Paris. In her bedroom. It had hung directly over her bed. She'd told him it was one she'd painted with someone. He'd been amazed how the beauty of the Point Arena Lighthouse had been captured so magnificently on canvas. The painting was so vivid it seemed that the waves from the Pacific were hitting the shoreline. He recalled visiting the actual lighthouse years ago with his parents.

"Bristol?"

She switched her gaze to him. "Yes?"

"Are you okay?"

She stood beside a lamp and the light illuminated her. He was thinking then what he'd thought when he'd first seen her. She was beautiful. In the bright light, he could study her. See more. Her dark hair was swept up and away from her face in a way that seemed to make her features even more striking. Especially with those earrings in her ears…

It was then that he remembered. He'd given her the earrings as a gift. It seemed the Christmas ornaments weren't the only thing she'd kept.

"You're ready to see him?"

"Yes."

She nodded. "He's asleep, so whatever you do, try not to wake him. Laramie can be a handful when awakened from his sleep. He doesn't like that very much."

"I won't wake him."

"Okay. Then follow me please."

She headed up the stairs and he followed, feeling his stomach knot with every step. This was crazy. He'd faced bitter enemies without flinching. Yet knowing that at the end of these steps was a child he'd helped to create had nervous tension flowing through him.

The moment they reached the landing she turned to him.

"This way. His bedroom is next to mine so I can hear him at night."

He nodded, inhaling her scent. It was soft, subtle—jasmine. He recalled that was her favorite fragrance and for those three days they'd spent together it had become his.

He hung back when she opened the door and entered the bedroom. She turned on a small lamp. His gaze raked the room. It had bright yellow walls and a mural of zoo animals gathered around an image of someone reading a book.

Then there was the toy box in the corner. He smiled, remembering how he would pull all his toys out of the box at the beginning of the day as a boy, only to have to put them back at the end. His parents always had a full-time housekeeper and undoubtedly, she'd figured the more she taught him to do in his playroom, the less she would have to do.

He watched Bristol move toward the bed. From the doorway he could see the small sleeping form beneath the blanket. A mop of dark curly hair peeped out and he instantly recalled the pictures he'd seen of himself as a child with the same mass of curly hair. His parents hadn't given him his first haircut until he was about four.

When Bristol stopped by the bed, he moved to where she stood as blood pounded in his temples. He looked down and his heart stopped. Suddenly, he was bombarded with emotions he couldn't keep in check. He was looking down at his child. His son.

His son.

A son he and Bristol had made together during their three days of heated passion. Three days he hadn't been able to forget. Three days, the memory of which had helped him maintain his sanity when any normal person would have lost it.

He had expected to feel something. But not this. Not this overflowing of emotions filling him to capacity, taking hold of his mind and heart. He might not have been interested in fathering a child before, but the thought that he'd fathered this one had intense pride tightening his shoulders then spreading all the way down to his gut.

Since his child was lying on his stomach, he could only see one side of his face. That was enough. His mind rang out with the words... *He's mine. All mine.*

Um, not quite, he thought, glancing at the woman by his side. His son was hers, too. That was a fact he couldn't forget.

She met his gaze. At that moment, something passed between them and this time it wasn't sexual in nature. It was an unspoken understanding that no matter what, this child—their child—would always come first. He understood and accepted the pledge.

"Does he sleep through the night?" he whispered. He had to say something. He wanted to know so much. He wanted to know everything.

A smile touched her lips. "If you're hoping he'd awake anytime soon, no such luck," she whispered back. "He usually fights sleep tooth and nail, but when he's out, he's out until the next day."

"May I come back tomorrow to see him? Spend time with him?"

She didn't answer. Why? All he needed was a yes or no, preferably yes. Instead, she whispered, "Let's go back downstairs and talk about it."

Talk about it? Did she think her answer would make him yell and risk waking up his son? What was there to talk about? This was his son. She'd said so. He'd believed her even without seeing all of him. Drawing in a deep breath, he hoped like hell there was not about to be any drama. The only true drama he enjoyed was of the SEALs kind.

He followed her out the door and back down the stairs. "Would you like a cup of coffee or a beer, Laramie?"

"A beer will be fine."

"I'll be right back."

In a way, he was glad she'd left him alone for a few moments to deal with all these emotions. Was she deliberately stalling? Would she try to deny him rights to his son? She'd said the reason she'd tried writing to him three years ago was because she'd wanted him to know she was pregnant. He'd just seen his child. Now what? Did she expect him to walk away? Should he consider obtaining an attorney so he could know his rights as a father? All he knew was that his son had his name. Bristol even had his name, although they weren't legally married.

He rubbed a hand down his face. The hour was late. Was he overthinking things? If he was, it wouldn't be the first time. He was a suspicious bastard by nature. He rarely took anything at face value.

She returned with a beer for him and a cup of tea for herself. He remembered how she would drink a cup of tea every morning and every night before bedtime. He would get all turned on just watching how she sipped her tea.

"Let's sit in there," she said, indicating the living room. "Although I loved my studio apartment in Paris, it's nice to have more room here, especially with Laramie."

She sat down but he remained standing. Her calmness kicked up the uncertainty inside him even more. Was this when she would tell him he could have no part in his child's life or that he would only get whatever part she chose to give him?

He opened his beer and took a huge swig. The cool liquid felt refreshing going down his throat. He glanced over at her and saw she was looking at him. It was as if she wanted to say something but was too nervous to do so. In that case, he needed to just come out and squash whatever ideas were formulating in her head here and now.

"I asked you upstairs if I could come back tomorrow

and you never gave me an answer. So I can only assume you have a problem with me doing so. In that case, I think you need to hear me out, Bristol."

He moved to stand a few feet from where she sat and met her gaze. "I want to see my son again. Every chance I get. I want to know him and I want him to know me. I want to be there for him. I want to be a part of his life. I'm not a man who will walk away from my child. I have rights as a father."

He paused before adding, "And just so you know, if you deny me those rights, I will fight you legally with every penny I have."

Eight

Bristol knew she needed to do something before she began crying. Already it was taking everything within her to fight back the tears glistening in her eyes. She doubted Laramie knew just how much his words meant to her.

A part of her had known that she'd fallen in love with him during their holiday fling for a reason. Although she hadn't gotten to know him in the way she would have liked, in her heart she'd believed he was a man with character. A man of honor. A man who believed in doing the right thing.

When she discovered she was pregnant, letting him know had been automatic because of what her mother had done to her father. But Bristol hadn't known, until this very minute, how Laramie would feel about their son. Whether he would accept him or walk away. Even when he'd said he believed Laramie was his and had wanted to see him, there hadn't been any guarantees as to what his reaction would be. But she could not deny him the right to see his son and if he'd walked out the door after doing so, it would have been his loss. Not hers or her child's.

But from what he'd just said so passionately, he didn't plan to walk out the door. He wanted to be a part of his child's life…just like her father would have wanted to be a part of hers had he known about her sooner. Laramie Cooper was proving there were decent men out there. Just like her father.

Tears she couldn't contain any longer wet her cheeks. Why was she getting so emotional? Especially now? She blamed it on the fact that the man she'd fallen in love with three years ago, the man she'd thought was dead, was not only very much alive but was here, in her home, standing in front of her and accepting his child without any hesitation. Of course that didn't mean he wanted to renew a relationship with her or anything; she understood that. That was fine. The most important thing was that he wanted a relationship with his son.

"Hell, Bristol, you're crying over what I said? Just because I want to be a part of my child's life?" Laramie asked in an incredulous voice.

More tears she couldn't control flooded her eyes, and she saw both anger and confusion in his features. She wasn't handling this very well and now she had him thinking the complete opposite from what she was feeling.

"I need to get some tissue," she said, quickly getting up to go into her kitchen to grab a few. Moments later, when she returned, Laramie was standing in front of her Christmas tree with his back to her. His hands were shoved into the pockets of his jeans. She wondered if he'd noticed the ornaments. She doubted he would ever know how much she'd come to treasure them. How each time she looked at one she was reminded of Paris.

"Laramie?"

He turned around and met her gaze. She could tell from his stance and his brooding expression that he was still angry, even more so. She needed to explain and the only way she could do that was to tell him everything. "I think we need to sit down and talk."

The look in his dark, piercing eyes said that as far as he was concerned, there was nothing to talk about, but he nodded anyway. She took a seat on her sofa again, but he said, "I'd rather stand."

She wished he would sit down. Then she wouldn't have to stare up at him. Wouldn't have to notice just how well-built he still was. How sexy he looked in jeans and a leather jacket. And she wouldn't have to notice how his eyes were trained on her. But she said, "Okay, if you prefer standing."

The room was quiet but she was convinced she could hear the pounding of her heart. "I might have confused you about a few things, Laramie," she said. "I would like to explain and hope in the end you'll understand."

She paused before saying, "Growing up, I never knew my father. Other kids had daddies and I didn't understand why I didn't. It was just me and my mom. One day… I believe I was eight at the time… I asked her about it. I wanted to know where my daddy was. She got angry with me and said I didn't have a daddy, that I didn't need one and not to ever bring up the subject of a father again. Her words were final and I knew it."

Bristol picked up her teacup and took a sip although the tea had cooled. "It was only after my mother died when I was fifteen that I moved from Houston to—"

"You lived in Texas?"

"Yes. I was born in Houston and lived there until I was fifteen."

He nodded. "I'm a Texan, as well. I was born in Austin."

She nodded and then continued her story. "When Mom died, I moved here to New York to live with my aunt Dolly. She was my mother's only sibling."

Bristol took a breath and then continued, "It was only then that I got up enough courage to ask my aunt about my father. I knew nothing about him. I didn't even know his name. But Aunt Dolly did. However, my mother had sworn her to secrecy. According to my aunt, my father and mother dated while in high school in Dallas but he broke things off with my mom to pursue his dream of studying art in Paris. My aunt said he asked my mother to go with him, but she refused, saying she didn't want to live in another country."

"Your father was an artist, as well?" Laramie asked as he leaned against a bookcase.

"Yes." Now might have been a good time to tell him her father was the famous artist known as Rand, but she didn't. Her father's identity wasn't important to this story.

"Imagine how excited I was when I found that out. When I learned where my artistic abilities had come from. It also explained why my mother never wanted me to pursue my art. I guess me doing so reminded her of him. Once I found out who he was, I wanted to connect with the man I never knew. The man my mom had kept from me."

She took another sip of her tea. "According to my aunt, my mother never told my father she had gotten pregnant. He didn't know he had a daughter. The reason Mom kept it from him was because she resented him for choosing Paris over her."

She paused again before saying, "I convinced my aunt that I needed to see my father. To let him know I exist. She prepared me by saying that he might not want a child, that he might question if I was really his. Aunt Dolly didn't want me to get hurt. But I didn't care. I needed to meet him."

She recalled that time and how desperate she'd felt. "One of the men at my aunt's church was a detective with the NYPD. He tracked down my father and discovered he lived in Los Angeles. I made the call to my dad the morning of my sixteenth birthday. Aunt Dolly talked to him first, to break the ice and introduce me. Then she handed the phone to me."

"What did he say?"

No need to tell Laramie it had practically been the same

thing he'd said when she'd told him about their child. "He said that he believed I was his and that he wanted to see me. To prove that point, he flew out immediately. In fact, he knocked on my aunt's door in less than eight hours." She smiled. "That was the best birthday present ever."

She fought back the tears that threatened to fill her eyes again as she said, "On that day, I began what was the happiest two years of my life. He told me that he wrote my mother but she refused to write him back. His letters were returned. She stopped all communication between them. When he returned to Dallas from Paris that first year for the holidays, he'd tried finding my mother but no one knew where she had moved to. Later on, he met someone else. He was still married to that woman when we met. They had two young sons. None of his sons were interested in art and he was glad that I was. We discovered we had quite a lot in common."

"Was he upset that your mom kept your existence from him?"

"Yes, very much so. He saw that as wasted years. Years when I could have been spending time with him. We tried to do everything we could together during those two years because that was all we had."

A bemused look appeared on Laramie's face. "Why was that?"

She swallowed, feeling the lump in her throat. "Because, although I didn't know it, my father was dying of cancer."

She drew in a deep breath as she held Laramie's gaze. "So as you can see, my actions regarding you and my son were based on my own experiences with my dad. That's why I wrote to you as soon as I found out I was pregnant. I didn't want to make the same mistake my mother made. You had a right to know about him, even if you rejected him. It would have been your decision. Your loss."

He didn't say anything for a minute. "I'm sorry about your father."

"Me, too. But we got to spend two years together. He made me feel so loved. So very special. He even asked me to change my last name to his, and I did. He also asked if I would come spend my last two years in high school with him in California. That meant leaving Aunt Dolly and I was torn about doing that, but she was fine with it and encouraged me to go. Although she never said, I think he confided in her and told her he didn't have long to live."

"And nobody told you?"

"No. Very few people knew about his condition. In his final days, I saw him getting weak and asked him about it, but he said he'd caught some kind of a virus. He only told me the truth during his last days. That's when he told me what was wrong and if I ever needed anything to contact Colin Kusac, his close and trusted friend." There was no need to tell him how much her father's wife had resented her presence and how mean she'd been at the reading of her father's will.

"So you ended up in Paris to study like he had?"

"Yes. He made that possible before he died. He wanted me to study at the same art academy." She had worked at that café in Paris not because she had to, but because she had wanted to. Her father had taken care of her tuition as well as provided her with a generous monthly allowance. Then there had been the proceeds from her mother's insurance policies. She had put all the money in a savings account. While growing up, her mother had taught her the importance of being independent and not wasteful.

"I had a wonderful father. I just wish I'd had more time with him."

Laramie didn't say anything for a moment, then he asked, "Do you resent your mother for standing in the way of that happening?"

She drew in a deep breath. "Not now, but for years I did. She wanted to hurt my father by keeping my existence a secret from him. She knew him and had known he would have wanted to become a part of my life, but she never gave him that opportunity. In the end, she not only hurt him but she hurt me, as well. I could never do that to my child. That's why I would never stand in the way of you developing a relationship with Laramie. I know the pain and heartbreak it could cause."

The only noise in the room was the sound of the logs crackling in the fireplace. "Thanks for sharing that with me, Bristol."

Telling him the story of her parents and her relationship with her father had drained her. Slowly standing to her feet, she said, "Now that we've gotten that cleared up, what time would you like to come meet Laramie tomorrow?"

An anxious smile touched Laramie's lips. "How soon can I come?"

She chuckled. "Laramie is an early riser so I'm usually up preparing breakfast around eight. You're welcome to join us if you like."

"I would love to."

She glanced at her watch. It was late. Almost midnight. "Do you want me to call you a cab?"

"No, I should be able to get one on the corner."

"Okay." She walked him to the door and watched as he put on his Stetson, while thinking how much more cowboy than SEAL he looked at that moment. "I'll see you in the morning then."

"Yes. In the morning. Oh, by the way, does Laramie have a favorite toy?"

She shook her head. "No. Like most kids his age he likes stuffed animals. He does have this thing for airplanes and he likes to color so he has a ton of coloring books. For his birthday one of Ms. Charlotte's sons, who also has a two-year-old, gave Laramie an electronic tablet. I'm trying to teach him how to play educational games on it."

He nodded. "What kind of tablet is it?"

Bristol told him the brand. Her heart missed several beats when Laramie stood in front of her, holding her gaze. As if to get her mind off what she was feeling, she thought of something. "It might get confusing with you and Laramie having the same first names. Can I start calling you Coop, or is that name restricted to just your team members?"

"No, it's not restricted so that's no problem."

"Good."

He shoved his hands into his pockets. "If there's a change of plans or if you need me for anything, you can contact me at the Marriott Hotel in Times Square. I'd like for you to have my personal number," he said, pulling out his cell phone. "What's yours so I can call you? That way you can have it."

She rattled off her phone number and when she heard her phone ringing in the purse she'd placed on the table earlier, she said, "I got it."

He nodded. "Now you have mine and I have yours."

She dismissed any significant meaning to that. He was merely providing her his number because of Laramie. "Good night, Laramie… Coop. I am so glad you are alive."

He smiled. "Me, too."

He stood there for a second, staring at her, before saying, "Good night, Bristol. I'll see you in the morning."

He turned and quickly moved down the steps.

Laramie entered his hotel room, feeling a happiness he hadn't felt in a long time. In addition to that, a rush of adrenaline was pumping furiously through his veins. What were the chances of the one woman he thought he would never see again, the one woman he thought about often, the one woman who'd helped him retain his sanity while being held hostage, would be here? In New York? And that he would run into her?

Well, he hadn't exactly run into her, but the circumstances surrounding their chance encounter still seemed unreal. And not only had he found out he had a son tonight, but he'd seen him. What a feeling! It was exhilarating, and he couldn't wait to share it with the guys.

He glanced at his watch. It was late. Almost midnight. But he knew Bane, Viper, Mac and Flipper would be up. However, Bane had triplets and Mac had four kids Laramie didn't want to wake up. To be on the safe side, he would text the four to call him.

Laramie also knew he needed to contact his commanding officer to let him know he would be taking his military leave after all. He wondered what would have happened had he not been in New York tonight. No telling when his and Bristol's paths would have crossed, if ever. He'd already missed two years of his son's life and he didn't plan to miss any more.

At some point he also needed to call his parents to let them know they were grandparents. He wondered how they would feel about that. They'd never hinted one way or the other if they wanted grandchildren. They hadn't ever nagged him about settling down or marrying.

After sending the text off to the guys, he removed his jacket and hung it in the closet before the first call came in. He recognized the number as Bane's. "You okay, Coop?" Bane asked with deep concern in his voice.

"Yes, I'm fine. But I do have some news to share. Hold on, I hear another call coming in."

The others began calling and they connected to their conference number so they could all be on the phone at once. "Okay, Coop, what kind of news do you want to share with us?" Viper asked.

"Don't tell us the commander gave you another top secret job. Another cockatiel for you to deliver to some very important person?" Flipper teased.

"Maybe it will be a dog this time," Mac kidded. "Or maybe a pet monkey."

Laramie took their jokes in stride; nothing could put a damper on his mood. "I ran into Bristol Lockett here in New York."

"Bristol Lockett? That woman we couldn't tear you away from in Paris three years ago?" Viper asked.

"If I recall," Bane said, "you went missing for three days because you were with her."

"And we couldn't wipe that damn smile off your face for almost a month," Mac interjected.

"So how was the reunion?" Flipper asked. "She still look good?"

"Yes, she's the same woman, Viper. I didn't know you were missing me so much during those three days, Bane. I don't recall smiling for almost a month, Mac. If I did, I had a good reason for it. And yes, Flipper, she still looks good and the reunion was great once she recovered from fainting."

"Why did she faint?" Bane asked.

Laramie settled down on the edge of the bed. "Bristol thought she was seeing a ghost. She'd assumed I was dead."

"Why would she assume that? Had she contacted your parents or something?" Viper asked.

"No. I never gave her any information about my family."

"Then why would she assume you were dead? No agency had the authority to release that information. Our mission in Syria was a top secret, highly classified covert operation," Mac said.

"Bristol tried writing to me and the letter was returned. She knew someone who had a friend at the State Department who told her I'd gotten killed in Syria."

"Someone breached classified information?" Flipper asked.

"The person who did it felt she needed to know. Like I said, she was trying to reach me."

"Why was she trying to reach you?" Viper asked.

Laramie paused before saying, "She wanted to let me know she'd gotten pregnant."

Everyone got quiet and Laramie knew why. They were trying to digest what he'd said. A smile touched his lips when he added, "Yes, what you're thinking is right. I have a child. A two-year-old son."

Nine

"Hungry, Mommy."

Standing at the stove while preparing breakfast, Bristol couldn't help but smile. Each morning her son woke up in a good mood. Hungry, but good. It didn't matter that he usually had a bedtime snack. He evidently slept that off every night.

"Mommy is almost done, Laramie. Please color me a picture."

"Okay."

She'd discovered early that Laramie liked marking up things, preferably with his crayon. When her walls became a target, she'd purchased him a coloring book. Now it was the norm for him to color her a picture in the book while he waited for breakfast. And since he was home with her every day, she used any free time she had to teach him things. He already knew his primary colors, how to count to ten and since she knew fluent French, she made that his second language by identifying things in both English and French. So far he was mastering both.

She had just finished cooking the eggs when the doorbell rang. Laramie ceased his chatter long enough to say, "Door, Mommy."

Wiping her hands on a kitchen towel, she turned and said, "Yes, I heard it." And from the way her heart was pounding in her chest, she knew who it was. Laramie… Coop. "I'll be back in a minute, sweetie."

Refusing to acknowledge the fact that she'd taken extra care with her looks this morning, she headed for the door. Coop was here to see Laramie and not her.

Before opening the door, she looked through the peephole. There was no way on earth she could dismiss just how incredibly handsome her son's father was. With his striking masculine looks she found it hard to believe some woman hadn't snatched him up by now. He'd said he wasn't married, but he didn't say whether or not there was a special woman in his life. She tried to push the thought out of her mind; it wasn't any of her business.

Their only connection, the only reason he was standing on her doorstep a little after eight in the morning, was Laramie. And from the looks of it, he was bearing gifts. She had a feeling her son would be getting an early visit from Santa.

Inhaling deeply, she opened the door. "Good morning, Coop."

Bristol looked even more beautiful in the daylight. Today her dark brown hair was flowing down her shoulders. And although she wasn't wearing lipstick, she'd put something on her lips to make them shine. Another thing different from last night was her outfit. Today she was wearing a pair of jeans and a pullover sweater. Was it a coincidence or had she remembered him once telling her that red was his favorite color?

The color really didn't matter because the woman standing in the doorway was too stunningly beautiful for words. He drew in a deep breath and pulled in her scent. She was wearing the same perfume from three years ago, from last night. He tried to keep memories of their holiday fling at bay so he could focus on their son. But then how could he, when the result of that fling was why he was here?

He recalled Mac's lecture. Mac, being the oldest of the group and the one who'd been married the longest, had given him advice last night. If Laramie's only interest in Bristol was his son, then he needed to make that point clear up front. Mac had known a lot of men who hadn't. Because of that, the women in those relationships assumed romance and the baby were a package deal.

As he tried to regain control of his senses, it occurred to Coop that while he'd been checking Bristol out, she'd been doing the same with him. He cleared his throat. "Good morning, Bristol. I hope I'm not too early."

"No, your timing is fine," she said, stepping aside to let him in. "I just finished cooking breakfast. I hope you're hungry."

Boy, was he ever, and it had nothing to do with food. The moment she'd opened the door, he'd felt it. The sizzle of attraction had been bad enough outside, but now, within the cozy confines of her home, it was stronger than ever. Did she feel it, too?

"Yes, I'm hungry."

He couldn't recall ever being swept away by a woman except for once in his life. And she had been that woman.

"Good, because I've made plenty. Laramie is up and as usual for this time of morning, he's in a good mood."

"Is he ever in a bad mood?" he asked, placing the gift-wrapped packages on her sofa.

She smiled and he wished that smile didn't cause a stirring in his gut. "Yes, whenever he's sleepy and tries like the dickens to fight it. That's when he becomes cranky."

She took in the numerous gifts he'd brought. "Looks like you went shopping."

He smiled. "I did. I was there when the gift shop at the hotel opened. I plan to do more shopping later today. It's hard to believe Christmas is in less than two weeks."

"Yes, it is."

They reached the kitchen and Coop stopped dead in his tracks. The little boy sitting at the table staring at him was a miniature of himself. The emotions he'd felt when he'd seen his son last night came back to hit him tenfold. Ms. Charlotte and Bristol were right. His son resembled him so much it was uncanny.

They shared the same skin tone, eye color and shape of nose, lips and ears. And then there was that mop of thick curly hair. Although Coop wore his hair cut low now due to military regulations, for years he'd worn it long, even during his teen years. His parents hadn't had a problem with it as long as he kept it looking neat. And he could tell, even though his son was sitting down, that he was taller than most two-year-olds. But then Cooper men were tall. He was six foot two and so was his father. His grandfathers on both sides had been six foot three.

"Who's that?" Laramie asked his mother loudly, pointing at Coop.

"It's not nice to point, Laramie." The little boy put his finger down but kept an I-am-sizing-you-up look on his little face.

"Laramie, this is your daddy. Can you say Daddy?"

"Daddy?" his son asked his mother, as if for clarification.

"Yes, Daddy."

The little boy nodded, looked back over at Coop and said, "Daddy."

Coop's heart missed a beat at hearing his son call him

that for the first time. He watched as Laramie began waving his hand, and then said, "Hi, Daddy."

Coop waved back. "Hi, Laramie."

And then as if Coop was being dismissed, Laramie picked up a crayon and began coloring in the book in front of him.

"You can go ahead and sit down, Coop."

Laramie snatched his head back up and scrunched up his face and said, "He Daddy, Mommy. Not Coop."

Bristol smiled. "You, and only you, can call him Daddy. I can call him Coop. You call him Daddy. Understand?"

Laramie nodded his head up and down. "Yes, Mommy."

Then to explain further she said, "I can also call him Laramie."

Laramie's face scrunched up again. "But that's me."

"Yes, but his name is Laramie, too."

Laramie then looked at his daddy. "You got my name?" he asked.

Coop decided not to say it was the other way around. Instead he would let Bristol handle this since she seemed to know how much their son could understand. "Yes, I have your name."

"But Mommy calls him Coop so he'll know when I am talking to him and not to you. Okay?"

Laramie nodded. "Okay." He then went back to coloring in his book.

Coop moved to the table and sat down. That got his son's attention again. Laramie looked over at him and with a stern face asked, "Clean hands, Daddy?" And to show what he meant, he held his hands out in front of him. "My hands clean."

"Oh." Coop got the message and glanced over at Bristol. "Where can I wash my hands?"

He could tell she was fighting back a smile when she said, "There's a bathroom right off the living room."

He stood. "Thanks." He headed to the bathroom to wash his hands. He had a feeling his two-year old son planned to keep him on his toes.

"Be still my hormones," Bristol muttered under her breath as she watched Coop leave the kitchen and head for the bathroom. Today he was wearing a pair of khakis and a pullover brown sweater. She was convinced that no matter what he put on his body, he was the epitome of sexy. There wasn't a single thing about him that didn't start her heart fluttering and send her female senses into overdrive. Then there was that self-assured walk he'd mastered. The man was true masculinity on legs.

"Daddy gone?"

She glanced over at her son as she placed the plates on the table. Was that sadness she saw in his little eyes? Of course, she had to be imagining things since Laramie had just met Coop. He couldn't have gotten attached already. She'd known Laramie would like Coop since he liked everybody.

"No, Daddy went to wash his hands."

Laramie nodded and then said, "Good." He then added, "Me got clean hands, Mommy." And just like he'd done for Coop, as proof of how clean they were, he held them out and flipped them over a few times.

She smiled and said, "Yes, you have clean hands, Laramie."

At that moment Coop returned and sat back down at the table. "Daddy back," Laramie said, smiling.

Coop returned his son's smile. "Yes, Daddy's back."

"Daddy, want to play some more?"

Coop, who was stretched on the floor, wondered how one little boy could have so much energy. He glanced at his watch. It was almost noon. Had he been here nearly four hours already? Breakfast had been delicious and he'd discovered just what a great cook Bristol was. When he'd complimented her she credited her aunt for making sure her culinary skills were up to par before she'd left New York to live in Paris.

After breakfast he helped Bristol tidy up the kitchen, although she'd said his help was unnecessary. But he'd wanted to help. Laramie had sat at the kitchen table, ignoring them while he colored.

Afterward they had gone to the living room. They'd placed most of the presents under the tree but there had been a few he'd let his son open now. Namely, more coloring books. To give him time alone with Laramie, Bristol had gone upstairs to her studio and closed the door. He felt good knowing she trusted him to take care of Laramie.

For a two-year old, his son was pretty darn smart. He spoke in understandable sentences and even knew how to speak French. During breakfast Bristol would lapse into French with Laramie. Coop appreciated that fact since he himself spoke several different languages, including French, and he enjoyed conversing with them in the language.

"Play games, Daddy."

Coop pulled himself up and looked at Laramie. He knew that his son didn't know the true meaning of the word *daddy*. To him it was just a name, but Coop hoped when Laramie got older it would come to mean a lot more. He wouldn't be around his son 24/7 because of the nature of his work as a SEAL. But he would be with him every chance he got.

That meant after every mission, he would head to New York. It no longer mattered that he liked California's weather better. His son was in New York and that's where he intended to be.

"He hasn't worn you out yet?"

He glanced up and saw a smiling Bristol standing in the entryway to her living room. He chuckled. "No, not yet."

"Well, you get a break since it's lunchtime."

As if Bristol had said a magic word, Laramie jumped up off the floor. "Lunch, Mommy?"

"Yes, Laramie. Lunch."

He was about to race for the kitchen when Coop stopped him and asked, "Clean hands?"

Laramie's small eyes widened. He then looked down at his hands. "No."

Coop nodded. "Come on, let's wash our hands."

Bristol watched them go, walking side by side. Father and son. It was a vision she'd thought she would never see, and seeing it now pulled at her heart. She recalled the telephone call she'd made to Dionne last night, to let her know Laramie was alive. It had taken her a full hour to tell her best friend everything, including how she'd fainted.

Then Dionne had asked her some tough questions. Namely, how she felt about Laramie and if she still loved him. Bristol had to explain that of course she still loved him but now her fears were greater than ever. She had taken news of his death hard and the grief had been so deep she'd sworn never to get that attached to another person again. It seemed all those she loved eventually died. Her mother. Her father. Her aunt Dolly. Was that why she was sometimes overprotective with her son? At least Margie thought that she was.

The work Coop did was dangerous. He risked his life constantly. Most of the time his whereabouts were unknown because the nature of his work was highly classified. There was no way she could make such a person a permanent part of her life. She couldn't imagine going through that sort of grief again. He'd beaten death once but the next time he might not be so lucky.

Dionne had asked Bristol the one question she couldn't answer. How could a woman stop loving a man like Coop?

She had no idea but she was determined to find out. She and Coop hadn't had a chance to sit down and talk, other than the discussion they'd had last night. She had no idea how long he would be in New York or what his plans were while he was here. He had said he wanted to spend as much time with Laramie as he could, and she didn't have a problem with that. She wanted her son to get to know his father.

She needed to get to know him, too. There was a lot of personal information about Coop that she wasn't privy to. She'd just learned last night that he was born in Texas. He rarely spoke of his parents but she knew they were alive. At least they had been alive three years ago.

"Mommy, hands clean now."

Coop and Laramie had returned. Now he was sitting high on Coop's shoulders with a huge grin on his face. "Okay, then, let's head into the kitchen for lunch."

Coop put Laramie down and as soon as his little feet touched the floor he took off toward the kitchen. He paused at the kitchen door long enough to look over his shoulder to say, "Come on, Mommy. Come on, Daddy. Laramie is hungry."

Coop burst out laughing as he walked beside her. "Did I imagine it or did he eat a huge breakfast a few hours ago?"

She chuckled. "No, you didn't imagine it. You'll find out just how much food he consumes. You'll never guess how much I spend on groceries."

He stopped walking and touched her arm. She couldn't contain the surge of sensations that settled in the middle of her stomach from his touch. "I will help you with that."

She shook her head. "Thanks, but I don't need your help. I told you last night that I don't want anything from you and I meant it." All she wanted was for him to have a relationship with his son.

"I don't agree with that."

She frowned, detecting his anger.

"We'll discuss this later, Coop. When Laramie takes his nap."

Coop nodded. "Okay. Do you need help with lunch? I can fix a mean peanut butter and jelly sandwich."

"No, thanks, I've got it covered. Today it's tuna sandwich and chips. He loves anything with seafood."

"So do I."

Bristol wondered if it would be the same way with Coop and Laramie as it was with her and her father. They had discovered so many similarities. She headed for the refrigerator, trying not to notice Coop's sexy walk as he moved to the table, where Laramie was already seated. She couldn't push to the back of her mind how he'd looked stretched out on her living room floor with Laramie. He had made himself at home and removed his sweater. No man had a right to such a sexy chest covered only by a T-shirt. She knew SEALs stayed fit, but he seemed to be working overtime doing so. And she tried not to think about how comfortable it felt having him here in her home with them. It was as if he belonged.

Air was nearly snatched from her lungs at the thought. How could she even think such a thing? There was no way Coop could be a permanent fixture in their lives. At least not hers. He was only here because of Laramie. Had there been more between them, he wouldn't have just stumbled across her the way he had. He would have looked for her after his rescue. But he hadn't. That reinforced her assumption that their holiday fling had been just that, a fling. Afterward he had moved on and not looked back. She knew she'd been out of sight and out of mind. He hadn't expected or probably hadn't wanted to ever see her again.

Like she told him, they would talk when she put Laramie to bed for his nap. There was a lot she and Coop needed to discuss. She had to reiterate that she wanted nothing from him. Hopefully, that would put him at ease that she wasn't going to hit him up for child support payments. However, she had a feeling he would want to pay them anyway, just because of the responsible person he was.

But she didn't intend to let him.

They also had to talk about her fake marriage to him. They needed to resolve that. Yes, she thought, as she began pulling the items out of the refrigerator for lunch. They definitely needed to talk.

Ten

Coop would be the first to admit that he'd been somewhat nervous upon arriving this morning, not sure of how his son would react to him. So far things were going great and he knew he had Bristol to thank for that.

As he settled back on the sofa, he thought about what she'd told him about her childhood. Specifically, growing up without knowing her father. And then only getting to spend a couple of years with him before he'd died.

After hearing her story, he wasn't sure what was worse. Having parents who were bitter toward each other or having parents like his who were obsessively into each other. If he had to choose, it would be the parents who were obsessively into each other. As far as he was concerned, her mother's resentment, bitterness and anger had only hurt Bristol. It was sad how one person's decision could change the lives of so many. He was glad Bristol had learned from her mother's mistake.

He couldn't help but smile when he remembered lunch. Laramie had cleaned his plate in record time. More than once, Bristol had to tell him to slow down so his food could digest. Coop hadn't been sure if Laramie knew what that meant until the boy began taking smaller bites of his sandwich.

It was obvious Bristol and Laramie had a routine. He hadn't put up a fuss when she'd mentioned it was time for his nap. Instead, he'd waved goodbye to Coop. But not before he'd asked if Coop would be there when he woke up. Before Coop could answer, Bristol had told Laramie not to expect him to be there because he had things to do. Was that her way of letting Coop know he was wearing out his welcome?

Hell, he hoped not. He'd placed a call to his commanding officer letting him know that he would be taking his holiday leave and would remain in the New York area. Like he'd told Bristol last night... He planned to spend as much time with his son as he could.

"I think he was asleep before his head hit the pillow. What did you do to tire him out?" Bristol asked, grinning as she returned to the living room.

He looked at her and thought those jeans she wore definitely displayed all her curves. Not all women could wear jeans and exude that kind of effect on a man. The kind that could shoot his libido into overdrive. The kind that made him remember, whether he wanted to or not, how things had been between them in Paris. How easily they'd connected. How insatiable their hunger for each other had been.

With effort, he brought his mind back to the conversation. Coop smiled. "He wanted to play hide-and-seek."

"Oops. I should have warned you about that."

In a way, Coop wished she had. Then he would have given his son restrictions about not hiding in certain areas. Coop hadn't set any rules, and Laramie had found a good place to conceal himself in his mommy's bedroom. He hadn't felt comfortable going into Bristol's room but since she'd left the door open he had seen enough to know it was neat as a pin and decorated in colors of mauve and gray.

And he had seen her bed.

It was the same one she'd had in Paris. Seeing that bed had made him recall everything they'd done and how they'd done it. It also made him realize that his son was conceived in that bed. Or it could have been the time he'd taken her against the refrigerator.

"How many times did you find him?"

Bristol's question interrupted his reverie. "Every single time."

No need to tell her that he'd had to coax Laramie out of his hiding place in her bedroom so he wouldn't have to go in there looking for him. That hadn't been easy. A promise to take him to the park one day soon cinched it.

He watched Bristol sit down on the chair and somehow she did it in a way that was a turn-on. He inhaled deeply, remembering for the umpteenth time that Bristol was off-limits. His presence here had nothing to do with her but everything to do with their son. No matter how many good memories he had of them together, no matter how hard he'd tried to find her in Paris, and no matter how attracted he was to her now, the bottom line was that Laramie was his focus.

A relationship with his son was the only thing that mattered. That meant he and Bristol needed to talk about a few subjects they'd skirted around.

Deciding not to beat around the bush, he said, "So let's talk, Bristol."

He could tell she was nervous. But whatever they discussed would be with the intent of putting their son's needs before their own. Unfortunately, Coop had plenty of needs.

He hadn't bedded a woman since his last assignment nearly eight months ago. No particular reason he hadn't done so other than the fact he'd been too busy trying to hire more men to help run the ranch in Laredo that he'd inherited from his grandparents.

Cooper's Bend was his favorite place in all the world and when he retired from being a SEAL, he planned to move there and make it his permanent home. He could retire after his twenty years with the military, which was what he planned to do. He had less than ten years left. Six more to be exact, since he'd entered the military at eighteen and could officially retire at thirty-eight. Then he would become the full-time rancher his grandfather had been. In the meantime, he had a good group of people running the place and went there from time to time to check on things.

It might be a good idea for him to consider moving there now. That would eliminate his need to find housing in San Diego to accommodate him and Laramie. The ranch, which sat on over six-hundred acres, was plenty big. He would love for Laramie to visit him at the ranch that held so many wonderful childhood memories for him. Hell, when his son got older, he could have his own horse.

"Yes, I think we need to cover a few things and come to an agreement," Bristol said, interrupting his thoughts.

"Okay. What do you want to cover?" he asked her.

She paused and then said, "I meant what I said about not needing anything from you where Laramie is concerned."

Already Coop knew that wouldn't fly. "I can't agree to that because Laramie is my responsibility, too. A responsibility I take seriously."

She opened her mouth to argue the point and he held up his hand to stop her. "Not negotiable, Bristol. It doesn't matter if you're able to take care of him yourself. What sort of man would I be if I didn't contribute to the welfare of my child?"

She didn't say anything and broke eye contact with him to gaze down at the floor. He knew she was thinking, probably of a way to counter what he'd said. As far as he was concerned she could think all she wanted, he wouldn't change his mind. As the only grandchild, he had inherited trust funds from both sets of grandparents. Also, his parents had established an endowment for him that he'd been eligible for when he'd turned thirty. He was yet to touch any one of them. In addition to all that money and the ranch, he was heir to RCC Manufacturing, Inc., a corporation founded by his parents over thirty-five years ago upon their graduation from Harvard. Considering all of that, there was no way in hell he would not contribute to his son's upbringing. In fact, he'd already left a message with his attorney to contact him. He intended to list Laramie's name on all his legal documents as his heir.

"I think we should compromise," she finally said.

He lifted a brow. "Compromise how?"

"You can provide for his future, such as setting up a college fund. I'll take care of any expenses for his well-being now."

Coop shook his head. "No. I still won't agree to that. I want to provide for my child's present and his future."

A frown marred her features. "Why are you being difficult?"

He returned her frown. "Why are you? Most men who father a child and are separated from them are required to pay child support."

"But usually only until they are eighteen. All I'm doing is asking you to start the support at eighteen."

He had news for her. He intended to take care of his child for the rest of his life. The trust funds he planned to establish for Laramie would assure that. The age of eighteen had nothing to do with it. He couldn't believe he was even having this conversation with her. Most women would want his monetary offering. Was he missing something here? "Can I ask you something?"

She nodded slowly, almost reluctantly, before saying, "Yes."

"You said you only met your father at sixteen. I don't

know anything about him, but did he wait until you were eighteen to begin providing for you?"

She stiffened. "He paid my entire tuition at the art school in Paris."

Cooper figured tuition at that school hadn't been cheap. "That's all he did? He actually waited until you were eighteen before doing anything?"

"Of course not."

"Then why would you expect me to? Evidently being an artist has you rolling in dough since you feel you don't need my help. That might be all well and good for you, but not for me. For me it's the principle of the thing. It's about doing my share in providing for a child I helped to create. So please don't ask me to consider doing otherwise."

Bristol's gaze held Coop's and she could tell from the determined look in his eyes that he would not back down on this. She wasn't privy to his income as a SEAL but she was certain he could use his money for better things…

Like what?

She drew in a deep breath when she suddenly accepted something. It was apparent that as far as Coop was concerned, nothing was better than taking care of his son. For Coop, it wasn't about the money. It was about taking care of his own. She'd gotten the impression three years ago that he wasn't extremely close to his family. But what she'd failed to realize was that her son was now his family and he wanted to not only be there for him but also contribute toward his well-being. For Coop, the contribution was essential. She got that now.

He'd been saying it all along, so why hadn't she been listening? Probably because, like her mother, she was determined to be independent and not depend on anyone for anything. She didn't have a problem with Coop being a part of his son's life physically, but she was trying to stop him from being a part of Laramie's life financially. Most men would have jumped at the chance to get out of paying some form of child support. But Coop wasn't one of those men.

Neither was her father.

And Coop was right. Randall Lockett hadn't waited until her eighteenth birthday to be a father to her. He'd immediately stepped in and, like a whirlwind, he'd changed her last name to his, bestowing upon her all the rights of being his offspring. He had taken her under his roof, adding her to his household.

She had enjoyed living with him in Los Angeles, even if it had meant moving out west, attending another school and making new friends. To her it had been worth it just to spend time with her father. He'd made sure she hadn't gone without anything. But the most important thing was the time they'd spent together. Nothing else mattered. Not the closet filled with new clothes, the private school or the international vacations. Not even the new sports car he'd given her.

"Okay, Coop," she finally said.

"Okay, what?"

She released a deep sigh. "Okay, we will share in the cost of raising Laramie."

"You don't have to sound so overjoyed about it."

She narrowed her gaze at him before she saw his lips tilt into a smile. He'd been teasing. Releasing another sigh, she said, "I'm not trying to be difficult, Coop. But when I had Laramie I knew he would be my entire world and that I would be the one he would depend on for everything. I thought you were dead. For the past two years, I've made it work. There hasn't been a decision I made without considering him. Even when I decided to quit my position with that magazine publisher to become an artist full-time. I'm doing okay financially."

No need to tell him about the ridiculously high commissions she received every month from her father's art. "I was raised by a single mother who worked hard and made sure we didn't waste money on frivolous things. I knew the difference between getting the things I really needed and denying myself those things I wanted that weren't essential."

She didn't say anything for a brief moment then added, "The reason I suggested you handle Laramie's future is because I think that's what upset my father the most with my mother…besides her keeping my existence from him. Knowing she hadn't adequately prepared for my future. I had to explain to him that it hadn't been her fault since there was no extra money to set up a college savings account for me. Mom was a teacher, not a six-figure-salary engineer. She had student loans to pay back. But still, we lived in a nice house in a good neighborhood. I thought we lived pretty good."

She smiled. "Mom said we were a team and always would be one. I was happy. I was content. At the time. I really didn't think of life being any better. It was years later that I found out just how complicated life could be."

Coop nodded. "Our son's financial well-being is something you don't have to worry yourself with anymore because I'm here to help." He leaned forward and rested his arms on his thighs. "There is that other item we need to discuss before I leave today, Bristol."

She lifted a brow. "What other item?"

He held her gaze. "The issue of our fake marriage."

Eleven

Coop could tell from the look in Bristol's eyes that she'd forgotten about that complication. That was unfortunate for her, since he clearly remembered. A woman claiming to be your wife was something that pretty much got stuck in your mind.

"I told you why I did it," she said in a defensive tone.

He leaned forward. "Yes, you did. But that doesn't mean we don't need to talk about it. Spinning that tale might have been okay when you assumed I was dead, but as you can see, Bristol, I'm very much alive."

When she didn't say anything, he asked, "What do you think we should do?"

She shrugged. "Why do we have to do anything? It's not as if anyone knows the truth but my best friend, Dionne, and her husband, Mark, who was working for the judge at the time."

"It's a lie, Bristol. And one thing about a lie, it can come back to haunt you when you least expect it."

She stood and began pacing. He watched her, trying to keep his mind on the issue at hand, but found it difficult to do so. Especially when her body was in motion. He should be noticing the sound of the wooden floor creaking beneath her feet or the way her hair brushed against her shoulders as she moved. However, he wasn't attuned to either of those things. Instead his total concentration was on her body. A body he remembered so well.

Coop couldn't watch her move those jeans-clad thighs without recalling a time he'd been between them. Recollecting a time when he'd tasted her. Touched her all over. He was so damn aware of every damn inch of her.

She suddenly stopped pacing and looked over at him. Why? Had she detected him staring? Should he sit there and pretend he hadn't been? He doubted he could, even if he wanted to. That would be trying to do the impossible where she was concerned.

"What do you suggest?" she then asked him.

Right now he thought about suggesting they go upstairs to her bedroom and get it on. Rekindle those days in Paris, if for no other reason than to prove he hadn't imagined it, that it had been as good as he'd remembered.

"There are only two options, Bristol. Either we pretend to get a divorce to end the fake marriage or we make the marriage real."

She came and sat back down. "There's absolutely no reason to make the marriage real, so getting a pretend divorce sounds good to me. All that involves is us saying we're getting a divorce. No paperwork needed." A huge smile touched her lips. "Great! That was an easy solution."

"Not quite."

She lifted a brow. "And why not?"

The muscles in his jaw tightened. "Because in the end you'll emerge smelling like a rose, but I'll be the scumbag. A man who deserted his wife and child for nearly two years, and then who turns around and divorces her."

His harsh description had her lifting a brow, which

meant she knew he didn't appreciate the position she was placing him in. "But I told you why I did it," she said.

"And now you want to take the easy way out."

Coop wondered why he was taunting her, especially when he truly didn't give a royal damn what people thought. They didn't know him. No, it wasn't the people he was concerned about. It was his son. When Laramie grew into manhood, what story would he hear about and believe? No matter how much quality time Coop would spend with his son, he ran the risk of Laramie one day wondering why he hadn't been there for them when it mattered the most. Hadn't Bristol said she'd wondered about it when she didn't know the real deal with her own father?

And, if he was honest, there was another reason he was suddenly thinking this way. It was about those memories he just couldn't shake. It was his attraction to Bristol that had been there from the start. This deep sexual chemistry they'd given in to in Paris.

He'd always prided himself on being a person who exuded total control. His SEAL friends often referred to him as the quiet storm. There was a coolness about him. Always calm. Always composed. Levelheaded to a fault. And beneath all that equanimity, he was watching, waiting, always on the lookout for the unknown. Considering the possibilities while fighting off the restlessness. But when he was provoked, all bets were off and he would kick ass like the best of them. Even more so. When pushed into a corner, he came out fighting.

What if at some point down the road Bristol met someone and decided to marry? How would that impact his relationship with his son? Would he have to stand in line for his son's attention? His affection? Was there a way to assure that didn't happen? Was he being a selfish bastard for wanting to make sure it never did?

"Coop?"

He blinked. Had he been staring at her while all those crazy thoughts rushed through his brain? And were they crazy? His steady gaze held hers. No, they weren't crazy. Irrational, yes. Crazy, no. There was a difference.

When she said his name again he answered, "Yes?"

"Are you okay?"

Now, that was a good question. Was he? To her he said, "I just realized how little we know of each other. How very little information was exchanged between us in Paris."

"We didn't do much talking," she blurted out. From the look on her face he knew she hadn't meant to say that. It didn't matter since what she'd said was true. Her hormones and his testosterone had been working overtime and the only thing they'd wanted to do was assuage the desire flowing between them. He hadn't wanted to know anything about her and she hadn't wanted to know anything about him. For those three days, pleasure had been the name of the game and they'd played it well.

"No, we didn't," he said. "And now we have a son to show for it. I want to get to know you."

"Why?"

"Because you are the mother of my child and there is a lot I don't know."

She lifted a chin. "Don't sweat it. The only thing you truly need to know is that I love him, will always take care of him and put his interests first."

He wondered if that was really all he needed to know. Maybe. Then maybe not. It had been one thing to arrive in New York a few days ago without a care in the world. His only thought had been how soon he could return to California. Now things had changed. He had a son. A real flesh-and-blood son. He also had a fake wife, who was the one woman he desired most. He could admit that no other woman had ignited his passion as quickly and as easily as Bristol.

Thoughts of her had sustained him. He recalled every single time he had touched her. How he had touched her. He remembered tasting her and how she'd tasted. How it felt to experience heaven while inside her. Their bodies locked together and hurtling into one orgasm after another.

"I'm not sure that's the only thing I need to know, Bristol," he said, finally addressing her earlier statement. "I need to know you."

She frowned. "No, you don't."

"Yes, I do. And you need to know me. Laramie needs to know me. He has grandparents that he needs to get to know and vice versa."

"I have no problem with that."

No, she might not. But would everything be on her terms? What if that guy Culpepper decided to come back around sniffing behind her the minute Coop was gone? His mouth pressed into a hard line at the thought.

"Can I ask you something, Coop?"

He looked over at her. "Yes."

"How do you feel about having a son? One you didn't know you had?"

He thought about her question, wanting to answer as honestly as he could. "I always liked kids well enough, Bristol. I get along fine with Mac's four. They call me Uncle Coop and all. But to be quite honest with you, I never intended to have any of my own because marriage wasn't on my radar. And having one out of wedlock was something I never intended to do. But now he's here. I've seen him and knowing he's mine and that you and I made him is so overwhelming. It's caused emotions I didn't think were possible to feel. It's not just about me anymore. Now it's about my child and you."

He saw the frown that touched her lips. "You don't need to concern yourself with me, Coop."

Boy, was she wrong about that. As far as he was concerned, she and his son were a package deal. The kind Mac had warned him about. But them being a package deal was Coop's choice, since it obviously wasn't hers. Nevertheless, he knew better than to try to convince her just yet. They would finish their conversation regarding their fake marriage later.

"When can I come back?"

"You're always welcome here, Coop. You're Laramie's father and like I told you, I would never keep you from sharing a relationship with him."

However, if she were to marry one day, a future husband might. He'd heard stories from Flipper about how one of his brothers had to constantly take his ex-wife to court for visitation rights. Just because this guy she'd married hadn't felt comfortable with Flipper's brother coming around whenever he'd wanted to see his daughter.

Coop didn't want to deal with that kind of problem. "I'd like to take you and Laramie to dinner tonight," he said.

"Dinner?"

"Yes, dinner. Is that a problem?"

"No, but other than McDonald's, I've never taken Laramie out to eat."

He liked the idea that his son's first time going to a restaurant would be with him. "There's a first time for everything, don't you think?"

Bristol recalled another time he'd told her that. It had been in Paris after he'd stripped her naked and she'd told him that no other man had been in her apartment before.

"So will you and Laramie have dinner with me tonight?"

"Where?"

"You pick the place."

She drew in a deep breath. Maybe going out to dinner wouldn't be so bad. "Laramie loves spaghetti and there's an Italian restaurant not far from here."

"I happen to like spaghetti, too, so that will work for me, if it works for you," he said.

"It will work for me if it's early. I need to have Laramie back here with a bath and into his pajamas no later than eight."

He nodded. "Will reservations at five o'clock be okay?"

"Yes. That's the time he usually eats dinner anyway."

Bristol was wondering why on earth she was paying so much attention to Coop's mouth when they should be figuring out details regarding Laramie. Why was she paying so much attention to his captivating eyes? To his masculine body? She saw men all the time but had never focused on any of those things. Why him? She knew the answer. Mainly because she knew how that mouth felt connected to hers.

She knew how it felt to be held within the scope of those eyes while desire streamed through her. And she knew all about that masculine body. How it felt to be beneath it. To feel the weight of it on her. To feel him inside her. Her breathing became choppy and she forced her gaze away from him.

"Are you okay, Bristol?"

Was she? She wanted to think she was, but honestly she wasn't sure. He'd been the last man she had slept with and now all those hot, delicious and wanton thoughts were trying to take over her senses. They really hadn't finished figuring out how to end their fake marriage. For some reason, she found the discussion draining and really didn't want to go back to it right now. There was no doubt in her mind he would bring it back up again.

However, there was something that had been on her mind since last night that she did want to discuss. "I'm fine, Coop, but there is something I've been wondering about."

"What?"

“Your friends. Those four guys I met who were with you in Paris. Mac, Bane, Viper and Flipper. Are they okay?”

A smile touched his lips. “Yes, they’re okay. I’m surprised you remembered them.”

“They were nice and—” she said, chuckling “—unforgettable. I liked them. I often wondered if they had gotten captured with you and if they’d lost their lives.”

“No, in fact they were part of the team that rescued me. If you recall, Mac was married when you met him. He and his wife are doing fine. Bane and his estranged wife renewed their vows and Viper is married now.”

“He is?”

“Yes, and happily so. Reminds us of that every chance he gets. Flipper is still Flipper. Happy-go-lucky and cheerfully single. Bane and his wife had triplets this year, almost six months ago.”

“Triplets?”

“Yes. Two boys and a girl. They want a huge family so I guess you can say they’re off to a good start.”

“I’m glad they’re all okay. When I got word that you’d been killed, I wondered about them. I take it the five of you are still close friends.”

“Yes, and we’re closer than ever. Even while I was being held hostage a part of me believed they would find me and get me out. And they did. We stay in contact even when we’re not on a mission. I talked to them just last night and told them I had seen you.”

“You did?”

“Yes. They remembered you, as well. I also told them I had a son. They’re happy for me.”

“Even though fatherhood wasn’t anything you asked for?”

“Doesn’t matter. I used a condom. Close to a dozen if you recall. Evidently one was defective. I regret that.” He paused and then said, "But under no circumstances do I regret Laramie."

She nodded. "Neither do I."

He inclined his head and looked at her. Under his close scrutiny she was tempted to cross her arms over her chest. She could feel her nipples hardening. "I keep thinking that things could have been different. You could have made another decision and not had him," he said.

She knew what he was hinting at. "Not having him wasn't an option for me. I admit becoming a mother was the last thing on my mind, but when I found out I was pregnant I knew I would keep my baby. When I mailed that letter to you, I had no idea how you would respond. It really didn't matter. I was doing what I thought was the right thing by letting you know. I was prepared to go solo regardless."

"And now you don't have to because I'm here."

For how long? she wondered. He was still a navy SEAL and could get called away on a mission at any time. A mission he might not return from. She'd already had to deal with news of him dying once; there was no way she could go through it again. That meant she had to fall out of love with him. But how could she do that?

He had made it pretty clear that he wanted to see Laramie as often as he could. So she'd be seeing him often, too. In that case, how could she begin the process of removing him from her heart? There had to be a way and she was determined to find it. She had lost her mother, her father and her aunt. The three most important people in her life were gone. Now she had Laramie. She lived for her son and that would be enough.

"I'll leave now so you can get some things done while Laramie is taking his nap. I'll be back around four-thirty."

"All right."

She moved to walk him to the door, but he just stood

there. Staring at her. More specifically, his gaze was fixated on her mouth. She saw it. Felt it. Her lips suddenly felt warm. Sensitive.

She knew she should turn away so her mouth wouldn't be the object of his focus. But the truth was, she couldn't. His assessing gaze was getting to her, and she couldn't do a single thing about it.

Bristol knew what he planned the moment he took a step in her direction but she didn't back up. She couldn't. It was as if she was rooted in place. Then he was standing directly in front of her. His eyes penetrating hers. His features fierce.

"I thought about you a lot, Bristol. During those eleven months while being held hostage."

His words made her heart flip several times. He had thought about her? "You did?"

"Yes. Thinking of you kept me sane…especially during those times I was being tortured," he told her quietly.

Oh, God! Tortured? There was an intense searing in the pit of her stomach. She couldn't imagine what he'd endured.

"I would close my eyes and remember each and every time I made love to you. Every single time I kissed you. We shared a lot of kisses over those three days."

Yes, they had. They'd shared a lot of things, including their bodies. He hadn't been the only one who'd remembered, although her situation hadn't been as difficult as his by any stretch of the imagination. Every time her child, their child, had kicked or moved within her womb, she would think of him. Mourn him. Grieve for him. She would also thank him for giving her his child.

"I need to kiss you," he said in a husky tone, reclaiming her attention. "I need to kiss you as much as I need to breathe."

And she needed to kiss him, as well. That was the shocking truth. No matter how independent she wanted to be, she needed to kiss him. Her eyes were focused on his lips with the same intensity that his had been on hers. She needed to feel the heat of her body against his.

She was succumbing to everything male that he represented.

"As you wish," Bristol whispered. She was the one who made the first move, standing on tiptoe, leaning in close and placing her mouth against his.

Twelve

Coop wrapped his arms around her and took over the kiss. The moment their tongues touched, getting reacquainted in the most passionate way, liquid heat seemed to spread through, burning him from the inside out.

His body leaped to life. He was now a man very much aware and filled with a yearning so deep it ached. Yet at the same time the yearning calmed the beast within him. Made him accept that Bristol could affect him in ways no other woman could.

He hadn't counted on her kiss being as greedy as his, her need just as insurmountable. Their tongues were mating in ways that sent a crackle of energy escalating between them. From the very first, he'd known she was different. He just hadn't known what role she would eventually play in his life. He had no idea that one day she would become the mother of his child.

He had given more of himself to her than he had to any woman. Even now he felt a need for her in every cell, in every pore. How could she get under his skin this way? To the point where he confessed to thinking of her while being held captive. Remembering her while being in pain.

He'd never shared that much about one of his missions with anyone. There had been no one to tell. His parents hadn't wanted to hear the gory details. And he hadn't been able to open up to the psychiatrist the military had ordered him to see. Only his SEAL teammates had known the hell he'd gone through. And now Bristol knew. Not everything but enough.

They needed to come up for air, so he slowly ended the kiss, pulling his mouth away on a guttural moan. Still needing a connection, he used the tip of his tongue to lick her lips from corner to corner, before grazing his jaw against her ear.

He dropped his hands and couldn't recall at what point his fingers had become buried in her hair. Now it looked unruly. Sexy as hell. The sight of her kiss-swollen lips made him even more aware of how much he wanted her. Desire pulsed through him and he felt hard as a rock.

He took a step back, because otherwise he would be tempted to sweep her off her feet and carry her upstairs to that bedroom he'd refused to enter earlier. "I'll be back to get you and Laramie around four thirty."

And then he headed for the door. He came close to making it out without looking back. But temptation was too much. Overpowering. He stopped and glanced over his shoulder. Bristol was standing there looking more beautiful than any woman he'd ever seen. There was heat in her eyes.

A hungry throb stirred inside him and he drew in a wobbly breath before forcing himself out the door and closing it behind him.

Bristol released a breath before burying her face in her hands. What on earth had she done? What on earth had she started? That kiss had made her come unglued. No, she'd lost her composure long before that kiss. The intensity of her sexual need had begun to affect her the moment Coop had walked into her house that morning.

She could no more deny the carnal attraction between them than she could refrain from breathing. And today, just a few moments ago in her living room, they'd both unleashed pent-up, held-back desires. Her body knew him, desired him, ached for him. Closing her eyes, she felt a surge of yearning trying to take over her senses again.

Opening her eyes, she refused to let it. At that moment she heard her cell phone ring and wondered who was calling. Coop had her number. Would he be calling her? There was no way he'd made it to the corner already. Maybe he'd decided dinner wasn't a good idea after all and was canceling. If that was true then she agreed with him. Sitting in a restaurant across from him might push temptation to a new level. She wasn't certain if their son would be enough of a buffer.

Pulling her phone out of the back pocket of her jeans, Bristol saw the caller wasn't Coop but Margie. She quickly clicked it on. "Yes, Margie?"

"You okay? You sound kind of breathless."

She swallowed. Did she? "I'm fine."

"I called to see how things turned out with your soon-to-be ex."

Bristol frowned, confused. "My soon-to-be ex?"

"Yes. You can divorce him on the grounds of desertion, you know. I can refer a good attorney you can use."

"Desertion?"

"Yes. At least that's what I call it. You thought he was dead. Granted I understand the military made a mistake, but if he had cared anything about you—even if he didn't know about your son—you were his wife. He should have moved heaven and earth to find you. Showing up now after all this time won't cut it."

Bristol didn't like what Margie was saying. But then her

manager didn't know the whole story. "Laramie and I have things to work out."

"What's there to work out? I talked to Steven and he's concerned about a dead husband reappearing. But I explained things to calm him down. I told him it was all a mistake and you would send your ex packing in no time. I assured him that there was no way you would hook up with Laramie again."

Frissons of anger ignited in Bristol's spine. Margie was believing just what Coop said people would believe about him. And it was all her fault. Furthermore, who gave Margie the right to tell Steven anything?

"Look, Margie, I have to go." It was either end the call or end their relationship, Bristol was just that mad.

Her manager didn't say anything for a moment, then added, "You sound upset, Bristol, and I hope it's not with me but with him. I'm aware you loved your husband. And I can understand you having feelings for him now. But I hope you're not thinking about tossing aside a chance with Steven for a man who didn't come looking for you."

Bristol lost it. "I don't know how many times I have to tell you that I'm not interested in Steven. Now goodbye."

She then hung up the phone.

Coop released a deep sigh the moment his hotel room door closed behind him. What a day. It had started out with him enjoying breakfast with his son and then it had ended after lunch with him kissing Bristol like he couldn't get enough of tasting her mouth.

He licked his lips. He still hadn't.

He never knew a woman's taste could mess with your taste buds and block out your other senses. But he had found out today. He just didn't understand it. Once he'd returned to his team to hang out for New Year's, after spending those three days with her, he'd been fine. She hadn't totally consumed his mind.

But he had thought about her…

And he had thought about her even more while being held hostage, because when your thoughts were filled with orgasmic pleasure it could erase the pain. The more those bastards tried to break him, the more he'd thought about Bristol.

Was that why he was so consumed with her now? He had thought about her so much that the memories of the time they'd shared in Paris were now a part of him? He rubbed his hand down his face. Maybe he was thinking way too hard.

He was removing his jacket when his cell phone rang. He recognized the ring tone. It was Bane. He pulled his phone from his pocket, chuckled and said, "With triplets, don't you have more to do with your time these days?"

Bane laughed. "No. That's where the benefits of belonging to a large family kick in. Everyone wants to help out. There haven't been triplets in the family since Quade's babies and everyone's excited. I couldn't tell you the number of visitors we've had. And more of them are planning to visit for the holidays. I told the family about your son. They're ecstatic and want pictures, so I need you to text me a few. You know the routine so get with the program."

Yes, he knew the routine. He had pictures on his phone of Mac's four kids. His phone was also filled with pictures of Bane's triplets. In the beginning, it seemed like Bane would text him a new picture every other day. Now it had decreased to only one a week. "No problem. I'm taking them to dinner and will take a photo then."

"I take it things are going well. I assume you had that talk you said you were going to have with her."

"Yes, I had it. She wasn't keen on the idea of sharing

support for our son. I had to explain that I don't operate that way. She didn't like it but she finally gave in."

"That's good. What did the two of you decide about the fake marriage?"

Coop rubbed the back of his neck when he remembered that particular conversation. "Bristol doesn't want to be married any more than I do. But we have Laramie to consider now. She suggested we just tell everyone we're getting a divorce. That will release her from the fake marriage. She sees that as the easiest and simplest way out."

"Is that what you want?"

Coop dropped down in the wingback chair. "No. But then marriage isn't what I want, either. At least it wasn't until I met my son. At first I convinced myself being a single dad wouldn't be a big deal since I'd be gone on missions most of the time anyway. But then I began thinking about those times I would be around. What if she began seeing someone who didn't want me to have access to my child the way I wanted?"

"You can work out visitation rights with an attorney, so there shouldn't be any problems with that. Why do I get the feeling there's more, Coop?"

Because there was more. It was at times like this that a part of him wished Bane didn't know him so well. He, Bane, Viper, Flipper and another friend by the name of Nick Stover had gone through the naval academy together. Mac had been a SEAL several years before any of them. For the longest time, Mac had come across like the big-brother SEAL looking out for them, like he figured they couldn't take care of themselves. Over time they'd learned how to look out for each other. A few years ago Nick had given up being a SEAL to take a job with Homeland Security after his wife had triplets.

He, Mac, Viper and Flipper had wondered if Bane would do the same thing because of his triplets. But Bane had assured them he wouldn't. Whereas Nick and his wife didn't have any family to help out, Bane had more family than the law allowed. Bane's triplets were the third set born in the Westmoreland family. There were Westmorelands all over the place. In several states, including Alaska.

Coop was close to all his team members but he and Bane shared a special bond because they'd been roommates at the academy.

"Yes, there's more," he finally said. "It's Bristol."

"What about her?"

"I'm more attracted to her than ever, man. She's beautiful. She's also headstrong, independent and a wonderful mother to Laramie."

"Sounds like you're falling for her all over again."

Coop leaned back in the chair. "To be honest, I don't think I ever stopped falling. I told you how she was constantly on my mind while I was in Syria and how those memories of us together were how I held on to my sanity."

"Did you tell her that?"

"Yes."

"And did you tell her that the minute the hospital released you to travel that you headed to Paris, hoping to see her?"

"No, I didn't tell her that. Maybe one day I will."

"Women like to know they were thought of. Remember how I kept all those cards and letters over the years for Crystal. It meant a lot to her."

He and Bane talked a little while longer. When they ended their conversation, he glanced at his watch. He needed to make another call, namely to his parents. He also needed to follow up with his attorney. Afterward, he would go to the hotel's fitness center and work off that delicious breakfast and lunch Bristol had prepared.

He thought about their kiss again. What he'd told Bane was the truth. He was attracted to her more so than ever.

Visitation rights with his son weren't the only thing he was concerned with. Visitation rights with his son's mother were also on his mind. The thought of her marrying someone else bothered him.

If it bothers you so much, then maybe you should marry her yourself.

What the hell! Why did an idea like that pop into his head? Anyone who knew him would attest to the fact that he wasn't the marrying kind. He liked his freedom. He enjoyed not answering to anyone but himself. He…

Loved his son.

His lips firmed in a straight line. Yes, he loved his son, but what did that have to do with desiring Bristol? Suddenly, he knew the answer. His love for his son affected everything. Even his son's mother.

He groaned in frustration. He had suggested the option of making the marriage real. She had immediately rebuffed it. At the time, it hadn't bothered him one iota. That idea hadn't been at the top of his list anyway.

So why was he thinking about it now?

Once again the answer was the same. He loved his son. Unlike his parents, who believed their love for each other weighed more than the love for their child, he didn't hold such beliefs. Although he'd seen his child for the first time only last night, more love than he thought he could ever have for any other human being had seeped into his heart and it was going to stay there.

He loved his parents. He loved his SEAL teammates as brothers. But the love he had for his child was so amazing that more than once today he'd had to pause to make sure he hadn't dreamed the whole thing.

That little face looked so much like him it was uncanny. Maybe the next time they would have a girl and she would look more like Bristol. Coop went still.

How could he even think what he just had? A daughter? With Bristol as the mother? Jeez.

He stood and began pacing. He was really losing it to even think such a thing. He needed to stay focused. The only person he needed to be thinking about was his son. But how could he think of his son and not think of his son's mother? The woman who'd given birth to him? The woman who made sure he got all the things he needed? The woman who was already teaching him a second language?

Hadn't he decided earlier today that they came as a package deal? But that had only been regarding financial support and nothing more. Hadn't it? Then why was he thinking all crazy? Why was he thinking beyond the financial to something even more? To marriage?

Because she's the woman you want.

Want and not love.

He knew love had nothing to do with it. Whatever feelings he had for Bristol were purely physical. That kiss today proved it, as well as the sexual chemistry surrounding them whenever they were together. That conclusion about the nature of their relationship didn't bother him and he doubted it bothered her.

Coop stood and checked his watch. He needed to go to the fitness center to work off his sexual frustrations, and he had plenty. When he arrived at her house to take them to dinner, maybe he would have worked some sense back into his brain.

Thirteen

"Daddy is back, Mommy?"

Bristol couldn't ignore the excitement in her son's voice. He had been disappointed when he woke up from his nap to find Coop gone. The light had come back into his little eyes only when she'd told him Coop would be back and would take them out to dinner to eat spaghetti.

Laramie had jumped with anticipation when he heard the sound of the doorbell. Now he was right at her heels as she moved toward the door. He was ready and she didn't want to admit it, but so was she. Her lips were still tingling from her and Coop's kiss earlier and she hadn't been able to paint for thinking of him.

And that wasn't good. She needed to get more than a grip. She needed to put things in perspective. When she did, that kiss would be placed on the back burner, where it belonged.

Looking through the peephole, she confirmed it was Coop. He looked handsome, just like the Texan he was proud to say he was. She opened the door and tilted her head to look up at him. Before she could say anything, Laramie, who'd managed to squeeze between her legs, said, "Daddy, you left me."

Her son's words had been spoken with such heartfelt pain that she understood why Coop reached down and pulled Laramie into his arms. She stepped back for him to enter. She was amazed at how quickly Laramie had taken to Coop. Maybe it was a male thing. Maybe he would get attached to any man. She wouldn't know because he rarely saw other men. Ms. Charlotte's sons came around every so often and Bristol hadn't dated since Laramie was born.

"I'll get his coat so we can go," she said, when Laramie sat down on the sofa.

"No rush," Coop said, glancing at her. "We have time."

She started to tell him that he couldn't get all emotional whenever Laramie flashed those sad brown eyes at him. Besides, due to the nature of Coop's job as a SEAL, there would be plenty of times when Laramie wouldn't see him. It was not like this would be Coop's address. He lived heaven knew where. But not here.

She crossed the room to the coatrack to get Laramie's jacket and heard what Coop was telling their son. He was being as honest as he could. "There will be days when Daddy will have to go away. Sometimes for a long time."

"How long?" Laramie asked his father. "This long?" Laramie then stretched his little arms out wide.

"Maybe even this long," Coop said, stretching out his own arms even wider.

"Oh." A disappointed pout curved Laramie's tiny lips.

Coop gathered his son close. "Just remember, I will always come back."

Bristol stopped. She had gone along with everything Coop had said until now. But considering the type of job he did, he couldn't promise that he would always come back. How dare he make such a promise to Laramie?

"Where you go, Daddy?"

"Far away. To keep you safe."

"Keep me safe?"

"Yes. Always."

Of course Laramie had more questions but Bristol had heard enough. She grabbed his coat off the coatrack, determined that she would have a talk with Coop when they returned from dinner, after she put Laramie to bed.

"Here's his coat," she said, returning to the living room to hand the coat to Coop.

There was no need for her to try and put on Laramie's coat since he was determined to stick to Coop like glue. The thought didn't bother her and she wasn't filled with even an ounce of jealousy. There was enough of Laramie to go around for the both of them. She thought it was sad her mother hadn't thought that way when it came to Bristol's father.

"Ready?"

She glanced over at Coop as she buttoned up her own coat. "Yes."

"I rented a car for us to use," Coop said, picking up Laramie.

"Just to go to the restaurant? We could have taken a cab."

"I plan to be in New York for a while and figured I would need one for you and Laramie."

She frowned. "Why would you need it for me and Laramie? If we need to go anywhere, we can take the subway like we always do."

"Not while I'm around," he said, heading for the door with Laramie.

Bristol didn't move for a moment, trying to push feelings of annoyance away. She was not used to depending on anyone except Ms. Charlotte. She should just accept what he'd offered as a kind and thoughtful gesture and let it go. Besides, her mother had always told her to pick her battles. What was foremost on her mind right now was the lie he'd told their son a few moments ago—that promise to always come back.

* * *

"Are you okay?" Coop asked Bristol, after she opened the front door. They were returning from dinner and he was carrying a sleeping Laramie in his arms.

"I'm fine. Why do you ask?"

"You were quiet at dinner."

She shrugged as she closed the door behind them. "I think Laramie did enough talking for the both of us."

Coop couldn't help but chuckle. That was true. His son had definitely been the life of the party. Their waitress had fallen in love with him and had been surprised at how well he conversed for his age. Laramie had eaten all of his spaghetti and clapped his hands afterward, saying how good it was.

Keeping his word to Bane about sending a picture, Coop had given their waitress his cell phone and asked her to take one of them. At first Bristol hadn't wanted to participate, saying it was about him and his son, and that his friends wouldn't want her included. He'd dismissed that assumption by reminding her how much they'd liked her when they'd met her in Paris.

The picture was perfect. They had looked like a family dining out together, enjoying their meal and each other's company. In addition to Bane, Coop had texted the photo to the others. Within minutes, his phone had blown up with their responses. They all thought Laramie was a mini-Coop just as he assumed they would. They also thought Bristol looked good. Really good. And texted him to tell her hello. They also said how good the three of them looked together. Funny, he'd thought the same thing.

He couldn't help but notice how little Bristol had said all evening. Was something bothering her? He knew she hadn't been keen on him renting a car just to have it available for her and Laramie, but surely she wasn't upset because of that.

"You want him upstairs, right?" he asked to make certain.

"Yes. I need to undress him for bed," she said, removing her coat. "It's past his bedtime. He lasted longer than I thought he would."

Carrying their son, he followed her up the stairs, trying not to notice the sway of her hips and the curve of her backside. But he did notice. He was a man after all, and didn't intend to feel guilty about checking her out.

He placed Laramie on the bed then watched while Bristol removed his clothes and put him in pajamas. Laramie opened his eyes once and gave his mother a droopy smile. "Love you, Mommy."

"Love you back, Laramie. See you in the morning." She leaned over and kissed him on the cheek. Then he drifted back to sleep.

Coop felt like an intruder to what was probably a usual bedtime exchange between mother and son. An exchange he was witnessing for the first time, one he felt no part of. He would have loved to dress his son for bed. But he hadn't been asked. Instead, he'd been delegated to the sidelines.

Bristol then glanced over at him and whispered, "We need to talk."

There was something in her tone. Whatever she wanted to talk about, he wasn't going to like it. "Okay."

She moved out of the room and he followed. In spite of his mixed emotions while watching Laramie's bedtime routine, Coop enjoyed walking behind Bristol. She helped keep his libido healthy. He thought now what he'd thought a number of times before. She looked good in jeans. He wondered if his son's birth was the reason behind all those curves that now looked even more delectable to him.

"Coffee or beer?"

Bristol's question thrown over her shoulder drew his attention. He had a feeling he would need something stronger than coffee. Probably even stronger than beer, so he would take the alcohol. “Beer.”

She kept walking toward the kitchen while he remained in the living room. With her no longer in sight, he turned his attention to the Christmas tree. He might be wrong but it looked like she’d added more ornaments than were there yesterday. The tree looked all bright and festive, recalling to his mind how perfunctorily the tradition was observed in his own family. His parents, or rather the housekeeper, put up a tree every year. And it remained up until New Year’s whether anyone was there to enjoy it or not.

He couldn’t help but recall his telephone call to his parents earlier today, to let them know about Laramie. They were surprised he’d been so careless with protection and his father had strongly suggested Coop get a blood test before claiming anyone. His mother had stated that if Laramie was truly his, then they would give the little boy all the love they’d given to Coop. He’d had to chuckle at that.

When his mother asked what was funny, he’d respectfully said nothing. They just didn’t get it, but at this point in his life, he didn’t care. His parents weren’t going to change and he was used to their behavior.

A part of him wondered if he would one day find his soul mate, like his father had. Coop knew well the story of how his parents had met in college and fallen in love, apparently at first sight. He often wondered if his parents had really planned for him, although they claimed they had. One thing was for certain, if Coop ever did meet his soul mate, he wouldn’t get so wrapped up in her that he wouldn’t love with equal intensity any child they’d made together.

He drew in a deep breath. Why was he thinking about soul mates? As far as he was concerned, one didn’t exist for him. Laramie would most likely be his only child. He was satisfied with that.

"Here you are."

He turned and Bristol handed him his beer. It was cold, but what he felt was the warmth of her hand when they touched. She had a beer for herself, as well. This was the first time he'd seen her drink beer instead of tea.

"I didn't know you drank beer," he said, tempted to reach out and touch that lone dimple in one of her cheeks.

"There's a lot you don't know about me, Coop."

She had him there. "What do you want to talk about?" he asked.

She moved past him to sit down on the sofa and, as usual, he watched her movements. He wanted to go sit beside her, but knew he shouldn't. For two people who'd made a baby together, they were as far apart as ever. He felt it. She was upset about something and he couldn't wait to hear what it was. He moved to sit down in the chair across from her.

"I want to talk about what you told Laramie."

He lifted a brow. "And what did I tell Laramie?"

The lamp in the room cast a soft light on her features. She wore her hair up in a ponytail with little curls fanning her face. He remembered her wearing a similar style three years ago. He'd taken the band out of her hair so it could fan around her shoulders. His fingers itched to do the same thing now.

"That you would always come back to him."

"I will."

She frowned. "You don't know that."

Now he was the one who frowned. "Do you think I'd deliberately stay away after seeing him? After getting to know him? You think I'd shuck my responsibilities? Even worse—that I could stop loving him and forget about him?"

"That's not what I'm insinuating, Coop. You're missing the point."

He leaned forward, needing to study her expression. To

try deciphering what the hell she was talking about. "So what is the point? Why don't I know that I will always come back to him?"

"Because."

He lifted a brow. "Because what?"

He watched her bury her face in her hands and draw in a deep breath before looking back up at him. The anguish he saw in her gaze made his insides clench when she said, "Because you could die."

Coop didn't say anything. Flashes of a time when everyone thought he had died, when he'd lived each day extremely close to death, filtered through his mind. He pushed the memories back and concentrated on the real fear he saw in Bristol's eyes. That was what he would address. "Yes, I could die. But so could you."

He saw the shiver pass through her before she lifted her chin. "Don't even try to compare what I do with what you do. I paint. You and others like you carry the weight of the world and all of the country's problems on your shoulders. You constantly put your life in danger, Coop. Do you deny that?"

He shook his head. "No, I don't deny it. But whenever I leave for any mission, I have every intention of coming back. Would you have preferred me to tell my son I won't be coming back?"

"No, but I wish you wouldn't make promises you might not be able to keep. If anything ever happens to you, I will be the one who has to explain what happened."

Why were they talking about him dying? Thanks to his son, he had every reason to live, not that he'd ever taken life lightly. But now he had someone in his life who made living doubly important. "I think you're going to the extreme with this, Bristol."

It was clear his words angered her. "You think I'm going to the extreme? You aren't the one who got word while four months pregnant that the father of her child was dead. Dead, Coop. I thought you'd died like all the others."

He frowned. "What others?"

"It doesn't matter. I prefer you don't make promises to Laramie you might not be able to keep."

He stood, feeling angry now, as well. "Then I suggest you do the same. Stop telling him at bedtime that you'll see him in the morning. Anything can happen to you overnight. You could even die in your sleep."

She narrowed her gaze at him. "Stop being ridiculous."

His jaw tightened. "Then I suggest you stop being ridiculous, too. There are no guarantees in life. People die every day. When your time comes, there's not a damn thing you can do about it."

She took a step forward. Got in his face. "I guess of all people you should know, since you had a chance to beat death."

Not good, he thought, meeting her eyes. He wished she didn't smell so good and he definitely preferred her not standing so close. As if it had a will of its own, his gaze moved from her face to her body. She was beautiful even when she was angry.

"And just what are you looking at?" she all but snapped.

Since she asked, he had no qualms in telling her. "You. Did I tell you how good you looked tonight?"

Fourteen

Bristol suddenly realized she might have made a mistake by getting in Coop's space. How had they gone from discussing his death to how good he thought she looked?

She angrily crossed her arms over her chest and then wished she hadn't when his gaze shifted to her chest. As if on cue her nipples hardened right before his eyes. She drew in a deep breath and took a step back. "I think it's time for you to go."

"Is it?"

"Yes."

"I thought you wanted to talk," he said, reclaiming the distance she'd put between them.

"I think we've said enough for tonight."

"Do you? Have you ever noticed we never seem to resolve anything when we talk?"

"And whose fault is that?" she snapped.

"Both of ours." A smile touched the corners of his mouth. "I agree that we've said enough for tonight."

"Good."

"No, Bristol, this is good." And then before she realized

what he was doing, he pulled her into his arms and lowered his mouth to hers.

Shivers of pleasure, the kind she only experienced with him, shot through every part of Bristol. Her eyelids fluttered shut, too overtaken by desire to remain open. When Coop slipped his tongue into her mouth, tasting of the peppermint candy he'd been sucking on earlier, she shuddered. More enjoyable shivers ran up her spine. Sensations consumed her. When his hands wrapped around her middle, she was pulled close to the fit of his hard, masculine body.

When she felt his engorged erection nestled in the juncture of her thighs, she couldn't help but moan. How could they have been talking about serious stuff one minute and kissing the next?

Heated pleasure nearly melted her where she stood. She should be fighting to hold on to her sanity, but she couldn't. Even thinking of it was almost impossible. His assault on her mouth was sensuous and unhurried. It was mind-blowing. It had awakened needs long ago forgotten. And when she thought she couldn't possibly handle anymore, he deepened the kiss and new sensations overtook her.

Suddenly he broke away and she moaned in protest. Looking into his eyes she saw a naked desire that nearly tripped her pulse. Thickened the blood rushing through her veins. The air shimmered around them with sexual undercurrents.

"I want you, Bristol."

His words, spoken in a deep voice, stroked over her skin like a warm caress. Her breathing became as rapid as her heartbeat. And she knew at that moment that kissing wasn't enough. Especially now that they'd been reminded of how it felt to become so enmeshed in each other. Sexual excitement curled her stomach at the memory. It wasn't about love…at least for him it wouldn't be.

For him, it was physical desire driving what was happening between them.

She, on the contrary, was driven by deep, never-ending love.

Two different drives. One final destination.

No need to deny what she truly wanted. "I want you, too, Coop."

As soon as the words left her lips, she was swept off her feet into strong arms and carried up the stairs.

Coop practically took the stairs two at a time with Bristol in his arms. He'd been unable to endure her form of passion any longer. Desire was clawing at his insides, making his need for her palpable. His need to make love to her was a pulsing, throbbing necessity he couldn't fight.

Entering her room, he went straight to the bed and placed her on it. Then he stood back and began removing his clothes while watching her remove hers. She pulled the sweater over her head and tossed it aside. He inhaled a sharp breath when he saw her breasts encased in a sexy black lace bra. Breasts his tongue had known and wanted to know again.

She unhooked the front clasp of her bra and his erection throbbed harder when the twin globes were freed. He'd always liked her breasts—their shape, size and texture. Coop was convinced if given the chance, he could devour those nipples 24/7.

He stopped taking off his own clothes just to watch Bristol finish taking off hers. He was mesmerized, captivated, so damn fascinated. When she removed her jeans, leaving herself only in undies, his erection got harder. She was wearing black panties that matched the bra.

Three words immediately came to mind. Gorgeous. Hot. Awesome.

"Is there a problem, Coop?"

Her voice snapped him back. He swallowed when he shifted his gaze to her face. "No, there isn't a problem."

"I was just wondering."

He didn't want her to wonder about anything. Especially about him being anxious to make love to her. He was convinced that somehow during those three days they'd spent together in Paris, Bristol had gotten into his blood. That had to be the reason he hadn't been able to forget her. The reason why thinking of her had kept him sane. What other reason could there be?

He quickly removed the rest of his clothes and then pulled out a condom from his wallet. He sheathed himself, knowing she was watching. It wouldn't be the first time she'd seen him do this and he didn't intend for it to be the last.

Bristol frowned when he got closer to the bed. Her fingers touched the scars that hadn't been there the last time they'd made love. From the look on her face he figured she knew where they'd come from. And then she did something he hadn't expected. Something that touched him deeply.

She leaned close and showered kisses over the scars. It was as if she wanted to kiss away any pain they might have caused him. When her mouth came close to his erection, he pulled back. He didn't want a reason to take off his condom. That was probably how she'd gotten pregnant the last time.

"I want to be inside of you, Bristol. I need it," he whispered hoarsely, climbing on the bed to join her.

"And that's where I want you, Coop," she said, wrapping her arms around his neck. "Inside of me."

Maybe she shouldn't have said that, shouldn't have so openly admitted her desire. Maybe she should not have been so brutally honest. But what else could she say when the juncture of her thighs throbbed for him? When her nipples were hard? When her heart was beating fast? When every nerve in her body shrieked with excitement and anticipation? When the moment she'd kissed his scars it was as if they'd become hers?

There was still a lot they didn't agree on and they truly needed to be downstairs talking instead of in her bedroom doing this. But then, maybe this was needed before they could have any sensible discussions. It was hard to sit down and talk like adults when said adults wanted to tear each other's clothes off, roll on the floor in front of the fireplace and mate like rabbits.

There was nothing that could hold her back from this. From giving herself to him like she'd done three years ago. So much had happened since then, but she didn't want to remember any of it…except for the birth of her son. That would always be a spot of joy in her life. But right now, at this instant, she wanted to be transported back in time. She wanted to experience once again how it felt when their bodies joined. When he proved to her just how much vitality he had. How much stamina.

When he showed her just how much he desired her. She could never get enough of that. His open display of need made sexual excitement curl her stomach. She felt light-headed with the effect of his masculine power.

"I plan to take this slow, Bristol."

His words had a shock effect to her system. Slow? He had to be kidding. She was so enthusiastic she was convinced that slow would kill her.

He touched her, using his fingers to unhurriedly skim across her skin, right beneath her breasts. His fingertips elicited sensations that made parts of her tingle. Lighting her up like a flame he intended to let burn gradually before sensuously snuffing it out.

The intensity of his gaze took her breath. She wasn't sure what emotions she saw in his penetrating look—except for one. The sexual vibes between them. They were stronger than they'd been in Paris. That was hard to believe because what they'd shared in Paris had been mind-blowing at minimum.

While his fingers were intent on driving her insane with lust, he increased her pleasure by leaning over and whispering, "I need to taste you."

She knew what he meant. He'd already kissed her. She knew he was referring to tasting her in another way. A way she remembered so well. A way that made the throbbing between her legs intensify. The one thing she remembered about Coop was that he never did anything without telling her beforehand, to make sure she was comfortable with what he wanted to do. He was not a man who exploited a woman's weak moments. There hadn't been any surprises in what he did, only in the magnitude of the pleasure his actions delivered.

She nodded. He took the motion as consent. Before she could draw her next breath, he lowered his head to her chest and slid a nipple into his mouth.

She purred. Of course he would start here, knowing exactly what he was doing to her and how he was making her feel. He was well aware that he could push her into an orgasm just from his mouth devouring her breasts. He'd done it before and, from the feel of things, he intended to do it again.

Suddenly, he pulled his mouth away and looked up at her. "Did you breastfeed our son?"

His question took her by surprise. "Yes."

He smiled as if the thought pleased him. She didn't have the mind to ponder why when his mouth went back to her breasts. Then, as if with renewed energy, he began sucking hard. Her womb contracted with every draw of a nipple into his mouth and her purr got louder.

She needed to touch him. She slid her hands over his shoulders and down his arms before bringing them back to cup the side of his face. Tingling sensations built between her legs. She was certain she was about to be pushed over the edge when he pulled back, lifted his head and said, "Not yet. Remember what I told you. I intend to make this slow so you can remember me for a long time."

She felt his body shift lower. Then he was touching her stomach, caressing it with gentle strokes. His hands moved lower and his fingers stilled when they touched the thin line of a scar.

"Because Laramie weighed so much I had to have a C-section," she said, explaining the bikini cut that was barely visible. Of course someone as observant as him would detect it.

He didn't say anything, but she felt his mouth when his tongue traced a path over the scar. He was kissing her scar like she'd done for his.

The air surrounding them became even more charged. And she was suddenly filled with so many emotions she felt completely out of whack.

Then he lifted her legs to fall over his shoulders while her hips were elevated with his hands. He nudged her knees open and then as if it was the most natural thing to do, eased his face between her legs and slid his tongue inside.

He kissed her with an expertise she found utterly amazing. His tongue went deep. It was thorough. And it was excruciatingly slow. It was as if he had all the time in the world to drive her mad with desire. The more she moaned, the more he tortured her, delving deeper with powerful strokes.

Then she had to fight back a scream when her body exploded into a gigantic orgasm.

Shivers ran through Coop as the thighs encasing his face quivered. He knew what that meant but he refused to stop. In fact, he needed to keep going because her taste was more potent now. Her taste was what he'd remembered, what he'd longed for, yearned for. His shaft throbbed with an urgency he hadn't felt since the last time he'd been with her.

He felt her tremors subside but he refused to let up. Doubted he could even if he wanted to. The taste of her juices flooded him with even more desire. When her thighs began trembling again, he knew she was reaching climax again.

When he'd seen that scar he had been filled with such profound emotion. They both had scars to show from their time apart. Hers had been a celebration of life, his had been a prologue to a death that never happened.

Those days were over. He was free and back in the land of the living. Back in Bristol's bed. The same bed where memories had been made before. The same bed where his son was created. Same bed, same woman.

He couldn't get enough.

When the last of the spasms wore off, Bristol wondered how she'd had mulitple orgasms so close together. Had she been that needy? That greedy? That hard up for sex?

If she'd just wanted sex she would have dated Steven, or any of the other men who'd hit on her over the years. But none of them had enticed her to open herself up this way. To invite them to her bed. To tell them she wanted them inside her. Only with Coop could she behave so boldly. And she knew why.

She was still in love with him.

Coop smiled down at her as his body straddled hers. Surely he didn't think she had the energy for another round of anything. Especially intercourse of the most intense kind. She was so tired she would probably fall asleep in the middle. But then she'd had two orgasms in less than twenty minutes. She owed him something and would fake it if she had to. He deserved his pleasure, as well.

She'd only faked it for one guy, her first time in high school. With Coop she'd never needed to fake a thing. He'd kept her blood pumping. Kept the primal attraction between them so real that she'd been ready whenever he'd been ready. She'd even been tempted to wake him up for more. But not this time. There was no way her body could endure another orgasm tonight. But for him, she would pretend.

"You're not about to go to sleep on me, are you?" he asked her, staring down at her.

She looked into his eyes and her body warmed under his intense regard. She lowered her gaze to his lips. Lips that were wet with her juices. Why did that cause a deep stirring in the pit of her stomach? Maybe it was because she recalled how his tongue had lapped her into consecutive orgasms.

"Ready to taste yourself?" he asked in a low whisper.

Blood rushed through her veins. He'd never asked her anything like that before. Taste herself? She knew how he would do it and imagining it aroused her enough that a low moan escaped her lips.

"Is that a yes?"

A sensual force seemed to overtake her. Where was his sexual aura coming from? Hadn't she thought of faking it just a minute ago? Now he was arousing her all over again with mere words. Laramie Cooper was too compelling for his own good. Definitely too sexy.

She should have known she couldn't fake anything with him because he had the ability to turn her on, even when she thought such a thing wasn't possible.

"Yes," she said.

Then he lowered his mouth to hers. The moment their lips touched, every hormone in her body crackled. She knew it was more than their combined tastes driving her over the edge. It was the masterful way his tongue dominated her mouth.

Her nerves did a pirouette, her brain sprinted and her stomach flipped.

He ended the kiss and looked down at her in a way that made moisture gather between her thighs. "You're ready for me again, Bristol?"

Yes, she was ready, even when she'd thought earlier there was no way she could go another round. Not only could she go, she intended to participate to the fullest and there wouldn't be anything fake about it. "Yes, I'm ready."

Her legs opened automatically, as if her body needed what he was giving. It had been three years since she'd done this and the last time had been with him. She slipped her arms around his neck and felt the large length of his erection touching her feminine mound.

Then he eased inside, inch by inch. His fullness encompassed her as he went deeper, filling her to the hilt. Her body stretched to accommodate him.

"You okay?"

She looked up and met his gaze. "Yes, I'm okay."

And honestly, she was. It was like a homecoming. The man she'd thought lost to her forever, the man she'd believed would never make love to her again, was doing just that. It was more than she could have hoped for.

"Thank you for my son," he whispered hoarsely.

And then he began moving while still holding her gaze, as if daring her to look away. She stared into his eyes while his body thrust inside her with a rhythm that released a sensual throb of desire in her veins. The sinfully erotic movement of his hips drew everything out of her, while at the same time demanding that she take as much of him as she could. Each hard thrust made her moan.

He kept moving at an unhurried pace, as if he wanted her to feel every single stroke. And she did. They were a perfect fit. She felt intense pleasure all the way to her bones.

The undercurrent flowing between them was explosive, hot with passion of the most mind-blowing kind.

Her body moved with his. Her inner muscles tightened around him. Together they were creating a sensual heat like she'd never felt before…not even the last time. She'd thought nothing could be more powerful than what they'd already shared. Bristol was proven wrong.

Then he increased his pace, refined his strokes and pumped into her with a vigor that made her entire body respond. She exploded the same time he did, and he covered her mouth to keep the scream from her lips.

They seemed to flow into each other. Her hips were connected to his. Their bodies were perfectly aligned as they experienced the throes of ecstasy together. When he finally released her mouth, she drew in a deep breath and clung to his shoulders. They rode the waves of pleasure together.

Moments later, he rolled off her and gathered her in his arms. His thumb stroked her cheeks. The last thing Bristol remembered before sleep overtook her was whispering his name.

Fifteen

Coop wasn't sure what awakened him, but he jerked upright in bed and glanced around before remembering where he was. Bristol's bed. He drew in a deep breath and rubbed his hand down his face before looking at the clock. It was three in the morning. The spot beside him was empty. He'd been sleeping so soundly that he hadn't noticed when Bristol got out of bed.

Where was she? He lay back down thinking she was probably in the bathroom. A few minutes later, when she hadn't returned, he got up and checked. She wasn't there. Had she gone to see about Laramie? Coop pulled on his jeans and left the bedroom to go to his son's room. He found his son sleeping, but Bristol wasn't there, either.

He was about to head downstairs when he heard a noise coming from the attic. He knew from playing hide-and-seek with Laramie that she'd converted the attic into her studio and that was where she did most of her painting. Was she painting this time of morning?

Coop walked up the six steps and found the door open. And there she was, standing in front of an easel. Was she wearing anything under that artist's cape? It was short and hit her at midthigh, which gave him a good view of her legs. She had a nice pair and like him, she was in her bare feet. He watched the look of concentration on her face. Her full attention was on whatever she was painting. Considering what they'd done tonight she should be exhausted. Obviously, she had a lot of energy.

She hadn't noticed him and he decided not to disturb her. Coop took in the room. It was huge. There were several built-in cabinets for her supplies. There was also a love seat, as well as a sink and counter that he figured she used as a cleanup station. The room had only one small window and he figured she wanted the least distractions possible while painting.

Coop was about to leave when he noticed several framed photographs on the wall. One was a photo of her and an older man. They favored each other and he figured the man was her father. He studied the man's features and tried to recall why he seemed so familiar.

Coop leaned in the doorway and recalled bits and pieces of what she'd told him about her past. Their son's middle name had been her father's first name. When they'd first met, her last name had been Lockett. He also remembered the story she'd told him about the two years she and her father had spent together before he'd died.

"That's a picture of you and your father, isn't it?"

His words had her swinging around so fast she almost dropped her paint brush. She released a nervous breath. "Coop, you scared me."

"Sorry," he said, entering the room. "I woke up and found you gone and wondered where you'd taken off to." It hadn't been his intention to stay the night at her house, but after making love that first time, they'd slept and had awakened to make love once more. Then they'd fallen asleep again.

She smiled over at him. "I didn't want to wake you. In

addition to painting during Laramie's nap time, I often paint late at night when he's asleep." She then broke eye contact and glanced at the framed photograph. "Yes, that's my father," she said proudly. He could hear the love in her voice.

"Randall Lockett was your father."

She snatched her gaze to him. "How do you know that?"

He could see the surprised look on her face. Was her father's identity supposed to be a secret or something? "I recognize him. I'm familiar with his work thanks to my parents, namely my mother. She owns several of his paintings."

"She does?"

"Yes."

He glanced at her easel and back at her before saying, "I even met him once when he came to Austin for an art show to benefit one of my mother's charities. I liked his work. I should have made the connection in Paris with your last name being Lockett and the two of you having similar styles. But it never crossed my mind." There was no need to tell her that the only thing that had been on his mind was getting her to the nearest bed.

"I can't believe you actually met my father."

He heard the excitement in her voice. "Yes, I was seventeen at the time and a senior in high school. It was the last event my mother sort of forced me to attend with her and my dad. In the end, I'm glad I went. He was a nice man. Very personable. Like I said, Mom has quite a few of your father's paintings and it was nice meeting the man who was getting so much of her money. I'm sure you know his work isn't cheap."

She chuckled. "Yes, I know."

"I remember that time well," he said. "I'd gotten word a few days before of my acceptance into the naval academy and was going away with my parents' blessing. I was relieved they hadn't placed any pressure on me to follow in their footsteps and take part in the family business."

"And what business is that?"

"RCC Manufacturing Company."

She lifted a brow. "RCC? I'm familiar with them. They're a huge operation based in Texas. I order a number of my art supplies through them."

He chuckled. "My parents would be happy to hear that."

"And you decided to become a SEAL instead of going into your family business?"

"Yes, that's right. I knew early on I wasn't cut out for the business-suit-and-tie crowd."

Coop glanced back over at the framed photograph and then back at her. "You seemed surprised that I knew Randall Lockett was your father, like it was supposed to be a secret or something. Was it?"

Bristol looked away from Coop to glance at the picture she'd taken with her father, one that she'd proudly hung on her wall. She wished Coop wouldn't stand there shirtless and in his bare feet. In jeans riding low on his hips and not quite zipped up all the way, with the snap undone. He looked way too sexy for her peace of mind.

She'd yet to answer Coop's question and she realized how little they knew about each other, even with all the intimacy they'd shared. She blamed it on the fact that whenever they were together they did little talking due to all the sexual chemistry surrounding them. Like now. She could feel it and she knew he did, as well.

She hadn't known so much need had been bottled up inside her. All it had taken was Coop unleashing it and she'd become a mad woman wanting to make up for lost time. Luckily for her, he'd been the same way. It was as if they hadn't been able to get enough of each other.

"It's not a secret per se. I just don't go around broadcasting it, so few people know. I don't want to use his name to build my own career as an artist, although I am proud to have been Randall Lockett's daughter."

"And I'm sure he was glad he was Bristol Lockett's father."

His words made her feel good. More than once, her father had told her how proud he was of her and all she'd accomplished. "Thank you for saying that."

"No need to thank me."

He moved around the room, looking at the easels showing various paintings she had done. She wasn't used to anyone invading her space, especially in here. For some reason his presence didn't bother her.

Another thing that didn't bother her, when maybe it should have, was how quickly they'd become intimate again. Had it been just the night before when he'd shown up at the gallery? She had wanted him immediately. Had needed him sexually. And he'd delivered, satisfying her.

It wasn't his fault that she had fallen in love with him years ago. Nor was it any of his concern that she was trying to fall out of love with him now. Sleeping with him hadn't confused the issue for her. She knew he didn't love her back.

She needed to get her mind off Coop, namely off his body, and transfer her thoughts to something else. She walked over to the coffeepot she kept in her studio and poured a cup. She then turned to him. "Would you like some?"

Her insides heated when his gaze roamed over her, making her realize just what she'd asked. She swallowed, thinking he'd had some already. A lot actually. But if he wanted more...she was game.

Drawing in a deep breath, she clarified, "Would you like a cup of coffee, Coop?"

He nodded slowly. "Yes, I'd love a cup."

She poured his coffee and he walked over to take the cup from her hand. Their fingers brushed and her stomach curled with pleasure.

"Thanks," he said.

"You're welcome."

They both took a sip of their coffees. Despite trying not to love him, she wanted to get to know him. Like she'd told him earlier, she was very familiar with his parents' company. It was on the Fortune 500 list, which meant he came from money. He'd said the reason he'd wanted to become a SEAL was that the work was a better fit for his personality. And he'd become a SEAL with his parents' blessing. She knew things didn't always work that way for the sons of important families.

"It's late. I hadn't intended to impose on you by spending the night. I'll leave now if you want me to."

She looked at him over the rim of her cup. Did she want him to leave? No, she didn't. "There's no need, unless you want to go. You'll probably be back in the morning for breakfast anyway."

He chuckled. "Only if I get an invitation."

"You have an invitation, Coop. I told you, you can spend as much time with Laramie as you want."

He nodded and took a sip of his coffee. "In that case, I'd like to ask you something."

"What?" she asked.

"What plans do you and Laramie have for the holidays?"

She thought about his question. "Just a quiet time at home this year. It will be Laramie's first Christmas where he understands that the holidays are special. I've been telling him that if he's a good boy, Santa will bring him something nice. He's been keeping his toys put away and getting better with potty training." She paused before asking, "Why did you want to know about my plans for the holidays?"

"Because I'm hoping I can join the two of you." He drew in a deep breath. "And before you ask, the answer is no. I had no plans to spend Christmas with my folks."

Bristol remembered the last holiday they'd spent together. At that time, he'd given her the impression that he and his parents weren't close. Now was just as good a time as any to ask him about it. After all, his parents were her son's only living grandparents. In fact, the only living relatives Laramie had besides her and Coop, as far as she knew. If anything were to ever happen to her or Coop…

She suddenly needed to know about the people who might one day be responsible for her son. "You're welcome to join us, but I want you to tell me about your parents, Coop. Laramie's grandparents."

He leaned against her art table, avoiding her stacks of supplies. "What do you want to know?"

She shrugged. "Mainly, why you never want to spend the holidays with them?"

A part of Coop wanted to think her question was simple enough. But when it came to his parents, nothing was simple unless you accepted them for who they were. He'd done that a long time ago.

"Come on, let's sit on the sofa and I'll tell you about them."

"Okay."

Together, they sat down. To be on the safe side, since she was too desirable for her own good, he sat at the other end of the sofa. He took a sip of his coffee and said, "I think my parents are swell people who after nearly thirty-five years of marriage still love each other deeply."

He chuckled. "I wouldn't be wrong if I were to say they were obsessed with each other. I was told by both sets of my grandparents—who are deceased now—that it had been that way from the first, when they'd met at Harvard.

Dad was from Laredo, Texas, and Mom from Laramie, Wyoming."

She lifted a brow. "Laramie?"

"Yes, and before you ask, the answer is yes. She named me after the city where she was born. She loved it that much and tried getting my father to move there after they were married. But he was a Texan through and through. He'd come from generations of ranchers, but he gave up that way of life, deciding not to follow in his father's, grandfather's and great-grandfather's footsteps as a rancher. He was the suit-and-tie kind. After college, he and my mom lived in Austin and started a business. Less than a year after graduating from college, the two of them were married. I was born three years later."

"No wonder your parents were so understanding about allowing you to have the career you wanted. They'd faced the same challenge."

"Yes, but my paternal grandparents weren't as understanding. They thought Dad was throwing away his legacy. Especially since my father was their only child."

He paused to take another sip of coffee. "I'm told that my mom's pregnancy with me was difficult. At one point, they thought she would die. My father was even told he might have to choose to either save his wife or his child. He picked his wife. But a top specialist arrived and assured my father he could save us both. He did. However, I think I was still a stark reminder to my dad of how close he came to losing Mom."

Bristol frowned, and he thought it was cute. "Surely, he didn't hold you responsible and mistreat you in any way."

"No, not at all. Dad was good. However, my parents' relationship took a turn. They were always close, but I think nearly losing Mom freaked Dad out. After that he was determined to spend every moment he could with her… for the rest of their lives. They take more trips than I can count every year, and they have a tradition of spending the holidays together somewhere—usually with friends in England. Like I told you before, I've never spent the holidays with my parents. I've always spent them with my grandparents on their ranch. And trust me, I had no complaints. My grandparents were the greatest. I loved being out on their ranch."

"Did you ever feel resentful of your parents for not spending time with you?"

He knew it was hard to understand his relationship with his parents, but for her he wanted to try to explain. "It's not that my parents never spent time with me, Bristol, because they did. They were very active in my life while growing up and there were a number of trips we took together."

He took another sip of coffee. "Thanks to them, I saw most of the world before my sixteenth birthday. There was never a time I didn't think my parents loved me. However, I always knew they loved each other more."

"And you didn't have a problem with that?"

"No. I had friends whose parents didn't even like each other, couldn't stand to be in the same room together. Some of their parents divorced as soon as they finished school and my friends knew they had been the glue that held their parents' unhappy marriages together. That wasn't the case with my parents. There was never any doubt in my mind that Dad and Mom loved each other to the moon and back."

He didn't say anything for a minute, then he added, "When they thought I was dead, they went bonkers. I think they got even closer, if such a thing is possible with them. When I was found alive, they refused to let me out of their sight at first. They even questioned if I should continue being a SEAL. I knew they were worried, but I wasn't used to all the attention, at least not from them. I couldn't wait until I finished my recuperation period to return to work."

She spun her cup in her hands and asked, "What happened to your grandparents' ranch?"

"They willed it to me, although they were fully aware of my career as a SEAL. But my grandparents also knew I would manage the ranch as well as become a SEAL. For the ranch, I hired the right people to take care of it until I retire from the military, which will be in about six years. Some of the men working at the ranch for me used to work for my grandparents and can be trusted."

She nodded. "What kind of ranch is it?"

"It was always a cattle ranch but thanks to Bane's family, the Westmorelands, I've added horses. Several of his family members own a horse breeding and training company. They needed another holding depot before shipping the horses off to be trained. That's where my ranch comes in. So, I guess my ranch is a horse ranch, as well."

"Do you go there often?"

"Not as much as I would like. When I do go there it's mainly to check on things. My men have everything pretty much under control."

"I'm glad."

A part of him believed she was, which made him say, "I want to show you and Laramie my ranch one day." He would tell her that much. He wouldn't tell her yet that he planned to make it his primary home for whenever Laramie visited.

She smiled and he felt a stirring in his stomach. "I'd love to see it, Coop. I know Laramie will, too. He loves horses."

"Then it's settled. I will take the two of you there after the holidays." Standing, he said, "I've kept you from your work long enough."

She smiled, standing, as well. "I'm okay. I was about to come to a stopping point anyway."

"You do this every night? Paint while Laramie sleeps?"

"Not every night. Just whenever the urge hits."

Funny, she should mention urges. At that moment, he was swamped with another urge. "Speaking of urges, Bristol," he said, setting his cup aside.

"What about them?"

"I feel one coming on myself."

She smiled. "You want to try your hand at painting?"

He chuckled. "No. It's not an urge to paint."

"Oh? What kind of urge is it?"

He leaned over and whispered in her ear. She smiled and placed her own coffee cup on the table. She moved closer and wrapped her arms around his neck. "In that case, I think we need to deal with these urges of yours."

"I agree." He swept her off her feet and headed toward her bedroom.

Sixteen

Coop felt something poke him against his nose and he snatched his eyes open. He saw a miniature pair of eyes and a little hand right in his face. "You in my mommy's bed," his son all but accused.

Yes, he was in Laramie's mommy's bed. Before Coop could open his mouth to assure his son that everything was okay, Laramie had pulled himself up on the bed and crawled over him, saying, "Move over, Daddy." The little boy then planted himself in the middle of the bed, unceremoniously separating Coop and Bristol like the parting of the Red Sea.

"Laramie!" Bristol said, quickly sitting up after coming awake. "Be nice."

"He in your bed, Mommy."

Bristol yawned and ran a hand through her son's curls. "I know and it's okay. Good morning, Laramie."

He wrapped his arms around his mother's neck. "Good morning, Mommy."

Then, as if satisfied, Laramie slid beneath the covers and closed his eyes.

Bristol glanced over at Coop and smiled. “Sorry about that.”

“Hey, don’t apologize. I take it he does this every morning.”

She nodded, pushing a mass of hair back from her face. “Yes. And as you can see it’s not quite six o’clock. He comes in here, gets in my bed and will go back to sleep for another hour or so, then he’ll wake up hungry. That’s how we start our day.”

For Coop that was a bummer because he’d planned to start his day by making love to her. Now, thanks to their son, those plans would be canned. But son or no son, Coop intended to get a good morning kiss. He leaned over and placed a kiss on her lips. “Good morning, Bristol.”

She smiled. “Good morning, Coop.”

He returned her smile. He’d liked waking up with her while in Paris and he liked waking up with her now. Even after making love to her multiple times last night, he still had a lot of sexual energy to work off and he knew only one other way to do so besides making love to Bristol.

“I’m going to the fitness center.”

She lifted a brow. “The fitness center?”

“Yes, back at the hotel. I’m used to working out every morning.” Usually he worked out twice a day. “I’ll be back for breakfast if that’s okay.”

“That’s fine. We’ll be here.”

“I’m counting on it.” He leaned over and kissed her again, this time a little longer, before easing out of bed. He slid into his jeans and went into the connecting bathroom. When he returned a few moments later, he saw she had drifted off to sleep with Laramie cuddled close.

As he finished dressing, he couldn’t stop looking at them. Something deep tugged at his heart. He wasn’t sure how to deal with all these emotions. For years, he’d stayed in control of all relationships he was involved in. Usually, none were for the long-term. He'd been determined that no woman would ever rule his heart.

He liked his freedom. Besides, his work as a SEAL wasn't conducive to a normal family life. He didn't know from one month to the next where a mission might take him or for how long he'd be gone. He'd always enjoyed the adventure, the excitement, the quest and, yes, even the danger. Definitely the danger. It was enough to get your blood pumping and your adrenaline flowing.

But, he thought, studying Bristol while she slept, she got his blood pumping and his adrenaline flowing, as well. And when he thought about what they'd shared last night, he couldn't help but smile. Then his smile widened and he knew why. He was happy. Truly happy. And the two people responsible for his happiness were sleeping in that bed. In the last forty-eight hours, his life had changed.

Already, he could admit he wouldn't want it any other way.

When he finished dressing, he walked back over to the bed to stare down at them. At her. He wondered if she had any idea what she did to him, what she had done to him three years ago. Resisting her hadn't been an option.

Bristol had gotten next to him without much effort and there hadn't been anything he could do about it.

Other than to fall in love with her.

That admission shook him to the core. He hadn't seen that coming. But now that he knew the truth, he had to accept it.

He loved her.

He drew in a deep breath. If he analyzed his behavior over the past three years, he probably would have realized he'd fallen in love with her the moment he and the guys had walked into that café in Paris. He'd seen her staring at him. He was certain he'd lost his heart then and there.

He'd left everyone at the table to approach her, determined to introduce himself before they could. Now his actions made sense. Love explained everything. Including the importance of those memories to his survival as well as why he'd returned to Paris looking for her as soon as he'd recuperated. When he'd accepted that she had been lost to him forever, he'd moved on. He'd been living a satisfied life but not a truly happy one.

There had to be a reason their paths had crossed in New York after all this time, a reason they had a child, who would always be a bond between them. And more than anything he also believed, whether she agreed or not, there was a purpose behind her decision to concoct a fake marriage and take his name.

He wanted Bristol and Laramie to always be a part of his life. He might not have planned for the recent turn of events, but now that he was faced with this little family of his, he had no regrets.

He was well aware that Bristol harbored reservations about making their marriage real, but he intended to get rid of whatever roadblocks stood in their way.

She didn't love him yet, but in the end she would. He was a determined man and when he came to a decision there was no stopping him.

He turned and walked out of her bedroom.

Bristol was in the middle of preparing breakfast when her phone rang. Was it Coop letting her know he wouldn't make it back for breakfast? Upon waking up again, Laramie had seemed a little disappointed that Coop had left. She had to admit, she was, too.

As she put the biscuits in the oven, she thought about how he'd found her in her studio working. He had been a distraction, but a welcome one. They had talked. But the one thing he hadn't said was whether or not he'd told his parents about Laramie. And about their fake marriage. If so, what did his parents think of all this?

When she grabbed the phone, she saw from the caller ID that it was Margie. "Yes, Margie?"

"Are you in a better mood today?"

Bristol raised a brow. "Was I in a bad mood yesterday?"

"I thought so. I might have upset you with those things I said about your husband. If I did, I'm sorry."

Bristol drew in a deep breath. Margie's words from yesterday had annoyed her. "There is a lot about my relationship with him that you don't know." And one of them was the fact he was not really her husband.

"Then enlighten me. Let's do lunch today."

Bristol nibbled on her bottom lip. Today was not a good day. She didn't like having to ask Ms. Charlotte to keep an eye on Laramie at the last minute. There might be a chance Coop would be available to watch him, but she couldn't depend on that. On top of those conflicts, she and Coop still had more to work through. They needed to decide how to move forward. He wanted to spend the holidays with them and she was fine with that. What she didn't want was what they'd shared last night muddying the waters.

She didn't want him to think that just because she'd allowed him in her bed she'd allow him into her life. That wasn't the case.

"Tomorrow will be better, Margie," she heard herself say.

"Okay, and tomorrow would it be a good time for you and Steven to talk?"

Margie's words got her attention. "Talk about what?"

Margie chuckled. "Honestly, Bristol, have you forgotten he represents a company who's a client? A client who made it possible for you to leave that boring job to stay home with your son and paint every day."

No, she hadn't forgotten, mainly because Margie refused

to let her. She just didn't understand why Margie couldn't see that Bristol and Steven didn't click. "Fine, as long as this is strictly a business meeting, Margie."

"What other kind of meeting would I arrange? You don't like Steven, I get that now, although for Pete's sake, I don't know why. But it's your choice. Call me later and tell me when would be a good time to get together tomorrow."

"All right. I'll talk to you later."

As soon as she clicked off the phone and placed it aside, her doorbell rang. "Daddy's back, Mommy!"

The excitement in her son's voice touched her. At least he wasn't annoyed like he'd been this morning when he'd discovered his favorite spot in her bed already occupied. Once he'd gone to sleep and woken back up, he'd been team Coop all over again. "Yes, sweetheart, I think your daddy is back."

Putting the kitchen towel aside, she left the kitchen and headed toward the door.

"Good morning. I got you this," Coop said, handing her a huge poinsettia. There was a florist shop by the hotel and when he'd seen it this morning he knew he wanted to get it for her.

"Thanks. It's beautiful, Coop."

"You're welcome. I liked it when I saw it. It looks healthy and there are leaves that will be turning red in a few days."

She smiled. "Come on in." She stepped aside. "I just put the biscuits in the oven."

"Biscuits? You can make biscuits?"

"Yes, thanks to Aunt Dolly."

He entered, pulling off his Stetson and hanging his jacket on the coatrack. "I knew you could cook but claiming you can make biscuits has elevated you to another level."

She smiled. "That's good to know."

He watched as she placed the potted plant on a small

table not far from the Christmas tree. It was hard to believe it was a week before Christmas, but in New York it was hard to forget the season. There seemed to be a Santa on every corner and all the light posts were decorated with wreaths.

"So, what do you think?" she asked, turning to stand beside the plant he'd given her.

His focus was on her when he said, "I wish I could have seen you pregnant."

"Where did that come from?" she asked, smiling.

"You asked what I thought and those were my thoughts while seeing you standing there, knowing my son is in the kitchen sitting at the table."

"Coloring."

He chuckled. "Yes, coloring."

She didn't say anything for a minute. "While pregnant, I looked like a blimp."

He crossed the floor to stop in front of her. He cupped her chin in his hand. "I bet you looked beautiful." He leaned down and brushed his lips across hers.

Then, as if she needed time to compose herself, she said, "The biscuits are about ready to come out the oven."

She hurried to the kitchen.

A couple hours later, Bristol stood in front of her easel. The sound of her son's laughter could be heard all the way upstairs, letting her know he was enjoying another day of Coop's company.

Her thoughts shifted back to breakfast. Laramie had been glad to see his father and had talked a mile a minute. Just like yesterday, after breakfast Coop had volunteered to help clean up the kitchen. Although she'd told him his help wasn't needed, he'd given it anyway. And she would inwardly admit there had been something comfortable about him helping with kitchen chores.

Her thoughts shifted to the poinsettia he'd given her. It was big and beautiful and looked like it belonged right in the spot she'd placed it. It had been so thoughtful of him to bring it for her, and it made her feel special, although she wished it didn't. The only other man who'd given her flowers had been her father. He had arrived at their first meeting with flowers and had given her flowers on her birthday ever since. Even after his death the flowers were delivered. They were always a beautiful bouquet and the card always said, "You are forever loved, Dad."

She wiped the tears from her eyes that always sprang up when she thought of her father and the little time they'd had together. But he was still making a positive impact on her life. The same way she believed Coop would make a positive impact on Laramie's life. He was spending time with their son and that meant a lot. Laramie would miss Coop when he left but he would look forward to his father's return.

If he returned...

She drew in a sharp breath as fear gripped her. She didn't want to think of the risk Coop took whenever he left on a covert operation, but she couldn't push it from her mind. Although he'd told her little about his work, he had explained to her in Paris that most of his missions were classified and couldn't be discussed. She wondered how families of navy SEALs dealt with not knowing from one day to the next the whereabouts of their loved ones and when they would return.

The sound of her cell phone snapped her out of her reverie. She grabbed it off the table and smiled when she saw the caller was Dionne. "Hi, what's up?"

"Just calling to check on you. Are you and my godson okay?"

Bristol smiled. "We're fine. Just getting used to having a male presence around." She thought of how Coop had looked, standing on her doorstep that morning wearing a Stetson, jeans, suede jacket and boots. You could take the man out of Texas but you couldn't take Texas out of the man.

"A hot male presence, right?"

She thought about what had taken place in her bed last night and hot was just one adjective she could use. Other descriptions definitely came to mind but since Dionne had said hot… "Um, you can't imagine just how hot."

"*Oui!* Tell me!"

Bristol laughed. "No details for now. I need to prepare Laramie's lunch."

"Okay, but you will tell me later."

"Yes, later."

"You sound happy, Bristol."

Did she? "It's the holidays. Of course I sound happy."

"Usually you're not cheerful this time of year. Those memories of your aunt…"

Yes, there would always be memories of her aunt, who'd died over the holidays. "I know. At least I was here when it happened."

"Yes, I was there, too. I got to meet her. She was so nice."

"She was super."

They talked about other things while Dionne brought Bristol up to date on her family and the other friends Bristol had left behind in Paris. "Bristol?"

"Yes?"

"Have you decided what you're going to do?"

Bristol frowned. "About what?"

"Your fake marriage. We went to a lot of trouble to make it seem real."

Bristol didn't say anything at first. She and Coop still hadn't decided how to proceed. "A fake divorce makes sense then, doesn't it? But then why waste money undoing something that wasn't real anyway?"

"Is that what he wants? To undo it?"

"I don't know what he wants. It only came up once. We need to talk about it again and make a decision," she said. "Everyone here thinks I was a widow and then out of the clear blue sky my husband reappears. It placed him in an awkward situation since he had no idea everyone thought we were married until I told him."

"Why not make it a real marriage under the pretense of renewing your vows?"

"Because there is no love between us."

Bristol knew what Dionne was going to say before she'd even said it. "There is love, Bristol, at least on your part. You loved him after Paris. Remember, I'm the one who told you he had died. I saw what that did to you and the grief you endured. You loved him too much. That much love doesn't just go away. There's no way you don't still love him."

Bristol opened her mouth to say that wasn't true, that she didn't still love Coop, but she couldn't lie to Dionne. "It doesn't matter. I intend to fall out of love with him."

"Why?"

Bristol drew in a deep breath. "You just said the reason. You saw the way I handled the news of his death and the grief I suffered as a result. I couldn't risk going through something like that a second time. I can't and I won't."

Seventeen

For the second night in a row Coop stood aside while Bristol tucked their son into bed. Today had been a full day of activities. After breakfast he'd stretched out on the floor and helped Laramie put Lego blocks together. Then after lunch he had bundled his son up in his boots and coat and they'd walked to the park.

Bristol had invited Coop to stay for dinner and now he couldn't help wondering if she would invite him to stay the night. She really hadn't invited him last night, but their need for each other had pretty much made the decision for them.

There was a strong possibility she might send him packing after they had the little talk he intended for them to have. It was time he forced her hand on a few things.

"Laramie wants to tell you good-night."

Bristol's words broke into Coop's thoughts and he moved from leaning in the doorway to where his son lay, barely able to keep his eyes open. His son, who had captured his heart the moment he'd heard he existed.

"Daddy, you stay. Sleep in Mommy's bed, okay?"

He couldn't help but smile. His son was giving him

permission even though Bristol hadn't done so. Instead of agreeing with Laramie, Coop said, "Good night, Laramie."

"Stay, Daddy. Sleep in Mommy's bed. Okay?"

Evidently Laramie wasn't going to let him off that easy. Was this the same kid who'd pushed his nose in this morning when he discovered Coop was in Bristol's bed? The same little fellow who'd crawled over him to claim his spot beside his mother?

"He will stay, Laramie. Now you need to go to sleep."

He glanced over at Bristol. Was that her way of giving him an invitation? But then all she'd assured their son was that he would stay, not necessarily that he would stay in her bed. Did that mean she planned to make him sleep on the sofa?

He'd tried deciphering her mood today. Although she'd been friendly enough, it had seemed as if she had a lot on her mind. That was fine. He had a lot on his, too. But still, he couldn't help wondering if she regretted the intimacy they'd shared last night. She hadn't mentioned it and neither had he.

"Love you, Mommy."

"Love you back, Laramie. See you in the morning." And just like the night before, Bristol leaned over and kissed him on the cheek. However, unlike last night, before drifting off to sleep Laramie said, "Love you, Daddy."

Coop felt a tug at his heart and a tightness in his throat. It boggled his mind how a child could love so easily. "I love you back, Laramie."

He and Bristol watched as their son drifted off to sleep.

When they left Laramie's room, Coop told her they needed to talk.

Did he regret sleeping with her last night? The morning had started off well…at least she'd thought so, when he'd returned and surprised her with that beautiful plant. However, since then he'd seemed quiet. More than once she'd noticed him studying her like she was a puzzle he was trying to put together. Why?

She looked across the room at him. He was staring at the Christmas tree. What was he thinking? She'd invited him to spend Christmas with her and Laramie. Then what? When would he be leaving New York for his next mission?

"Ready to talk?"

She wondered why he was asking her when he was the one who initiated the meeting. "I'm ready if you are."

He nodded and sat in the chair across from her. He looked at her for a few moments then he said, "I spoke with my attorney today."

"Oh? Why did you feel the need to do that?"

He leaned back in the chair and the fabric of his jeans emphasized his masculine thighs. She wished she didn't notice such things, but she did.

"Laramie is my heir and I wanted to include him in all my important documents."

"I see."

"I also needed legal advice on my rights as his father."

Bristol raised a brow. "Your rights?"

"Yes."

She frowned. "I don't understand. I thought I made it clear that I would never deny you access to Laramie and you could spend as much time with him as you want."

"Yes, but what if you decide to marry one day and your husband feels differently?"

"I don't ever plan to marry, so you have nothing to worry about."

"You don't know that."

"I don't know what?"

"That you never plan to marry. Things happen. You might change your mind."

Her frown deepened. "That won't happen."

"You can't be sure," he countered.

"Yes, I can."

He shook his head. "No, you can't. And because you can't, my attorney suggested that I take steps to protect my rights as Laramie's father by filing for joint custody."

Coop watched her lean forward in her seat, at full attention. Her eyes widened. "Joint custody?"

"Yes."

"That's crazy. You're not in this country most of the time. How can you even think about joint custody?"

"How can I not think about it, Bristol? In a way, it will make things easier on you."

"How do you figure that?" she asked, glaring at him.

"You will know what times during the year he will be with me and when he will be with you. One thing I'd like is to swap holidays every year."

"Swap holidays?" She asked the question like what he was requesting was the craziest thing she'd ever heard.

"Yes. I told you about the ranch I inherited from my grandparents. I want him to spend the holidays with me there next year. That will free you up to do whatever you want to do."

"Free me up? To do. Whatever I want. To do?"

She had enunciated each phrase. He could tell from the sound of her voice that her anger was increasing. "Yes. I figure with me pitching in, you'll be able to paint more. While I'm away as a SEAL, I plan on hiring a full-time nanny who—"

"A full-time nanny? You've got to be kidding." She inhaled and exhaled a few times and he knew she was trying to get her anger under control. "What's going on, Coop? What are you trying to do?"

He had no problem giving her an answer. "I'm trying to give you a reason to make our marriage real."

* * *

Bristol's pulse jumped a few notches as she inhaled deeply. "Why?" she asked him. "Why should we make our marriage real?"

He shifted again in his seat and she wondered if he'd done it on purpose to distract her. Did he have any idea how his movements always increased her hormone level?

"The foremost reason is our son. I just cited complications that could arise if we aren't married. Knowing I have a child is a game changer for me. It was never my intent to father a child until later in life, and like I told you, I don't regret him, Bristol. I appreciate everything you went through to bring him into this world. And just so you know, if the situation had been different and I hadn't been held hostage, if I had gotten your letter, you would not have been alone. I would have come to you. I would have been there for you and for my child."

"But how would you have been there, Coop? You're a part of the military's special services. When you leave on one of your missions you have no idea when you'll get back."

"True, but I would have taken the time off. The entire nine months if I had to. I would have made sure I was there for you. You would not have gone through your pregnancy alone."

He didn't say anything for a few moments. "I believe in accepting my responsibilities, Bristol, but, just so you know, I would not have asked you to marry me just because you were having a baby. I would have done right by my child and by you, but I would not have suggested marriage between us unless I thought it would work."

At least he was honest, she thought. "So given that, why do you think it will work now? We don't even know each other."

"We know enough and over the past couple of days

we've found out more. We could be together for years and not know everything. Besides, I enjoy getting to know you."

He shifted again and her gaze followed the movement. "I know you are a good mother. As far as I'm concerned, you're the best. I can't think of anyone else I'd want to be the mother of my child. I watch you with Laramie and I know how much you love him and will always put him first. A part of me wants to envy that closeness, but I can't. I want to be a part of it, Bristol. You've given Laramie something special. A home."

His words reminded her of something her father had said. Even though her mother had robbed him of time with Bristol, in the end, he couldn't resent her mother when his heart was filled with gratitude to her for shaping Bristol into the woman she was. One who was loyal and independent. Not spoiled or selfish. Although her father had never said so, she knew he'd compared her to his other two kids. After living in their household for almost two years, she could plainly see that his wife's parenting skills had been vastly different from her mother's. Krista Lockett hadn't known how to tell her sons no.

"To me marriage is more than a piece of paper," he said, interrupting her thoughts. "I can't help but believe that, especially when I see my parents together and how they interact with each other. Even if there wasn't all that love, I believe there would still be trust, respect and friendship between them."

Unfortunately, Bristol thought, she'd never witnessed any such thing between a married couple. It had always been just her and her mother, and her mother had rarely dated. The few times she had, Bristol hadn't been introduced to the men. When she'd asked her mother about it, all she'd said was that until she met someone special, there was no reason to introduce her dates to her daughter. Evidently her mother never met anyone special. And as for her father's marriage to Krista, Bristol could honestly say she'd never felt any love in their relationship. They'd shared the same bedroom but that was about all. They'd lived separate lives.

Bristol drew in a deep breath as she thought about what Coop had said. Yes, there was trust and respect between them. She'd trusted him enough three years ago to invite him into her home and she still trusted him. She also respected him. In just two days he had made an impact on his son's life. And there was his love for his country and his willingness to put his life on the line to protect it. There was no doubt in her mind they could be friends as they got to know each other. Sex between them was good.

But what about the love?

That was something he hadn't mentioned. He didn't love her, whereas she'd loved him almost from the start. A part of her truly believed she'd fallen in love with him the moment she'd seen him in Paris. There was no way she would have agreed to an affair if she hadn't loved him.

But none of those feelings mattered because all the love, respect, trust and friendship in the world couldn't erase how she'd felt when she'd thought he'd died. That was a period in her life she couldn't relive. Somehow, she needed to make him understand that.

"What you said might be true, but there's a reason I can't marry you, Coop, and it's one I can't get beyond."

He lifted a brow. "And what reason is that?"

She met his gaze, held it and said, "You might die."

Eighteen

"You might die..."

Coop stared at her, recalling their conversation last night when she'd said the same thing. Why was she so hung up on the possibility of him dying?

Something else he recalled her saying last night was that three years ago she'd thought he'd died like the others. At the time, he'd wondered what others she was talking about. Now he had an idea who they were. Her mother, father and aunt. All the people she'd ever cared about and loved.

His heart pounded hard in his chest. Did that mean she cared deeply for him, that she loved him?

What if he was right? The thought that she could love him as much as he loved her was more than he could have hoped for. There was only one way to find out.

"I vividly remember having this conversation with you last night. Why are you so obsessed with the possibility of me dying, Bristol? Why are you so convinced I won't come back to you and Laramie?"

He watched her closely, saw how she went still, saw the stark look of fear come into her eyes. Their gazes locked for a minute longer and then she rubbed her hand down her face before meeting his eyes again. Then he saw the tears she was fighting to hold back.

"Talk to me, Bristol. Tell me," he said softly.

Bristol's mind shifted to that day when Dionne had arrived at her apartment and told her what she'd found out about Coop. How could she make him understand how she'd felt and why there was no way they could have a real marriage?

There was no way she could go through something like that again.

"When I thought you had died," she said, trying not to choke on the words, "I thought I was going to die, as well. It came as such a shock. I experienced pain like I'd never felt before. It was deeper than when I lost my mom, my dad and Aunt Dolly. And I felt so alone."

She fought back her tears to continue. "Then I suddenly felt my baby…our baby…move for the first time. It was like he was trying to reassure me that things would be all right. But the thought that I'd lost you was more than I could bear. Even when I told myself that I never had you, that all we'd had was a holiday affair and that I probably would not have seen you again anyway, it didn't matter. The thought of you dying like the others nearly destroyed me. It was only when I finally came to grips with the fact that I was having a baby…your baby…a baby that would always be a part of you, that I was able to move on with my life."

Coop stood and walked over to her, extending his hand out to her. She took it and he gently tugged her off the sofa and into his arms. It was only then that she realized she hadn't been able to hold back all her tears. A few were streaming down her face. How awful it was for him to see her like this, crying over a man who'd meant more to her than she'd meant to him. But when he tightened his arms around her, pulling her deeper into the warmth of his embrace, it didn't seem to matter.

"Knowing you cared that much means a lot to me, Bristol. Like I told you, you were never far from my thoughts when I was captured. Thoughts of you are what helped me survive."

"Why?" she asked, wanting to know why he'd thought of her.

"Because during those three days we were together, you made a lasting impression on me."

Like he'd made on her, she thought. However, he'd gone a step further in making her fall in love with him.

He pulled back and looked at her, forcing her to meet his gaze. "And as you can see, I am very much alive. No matter how much torture they inflicted on me, I refused to let those bastards break me—because of you."

She lifted a brow. "Because of me?"

"Yes. I convinced myself that I had to survive for you. That once I was rescued I had to get back to you."

Too bad he hadn't meant that, she thought.

"By the time I made it to Paris, you had left."

Bristol went still as she stared at him. "What did you say?" She was convinced she'd heard him wrong.

"After getting rescued I had to comply with military procedures and get both physical and psychiatric evaluations. That took about three months. Then I flew to Paris to see you. Your landlord said you'd moved back to the States and hadn't left a forwarding address."

Bristol's head began spinning. "You went to Paris looking for me?"

"Yes."

"But why?"

He gently cupped her chin in his hand. "I had to see you again and let you know those three days with you meant everything to me."

"They did?"

"Yes, and I just didn't know the depth of what they meant until I saw you again the other night. But it really hit me this morning when I saw you and Laramie in bed, sleeping. Then I knew for certain."

"What did you know?"

He dropped his hands from her face to wrap them around her waist. "That I had fallen in love with you."

His words made her head spin even more. "What did you just say?"

He smiled down at her. "I said I fell in love with you, during that time in Paris. I tried to convince myself it was about the sex, and maybe it was at first. But by the time I left your place I felt an attachment to you I've never felt to any other woman." A smile touched his lips. "Who knows? Maybe my body knew I'd left something behind with you that I've never left with another woman, my baby."

"Oh, Coop," she said, feeling more tears well in her eyes. "I love you, too, but I'm so afraid I might lose you again."

He pulled her into his arms and tightened his hold on her. "Shh, sweetheart, it's okay. In life there are no guarantees, we know that. That's why it's important to enjoy our time together. If nothing else, being close to death so many times has taught me not to sweat the small stuff and to appreciate life. Living it to the fullest is what I want to do with you and our son. Please don't deny me that."

He paused before adding, "You gave me the hope and the will to live before, which was how I survived that hellhole. And you will continue to give me hope whenever I go out on any covert operation, Bristol. Now I have two people to come back to. Both you and Laramie. The two people I love the most."

His words meant everything. They were what she'd needed to hear. But could she get past the thought of losing him again?

She tightened her arms around him knowing she had to get beyond those fears. For her sake, for his sake and for their son's. She had to be strong and believe there was a reason their lives had reunited after all this time.

She pulled back and went on tiptoe to place her lips to his. The moment their lips touched, intense heat consumed her. She felt it spreading to him. He tightened his hold on her.

His masculine scent invaded her nostrils as he took her mouth with an urgency that made her weak in the knees. When she shifted she felt the hardness of his erection pressing against the juncture of her thighs.

Bristol released pleasured moans with every stroke of his tongue. She needed this. She had to think positively and believe they'd been reunited for a reason. For a purpose. They would do what her parents didn't do and raise their child together.

He deepened the kiss and she felt it all the way to the bone.

Suddenly, he pulled back and looked deep into her eyes. "I need more."

She needed more, too. "Then take more. Give me more."

Nothing else needed to be said. He swept her off her feet and into his arms and carried her up the stairs.

"I love you, sweetheart," Coop said, after making love to Bristol again.

He pulled her into his arms and glanced over at the clock. They'd made love three times since coming upstairs and had gotten little sleep in between. If the other morning was anything to go by, he figured his son would be invading this room in a couple hours, and Coop and Bristol still needed to talk.

Coop knew she was about to drift off to sleep and he needed to get her attention. "Bristol?"

"Um?"

"Will you marry me?"

She didn't say anything at first, then she looked up at him. "I can't let fear have power over me, right?"

He nodded. "Right."

A smile touched the corners of her lips. "Then yes, Coop. I will marry you."

A huge smile touched his features. "How soon?"

She chuckled. "Can we get through the holidays first?"

He shrugged. "I guess we can."

She kissed him on the cheek. "Thanks for being so accommodating." Then she asked, "When do you have to leave for another mission?"

"End of January, and I want us married before I leave."

"That shouldn't be a problem," she said.

"As far as anyone knows, we are renewing our vows. There will only be a few who know the truth."

"Your teammates?"

"Yes, and my parents. I told them I loved you and if nothing else, they understand the love between two people and how strong it can be. They can't wait to meet you and Laramie."

She eyed him skeptically. "You sure about that?"

"I'm positive." And he was. Once the initial shock wore off, his parents had called him back. They were excited and happy to have a grandchild. Coop figured they must have decided Bristol couldn't be all bad since she hadn't shown up trying to claim any of his inheritance on behalf of her child after she'd gotten word he was dead.

"And since we won't have time for a real honeymoon until later, I thought it would be nice if I took you and Laramie to my ranch for a week or two before I head out. We can hire an interior decorator to spruce the place up while I'm gone."

"I'd love that. Would you prefer living there more so than here?" she asked him.

"Wherever you want to live is fine with me. We can even do both if you like."

"Yes, that might be best. But for some reason I think I'm going to like your ranch."

He hoped she did. He wanted Laramie to love Cooper's Bend as much as he had while growing up.

"You will check out of the hotel and move in here with us, right?"

He chuckled. "Yes, I'll move in here with you and Laramie and we will spend the holidays together."

"Good."

He pulled her closer. She was right, all was good, and as long as he had her in his life, everything would continue to be good.

Everything would be perfect.

Epilogue

"I now pronounce you husband and wife. Laramie Cooper, you may kiss your bride."

Coop pulled Bristol into his arms and all he could think about was that she was now truly his. Legally so. When he felt a pull on his pants he broke off the kiss to glance down at his son.

"I want to kiss Mommy, too, Daddy."

Everyone laughed when Coop lifted his son up to kiss Bristol, as well.

He then glanced around. It had been a small wedding at the church Bristol attended. All his teammates had arrived yesterday with their wives, including Bane and Crystal. Coop's parents had gushed all over their grandson and Laramie enjoyed being the center of their attention.

Ms. Charlotte and her four sons attended and Coop was glad to meet them. Bristol hadn't told him that all four worked for the New York Police Department. They assured Coop that whenever he was gone they would keep an eye on Bristol. It wouldn't be a problem since she lived next door to their mother and they routinely checked on her anyway.

Coop's mother had walked into Bristol's home that

morning and her gaze had immediately latched on to the huge painting over her fireplace. When she asked Bristol about it, Bristol confessed it was a painting she and her father had done together. It was then that she'd told his mother who her father was. Coop thought he was going to have to pick his mother up off the floor. His very sophisticated mother had gotten giddy at the thought that her future daughter-in-law was the daughter of the famous artist, Randall Lockett.

The reception would be held in the church's dining hall, and tomorrow the three of them would fly to his ranch in Laredo. He couldn't wait to introduce his wife and son to ranch life at Cooper's Bend.

They would take a honeymoon when he got back from his next mission. Ms. Charlotte had agreed to watch Laramie for a week while they went to Jamaica.

"Ready to go to the reception Ms. Charlotte set up for us?" Bristol asked him.

Holding their son in his arms, Coop smiled at her. "Yes, sweetheart, I am ready. When it comes to you, I will always be ready."

"Thanks for inviting me, Bristol."

She smiled up at Colin Kusac. They had exchanged phone numbers that night at the gallery when she'd reunited with Coop. When Mr. Kusac had called to check up on her a few days later, she'd learned that just as she'd suspected, he was the person carrying out her father's wishes to make sure she got flowers every year on her birthday. He had explained that Randall had asked that of him before he'd died and Mr. Kusac had promised he would do so.

He'd also told her that he'd promised her father he would check on her from time to time. He confided that he knew how she'd been while living in Paris; and that when she returned to the United States to have her baby, he'd known about that, as well. He'd seen that night at the gallery as an opportunity to talk to her himself. She had discovered that Mr. Kusac—Colin—was one of the wealthiest men in New York and had come from old money.

"Thanks for standing in for Dad and giving me away."

"Thanks for asking me. I was honored to do so. Randall would have been proud of you today."

"Thank you."

They talked for a while longer and then the wives of Coop's teammates came up to say hello. She liked all the wives—Crystal, who was married to Bane, Layla, who was married to Viper, and Teri, who had been married to Mac from the start. They assured Bristol that she wasn't the only one with fears—that was part of being a SEAL wife. They would be part of her support team and would be there whenever she needed them. They even invited her to visit them at their homes. Everyone was excited when Viper and Layla announced they would be having a baby come early summer. They exchanged numbers with her and she knew they were women she would get to know as friends.

No sooner had the women walked off than Margie appeared, all smiles. Bristol knew why.

"I can't believe your husband is connected to so much wealth. Who would have thought his parents would be *those* Coopers. And that he's their heir."

"Yes, who would have thought?" Bristol smiled, knowing how Margie's mind worked.

"You did good, choosing him over Steven."

Bristol decided not to say that Steven hadn't even been in the running. When Margie left, Coop appeared at Bristol's side. "A car will be picking us up in a few minutes for the airport."

His parents' jet would fly them to Texas, where they

would stay for a week on a short vacation with Laramie. After Coop had told Laramie about the horses, their son had been bubbling over with excitement to visit the ranch.

Not caring that they had an audience, Coop pulled his wife into his arms and whispered, “I love you.”

She smiled up at him. “And I love you, too.”

And she meant that from the bottom of her heart.

* * * * *

AN HONOURABLE SEDUCTION

BRENDA JACKSON

To the man who will forever be the love of my life,
Gerald Jackson, Sr.

To all of my readers who asked for Flipper's story.
This one is for you!

To the Brenda Jackson Book Club/Facebook fans.
Over 4,000 strong and after fourteen years,
you guys still rock!

Many waters cannot quench love;
rivers cannot sweep it away.
—*Song of Solomon* 8:7

Prologue

The Naval Amphibious Base
Coronado, San Diego, California

"What kind of trouble have you gotten into?"

David Holloway, known to his Navy SEAL teammates as Flipper, glanced at the four men surrounding him. They were like brothers to him. More than once they'd risked their lives for each other and they would continue to have each other's backs, on duty or off. That bond was what accounted for the concerned looks on their faces. He wondered how they'd known he'd been summoned to the admiral's office.

"Let's hope I'm not in any trouble, Mac," Flipper said, rubbing a hand down his face.

He had to admit he was wondering what was going on, just like they were. Usually, you were only summoned to a meeting with the admiral when you were getting reprimanded for some reason, and he never got into trouble. At least he *rarely* did. As the son of a retired SEALs commanding officer and the youngest of five brothers—all Navy SEALs—he knew better.

"Maybe there's an event on the base and he wants you to escort his daughter now that you're the single one among us," Coop said, grinning.

Flipper didn't grin back. They'd seen Georgianna Martin, the admiral's twenty-three-year-old daughter. She was beautiful, but they'd heard the horror stories from other teammates who'd been ordered to take her out on dates. According to them, those evenings had been the dates from hell. The young woman was spoiled rotten, selfish as sin and had an attitude that sucked. That's why Flipper didn't find Coop's comment at all amusing. He hoped that wasn't why the admiral wanted to see him.

It didn't surprise Flipper that it was Mac who'd asked if Flipper had gotten into trouble. Thurston McRoy—code name Mac—was older than the other four men on the team, who had all started their careers as SEALs around the same time. Mac had been a SEAL five years before the rest of them. Mac seemed to like to think he was the big brother looking out for them, almost like he figured they couldn't take care of themselves. He was forever giving them advice—even when they didn't ask for it.

In addition to Mac and Flipper, their SEAL team included Brisbane Westmoreland, code name Bane; Gavin Blake, whose code name was Viper; and Laramie Cooper, whose code name was Coop.

Flipper checked his watch. "Since I have a couple of hours to spare before meeting with the admiral, let's grab something to eat," he suggested.

"Sounds good to me," Bane said.

Less than an hour later, Flipper and his four teammates shared burgers, fries and milkshakes at one of the most popular eating places on base. They decided to sit outside at one of the café tables in the front instead of inside where it was crowded since it was such a beautiful May day.

No one brought up his meeting with the admiral again or the notion of him taking the admiral's daughter on a date. He was glad. Instead, the guys had more important things to talk about, namely their families.

Bane's wife, Crystal, had given birth to triplets last year and he had new photos to share, so they passed Bane's cell phone around.

Viper's wife, Layla, was expecting with only a few months to go before Gavin Blake IV would be born. Viper was excited about becoming a father, of course.

Like Bane, Mac had plenty of photos to share; he was married and the father of four.

And Coop had a two-year-old son he hadn't known about until he'd run into his old girlfriend about six months ago. They'd reconnected, gotten married and were now a happy family.

Earlier in the week, the teammates had gotten word from their commanding officer that next week was the start of a four-month leave. For Flipper, that meant heading home to Dallas and he couldn't wait. His mother had a birthday coming up and he was glad he would be home to celebrate.

"I don't care what plans you all are making for your leave, just as long as you remember my mom's birthday celebration. I understand you not showing up, Viper, with a baby on the way. The rest of you guys, no excuses."

"We hear you," Bane said, grinning. "And we will be there."

When Viper ordered another hamburger, everyone teased him about being the one to eat for two instead of his wife. And then everyone talked about what they planned to do with their four months off.

It was two hours later when Flipper walked into the admiral's office. He was surprised to find Commanding Officer Shields there as well. Flipper saluted both men.

"At ease. Please have a seat, Lieutenant Holloway."

"Thank you, sir," he said, sitting down. He was used to being under his commanding officer's intense scrutiny, but there was something in the sharp green eyes of Admiral Norris Martin that was making him feel uncomfortable.

"You come highly recommended by your commanding officer here, Lieutenant Holloway. And the reason I asked to meet with you is that we need you. Your country needs you."

Flipper was happy to step up. He was a Navy SEAL, and the reason he'd enlisted, like his father and brothers, was to protect his country. "And what am I needed to do, sir?" he asked.

"Our investigators have provided intelligence and a preliminary report that says acts of espionage are happening in Key West. Someone is trading valuable government secrets to China."

Flipper didn't respond immediately.

The one thing he hated was a traitor, but he'd discovered that for the right price, a number of American citizens would perform acts of treason. He understood that. However, what he didn't understand was why he'd been singled out for this meeting. He was part of a SEAL team. He didn't work in naval intelligence.

Confusion must have shown on his face because Admiral Martin continued, “The report was given to me, but I don’t believe it.”

Flipper raised a brow. “You don’t believe a report that classified documents are being traded in Key West, sir?”

“Oh, I believe all that, but what I refuse to believe is that this suspect is guilty of anything.”

“Is there a reason why, sir?”

“Here is the information,” said Commanding Officer Shields, speaking for the first time as he handed Flipper a folder.

Flipper opened it to find a picture of a very beautiful woman. She looked to be around twenty-four, with dark, sultry eyes and full, shapely lips. Then there was her mass of copper-brown spiral curls that flowed to her shoulders, crowning a cocoa-colored face. A pair of dangling gold earrings hung from her ears and a golden pendant necklace hung around her neck.

He knew he was spending too much time studying her features, but it couldn’t be helped. The woman was strikingly beautiful.

Reluctantly he moved his gaze away from her face to check out the background of the photo. From the tropical vegetation captured by the photographer, she seemed to be on an island somewhere. She stood near a body of water that showed in the corner of the eight-by-ten photo. Scribbled across the bottom were the words:

Miss you, Godpop 1

Love, Swan

Swan? It was an unusual name, but it fit.

He moved to the next document in the file. Attached to it was a small family photo that showed a tall Caucasian man with sandy-brown hair and brown eyes standing beside a beautiful woman who closely resembled Swan. Her mother. In front of the couple was a beautiful little girl who looked to be around eight.

Flipper studied the child's face and knew that child had grown up to be the gorgeous woman in the first photo. The shape of her face was the same, as were her eyes. Even as a child, she'd had long curly hair.

The family photo was clipped to a profile of the young woman. As he'd guessed, she was twenty-four. Her name was Swan Jamison. She was an American, born in Key West. Presently, she owned a jewelry store on the island. That was all the information the document provided.

Flipper lifted his gaze to find his commanding officer and the admiral staring at him. "I assume this is the person naval intelligence believes is the traitor."

"Yes," Admiral Martin said. "She's my goddaughter. I am Godpop 1."

"She's my goddaughter as well," added Commanding Officer Shields. "I am Godpop 2."

Flipper's gaze moved from one man to the other. "I see, sirs."

Admiral Martin nodded. "Her father was part of our SEAL team and our best friend. His name was Andrew Jamison."

Flipper had heard that Commanding Officer Shields and Admiral Martin were part of the same SEAL team a number of years ago.

"Andrew was the best. He lost his life saving ours," said Commanding Officer Shields. "He didn't die immediately, and before he died, he made us promise to look after his wife, Leigh, and his daughter, Swan." The man paused and then said, "Over twenty-eight years ago, when we were taking some R & R in Jamaica, Andrew met Leigh, who was a Jamaican model. They married a year later, and he moved her to Key West, where our team was stationed. After Andrew was killed, Leigh returned to Jamaica. When Swan graduated from high school, she returned to the Keys and moved into her parents' home."

"How old was she when her father was killed?" Flipper asked.

"She was fifteen," Admiral Martin said. "Swan was close to her dad. Leigh was so broken up over Andrew's death that she didn't want to live in the States without him, which was why she returned to Jamaica. She passed away two years ago."

Flipper's commanding officer then took up the tale. "Leigh sent for us before she died of stomach cancer, asking us to look out for Swan after she was gone. We would have done that anyway, since we always kept in touch with both Leigh and Swan. In fact, Swan rotated summers with us and our families even after Leigh returned to Jamaica. We took our roles as godfathers seriously. We were even there when Swan graduated from high school and college."

"Did Swan have any American grandparents?" Flipper asked.

He saw both men's lips tighten into frowns. "Yes. However, her paternal grandparents didn't approve of their son's marriage to Leigh," said Commanding Officer Shields.

"So they never accepted their granddaughter." It was more of a statement than a question.

"No, they never did," Admiral Martin confirmed. As if it was a topic he'd rather change, the man added, "We've been given some time to find out the truth, but not much. Luckily, Swan's Godpop 3 has a high-level position at naval intelligence. Otherwise, we wouldn't know about the investigation. We have thirty days to prove Swan is not a traitor and identify the person who is. That's where we need your help. Instead of releasing you to go home as we're doing for the other members of your team, we are assigning you to a special mission, Lieutenant Holloway. You are being sent to Key West."

One

Key West, Florida

Swan Jamison was beside herself with excitement as she opened the huge box on her desk. Although it contained only her jewelry-making supplies, the package served as affirmation that while rebuilding was still taking place in certain areas, the majority of the island had recovered from the hurricane that had hit eight months ago.

"Anything for me?" Rafe asked, sticking his head through the office door.

Her shop was in a very trendy area so she could capitalize on the tourists visiting the island. To help with high operating costs, she leased out one of the large rooms in the back. Rafe was her tenant, who'd converted the back room into a tattoo shop. On some days, he got more customers than she did.

"Nothing for you, Rafe, just supplies for me." She

checked her watch. “You’re early today.” Usually he didn’t open up until noon.

“I have a special appointment at ten thirty and I need to ready my ink.” And then he was gone. Rafe didn’t say a whole lot except to his customers.

The door chime alerted her that *she* had a customer. Jamila, who worked part-time and usually only in the mornings, had taken time off for a day of beauty—hair, nails, pedicure, bikini wax, the works. Her boyfriend worked on a cruise ship that was due in port tomorrow. Swan was happy for Jamila and happy for herself as well. The cruise ships always brought in tourists who wanted to purchase authentic handmade jewelry.

She walked out of her office as a man perused her jewelry display case near the door. That was good. While he checked out her jewelry, she would check him out.

He had a nice profile. Tall, broad shoulders that looked good in a T-shirt and a pair of muscular thighs that fit well in his jeans. He had diamond-blond hair that was neatly trimmed and his hands were the right size for his body.

There was something about the way he stood, straight and tall, that all but spelled out *military man*. And the way his legs were braced apart, as if he had to maintain his balance even on land, spelled out *navy*.

Too bad. She didn’t do military men. In all honesty, lately she hadn’t done men at all. Too busy.

And then there was the issue of Candy’s divorce. Swan knew she shouldn’t let what had happened to her best friend darken her own view, but Swan was known to claim whatever excuse suited her and that one did at the moment.

And speaking of the moment, she had looked her

fill. She needed to make her first sale of the day. "May I help you?"

He turned and looked at her, and every cell in her body jolted to attention.

Wow! She'd seen blue eyes before, but his were a shade she'd never seen. They were laser blue; the intense sharpness of the pupils captured her within their scope. And his features… Lordy! The man had such gorgeous bone structure! There was no way a woman had ever passed by him and not taken a second look. Even a third, while wiping away drool.

"Yes, you can help me."

And why did he have to sound so good, too? The sound of his voice—a deep, husky tone—made her throat go dry.

"All right," she said, walking over to him. She knew she had to get a grip. Her store had been closed for two months due to the hurricane, and now that the tourists were returning, she needed to catch up on sales.

"And how can I help you?" She didn't miss the way he was looking at her. She saw interest in his eyes. There was nothing wrong with that. She took pride in her appearance because she had been raised to do so. Leigh Rutledge Jamison, who'd been a Jamaican model, had taught her daughter that your appearance was everything.

Pain settled in Swan's heart. She missed her mom so much.

"I'm looking for a gift for someone."

Swan nodded as she came to stand beside him. Not only did he look good and sound good, but he smelled good as well. She glanced down at his hand and didn't see a wedding ring. He was probably buying a gift for his girlfriend or soon-to-be fiancée.

"What do you have in mind?"

"What do you suggest?" he asked her.

"Well, it depends," she said, looking into those gorgeous eyes.

"On what?"

"What the person likes. I make jewelry from stones, but as you can see, there are a number of them, in various shades, colors and styles."

He smiled and Swan felt a tingling in the pit of her stomach when a dimple appeared in one of his cheeks. "I honestly don't know what she likes. Her tastes change from year to year. It's hard to keep up."

Swan nodded. "Oh. Sounds like the two of you have known each other for a while."

His smile widened even more. "We have. I would have to say I've known Mom all my life."

"Your mom?"

"Yes. Her birthday is next month. I was passing by your shop and thought I would drop in to see what you had."

A racing heart for starters, Swan thought. So the woman he was thinking about buying jewelry for was his mother. "Well, I'm glad you came in. Let me show you what I have."

"All right. There looks to be a lot of nice pieces."

She appreciated the compliment. "Thanks. I made most of them myself."

"Really? Which ones?"

She led him to the area set aside for Swan Exclusives. "These. Most of the stones come from India, Argentina and Africa."

He leaned in to look. "You did an excellent job."

Whoever said flattery, especially coming from a

good-looking man, would get you anywhere knew just what they were talking about. "Thank you."

"I'm David, by the way. David Holloway." He offered her his hand.

She took it and tried to ignore the sensations that suddenly flowed through her from the contact. "Nice to meet you, David." She quickly released his hand. "And I'm Swan."

"The name of the shop."

"Yes."

"It's a unique name."

"Yes, my parents thought so. On their first date, my father flew Mom from Jamaica to New York to see *Swan Lake*."

"Some date."

"Yes, he was trying to impress her."

"I take it he did."

Swan chuckled. "Yes, because he actually flew them there. He had his pilot's license."

"Now I'm impressed."

She didn't like bragging about her father but there were times when she just couldn't help it. "He served in the air force—that's where he learned to fly. And then he went into the navy after deciding he wanted to be a SEAL. That's when he met Mom, while he was a SEAL. She hadn't known about his stint in the air force until the night he rented a plane to fly them to New York."

Why was she telling him all this? Usually she wasn't chatty. "What about this one?" she asked as they moved to another glass case. "I call this piece *Enchantment*."

"Why?"

"Look at it," she suggested, leaning closer to the glass. He followed suit. "This is one of my favorite pieces because the teardrop gemstone necklace is pretty similar to my very first piece." No need to tell him that she'd made that one for her own mother.

"It is beautiful."

Something in his tone made her glance over at him, and she found him staring at her and not at the jewelry in the case. His eyes held her captive and their gazes met for a minute too long before she broke eye contact with him.

She swallowed. "So are you interested...in this piece?" She wanted to ignore the way her stomach seemed to be filled with all kinds of sensations, but she could not.

"I'm interested in a lot of pieces, Swan, but I'll start with this one."

Swan Jamison was even more beautiful than the photograph he'd seen last week.

The photographer hadn't fully captured the rich creaminess of her skin. And the shade of red lipstick she wore today seemed to make her lips plumper, more well-defined. Luscious.

He had read the dossier on her. He knew his commanding officer and Admiral Martin were operating based on a personal connection with her. He was not. If Miss Jamison was guilty of any wrongdoing, he would find out. And if she wasn't the one handing out classified data to China, then he would discover who was.

"So you want to buy this particular piece?"

Her question brought his thoughts back to the present. "Yes."

"Wonderful. I think your mother will like it."

"I'm sure she will. What about earrings?"

She lifted a brow. "Earrings?"

"Yes. Do earrings come with the necklace?"

"No, but I can make you some."

He'd been hoping she'd say that. "When?"

"It will take me a couple of days. The cruise ship docks tomorrow, so the shop will be busy. Two days from now will work for me, unless you need them sooner."

"No, I can wait. My mother's birthday is next month."

He would have an excuse to return to her shop.

Flipper watched her open the case and pull out the necklace. He knew his mother was going to love it.

"If you don't mind, please complete this ticket," she said. "And I will need full payment for the earrings before I make them."

"That's no problem," he said, taking the document from her.

After he completed the form, he handed it back to her. She glanced at it. "So you're from Texas?"

"Yes. Dallas. Ever been there?"

"Yes, once. I thought it was a nice city."

"It is. I was born and raised there."

"And what brought you to Key West?" she asked him.

"Work, at least for the next thirty days." That wasn't a total lie.

"Hurricane relief?"

"Something like that."

"You're military?"

"At one point but not now." He would let her think he was no longer military.

"I knew immediately."

He lifted a brow. "How?"

She shrugged. “Military men are easily recognized, at least by me.”

“Because your dad is military?”

“He *was* military. Dad died years ago in the line of duty.”

“I’m sorry.” Flipper was always sorry whenever a fellow soldier lost their life.

“Thank you. Your package will be ready in two days, David. Your mobile number is on the form you completed. If I get to it sooner, I will call you.”

“Two days is fine. I’ll be back.”

“’Bye, David.”

“’Bye, Swan.” He then turned and walked out of the shop.

As much as he wanted to invite her out to lunch today, he knew he couldn’t rush things. He needed to earn her trust, even though he had less than thirty days to prove her innocence and determine who had no qualms about making her look guilty.

Swan was cheerful that night as she let herself into her home. Sales today had been better than normal. A tour group from New York had converged on the island and they’d come to spend money. She’d been happy to oblige.

Opening a jewelry shop had been a risky business move, but one that had paid off. She’d earned a degree in business management from the University of Miami and returned to the island after college to work as a manager at one of the elite hotels on the island. She’d enjoyed her job but had felt something was missing in her life. She hadn’t been using her jewelry-making talent.

She’d promised her mother on her deathbed that she would find a way to use that talent.

Even after taking care of all her mother's funeral expenses, there had been more than enough money left to buy a little storefront. It had been a good investment because of its location. Some days were busier than others. This had been one of those busy days.

Now she was ready to wind down for the evening. She pulled her hair back in a ponytail and eased her feet into her favorite flats before heading to the kitchen for a glass of wine. As she did so, she couldn't help but think about her first customer of the day.

David Holloway.

He was a cutie, she had to give him that. And the memory of those eyes had stayed with her most of the day.

David Holloway had come into her shop to buy a birthday gift for his mother. How sweet. His mother was lucky. A lot of men didn't even remember their mothers' birthdays. She'd dated quite a few of those men and never developed lasting relationships with any of them. She figured if a man didn't treat his mother right, then there was no hope for a girlfriend.

As she opened the French doors to step out on the patio, she again remembered those blue eyes and how she'd felt whenever she'd looked into them. No man's eyes had ever made her feel that way before.

The effect was unsettling.

Okay, so what was wrong with her? Cutie or no cutie, she normally didn't get caught up over a man. She dated when it suited her, but she would admit that no one had suited her lately. At least not since her best friend, Candy, had left Key West to go live in Boston. Candy had refused to live on the island with her ex and his new wife—the one he'd married before the ink had even dried on the divorce papers.

Refusing to dwell on how shabbily Donald Knoll had treated Candy, Swan looked out at the water. It was calm tonight. When she had evacuated due to the hurricane, she hadn't known what to expect when she returned. Between her home and her shop, there had been some damage, but not as much as she'd feared.

The thought of losing her home had been devastating. This was where her father had brought her mom after they'd married. This home held so many childhood memories—of her father leaving on his missions as a Navy SEAL, of how happy she and her mother would be whenever he returned.

But then he hadn't returned.

Swan felt a knot in her throat as she recalled that day. She'd never seen that sparkle in her mother's eyes again. Swan recalled her mother telling her once that when you met a man who could put that sparkle in your eyes, then you knew he was a keeper.

Swan often wondered if she would ever find her keeper.

She had plenty of time. Besides, she needed to rethink her opinion about men first. If what Don had done to Candy wasn't enough to keep her single, all Swan had to do was remember William Connors, the businessman she had met while working at the hotel.

At the time, he had convinced her he was a bachelor without a care in the world but claimed that he wanted to make her Mrs. William Connors one day.

For some reason, Candy hadn't trusted him. She had a friend who worked for a private investigator check him out. Swan had been devastated when the investigation revealed there was already a Mrs. William Connors, along with three Connors children.

William had been playing her. He had been a lesson well learned. Her only regret was that she'd shared her body with him. She'd been young, naive and impressionable. He had been her first and he should not have been.

She was not naive now and she went into relationships with caution and even a little mistrust. Her mother once told her that being mistrustful wasn't a good thing. Swan knew she would have to learn how to trust again.

She took another sip of wine. Unfortunately, she hadn't gotten there yet.

"So how did things go, Flipper?"

"Have you met her yet?"

"Does she have a traitorous face or just a pretty one?"

"Do you think you'll be able to prove she's innocent?"

Flipper heard the questions coming at him nearly all at once. While unpacking, he had placed his mobile call on speaker to engage in a five-way conversation with his SEAL teammates.

"I think things went rather well, Mac. And yes, I met Swan Jamison today, Viper. I went into her jewelry store to purchase Mom a birthday gift."

Flipper eased open the dresser drawers to place his T-shirts inside. "She doesn't have a traitorous face or just a pretty one, Coop. The woman is simply gorgeous. Beautiful beyond belief. And yes, I hope to prove she's innocent, Bane, because Commanding Officer Shields and Admiral Martin truly believe she is."

"What do you believe?" Viper asked.

Flipper leaned against the dresser for a minute and thought about Viper's question. "Too early to tell."

"Did you ask her out on a date?" Coop wanted to know. They could hear Coop's two-year-old son, Laramie, chattering in the background.

"No, not yet." Flipper's attraction to her had been instant. He'd felt it the moment he looked into her face. Discussing her now wasn't helping matters. All it did was force him to recall what a beautiful woman she was—a woman he would have to spend time with in order to discover the truth.

"Then how do you plan to see her again if you don't ask her out?" Mac wanted to know, interrupting Flipper's thoughts.

"I ordered a pair of earrings to go with the necklace I bought for Mom. She has to make the earrings and I'll make my move when I pick up my purchases in two days."

"And if she turns you down?" Viper asked.

"Not an option. I now have less than thirty days to get this all straightened out."

"We should be there with you, watching your back," Bane said.

"No, you guys are just where you need to be, which is home with your families. I've got this."

"Well, some of our families don't appreciate us being home," Mac grumbled.

Flipper rolled his eyes. They'd all heard the complaints from Mac before. After every extended mission, their teammate went home to an adjustment period, where he would have to get to know his wife all over again and reclaim his position as head of the house. Sometimes the adjustment didn't go over well. Mac had a strong personality and so did Mac's wife, Teri. "Do we have to send both you and Teri into the time-out corners?"

"Hell, I didn't do anything," Mac exclaimed.

Flipper chuckled. "Yeah, right. You better get your act together, Mac. No other woman is going to put up with your BS."

"Whatever. So what did you notice about the place today?"

Mac was changing the subject and Flipper decided to let him. "Everything matched the architectural report I was given. Even with the repairs due to the hurricane, there were no major changes. Front door. Back door. High windows. Glass storefront. No video cameras outside. There are several rooms in back. One is being used as a tattoo parlor. I didn't see the person who runs it. I think I'll go out tonight and do a little more investigating," he said, sliding into a black T-shirt.

"Be careful, Flipper," Viper said. "Although you might not have seen any video cameras, that doesn't mean there aren't any."

"I know. That's why I'm wearing my Pilf gear."

Everybody knew how much Flipper liked digital technology. In addition to all the futuristic developments the military used, Flipper had created a few of his own high-tech gadgets behind the scenes. Some had been so impressive the federal government had patented them as Pilf gear to be used by the military. Pilf was the name Flip spelled backward. On more than one occasion, Flipper had been offered a position with the Department of Defense's Research and Development Department and had turned down each offer, saying he loved being a Navy SEAL more.

"We don't give a damn if you plan to parade around naked tonight, Flipper. Be careful."

He knew Mac was in his big-brother mode. "Okay, Mac. I hear you and I will be careful."

"Call to check in when you get back to the hotel tonight," Bane said.

"It will be late and I wouldn't want to wake up any babies, kids or a pregnant woman. I'll text everyone."

A short while later, wearing undetectable military gear under his clothing, Flipper left his hotel using the stairs.

Two

Two days later, Swan didn't leave the shop for lunch. Instead she accepted Jamila's offer to bring her something back from the sandwich shop on the corner. Although she'd tried convincing herself her decision to hang around had nothing to do with the fact that David Holloway would be returning today to pick up his items, she knew it did.

And her anticipation was so bad that every time the door chimed, her heartbeat would kick up a notch, only to slow back down when someone other than him walked in. She checked her watch. The shop would be closing in an hour. What if he didn't make it before closing time? What if…?

The door chimed, and her heart nearly stopped when David Holloway walked in.

She'd told herself the man hadn't *really* looked as good as she remembered from that first day, but now she saw that he did. In fact, today he looked even better than she remembered. Maybe it had something to do with the unshaven look. Men with a day-old beard had sex appeal. But it could also be his tan, which indicated he'd probably spent the last couple of days lying in the sun.

If he'd been at the beach, there was a good chance he hadn't been there alone. But didn't he say he was in the Keys working?

Why did she care?

She quickly dismissed all those questions from her mind as she continued to watch him walk toward her in a strut that had blood rushing through her veins. His blond hair and blue eyes seemed brighter against his tanned skin. He was deliciousness with a capital *D*.

But then that capital *D* could also stand for *dangerous* if she wasn't careful. Or it could stand for *delusional* if she didn't get control of her senses. Right now, she would play it safe and claim the capital *D* stood for *David*. She couldn't allow herself to think any other way for now, no matter how tempting.

She smiled. "Hello, David."

"Hi, Swan."

"Your tan looks nice."

He chuckled. "So does yours."

She grinned. "Yes, but mine's permanent."

"I know and I like it."

She didn't say anything to that because she understood what he was implying. He was letting her know he had no problem with interracial dating. She didn't have a problem with it either. Neither had her father, although his family had had conniptions about his marriage to Swan's mother. She pushed that thought to the back of her mind, refusing to dwell on an extended family that had never accepted her or her mother.

She reached behind the counter and retrieved a box. "I hope you like the way the earrings came out." She opened it to show him the final earrings.

"Wow!" He ran his finger over the stone that came closest to matching the color of his eyes. "You're very gifted."

"Thank you, and I believe your mother will love them."

"I'm sure she will. I think I've outdone my brothers this time."

She closed the box and placed it, along with the one containing the necklace, into a shopping bag. "You have brothers?"

"Yes, four of them. I'm the youngest."

"My goodness. Any sisters?"

"Not a one. Three of my four brothers are married, so I have sisters-in-law. They are the best."

"And the fourth brother is still single?"

"He's divorced but has a beautiful little girl. And she's my parents' only granddaughter. They have six grandsons."

"Sounds like a nice family. Is your father still alive?"

"Yes, Dad is still alive. He and Mom own a medical supply store."

She nodded as she offered him the bag. "Here you are, David. Thanks again for your business."

He accepted the bag. "Thanks. Now that this is taken care of, there's something I want to ask you, Swan."

She lifted a brow. "What?"

"Would you go out to dinner with me tonight?"

Normally Flipper was good at reading people, but he was having a hard time reading Swan. He definitely needed to remedy that. Although both Commanding Officer Shields and Admiral Martin were convinced of her innocence, the jury was still out for him. He had to remain impartial and deal with the facts, not speculations.

For two nights, he'd searched the area around her shop. Getting inside without triggering her alarm hadn't been easy, but he'd done it. Once he'd picked up the location of the interior security cameras, it was a small matter to make sure he stayed out of their range and within a certain perimeter until he could deactivate them and do what he needed to.

"Go to dinner with you?"

"Yes."

She was apparently mulling over his invitation in her mind and he would give her time to do that. He had no problems studying her while he waited for her answer. Today she looked even prettier than the other day. He figured it had to be the lighting in this place.

"Yes, David. I'll go to dinner with you. You name the restaurant and I'll meet you there."

She wasn't going to give him her address and he had no problem with her being cautious. Little did she know he already knew where she lived and had visited yesterday while she'd been here at her shop. She had a beautiful home on the ocean. Inside it was as neat as a pin with no clutter. She'd even made up her bed before leaving.

"I noticed a restaurant off the pier. Summer Moon. I've heard only good things about it since I've been here." And he knew the place was within walking distance from her home.

"Everything you've heard is true. Summer Moon is fabulous and one of my favorite eating places. I'd love to join you there. What time?"

"What about seven? Will that be a good time for

you?" He figured since it didn't get dark until close to nine, he wouldn't have to worry about her walking to the restaurant in the dark. After dinner, he would walk her home or put her in a cab regardless of the fact that she lived only a few blocks away.

"Seven is perfect."

"Good. I'll see you then."

Swan watched him walk out of the shop.

David had the kind of tush that made a woman want to squeeze it…after doing all kinds of other things with it.

She jumped when fingers snapped in her face. Frowning, she looked at Jamila. "What did you do that for?"

"To keep you from having an orgasm in the middle of your shop."

Swan rolled her eyes. Jamila, the attractive twenty-two-year-old green-eyed blonde, evidently thought reaching a climactic state was that easy. "It would take more than ogling a man for that to happen, Jamila."

"I don't know. Your eyes were about to pop out of their sockets and your breathing sounded funny."

"You're imagining things."

"Denial can be good for the soul, I guess. So who is he?"

Swan and Jamila had more than an employer-and-employee relationship. Their friendship had started when Jamila first moved to the island a couple of years ago and patronized Swan's. It didn't take long to discover that Jamila liked nice things and decided Swan's was one of her favorite places to shop. Last year, Jamila had been looking for work after she lost her job as a day cruise ship captain.

As far as Swan was concerned, it hadn't been Jamila's fault when an intoxicated customer had tried coming on to her and she'd kicked him in the balls. Surgery had to be performed and the man had sued the ship company. They'd settled out of court but not before firing Jamila for all the trouble she'd caused.

Jamila had gotten an attorney herself so she could not only sue her former employer for an unfair firing but also sue the intoxicated customer. To avoid negative publicity, her former employer wanted to settle out of court with her as well. The intoxicated customer was also trying to settle since the woman he'd been with on the ship hadn't been his wife. If things worked out in Jamila's favor, she wouldn't need a job at Swan's much longer.

"He is a customer who came into the shop a couple of days ago to buy a gift for his mother."

"His mother and not his wife?"

"He says his mother."

Jamila snorted. "Men lie all the time."

How well she knew, Swan thought. Then she wondered why Jamila was men-bashing today. This wasn't the first comment of that type she'd made since arriving to work. Her boyfriend had come to town a couple of days ago with the cruise ship, right? So what was going on?

Swan decided not to ask. She didn't want to hear another sad story about a man that would ruin her date tonight with David. It was a date she was definitely looking forward to. She figured going out to dinner with him wouldn't be risky as long as she kept things in perspective.

She knew what could happen if she let her guard down when it came to a man.

* * *

Flipper deliberately arrived at Summer Moon early so he could see when Swan arrived. His stomach felt floaty the moment she turned the corner from the street where she lived.

Be still, my...everything.

She was wearing a printed sundress and a pair of high-heeled sandals, but what caught his attention—and was still holding it tight—were her long shapely legs that seemed to go on forever. He would love to see where they stopped under that dress. He forced that thought to the back of his mind.

But the closer she got, the more that thought wiggled back to the forefront. He shouldn't let it. He was on assignment and she was the subject of an investigation. He shouldn't see her as temptation. Letting his guard down around her could be a dangerous and costly mistake. He had to keep his head screwed on straight, no matter how innocent she seemed and how beautiful she was, and she was definitely one gorgeous woman.

Men, even some with female companions, were giving Swan second looks, and Flipper tried to downplay his anger. He had no right to be upset about other men checking her out when he was checking her out himself. The best thing to do to control his crazy reaction was to stop looking at her, so he glanced down at his bottle of beer and thought about the reports he'd finished reading a short while ago on her employee and her tenant.

Jamila Fairchild had worked for Swan for a year. He knew all about her former job as a captain of a day cruise ship, why she'd gotten fired and her litigation against not only her former employer but also the man who'd caused the ruckus in the first place. Naval intelligence hadn't left any stone unturned in Ms. Fairchild's report and she'd come up clean. Flipper would verify that she was.

Then there was Rafe Duggers, the tattoo artist. Although his parlor was located inside Swan's shop, there was a back door for his customers to use without entering through the jewelry shop. Flipper hadn't gotten a chance to look around the tattoo parlor and he intended to do another visit in a few days. Rafe was too squeaky-clean to be true.

No wonder naval intelligence was trying to point the finger at Swan. After all, it was her shop and they had somehow traced activity as originating there. But how? When? He hadn't found anything.

He had searched Swan's office, the small kitchen in the back, the bathrooms and another room that she used as a workshop where she made her jewelry. He'd come up with nothing, even after checking out her computer. So what were the grounds for accusing her?

Flipper's mind flicked back to Swan and he stood when the waiter escorted her to his table. "Hello, Swan. You look nice."

"Thanks and so do you. I was trying to be early and you still beat me here," she said, sitting down across from him.

"I was thirsty," he said, sitting back down and indicating the beer. Now that she was here and sitting directly across from him, he was more than thirsty. If he wasn't careful, he could have a full-fledged attack of desire. She had a pair of beautiful shoulders and her skin appeared soft and smooth to the touch.

Then his mind drifted to wanting her and he quickly snatched it back. "You walked here. Does that mean you live close by?" he asked, deciding it was best to keep the conversation moving.

"Yes, not too far," she said. He knew she was deliberately being evasive.

The waiter handed him another beer and gave them both menus. "What would like to drink, miss?" the waiter asked her.

"A glass of Moscato please."

When the waiter left, she glanced over at Flipper before picking up her menu. "You're not working so hard that you're not enjoying the Keys, are you?"

"I'm doing a bit of both. I admit the ocean is beautiful tonight."

She smiled. "I think it's beautiful every night."

He nodded as he took another sip of his beer, straight from the bottle. "So are you a native or a transplant?"

"A native. I was born and raised right here on the island in the same house I live in now. My mother never made it to the hospital before I was born."

He raised a brow. "She didn't?"

"No. Mom came from a part of Jamaica where the belief was that when it comes to delivering a baby, a midwife is better than a medical doctor. My father promised to find her a midwife here. Otherwise she would have insisted that I be born in Jamaica and he didn't want that. He wanted me born in America."

"So he was able to find a midwife?"

"Yes, but I was born a few weeks early and the midwife wasn't here."

"So who delivered you?"

"My dad, with the help of three of his closest military friends. They were stationed at the base here and were visiting, watching a football game at the time. Needless to say, over the years I've gotten four different versions of what happened that night. My mother didn't remember a thing other than it took four men to deliver me. Although Godpop 1 claims my father passed out trying to cut the umbilical cord."

Flipper laughed. He then asked, "Godpop 1?"

"Yes, my father's three closest friends, the ones who assisted that night, became my godfathers. That's how I distinguish them. Godpop 1, Godpop 2 and Godpop 3."

Flipper nodded. No wonder the three men felt such strong ties to her. "You're lucky to have three godfathers. I don't have a one."

"Yes, I'm lucky," she said, after the waiter set the glass of wine in front of her. "They were my and Mom's rocks after we lost Dad, especially when my grandparents showed up at the funeral trying to cause problems."

Then, as if she realized she might have shared too much, she asked, "So what do you plan to order?"

Swan thought David had picked the right place for them to have dinner. When he asked for recommendations on what to order, she suggested Summer Moon's crab cakes and, as usual, they were delicious. The mango salad was superb, and after dinner they enjoyed listening to the live band.

When the band played their last song, she glanced over at David to discover him staring at her. The intensity in his gaze nearly scorched her and she took a sip of her wine. "Thanks for dinner, David."

"Thank you for accepting my invitation. The place is about to close. Are you ready to go?" he asked her.

"Yes." Because she knew he would suggest that he walk her home, she added, "If you still have a little bit of energy, I'd like to treat you to something."

He lifted a brow. "What?"

"A laser show that officially kicks off the summer season. It's a short walk from here." Since it was in the opposite direction from where she lived, she would have no problem catching a cab back later—alone.

He smiled as he beckoned for the waiter to bring their check. “Then by all means, let’s go.”

Once the show began, it didn’t take Swan long to decide that David was wonderful company. She could tell he was enjoying the laser lights as much as she was.

She attended the event every year and it seemed the displays only got better and better. Each year, they honored a different state and tonight that state was New York. The New Yorkers in the crowd showed their happiness with whistles and shouting. And when a huge display of the Statue of Liberty flashed across the sky in a brilliant variety of colors, Swan caught her breath.

After that, the showrunners took the time to honor the servicemen in attendance with a flag salute. She couldn’t hold back her tears as she remembered how much her father had loved his country and how, in the end, he’d given his life for it and for her.

David must have detected her weepy state. He pulled her closer to his side.

“Sorry,” she said. “I get all emotional about our servicemen and servicewomen, especially those who sacrifice their lives.”

“You sound very patriotic.”

She pulled back and looked up at him. “Of course I’m patriotic. Aren’t you? You did say you used to be in the military, right?”

“Yes, I’m very patriotic,” he said, wrapping his arms around her. She wished she didn’t think the arms around her felt so strong and powerful.

“I thought you would be, but you said I sounded patriotic as if you thought that perhaps I wasn’t.”

"I apologize. I didn't mean it that way. I'm glad you're so patriotic."

She nodded, accepting his apology. Scanning the area around them, she said, "They are serving complimentary wine coolers over there. Let's go grab a couple."

"Sure thing." He placed his hand on the small of her back.

The contact sent a rush of desire through her that was so strong she had to force herself to breathe. Swan quickly glanced up at him and noticed he'd been affected by the feeling as well. However, he hadn't removed his hand.

Instead, he pressed his hand more firmly into her back and she felt him urging her away from the crowd and toward a cluster of low-hanging palm trees. Once they stood in the shadows, he turned her in his arms, stared down at her for a long moment and then lowered his mouth to hers.

The moment their lips touched, he slid his tongue inside her mouth, and she recalled her thoughts from earlier that day. He was delicious—and dangerous—with a capital *D*. And it wasn't just because he tasted of the beer he'd consumed at Summer Moon, but because he tasted like a hot-blooded man. All the sexiness she'd seen in him was reflected in his kiss.

When she began kissing him back, he wrapped his arms around her and deepened the exchange by crushing his mouth to hers.

She didn't mind his eagerness. In fact, she welcomed the pleasure of his hunger, his taste, which was getting more provocative with every stroke of his tongue. It had been a while since she'd been kissed, and certain parts of her were reminding her of just how long it had been. Not only that, those certain parts were goading her to keep up with the forceful demands of his mouth. She hadn't been kissed so thoroughly or possessively before in her life. Or so passionately.

Swan wasn't sure how long they stood there kissing. It wasn't until they heard the sound of fireworks that they disengaged their mouths. She glanced up as more fireworks exploded in the sky. Instead of looking up, David trailed his tongue along her neck and collarbone with wet licks.

"Say you'll go out with me again, Swan."

There was no way she wouldn't say it. She looked at him and saw deep desire in the eyes looking back at her. "Yes, I'll go out with you again."

"Good."

And then he lowered his head and kissed her again.

Flipper had tried everything possible to get to sleep. He'd counted sheep, counted backward, rolled his eyes for a full thirty minutes and had even tried hypnotizing himself. None of those things helped.

He couldn't remember ever feeling this tight with need. So here he was, close to four in the morning, and still wide awake. Nothing he did could erase the taste of Swan from his mouth and the act of kissing her from his mind.

The kiss would complicate his mission, but it hadn't been an act. It had been the most real thing he'd done in a long time. He had wanted that kiss. Needed it. It had been inevitable.

Sitting across from her at dinner and watching the movement of her mouth had caused a throbbing need to erupt in his gut, making him rock hard. There had been no way to ignore the delicious heat of carnal attraction spiking between them.

And the patriotism he'd seen in her eyes when she'd gotten teary-eyed in support of servicemen, and then when she'd told him about her work with the city to find lodging for homeless vets, hadn't helped. Neither had the fact that she'd looked stunning and had smelled irresistibly hot tonight.

Kissing her had made his entire body feel alive. Had revved up his passion to a degree that his libido had him tied in knots and had his pulse tripping. He could feel himself riding the fine edge of intense desire heightened by more sexual energy than he'd felt in a long time.

While kissing her, he hadn't cared that they could have been seen in spite of the low-hanging trees. He'd been beyond the point of caring. He'd been tempted to drag her to the ground right there.

Damn. How was he going to clear her of anything when the only thing he'd wanted to clear her of was her clothes?

He had access to women whenever he needed them. There were always women who went bonkers for men in uniform and he had no problem engaging in one-night stands. Those types of relationships had always been the way to go for him. He liked being single, coming and going as he pleased, with no one to worry about but himself.

It had been a long time since any woman had kept him up at night and that wasn't cool.

Grabbing his phone he texted the message: If anyone is awake. Call me.

Within seconds, his phone rang. It was Bane. "What's going on, Flipper?"

"Why are you up?" Flipper asked his friend.

"Feeding time. Crystal and I rotate."

"Oh? You're breastfeeding now?"

"No, smart-ass. The trio are on bottles now. What are you doing up?"

Flipper stretched out across the bed. "I couldn't sleep. I tried everything. I even tried to hypnotize myself."

Bane chuckled. "I guess it didn't work."

"No, it didn't work."

"So why can't you sleep, Flip?"

He wasn't one to kiss and tell, no matter who the listener was, so he said, "I still haven't figured out anything about the situation down here and the CO and the admiral are depending on me."

"Maybe they're going to have to accept naval intelligence's report that she's guilty."

"I don't think so." Flipper paused. "She cried tonight."

"What do you mean, she cried?"

"Today was the first day of summer and there's an annual laser show to commemorate the change in season. One of the laser displays was a salute to New York, where they did an awesome light replica of the Statue of Liberty and American soldiers. She got emotional and cried. Dammit, Bane, a person who is betraying their country doesn't cry for those in the service. Call me a sucker for tears but I don't believe she has a traitorous bone in her body."

"Then it's up to you to prove it. What about those two people who hang around her shop?"

"The woman who works for her and the tattoo guy? Both seem clean. But I will dig further. I have to."

"Okay, but make sure while you're digging for answers that you're not burrowing yourself into something you can't handle."

"What do you mean?"

"I think you know what I mean, Flip. You were sent there to prove her innocence—not to prove she has a passionate side. Remember that. Good night."

Flipper clicked off the phone and rubbed a hand down his face. Little did Bane know that after the kiss with Swan tonight, Flipper was driven to do more than prove her innocence, or her passion.

He wanted to possess Swan completely.

And he had a feeling the desire wasn't one-sided. He'd seen the look in her eyes during dinner. He'd felt how her body had responded to his touch. He was certain the same sensations that rushed through him had affected her, too. Kissing her had been inevitable, something they both wanted and needed.

The genie called desire was out of the bottle and Flipper honestly didn't know how to get it back inside.

Three

Swan pushed away from her desk and took another huge gulp of ice-cold lemonade. It had been that way for her all day. Instead of concentrating on the online orders she needed to fill and ship out, her mind was wrapped around that kiss from last night.

All she had to do was close her eyes to remember every single detail, specifically every sensuous lick of his tongue inside her mouth. Even now, the memory sent multiple sensations coursing through her body, causing pleasure the likes of which she'd never encountered before.

She looked up at the sound of a knock on her door. "Yes?"

Jamila stuck her head in. "Mr. Make-you-have-an-instant-orgasm is back."

Swan didn't need to ask Jamila what she meant or who she was talking about. "Any reason you can't wait on him?"

Jamila smiled naughtily. “I could use the pleasure but he specifically asked for you.”

Swan nodded. “I’ll be out in a minute.”

“Okay, I will let him know.”

Swan reached over and took another gulp of her lemonade. She didn’t want to admit it, but after that kiss last night, David could become an addiction. Besides putting down a gallon of lemonade, she’d been twitching in her seat most of the day, thinking that if his tongue could do that to her mouth, then Lordy…she could only imagine what else he would be able to do…

She quickly stood, refusing to go there even as a naughty part of her mind wished that he would. Leaving her office, she rounded the corner and stopped.

David stood in the middle of her shop wearing a pair of khaki shorts and a muscle shirt. The sight of his muscled abs and strong legs made Swan bite back a groan. Just when she thought he couldn’t get any sexier, he’d proved her wrong.

He must have heard the sound of her footsteps because he turned and smiled.

As if on cue, she smiled back. “Hello, David, you came to make more purchases?” Hopefully he would take the hint that she didn’t expect him to just drop by without a reason.

“Yes. I’m buying jewelry for my three sisters-in-law and would love for you to offer suggestions.”

Swan couldn’t help but smile since she liked making sales. What store owner wouldn’t? “I’d love to help you pick out pieces of jewelry for them.”

An hour later, Swan stood at the cash register to ring up all of David’s purchases. With her assistance, he’d selected some really nice pieces, with a number of the stones chosen specifically because that’s what he’d said they would like. Then he wanted earrings to complement the necklaces, which he paid for in advance. They decided to select stones for the earrings tomorrow since they'd spent a lot of time on the necklaces today and her shop would be closing in less than an hour.

From their conversation, she knew the Holloways were a close-knit family. He'd even pulled out his phone to show her pictures of his young niece and nephews.

"No pressure for you to marry?" she asked when he tucked his phone back into the pocket of his shorts.

"None. My parents have been married for more than forty years and are still very much in love. They make sure their kids and grandkids know that. They believe we will know when it's time for us to marry without any pressure from them. We'll be the ones to have to live with the people we choose. They just want all their children to be happy."

She nodded. "I like the way your parents think. I want to believe that, had my parents lived, they would have a similar philosophy. Dad used to tell me all the time that he wanted me to grow up and be whatever I wanted to be and do whatever I wanted to do, and that he and Mom would always have my back."

She suddenly felt a deep sense of loss. "Appreciate your parents, David. You never know how truly great they are until they're gone. But in all honesty, I think I've always known I had great parents."

At that moment, he did something she wouldn't have expected from him—he reached out and took her hand. "They sound great and I know they're proud of your accomplishments."

"Thanks." That was a nice thing for him to say. To avoid thinking about just how nice he was, she slid the bag with his purchases toward him and gave him the credit card slip. He signed it and gave it back to her.

"How would you like to go to happy hour at Danica's with me?"

After talking about her parents and missing them like crazy, she could use more than just an hour of happiness. She would love to be able to have a lifetime of that feeling.

It wasn't that she was *unhappy*, because she wasn't, but there were times when she wondered if maybe there was more out there for her than what was currently in her life. Perhaps she was shortchanging herself on some things. What those things were, she had no idea.

"I would love to go but good luck getting a table at Danica's. They have the best hot wings and are always crowded, *especially* for happy hour. I think the entire island heads over there at five."

"Since I know you don't close your shop until five, how about if we meet over there at five-thirty? I guarantee we'll have a place to sit."

"Um, sounds like you might have connections, David Holloway."

"We'll see." He took the bag and turned to leave, and just like before, she watched his movements until he was no longer in sight.

"Wow. You do have connections, don't you?" Swan said, sliding into a stool at the bar. "I've been here a number of times and the best seat I've ever gotten is at one of those tables outside."

Flipper smiled. Like at Summer Moon, he'd arrived early and was waiting for her. He liked seeing her stroll down the sidewalk looking as beautiful as ever.

Today she was wearing a pair of shorts and a pretty

top. Her legs were long and shapely and he could imagine them wrapped around him while…

Whoa, he didn't need to go there. Ever since that kiss, he'd been trying *not* to go there—no matter how tempted he was to do so. Quickly, he changed the direction of his thoughts.

"I know Danica personally," he said, trying hard to keep his naughty thoughts in check.

She lifted a brow. "Really? How?"

There was no way he would tell her the whole story. Danica was the godmother of former SEAL team member Nick Stover. Nick had given up being a SEAL a few years ago to take a job with Homeland Security after his wife had triplets. Instead of the whole history, Flipper gave her a modified version. "Her godson and I used to work together."

"Oh." The bartender chose that moment to take their drink order.

"I know you used to be in the military at one point but what do you do now?" she asked once the bartender had walked away.

Flipper had expected that question sooner or later and had a prepared answer. "I travel a lot and my job deals with ocean marine work. I guess you can say I'm a specialist in that area."

"Sounds interesting."

He chuckled. "Trust me, it is."

The bartender set their beers in front of them along with a huge plate of hot wings. They dug in.

"Your assistant at the store seems nice," Flipper commented. "I hope she didn't get offended when I asked specifically for you."

"No, very little offends Jamila, trust me."

"You've known her a long time?"

If his question seemed odd, she didn't mention it. "We met a couple of years ago when she moved to the island. The first time she came into my shop she nearly bought out the place. Like you, she has a huge family living up north and wanted to buy holiday gifts for everyone. Thanks to her, I made my month's quota in that one day. She earned a friend for life."

Flipper took a long swig of his beer. What Swan had just told him was interesting. Based on the naval intelligence report he'd read, Jamila didn't have any family. No parents, siblings, aunts, uncles or cousins. She'd been adopted and her adopted parents had been killed in a car accident in her last year of high school. And they hadn't lived in the north but out west in California.

Why had Jamila lied?

"So you hired her that day?" he asked, grinning, trying to make a joke of what she'd told him.

"No, she had a job as a ship captain at one of the day cruise companies in town. When things didn't work out for her there, I hired her on part-time."

He'd read the report and knew why Jamila had been let go and knew about her pending lawsuits. There was a big chance both cases would be settled out of court in her favor. "Is the reason she's part-time because she's a student?"

"Sort of. She saw how much money Rafe makes and—"

"Rafe?" He knew who Rafe was, but Swan didn't know that.

"Yes, Rafe. He rents space in my shop where he operates a tattoo parlor. He's good and always has a steady stream of customers. Some are so pleased with his work that they recommend him to others. I've known people to fly in just to use his services."

She took a sip of her beer, grinned and added, "Jamila decided to give him some real competition by becoming a tattoo artist as well. I have to admit she's pretty good. But Rafe doesn't seem worried. He even allows her to assist him sometimes. I guess you can say he's taken her under his wing. I think that's nice of him."

Flipper took another swig of his beer. "Yes, that is nice of him. Real nice."

Later that night, as they waited for a car at the taxi stand, Swan turned to face David. "I had a wonderful time this evening."

Once again, she had enjoyed his company and hated that their time together was about to end. It didn't come as a surprise to her that the sexual chemistry between them was more explosive than ever. The kiss they'd shared the night before had ignited something within her. From the way she'd noticed him looking at her, she believed something had ignited within him as well.

More than once, her smooth bare legs had brushed against his hairy ones. The sensual contact had sent a gush of desire through her.

The first few times it happened, she'd pulled away. But finally, she'd decided not to pull her legs back and he'd given her one of those *I know you did that on purpose* looks and she had smiled innocently and sipped her beer.

He had initiated the next physical contact and she could envision his mind at work trying to decide how to push her sensual buttons. She doubted he could push them more than he was already.

"I'm glad I got to meet Ms. Danica. After all the years I've been living here, this was my first time meeting her. She's nice."

"Yes, she is."

"And I definitely appreciate this," she said, holding up the bag of hot wings the older woman had given Swan to take home.

"I think she appreciated how much you enjoyed them."

She chuckled. "You're probably right."

"What do you have planned for later?" he asked in a deep, husky tone that seemed to have dropped a purposeful octave.

He had taken her hand when they left Danica's to walk to the taxi stand. The feel of his fingers entwined with hers had stirred something within her, something that grew with every step they took. She was aware of every detail about him as they walked together. Because of his long legs, more than once he had to slow his pace so she could keep up with him.

Swan could have walked home but figured he would suggest walking there with her. She was still cautious about letting him know where she lived. When she left Jamaica to begin living on her own, her mother had drilled into her the danger of letting a man know where you lived too soon. In her heart, Swan felt David was safe, but still…

"It's near the end of the month and I need to work on the books for my accountant." No need to mention she had tried doing that very thing today at work and hadn't been able to concentrate for remembering their kiss from last night.

"How about dinner tomorrow night?" he asked her.

She didn't answer right away. Instead, she broke eye contact with him and glanced down at the sidewalk. Hadn't they seen each other enough these last few days?

Where was this leading? Wasn't he leaving the Keys in less than a month?

She glanced back at him. "Why? We've gone out twice already. I wouldn't want to dominate your time."

"You're not. And the reason I want to take you out again is because I enjoy your company."

She certainly enjoyed his. "Can I ask you something, David?"

He nodded. "Yes?" Considering her history with William, it was something she probably should have asked David before going out on their first date. She'd discovered the hard way that a man not wearing a wedding ring didn't mean anything these days.

"What do you want to ask me, Swan?"

She met his gaze and hoped she would be able to see the truth in his eyes. "Do you have a wife or a significant other?"

Instead of guilt flashing in his eyes, she saw surprise. "No. I'm not married and I've never been married. I dated a woman for years but because of my frequent travels, she decided to end things. That was over six years ago." He then leaned against a light post and asked, "What about you, Swan? Have you ever been married or is there a significant other?"

"Of course not."

He nodded slowly. "Then I assume there is a reason you thought that maybe I was in a relationship?"

"I needed to be sure."

He didn't say anything. Instead, he looked at her as if tumbling her answer around in his head. "But like I said, I assume there is a reason you needed to know."

"Yes." However, she didn't intend to go into any details.

"Well, rest assured there is not a Mrs. David Holloway out there anywhere. Nor is there any woman wearing my ring. Satisfied?"

"Yes."

At that moment, a taxi pulled up. "Thanks for dinner again." She was about to move toward the taxi when he reached out, took hold of her hand and tugged her to him. He lowered his mouth to hers and kissed her quickly but soundly on the lips.

"I'll see you tomorrow," he said, his words a soft whisper against her wet lips.

"Tomorrow?" she asked in a daze from his kiss.

"Yes, we're supposed to go over designs for the earrings, remember?"

It was hard to remember anything after a kiss like that. "Yes, I remember," she said.

"Then I'll see you tomorrow."

She nodded, and when he opened the door for her, she quickly got into the taxi and headed home alone.

The moment Flipper entered his hotel room he went to the small refrigerator beneath the wet bar and pulled out a beer. Just then it didn't matter that he'd already drank a couple at Danica's. He needed another. There was just something about Swan that was getting to him, touching him on a level he wasn't used to when it came to women. He had truly enjoyed her company tonight.

He and his SEAL teammates had just returned from a two-month mission in South Africa and more than anything he had needed to unwind. He would be home in Texas doing just that had he not been summoned to the admiral's office.

So here he was, and although he was in Key West on official military business and he was supposed to be investigating Swan, he loved spending time with her.

Tonight, when she'd met Danica, it had been priceless. You would have thought Swan had met a Hollywood celebrity. He had sat there while the two women conversed, immediately as comfortable as old friends.

The sound of Swan's voice had been maddeningly sexy with a tinge of sweetness that had stroked his senses. For the first time since returning to the States, he had allowed himself to uncoil, to loosen up and relax while appreciating the richness of her personality. Her persona was uniquely hers and the sensuality of her very being called to him in a primitive way.

And that wasn't good.

Taking a huge swig of his beer, he switched his thoughts to what he should be focused on—what she'd told him about Jamila and Rafe. Remembering what she'd said, he pulled his phone out of the pocket of his shorts and with one click he connected to his friend Nick Stover.

"This better be good, Flipper. Natalie is taking an art class at the university tonight and I have babysitting duties."

Flipper couldn't help but smile. Like Bane, Nick had triplets and from the sound of the noise in the background, the triplets had him. "Stop whining. Taking care of a trio of three-year-olds can't be too bad."

"Then you come do it."

"Sorry, I'm on assignment."

"So I hear. In the Keys, right?"

He figured for Nick to know that much meant he'd either talked to Bane, Viper, Mac or Coop. "Yes, I'm in Key West."

"While you're there, be sure to stop by Danica's. Give her a hug for me."

"I did that already. Tonight, in fact."

"Good."

"I think she has more photos of the triplets than you do."

"I wouldn't doubt it. So if you can't be a backup babysitter, why are you calling?"

"When you arrive at your cushy job at Homeland Security tomorrow, there are two people I need you to check out for me. I've read naval intelligence reports on them, but something isn't adding up. Call me a suspicious bastard, but after that situation with Bane, when those traitors within the agencies were exposed, I'm not taking any chances."

He then told Nick about the discrepancies between what the reports said and what Swan had told him. "Somebody is lying. Either Jamila lied to Swan or someone falsified the report, and I want to know which it is."

Four

"He's *baaack*," Jamila said.

Swan pushed away from her desk. She didn't have to ask who Jamila was talking about. "I was expecting him," she said in what she hoped was a professional tone. "He needs to look at designs for earrings."

"If you say so. I'll send him in here."

Swan was about to tell Jamila they could use the computer out front, but Jamila was gone after closing the door behind her.

Standing, Swan inhaled deeply. How she had finished the books last night, she wasn't sure. Thoughts of David had been stronger than ever after their night out. When she'd gone to bed, she had dreamed about him. Okay, she'd dreamed about him before, but the dreams last night had been so hot it was a wonder they hadn't burned her sheets. She had been tempted to do something she hadn't done in a long time, reactivate her vibrator.

She drew in a deep breath when she heard the knock on her door. "Come in."

And in walked David, looking sexier than he had the other times she'd seen him. Last night, to stay focused, she had come up with every reason she could think of for why she shouldn't be attracted to him and why a relationship with him wouldn't work.

She'd even thrown in the race card. But of course that was thrown out when she remembered her parents and how happy they had been together. Yet she also couldn't forget how her father's family had ostracized him for his choice in love. Would David's family be the same way? There was no reason to think they wouldn't. And wasn't she getting ahead of herself for even throwing love in the mix?

"Hello, David."

"Swan." He glanced at her desk, taking in all the folders spread across it. "You're busy."

"That's fine. Besides, I need to get those earrings ready for you."

Now that he'd seen her desk, it would make perfect sense for her to suggest they use the computer out front to design the earrings. But now that she had him behind closed doors, she liked it.

Not that she planned on doing anything about having him here.

"Please have a seat while I clear off my desk." Today he was wearing jeans and she couldn't help but watch how fluidly his body eased into the chair. How the denim stretched across a pair of muscular thighs. She quickly switched her gaze before he caught her looking.

"Nice office."

"Thanks." She closed the folders and placed them in her inbox tray. She then glanced over at him and caught him looking at her. She followed his gaze and soon figured out why he was staring.

She was wearing a skirt with a V-neck blouse, and when she'd leaned over to place the folders in the tray, her shirt had shown a portion of her cleavage. Instead of calling him out for trying to cop a view of her breasts, the fact that he was interested sparked a distinct warmth between her legs.

She quickly sat down. "Now if you would roll that chair over here, I am ready." Too late, she realized how that sounded and quickly added, "To look at designs."

He smiled. "I know what you meant."

He rolled his chair behind her desk to place it right next to hers. When he sat down, their legs touched. Moving away would be pretty obvious so she let the denim of his jeans rub against her bare legs.

"Now, then," she said, trying not to notice how good he smelled. "What do you think of these?" she asked, bringing up a few designs on the computer screen.

When he didn't answer, she glanced over at him and found him staring at her. Sitting so close to him, she could look directly into his laser-blue eyes. It was as if his gaze was deliberately doing something to her, causing a surge in her breath and arousal to coil in her core. She saw the dark heat in his eyes and desire clawed at her even more.

"May I make a suggestion?" he asked in a voice that seemed to wobble in a sexual way.

"It depends on what that suggestion is," she heard herself say.

He leaned in a little closer and whispered, "I want to kiss you again. Only problem is that I don't want to stop until I get enough. And I'm not sure I would."

She had been staring at his lips, watching how they

moved while he talked. She slowly dragged her gaze back up to his eyes. She saw need flare in his gaze at the same time that anticipation for his kiss thickened the air flowing in and out of her lungs.

"I don't know what to say."

"Don't say anything, Swan. Just bring your mouth closer to mine."

She knew she shouldn't, but she found herself doing it anyway.

Flipper drew in a deep breath when Swan's lips were almost touching his. He flicked out his tongue and she gave a sharp intake of breath when he began licking her lips from corner to corner with the tip of his tongue.

"What are you doing?" she asked on a wobbly breath.

"Since you asked..." He captured her mouth and when she closed her eyes on a moan, he reached up and cradled her face in his hands while he kissed her with a greed he didn't know was in him.

What was there about her that made him accept the primitive part of himself that wouldn't be satisfied until he made love to her? Was it because she crept into his dreams at night and into his every waking thought? Or was it because an arrow of liquid heat shot straight to his groin whenever he saw her? Or could he blame it on the fact that whenever she touched him, he burned? She made him edgy and aroused him as no other woman could.

It was all of those things and more.

Right now, he didn't know how to back away. So he didn't. Instead he accepted the stream of heat in his gut and the crackle of energy passing between them.

Their lips were copulating in a way that sent blood coursing through his veins like a raging river. It was raw, hot and explosive, causing a hot ache to erupt in his gut. It wouldn't take much to lose control and take her here on her desk. At that moment, his entire body was tight with need, totally entranced by everything about her.

The phone rang and they quickly broke off the kiss, drawing in deep breaths of air. He watched as she reached across her desk to press the speaker button. "Thank you for calling Swan's."

At first, no one said anything and then a deep male voice said, "Swan? Are you okay? You sound out of breath."

He watched as she pulled in another deep breath before a smile touched her lips. "I'm fine, Godpop 1. How are you?"

Knowing who she was talking to on the phone was like a pail of cold water drenching Flipper. He was quickly reminded why he'd been sent to Key West. His admiral would have him court-martialed if he knew what Flipper had just done with his goddaughter. If the man had any idea how many times Flipper had kissed her already and how each time he'd wished they had gone even further…

She turned off the speaker so he heard only one side of the conversation, and from the sound of her voice, he knew she was happy about receiving the call.

Feeling a tightness in his crotch from his still-aroused body, he got up from the chair and walked to the window. If she could have this sort of effect on him just from a kiss, he didn't want to think about what would happen if he were to make love to her. Just the thought of easing his body into hers had his stomach churning and caused an ache low in his gut.

Knowing he needed to think of something else, he

glanced up into the sky. It was a beautiful day. Monday was Memorial Day and he wondered if Swan had made any plans to celebrate. He'd heard there would be a parade and unlike some places in the States, where stores remained open on Memorial Day, the laid-back businesses in the Keys closed up for one big party.

He liked the Keys. When he retired from being a SEAL, he could see himself moving here to live out the rest of his days. The island was surrounded by the ocean and they didn't call him Flipper for nothing. He loved water. Being in it and being a part of it. Living this close to the sea would certainly be a plus for him. But then there was the question of how he would deal with Swan if he chose to retire here. Even if he could prove she was not guilty of espionage, there was always that possibility she would hate his guts regardless of the outcome, because he had not been truthful with her.

"Sorry about that, David."

He turned, not caring that she could see his still-hard erection. It was something he couldn't hide even if he had tried. Was she sorry they'd been interrupted or was she regretting that they'd kissed in the first place? He hoped it was the former because he doubted he could ever regret kissing her. "I take it that was one of your godfathers?" he asked, knowing it had been.

She was staring at him below the waist, but after his question, her gaze slowly moved upward to his face. "Ah, yes, that was one of my godfathers. The other two will be calling sometime today as well. It always works out that they all call within twenty-four hours of each other."

He nodded and slowly walked back over to his chair to sit down. "I know you're busy so let's look at the designs."

Had he just seen a flash of disappointment in her eyes? Did she want them to continue what they'd been doing before she'd gotten that call? Didn't she know how close they'd both been to going off the edge and falling into waters too deep to swim out of? Even for him, a SEAL master swimmer.

Somehow they got through the next half hour looking at earring designs. Just as each one of the necklaces were different, he wanted the earrings to be different as well and reflect each one of his sisters-in-law's personalities.

When he was satisfied with his choices, he stood, convinced he needed to rush back to the hotel and take a cold shower. Sitting beside Swan and inhaling her scent without touching her was one of the most difficult things he'd had to do in a long time.

She was so female that the maleness in him couldn't help responding to everything about her. A part of him felt drugged by her scent and the intense physical awareness of her. Even now, desire was racing through his bloodstream.

"I owe you additional monies, right?" he asked. A couple of the designs he'd selected cost more than what she'd originally estimated.

"Yes. I'll let you know the difference after I finish designing them, when you pick up everything."

He hadn't missed the fact that when he stood her gaze had immediately latched on to his crotch once again. Was she still hoping to see him with a hard-on? If that was true, then she wasn't disappointed. He could get aroused just from looking at her.

And why did she choose that moment to lick her lips? She had no idea that seeing her do such a thing sent the pulse beating in his throat and desire hammering against his ribs.

On unstable legs and with an erection the size of which should be outlawed, he moved around her desk and looked at her. "Yesterday I asked you to go to dinner with me again, but you never gave me an answer."

He figured that seeing how aroused he was, she probably wouldn't give him an answer now either. She surprised him when she said, "Yes, we can dine together this evening."

He nodded. "Okay, you get to pick the place."

She took a slip of paper off her desk, wrote something on it and handed it to him. He looked at it and he must have stared at it too long, because she said, "It's my address, David. I'm inviting you to dine with me this evening at my home."

He broke eye contact with her to glance back down at the paper she'd given him. He looked back at her while trying to downplay the heat rumbling around in his gut.

"Do you need me to bring anything?" he asked her.

"No, just yourself."

Swan glanced around her home and felt the knots beginning to twist in her stomach. She hoped she hadn't made a mistake inviting David here.

Today marked a week since they'd met and if she was going to continue to see him while he was on the island, she couldn't take advantage of his thoughtfulness and expect him to invite her out without ever returning the kindness. However, more than anything else, she needed to keep things in perspective. She needed to remember he was someone she could have a good time with and that's it.

She didn't want anything more than that.

One day, she would be ready to explore her options and consider a future with a man, but that time wasn't now. She liked being single and responsible only for herself.

She knew from Candy that a serious relationship was hard work. And on top of all that hard work, you could assume you had the right person in your life only to discover you didn't. By then, you would have opened yourself up to hurt and pain in the worst possible way.

The thought that a man had caused her best friend that kind of agony bothered Swan whenever she thought about it. Candy loved Key West as much as Swan did, and for a man to be the reason she had moved away was disheartening.

Swan tried telling herself that not all men were like Candy's ex, Don, or like William. On days when Swan wanted to think all men were dogs, all she had to do was remember her dad.

Andrew Jamison was the yardstick she used to measure a good man. She'd watched how he had treated her mother, had seen the vibrant and sincere love between them. She had not only seen it, but she'd felt it as well. Both her parents had been demonstrative individuals and Swan had often interrupted them sharing a passionate kiss or embrace.

She still felt it here, within the walls of her house and in the very floor she walked on. All the love that had surrounded her while growing up was in this house she now called home.

She was glad her mother hadn't sold it after her father died, when Leigh had made the decision to move back home to Jamaica. Instead, she had kept the house, knowing one day Swan would want to return. It was almost too spacious for one person but Swan knew she would never sell it or move away. This house had everything she needed.

She could see the water from any room, and at night, whenever she slept with the window open, the scent of the ocean would calm her.

Her favorite room in the house was her parents' old bedroom, even though she had not moved into it. It had floor-to-ceiling windows and a balcony she liked sitting on while enjoying her coffee each morning. A couple of years ago, she'd had the balcony screened in to keep the birds from flying into her house, although she loved waking up to the sound of them chirping every morning.

Although neither one of her parents would tell her the full story, Swan knew her father had come from a wealthy family. And she knew he had been disowned by them when he had fallen in love with her mother and refused to give her up. Before dying, Leigh had given Swan a beautiful leather-bound diary to read after her death. That's what had helped keep Swan sane, reading the daily account of her mother's life and love for her father and believing they were now back together.

For weeks following her mother's death, Swan had wanted to be alone to wallow in her pity and read about what she thought was the most beautiful love story that could exist between two people. Her mother had always been expressive with the written word and Swan enjoyed reading what she'd written.

It had made Swan long for such a man, such a love. Maybe that's why she had been so quick to believe in William and why, once she'd found out about his duplicity, she'd been so reluctant to get serious with a man since.

From her mother's diary, Swan discovered her mother's appreciation for her husband's agreement to make Key West their home. The people on the island embraced diversity and tolerated different lifestyles.

Swan had read the account of when her father had been stationed at a naval base in Virginia and had sent for her mother to join him there. In the diary, her mother had written about the hateful stares they would receive whenever they went out together. The unaccepting and disapproving looks. The cruel words some people had wanted them to hear.

Her father hadn't tolerated any of it and hadn't minded confronting anyone who didn't accept his wife. But to avoid trouble, Leigh had preferred to live in Key West, where people's issues with an interracial marriage were practically nonexistent.

However, people's attitudes never kept Leigh from leaving the island to join Andrew whenever he would send for her. Oftentimes, Leigh would take Swan along and they would both join Andrew in different places for weeks at a time.

When she heard the sound of the doorbell, Swan drew in a deep breath. The time for memories was over. The only plans she had for *this* evening were for her and David to enjoy the meal she'd prepared and later enjoy each other's company.

She had no problem with them deciding what the latter entailed when that time came.

"Hello, David. Welcome to my home."

Flipper pushed from his mind the thought of how Swan would feel if she knew this wasn't his first time here. How she would react if she knew he had invaded her space without her knowledge. If she ever found out the truth, would she understand it had been done with the best of intentions? Namely, to keep her from wasting away in a federal prison after being falsely accused of a crime?

He forced those thoughts to the back of his mind as he smiled down at her. She looked absolutely stunning in a wraparound skirt and yellow blouse. “Hi. I know you said I didn’t have to bring anything, but I wanted to give you these,” he said, handing her both a bottle of wine and a bouquet of flowers.

He had decided on the wine early on, but the flowers had been a spur of the moment thing when he’d seen them at one of those sidewalk florist shops. Their beauty and freshness had immediately reminded him of Swan.

“Thank you. The flowers are beautiful and this is my favorite wine,” she said, stepping aside to let him in.

He chuckled. “I know. I remember from the other night.” There was no way he would also mention having seen several bottles of Moscato in the wine rack the time he had checked out her house.

He glanced around, pretending to see her home for the first time. “Nice place.”

“Thanks. I thought we would enjoy a glass of wine and some of my mouthwatering crab balls out on the patio before dinner.”

“Mouthwatering crab balls?”

“Yes, from my mom’s secret recipe. You won’t be disappointed,” she said, leading him through a set of French doors. The first thought that came to his mind when he stepped out on her patio, which overlooked the Atlantic Ocean, was that it was a beautiful and breathtaking view. This had to be the best spot on the island to view the ocean in all its splendor.

He recalled how, as a boy, he would visit his cousins in California and dream of one day living near the beach. Over the years, being stationed in San Diego had been the next best thing. He owned an apartment close to base that was within walking distance of the beach.

However, his view was nothing like this. All she had to do was walk out her back door and step onto the sand. It was right there at her door. If he lived here, he would go swimming every day.

He glanced over at her. "The view from here is beautiful."

"I love this house and appreciate my mother for not selling it when she decided to move back to Jamaica after Dad died. She got a lot of offers for it, believe me. So have I. Mom said being here without Dad was too painful, but she knew I'd feel differently. For me, it was just the opposite. Being here and recalling all the memories of when the three of us shared this place makes me happy."

Hearing how the loss of her parents affected her made Flipper appreciate his own parents even more. Colin and Lenora Holloway had always been their sons' staunch supporters. Their close and loving relationships had been the reason none of their sons had had any qualms about settling down and marrying. All the marriages had worked out, seemingly made in heaven, except for his brother Liam's.

When Bonnie had gotten pregnant, Liam had done the honorable thing by marrying her. Bonnie had always been a party girl and didn't intend to let marriage or being a mommy slow her down. While Liam was somewhere protecting his country as a Navy SEAL, Bonnie was conveniently forgetting she had a husband.

No one, not even Liam, had been surprised when he returned from an assignment one year and she asked for a divorce. Liam had given it to her without blinking an eye. Since then, Bonnie had remarried, which had introduced another set of issues for Liam. He was constantly taking Bonnie to court to enforce visitation rights to see his daughter because the man Bonnie married didn't like Liam coming around.

Flipper had no qualms about marriage himself, but he had too much going on right now. Namely, resisting the temptation of Swan while he continued his investigation. That was his biggest challenge. The more he was around Swan the more he liked her and the more he wanted to prove her innocence. It was hard staying objective.

"Here you are," she said, handing him a cold bottle of beer. "I figured you would like this instead of the wine."

He smiled. Like he had picked up on her drinking preferences, she had done the same with him. "Thanks. I've never been a wine man."

She chuckled. "Neither was my dad. That's how I knew when it was time for him to come home because Mom would have his favorite beer in the fridge."

He opened the bottle, took a sip and noticed her watching him. He licked his lips, liking the taste of the beer, which was the brand he'd chosen the other night at Summer Moon. When he took another sip and she continued to watch him, he lifted a brow. "Is anything wrong?"

She smiled. "No, nothing is wrong. I just love to watch how you drink your beer."

He chuckled. That was a first. No woman had ever told him that before. "And how do I drink it?"

"First there's the way your mouth fits on the beer bottle. I find it very sensuous."

He tried ignoring the quiver that surged through his veins at the tone in her voice. "Do you?"

"Yes. And then there's the way you drink it like you're enjoying every drop."

"I am."

"I can tell." Then, as if she thought perhaps she'd said too much, she took a step back. "I'll go get those crab balls for you to try."

When she turned to leave, he reached out and touched her arm. He couldn't help it. The air all but crackled with the sexual energy between them. "Come here a minute before you go," he said, setting his beer bottle aside. "Although I do enjoy drinking beer, I've discovered I enjoy feasting on your mouth even more."

And then he lowered his mouth to hers.

Perfect timing, Swan thought, because she needed this. She'd wanted it the moment he tilted his beer bottle to his mouth and she'd watched him do so. And now he was doing her. Showing her that he was enjoying her mouth more than he'd enjoyed the beer. Just like he'd said.

There was a certain precision and meticulousness in how he mastered the art of kissing. First, as soon as his tongue would enter her mouth, he would unerringly find her tongue, capture it with his own and begin gently sucking in a way that made the muscles between her legs tighten. Then he would do other things she didn't have a name for. Things that made desire flow through her like sweet wine, kindling heated pleasure and burning passion within her.

He rocked his thighs against her and she felt him pressed against her. His arousal was massive. Instinctively, she moved her hips closer, wanting to feel him right there, at the juncture of her thighs.

When he finally pulled his mouth away, she released

a deep, satisfied breath. Her mouth was still throbbing and there was an intense ache in her limbs. Right now, their heavy breathing was the only sound audible, and the laser-blue eyes staring down at her sent a tremor to her core.

She licked her lips when she took a step back. “Ready for a few crab balls?”

“Yes,” he said, after licking his own lips. “For now.”

Five

He wanted her.

Flipper knew he shouldn't, but he did. All through the delicious dinner Swan had prepared and while engaging in great conversation with her, the thought of just how much he wanted her simmered to the back of his mind. Now with dinner coming to an end, desire was inching back to the forefront. Images of her naked tried to dominate his mind, the thoughts made him shift in his chair to relieve the ache at his crotch.

"Ready for dessert, David? I made key lime pie."

Right now, another kind of dessert was still teasing his taste buds. "Yes, I would love a slice, and dinner was amazing by the way. You're a good cook. My mother would absolutely love you."

Too late, he wondered why he'd said such a thing. From the look on her face, she was wondering the same thing. So he decided to clean up his mess by adding, "She admires other women who can cook."

Swan smiled. "You don't have to do that, David."

"Do what?"

"Try to retract the implications of what you said so I won't get any ideas."

He *had* done that, but not for the reason she thought. He'd done so because it wasn't right for either of them to think something was seriously developing between them. More than likely, she would hate his guts when she learned why he was really in Key West, when she discovered she was his assignment and nothing more. He couldn't tell her the truth, but he could certainly set her straight on what the future held for them.

"And what ideas do you think I wanted to retract?"

"The ones where I would think we were starting something here, the ones that meant I would be someone you'd take home to meet your mother."

He sat down his glass of ice tea, which she had served with dinner. "Any reason why I wouldn't want to take you home to meet my mother *if* we shared that kind of a relationship, Swan?" Although he didn't think he needed to let her know—again—that they didn't share that kind of relationship, he did so anyway.

"Honestly, David, do I really have to answer that?"

"Yes, I think you do."

She stared at him for a minute. "I'm well aware when it comes to interracial relationships that not all families are accepting."

He chuckled. "My family isn't one of them, trust me. Interracial or international, we couldn't care less. My brother Brad met his wife, Sela, while working in Seoul, South Korea, and my brother Michael met Gardenia in Spain. Like I told you, my parents would accept anyone who makes us happy, regardless of race, creed, religion, nationality or color."

She didn't say anything to that. Then she broke eye contact with him to glance down into her glass of tea. Moments later, she raised her gaze back to him.

"My father's parents didn't. They threatened him with what they would do if he married Mom and they kept their word. They disowned him. Still, my mother reached out to them when Dad died to let them know he'd passed. They came to his funeral but had no qualms about letting Mom know they still would not accept her. They would only tolerate me since I was biracial. They even tried forcing Mom to let me go back with them. That's when my godfathers stepped in."

Flipper shook his head, feeling the pain she refused to acknowledge, the pain she'd obviously felt because of her grandparents' actions. But he'd heard it in her voice nonetheless.

"It's sad that some people can be such bigots. At the risk of this sounding like a cliché, some of my closest friends are black," he added, immediately thinking of Bane, Viper and Coop. Like her, Mac was of mixed heritage and had a white mother and black father.

"I'm sure some of your closest friends are, David."

He wondered if she believed him. One day, she would see the truth in his words. Then it suddenly occurred to him—no, she would not. There would be no reason for her to ever meet the four guys who were just as close to him as his biological brothers.

"I'll be back in a minute with the pie," she said. Then she stood and left the room.

Flipper watched her leave, feeling that he hadn't fully eradicated her doubts the way he'd wanted to do. That bothered him. He didn't want her to think he was one of those prejudiced asses who believed one race of people was better than another. What her grandparents had done to her father and mother, as well as to her, was unforgivable. Regardless of how she'd tried to come across as if their actions hadn't hurt her, as if they still didn't hurt her, he knew better.

She needed a hug right now.

He pushed back his chair and left the dining room to enter her kitchen. Instead of getting the pie like she'd said she would do, she was standing with her back to him, looking out the kitchen window at the ocean. And he could tell from the movement of her shoulders that she was crying.

"Swan?"

She quickly turned, swiping at her tears. "I'm sorry to take so long, I just had one of those miss-my-daddy-and-mommy moments."

He crossed the room to her, knowing that her tears were about more than that. He knew it and he intended for her to know he knew it. "Not wanting to get to know you—that was your grandparents' loss, Swan."

She gazed into his eyes and nodded. "I know, David, but their actions hurt Dad, although he never said it did. I knew. Mom knew, too. I think that's one of the reasons she loved him so much, because of all the sacrifices he'd made for her. That's why she did anything she could to make him happy so he would never regret choosing her. But it wasn't fair. He was a good man. Mom was a good woman. They deserved each other and should have been allowed to love freely and without restrictions, reservations or censure. It just wasn't fair, David."

And then she buried her face in his chest and cried in earnest. Wrapping his arms around her, he held her, leaning down to whisper in her ear that things would be all right. That her parents had had a special love, one she should be proud of, one the naysayers had envied.

Emotions Flipper hadn't counted on flowed through him as he continued to stroke her hair and whisper soothing words next to her ear. Inwardly, he screamed at the injustice of trying to keep someone from loving the person they truly wanted to love. It was something he'd never understood and figured he never would. And never would he accept such a way of thinking from anyone.

Swan knew she should pull out of David's arms, but found she couldn't do it. Being held by him felt good. His fingers, the ones that were stroking through the strands of her hair, seemed to electrify her scalp. They sent comforting sensations all through her—and something else as well. A need that he was stroking to fruition. As a result, instead of pulling out of his arms, she closed her eyes and enjoyed being held by him while inhaling his masculine scent.

She wasn't sure how long they stood there, but it didn't take long for her to notice his breathing had changed. But then so had hers. His touch had shifted from comforting to passionate. He was using the same strokes, but now the feelings within her were beginning to build to an insurmountable degree of desire.

Opening her eyes, she lifted her head to stare up at him. The minute she did, she caught her breath at the intense yearning she saw in his gaze. That yearning reached out to her, jolted her with a level of throbbing need she hadn't known existed. She'd heard of raw, make-you-lose-your-senses passion, but she had never experienced it for herself.

Until now.

"David…" She said his name as something burst to life in the pit of her stomach. It made a quivering sensation rise at the back of her neck. He implored her with his eyes to follow this passion, as if letting her know he understood what she was experiencing even if she didn't.

"Tell me what you want, Swan," he said in a deep voice while gently caressing the side of her face. "Tell me."

The intensity in his eyes was burning her, scorching her with the sexual hunger that was coming to life inside her. She wanted more than his erection pressing hard against the apex of her thighs. She wanted him on top of her. She wanted him to slide into her body and begin thrusting in and out. She needed to lose herself in more than just his arms.

Suddenly, she felt emboldened to tell him just what she wanted. "I want you, David. In my bed."

Flipper wanted to be in her bed as well. Lord knows he shouldn't want it, but he did. He would have to deal with the consequences later. He felt too tight and hot to try to fight the demands his body was making. Sweeping her into his arms, he quickly walked out of the kitchen and headed toward her bedroom.

"You think you know where you're going, David?"

He slowed his pace, remembering that she had no idea that he knew the layout of her home. Not only did he know where her bedroom was located, he knew the blueprint of the plumbing underneath her floor. He looked down and met her gaze, grateful she wasn't suspicious. "I figured you would stop me if I went in the wrong direction."

"Yes, I would have stopped you, but you're going the right way."

"Good." When he resumed his swift pace, it didn't take him long to reach her bedroom.

Swan had gotten next to him in a way he hadn't counted on happening. Seducing her had not been part of the plan and he should not have allowed things to get this far. He didn't want to think of the major complications involved, and not just because she was the goddaughter of three top naval officers.

But something was happening that he hadn't counted on. His mind and body were in sync and a rare sexual aura was overtaking him. He could no more stop making love to her than he could stop being a SEAL. For him to even make such a comparison was pretty damn serious.

Instead of placing Swan on the bed, he eased her to her feet, loving the feel of her soft body sliding down his hard one. "If you're having second thoughts about this, Swan, now's the time to say so."

She shook her head and then in a wobbly voice, she said, "No second thoughts, David."

Hearing her affirmation spoken with such certainty, Flipper released a low, throaty groan as he lowered his mouth to kiss her again, needing the connection of her lips to his as much as he needed to breathe. Wrapping his arms around her waist, he pulled her body closer to him as he deepened the kiss, wanting her to feel his erection, the hard evidence of his need for her.

He had never wanted a woman with this much intensity in his life, and he had no idea why Swan was having this kind of an effect on him.

Why she, and no other woman before her, had tempted him to cross a line during a mission. His mind didn't function that way. He had yet to prove her innocence, so technically, she was still naval intelligence's prime suspect, but at the moment that didn't matter. For all he knew, he could be about to sleep with the enemy.

But right now, that didn't matter either because deep down, a part of him believed she was innocent.

What was happening between them was definitely out of the realm of normal for him. He'd known he would have to get close to her, but he hadn't counted on this—his intense desire to do inappropriate, erotic and mind-blowing things to Swan Jamison.

But he wanted her and there would be no regrets. At least not for him, and based on what she'd just said, there would be no regrets for her either.

The moment he ended the kiss, his hands were busy removing her skirt, followed by her blouse, and when she stood in front of him in her lacy panties and bra, he couldn't help but growl his satisfaction. She looked sexy as hell and the rose-colored ensemble against the darkness of her skin was stunningly beautiful. *She* was beautiful.

He reached up and traced a finger along the material of her boxer-cut panties. This style on a woman had never done anything for him. Until now.

"You should have been a model," he said in a deep, throaty voice, filled with profound need and deep appreciation. She had such a gorgeously shaped body.

"My mother used to be a model. I was satisfied with being a model's daughter."

"And a strikingly beautiful one at that," he said, lowering to his knees to rid her of her panties. He couldn't wait to touch her, taste her and do all those erotic things to her he had dreamed of doing over the past few nights.

He breathed in deeply, getting more aroused by the second while easing her panties down a pair of long, beautiful legs.

After tossing her panties aside, he leaned back on his haunches and gazed at her, seeing her naked from the waist down. Her small waist, her stomach, the shape of her thighs and longs legs were perfect. She was perfect.

After looking his fill, he leaned forward and rested his forehead against her stomach, inhaling her luscious scent. He loved the way it flowed through his nostrils, opening his pores and causing his body to become even more erect.

And then he did something he'd wanted to do since their first kiss. He used the tip of his tongue to kiss her stomach, loving the indention around her naval and tracing a path around the area. Then he shifted his mouth lower, licking his way down and enjoying the sound of her moans.

When he came to the very essence of her, he licked around her womanly folds before leaning in to plant a heated kiss right there. It was as if sampling her special taste was as essential to him as breathing. His hands held firm to her thighs when he slid his tongue inside of her, loving the sound of his name from her lips.

Then he went deeper, using his tongue to taste her, claim her and brand her. The latter gave him pause but not enough to stop what he was doing. He'd never claimed a woman as his own and had never thought about doing so. But with Swan, it seemed such a thing wasn't just desired but was required.

And he didn't want it any other way. She was the first woman he wanted to claim. Forcefully, he pushed to the back of his mind what it could mean to make any woman his and decided he would dwell on that aspect of things at a later time. For now, he wanted to focus on the delicious, succulent, enjoyable taste that was Swan.

He took his time, wanting her to know just how much he loved doing this to her. He wanted her to feel the connection his tongue was making with her flesh. However, he wanted her to do more than feel it, he wanted this connection absorbed into her senses, into her mind, into every part of her body.

Moments later, Flipper knew he'd achieved his goal when he felt her fingers dig into his shoulder blades, followed by the quivering of her thighs. Tightening his hold on her hips, he knew what would be next and he was ready.

She screamed his name when she was thrown into an orgasmic state. Her fingernails dug deeper into his skin, but he didn't feel the pain because knowing he was giving her pleasure made him immune to it. What he felt was a desire to take things to the next level, to slide into her body and go so deep it would be impossible to detect where his body ended and hers began.

He finally pulled his mouth away and looked up at her, saw the glazed look in her eyes. Without saying a word, he traced his fingers around the womanly mound he'd just kissed before inserting his finger inside of her. She was ultra-wet and mega-hot and he had every intention of capitalizing on both. The orgasm she'd just experienced would be small in comparison to the one he intended to give her.

Pulling his finger from her, he licked it clean, knowing she was watching his every move. "Sweet," he said softly, holding her gaze.

He slowly eased to his feet and reached behind her to

remove her bra. When she stood totally naked in front of him, he feasted his gaze on her. “And I’m about to show you just how sweet I think you are, Swan.”

Six

Swan was having difficulty breathing and the blue eyes staring at her made getting air to flow through her lungs even more difficult. Never had she felt this energized from a sexual act. And when David got to his feet and leaned in to kiss her, letting her taste herself on his lips, she felt weak in the knees. But he held her around the waist, holding her up as he kissed her more deeply, making her wish the kiss could last forever.

She released a low disappointed groan in her throat when he pulled his mouth away.

"Don't worry, there's more coming."

He swept her off her feet and carried her over to the bed, placed her on it and joined her there.

"You still have clothes on," she said, reaching out to touch his shirt.

"I know and they will be coming off. Right now, I just want to lie here with you and hold you in my arms."

She smiled at him. "You're not going to fall asleep on me, are you?"

Chuckling, he said, "Asleep? With you lying beside me without a stitch of clothes on? Sleep is the last thing I'd be able to do, trust me."

He'd already pleasured her with his mouth, so she couldn't help wondering what was next. She soon discovered his intent when he reached over and cupped her breasts.

"You are perfect," he said in a deep husky voice.

The words triggered a memory of overhearing her father whisper the same compliment to her mother, after she surprised him with a special dinner after he returned home from one of his missions.

Swan knew she was far from perfect. Those were just words David was speaking. But still, hearing them filled her with joy. Maybe she shouldn't let them, but they did.

Then any further thoughts dissolved from her mind when David eased a nipple between his lips. She moaned at the pleasure she felt all the way to her toes. Just when she thought she couldn't stand anymore, he began torturing her other nipple.

When he finally eased away, she opened her eyes to watch him undress. When he removed his shirt, she saw the tattoos covering his tanned skin on both of his upper arms—huge dolphins emerging from beautiful blue ocean waters. Another tattoo of even more dolphins was painted across his back in beautiful vivid colors. She'd never been into tattoos but she thought his were stunning.

"I like your tattoos," she said.

He glanced over at her and smiled. "Thanks."

When he lowered his shorts, her gaze moved to the area between a pair of masculine thighs. His shaft was massive and marvelously formed. Just the thought of him easing that part of himself inside of her sent her pulse skyrocketing.

"You okay?"

She lifted her gaze to his. She wasn't sure if she was okay. A thickness had settled in her throat when she saw how he was looking at her. Not only did he intend to join his body with hers, she had a feeling he planned to keep them connected for a while.

"Yes, I'm okay."

Swan continued to check him out, thinking he had a mighty fine physique. His body was all muscle and it was obvious that he worked out regularly. A man didn't get those kinds of abs if he didn't.

She watched as he pulled a condom from his wallet and sheathed himself in a way that was so erotic, she felt herself getting wetter between the legs just watching him. Then he was strolling back toward the bed. To her.

"I'm about to make sure you feel more than okay," he said, reaching down and easing her up to rest her chest against his. Her breasts were still sensitive from his mouth and rubbing them against his chest caused a multitude of arousing sensations to swamp her.

"What are you doing to me?" she asked in a ragged breath, barely able to get the words out.

"Anything you can imagine," he whispered, lowering her back on the mattress and then straddling her. He stared down at her as he gently moved her legs apart. She felt him, that part of him, lightly touch her feminine folds and then he was rubbing back and forth across them, sending even more sensations racing through her bloodstream.

"Trying to torture me, David?"

"No, trying to pleasure you. Ready for me?"

The movement of his manhood against her was making it impossible for her to concentrate. "What do you think?"

"You're wet and hot, so I think you're ready." And then he entered her in one deep thrust.

She gasped at the fullness and was glad he'd gone still for a minute. This gave her the chance to feel him fully embedded deep within her. It had been a long time for her and her inner muscles were greedily clamping on to him, tightening their hold.

"You're big," she whispered.

"You're tight," was his response. "But we're making this work."

And he did. First he began moving again, gently sliding in and out of her. That only lasted a few seconds before he picked up the pace and began thrusting harder.

She responded by wrapping her legs around his waist. Then he lifted her hips to receive more of him. When he established a slow and deep rhythm, touching areas in her body that hadn't been touched in a long time, or ever, she fought back a scream. She grabbed hold of his hair and pulled it, but he didn't seem to mind.

"Rule number one, Swan. Don't hold back."

Was he kidding? It wasn't a matter of holding back. It was more like she was trying to keep her sanity. David was so powerfully male that he was pushing her over the edge with every deep stroke. Every cell within her vibrated in response to his precise thrusts.

"Hold on, baby. Things are about to get wild."

Flipper had given Swan fair warning. When he began pounding harder, making strokes he'd never attempted with another woman—going deep, pulling out and then going deep again—he felt a quivering sensation start at the base of his testicles and move toward her womb with each and every thrust. He had to hold on tight to her to keep them on the bed. He was determined to show her wild.

Simultaneously, he leaned down to have his way with her mouth, licking it corner to corner and then inserting his tongue inside with the same rhythm he was using below.

What he was feeling right now was more than off the charts, it was out of the atmosphere. When she finally let go and screamed his name, the sound vibrated in every part of his body, especially in her inner muscles. They clamped down on him, trying to pull everything out of him while her hands tightened even more in his hair.

"David!"

She screamed his name again. The sound drove him. He wanted more of her. Wanted to go deeper. Throwing his head back, he felt the veins in his neck strain. There was pain but not enough to dim the pleasure.

And he knew at that moment Swan had gotten under his skin in a way no other woman had.

He began rocking hard into her with an intensity that made him go deeper with every thrust. Then he was the one hollering out in pleasure, saying her name as an explosion ripped through him. Then like a crazed sexual maniac, he leaned in to feast on her mouth and breasts. It was like his desire for her could not end.

"David!"

He knew she was coming again and, dammit to hell, so was he. Marveling at such a thing, he tightened his hold on her. His control had not only gotten shot to hell and back but had died an explosive death as the result of the most powerful orgasms he'd ever endured.

This was what real lovemaking was about. No holds barred. No restrictions. Every part of him felt alive, drained, renewed. The room had the scent of sex and more sex. But that wasn't all. Emotions he'd never felt before touched him and swelled his heart.

He quickly forced those emotions back, refusing to go there. Knowing he couldn't go there.

The husky sound of deep, even breathing made Swan open her eyes. She was still in bed with David. Their limbs were entangled and his head was resting on her chest as he slept.

This man had been the most giving of lovers. He didn't come until he made sure she came first. He had kissed every part of her body, some parts more than others, and he had stoked passion within her in a way that had made her reach the boiling point. No man had ever made love to her with such intensity.

He had warned her about them getting wild. As far as she was concerned, they had gotten more than wild, they had gotten uninhibited, untamed. She hadn't known she had so much passion within her. He had brought it out and made her do more than own it. He had made her so aware of it that she doubted she could undo what he'd done.

David Holloway had done more than push a few of her buttons. He had turned on all the lights.

That thought made her smile and pull him closer. Feeling exhausted, she closed her eyes and drifted into sleep.

Flipper slowly opened his eyes, taking in the sight and scent of the woman lying beside him, snuggled close to his body. He was so sexually contented, he could groan out loud. He didn't. Instead he tightened his arms around her.

Things had gotten wild. They had finally fallen asleep after four rounds of the most satisfying love-making possible.

While making love with Swan, he had discovered there was a vast difference in making love to her versus making love to other women. He'd known it before but she had made that point crystal clear tonight.

With other women, he'd usually had one goal in mind—seeking sexual pleasure and making sure she got hers. With Swan it had been about that, too, but it had also been about finding closeness. No other woman had made him want to stay inside her. It had only been the need to replace condoms that had forced him from Swan's side. And then he had been back inside her in a flash…like that was where he belonged. Hell, he was still thinking that way and the twitch in his aroused manhood was letting him know just what he desired.

Flipper was known to have a robust sexual appetite. When you lived your life on the edge, engaging in covert operations as his team did, then you needed a way to release.

Usually, unerringly, he found his release in some woman's bed. He made sure she knew it was one and done. Due to the nature of his occupation, he didn't have time for attachments or anything long-term. Some SEALs did; he didn't. He'd tried it once and it hadn't worked out. Now he preferred being a loner. It didn't bother him that he was the lone single guy among his close friends. To each his own.

So how could one night in Swan Jamison's bed have him thinking things he shouldn't be thinking, especially considering why he was in Key West in the first place?

It had everything to do with the woman he'd had mind-blowing sex with for the past four hours or so. Now he saw her as more than an assignment. Now she was also a woman who had the ability to match his sexual needs one-on-one, something he found invigorating and energizing on all levels. He was a totally physical male and Swan Jamison was wholly, utterly female. Almost to the point that she'd blown his ever-loving mind.

Now she was sleeping peacefully while he was lying here thinking, knowing his honor was being tested. As a military man, he always did what was honorable. On top of that, his mother had drilled into all five of her sons that honor was not just for their country but extended to humans just as much, especially women. Why had that thought settled deep into his mind now?

One reason might be that he'd read the report on her. He knew about those elderly people residing at the senior living complex that she visited on her weekends off and how she'd championed so hard for the homeless. She was working with the mayor to help find funding to build a housing complex for them.

She was a caring person. He'd witnessed her love for her country, for her father, that night at the fireworks and the more he was around her, the more he believed in her innocence.

She made a sound now and he glanced down and met beautiful brown eyes staring at him. Immediately his senses connected with those eyes. She trusted him. He could see it in the gaze staring back at him. Otherwise he would not be here in her bed.

What would she think when she learned the truth? Would she still trust him? He pushed the thought to the back of his mind.

She gave him a beautiful, sleepy smile that melted

his insides. Made him wish he had come here to the Keys for a real vacation, a much-needed one. He wished he had entered her shop with no ulterior motive but to do as he claimed, which was to buy his mother a birthday gift. He would still have tried his hand at seducing her, but things would have been different. Specifically, he wouldn't feel as if his honor was being compromised.

"You didn't try my key lime pie," she whispered.

"We can get up and eat some now if you want," he said.

"No, I like being just where I am. We can always eat some later…or even for breakfast."

He leaned down and brushed a kiss across her lips. "Um, breakfast sounds nice. Is that an invitation to stay the night?"

"Only if you want to."

He wanted to. And when he brushed another kiss across her lips, he slid his tongue inside her mouth to kiss her deeply and let her know how much he wanted to stay.

He knew at that moment that his commanding officer and the admiral weren't the only ones with a personal interest in Swan Jamison. He now had a personal interest in her as well.

Seven

The next morning, Swan woke up to bright sunlight flowing in through her window and a powerfully male body sleeping beside her.

Last night was rated right up there with *Ripley's Believe It or Not*. It had been just that spectacular. They'd made love a couple more times before getting up after midnight to eat the pie she'd prepared for dessert. After clearing off the table and loading the dishes into the dishwasher, he'd suggested they walk on the beach.

So at one in the morning, they had strolled hand in hand along the water's edge. It had been a beautiful night with a full moon in the sky. The breeze off the ocean had provided the perfect reason for him to pull her close while walking barefoot in the sand. He told her more about his family; namely about his parents' medical supply company.

Then at some point, they began talking about her

company and she found herself telling him just about everything about jewelry making. He was curious about her stones and complimented how beautiful they were and inquired how she was able to create so many pieces.

No man had ever taken an interest in her work before and she was excited that he thought what she did for a living was important. She had found herself explaining the day-to-day operations of Swan's. He couldn't believe how she found the time to handcraft a number of the items sold in her shop.

David also thought it was great that Rafe, through his connections with a huge distributor in California, was able to get some of Swan's more expensive stones at a lower cost and had even helped her save on shipping by including them in the packaging with his ink.

She glanced over at him now as he shifted in bed. He kept his arms wrapped around her while he slept. She studied his features and saw how relaxed he looked.

She drew in a deep breath, still amazed at the depth of what they had shared last night. It had been the most profound thing she'd ever experienced with a man. Making love with David had touched her in ways she hadn't thought possible. He had made her feel things she hadn't ever felt before and those things weren't just sexual in nature. While in his arms, she had felt safe and secure. Protected.

As far as she was concerned, what they'd shared last night was more compelling and meaningful than any other time she'd shared with a man, even more meaningful than the time she'd spent with William. She'd never really allowed herself to fully let go with William. Now she could admit to herself that she'd known in the back of her mind that something didn't add up with him.

Yet she'd been so desperate for companionship after

losing her mother that she had wanted to believe William was honest, even though he'd seemed too good to be true. She was glad Candy had become suspicious when he'd never wanted them to be photographed together or when he'd insisted that they spend the night at Swan's place instead of the hotel.

At the time, his requests hadn't bothered her because she hadn't wanted her employer or her coworkers to get in her business. But Candy had seen through all that and knew something in the milk wasn't clean, as she would often say. It had been Candy who'd unveiled her own husband's secret affair with a flight attendant. And once confronted, Don hadn't denied a thing. He'd said he was glad she'd found out because he wanted a divorce.

Pushing thoughts of Don's and William's betrayals to the back of her mind, Swan continued to study David. She couldn't help but recall the number of times he'd made her climax. Now that was simply amazing all by itself.

She was enjoying her time with him, even knowing it wouldn't last. Later this month, he would leave the island and she would probably not hear from him again. She knew that, accepted it. She had long ago learned to live for the now and not sweat the small stuff. Especially those things she couldn't change.

"You're awake."

She couldn't help but smile at the slumberous blue eyes staring at her. The dark shadow on his chin made him look even sexier. "Yes, I'm awake. I guess I should be a good host and prepare breakfast before you leave."

"Um, I've overstayed my welcome?"

"No, but today is Sunday and I have a lot to do."

"Maybe I can help you."

"You don't know what I'll be doing."

He reached out and pushed her hair back off her shoulders so he could completely see her face. “Then tell me.”

She gazed into his eyes. “The shop is closed on Sundays and I use my day off to visit Golden Manor Senior Place. My mom used to do volunteer work there when we lived on the island years ago. I would go with her on Sundays to visit everyone. I guess you could say it’s become a family tradition that I decided to continue.”

“I think that’s a wonderful thing you’re doing. I’m sure the residents there appreciate it.”

“Yes, they do, although those who knew my mom are no longer there. They’ve passed on. I’m establishing new relationships and friendships.”

“Good for you. I’d love to join you.”

“You would?” she asked, surprised.

“Yes, and don’t worry about preparing breakfast. I’ll go home and refresh and be back here within an hour. We can grab breakfast somewhere before heading over. Afterward, we can spend more time on the beach. I enjoyed the walk last night with you.”

And she had enjoyed it, too. The thought that he wanted to spend more time with her made her feel really good inside. “Okay, that sounds wonderful.”

“I’m glad you think so, and before I leave…”

“Yes?”

He leaned over to kiss her and she knew where things would lead from there. She looked forward to getting wild again with him.

Flipper clicked on his phone the minute he walked into his hotel room. He noted several missed calls since he’d deliberately cut off his phone last night. One was from the admiral, who was probably calling for an update. But first Flipper would return the call to Nick.

"Flipper, should I ask why I couldn't reach you last night?"

"No, you shouldn't," Flipper said, flopping down in the nearest chair.

"You have heard the saying that you shouldn't mix business with pleasure, right?"

Too late for that, Flipper thought, running a hand down his face. Instead of responding to Nick's comment, he said, "I hope you have something for me. There's another angle I want you to check out."

"Okay, and yes, I have something for you. I found out the initial investigation was handed off to a group of civilian investigators, which means naval intelligence didn't rank it at the top at first."

Flipper was very much aware of the part government bureaucracy played in certain investigations. If someone thought a case should be under naval intelligence's radar, then they made sure it got there. "Why?"

"Not sure yet, but first, let's talk about Jamila Fairchild."

Flipper leaned forward in his chair. "Okay, let's talk about her. What do you have?"

"Not what you obviously think. What she told Swan was the truth. She does have a huge family who lives in the north."

Flipper raised a brow. "Then who made the error in the report from naval intelligence?"

"Don't know, but it's worth checking out, although I don't think it's anything suspicious on Ms. Fairchild's end. Especially when I tell you who her family is."

"And who is her family?"

"Her mother's brother is Swan's grandfather."

A frown covered Flipper's face. "The grandfather who disowned Swan's father?"

"Yes, from what I've gathered. But I can find no record of her grandfather ever reaching out to her."

"Interesting."

"Yes, it is. I take it Swan Jamison doesn't know about the family connection."

"No, she doesn't." Flipper decided not to try to wrap his head around this bit of news just yet. Instead he asked, "What about Rafe Duggers?"

"Personally, I think something is going on with him."

Flipper lifted a brow. "What?"

"First of all, certain aspects of his info are sealed."

"Sealed?"

"Yes. I would think if naval intelligence was checking into something related to Swan and her story, they would see that sealed record for her tenant as a red flag. For them not to have flagged it raises my own suspicions about a few things."

That raised Flipper's suspicions as well. Was Rafe a double agent? Someone working undercover? Was someone in naval intelligence deliberately setting Swan up as the traitor? If so, why?

"You weren't able to find out anything about him?"

There was a husky chuckle. "I didn't say that. There are ways to find out anything you want when you know how to do it."

And Nick knew how to do it. He'd been an amazing SEAL, but as far as Flipper was concerned, Nick's natural investigative talents were better served at Homeland Security. "When will you let me know something?"

"Give me a couple of days. In the meantime, don't say anything to anyone about my suspicions about Duggers."

"Not even the CO and admiral?"

"Not even them for now. You mentioned Swan had a third godfather who was someone high up at naval intelligence. Was his identity revealed to you?"

"No, it wasn't but then I didn't ask," Flipper said.

"It wasn't hard to find out," Nick replied. "All you have to do is find out who Andrew Jamison's SEAL teammates were at the time he died and do a little research to determine where they are now."

"I take it you've done that."

"Yes, and would you believe Swan Jamison's third godfather is Director of Naval Intelligence Samuel Levart?"

Flipper would not have considered Director Levart in a million years, but it all made sense now. In order for someone to have delayed making formal charges against Swan, that person would have to be someone in power. The admiral had alluded to as much. "Swan doesn't know how favored she is to have three powerful men in her corner."

"Yes, but we both know it wouldn't matter if one of her godfathers was the President. If naval intelligence believes they have enough evidence to prosecute her, they will," Nick said.

Flipper knew that to be true. Now more than ever he had to find the person intent on framing Swan. To him, it was beginning to look like an inside job.

"So what else do you have for me to check out?" Nick asked, reclaiming Flipper's attention.

"It's about something Swan told me." He then shared with Nick the information about Rafe Duggers's association with some huge distributor in California. "I need you to check that out."

"I will. I know time is of the essence so I'll get back to you soon, Flipper."

"Thanks, I appreciate it."

"If you're so concerned about me, then why not return to the Keys and keep an eye on me, Candy?" Swan asked. She moved around her bedroom getting dressed while talking to her friend on speakerphone.

"You know why I won't return, just yet. But I did hear something that's interesting."

"What?" Swan asked as she shimmied into her skirt.

"I talked to Francola the other day and she said Marshall mentioned to her that Don is thinking about moving away from the island."

Swan paused. Francola and her husband, Marshall, had been close friends of Don and Candy's while they were married. The two couples often did things together. Personally, Swan didn't care much for Francola because the woman had been aware Don was cheating on Candy but hadn't told her friend. "I would take anything Francola says with a grain of salt these days," Swan said as she continued dressing.

"I know you still fault her for not telling me about Don and I admit I was angry with her, too, but now I understand her not doing so."

"Do you?"

"Yes. Her relationship with me is not like our relationship, Swan. You and I have been best friends since grade school and we have no secrets. You would have told me about Don had you suspected anything."

"Darn right."

"Well, Francola and I didn't have that kind of relationship. We only met through our husbands, who worked together. Besides, I'm not sure I would have believed her even had she told me. I would have been in denial." Candy paused. "Now, enough about me. Tell me more about this David Holloway."

Swan smiled while putting hoop earrings into her ears. "He's a real nice guy. Thoughtful. Considerate. Handsome as sin." She glanced over at her made-up bed. Although there were no signs of anyone sleeping in it last night, it didn't take much for her to remember all the wild action she and David had shared under the sheets. "And he's great in bed. More than great. He's fantastic."

"Just be careful, Swan. Protect your heart."

Swan slipped her feet into her sandals. "My heart? It's not like I'm falling for the guy, Candy."

"Aren't you? I can hear it in your voice. You like him a lot."

Yes, she did like him a lot. "It won't go beyond me liking him," she said, trying to convince herself of that more so than Candy.

"Can you honestly say that?"

"Yes, because I can't let it. His work brought him to the island and he'll be leaving soon. In less than thirty days."

"Doesn't matter."

Swan knew for her it *did* matter. She only wanted short-term. The last thing she wanted was to do long-term with any man.

Eight

"I enjoyed my time with you today, Swan," Flipper said, looking down at her.

They'd had brunch at Summer Moon before heading to the senior living complex where they spent the next four hours. She assisted the staff by reading to groups of people and even taking a few of the seniors for walks around the complex. Some, she'd explained, had family who rarely visited so she had become like their surrogate granddaughter.

On the flip side, considering what she'd missed out having in her life, he couldn't help but wonder if they had become her surrogate grandparents.

From the moment she walked into the facility, everyone brightened up when they saw her. It was amazing to him. She knew just what to say to elicit a smile or to get them to engage in more conversation. The majority of the seniors knew her by name and he couldn't help noticing a number of the women wearing what looked like necklaces she'd made.

When he inquired about the necklaces Swan confirmed they were her designs but she had taught the women to make them from stones she'd given them. It had taken longer than normal since a lot of the older women's hands weren't as nimble as they used to be.

After leaving the nursing home, they'd grabbed lunch at a sidewalk café before returning to her house where they'd spent the rest of the day on the beach. Later, after ordering takeout for dinner from Arness, they were back at her place.

No matter how tempting Swan was making it for him to stay longer at her place, he would leave when it got dark. The information about Rafe Duggers's sealed records bothered him and he'd decided to poke around in the tattoo parlor later that night to see what he could find.

He glanced over at Swan as she sat across the table from him eating dinner. Earlier today, when he had returned to take her to breakfast, she had opened the door looking fresh and perky and dressed simply in a pair of shorts and a tank top. Seeing her dressed that way reminded him of just what a gorgeous pair of legs she had, as well as how those same legs had wrapped around him while they'd made love that morning and the night before.

When they had gone swimming, she'd worn one of the sexiest two-piece bathing suits he'd ever seen. He had totally and completely enjoyed his day with her. They would be attending the Memorial Day festivities together tomorrow in town, which included a parade.

Because he needed some investigative time, he'd

come up with an excuse for why he couldn't see her a couple of days this week. Time was moving quickly and he had yet to find anything to clear her of wrongdoing.

Because of Nick's warning, Flipper hadn't told Admiral Martin everything when he'd called him back yesterday. Namely, he'd left out the discrepancies between what Nick had found out and the actual reports from naval intelligence. Until Flipper discovered what was going on, he would follow Nick's advice and keep that information to himself for now.

"Although I won't be seeing you for a few days because of work, will you still be on the island?" Swan asked.

It was hard not to be totally truthful about why she wouldn't be seeing him. She was the last person he wanted to be dishonest with but he had no choice. His goal had always been to prove her innocence and now that was doubly true. He would check out the tattoo shop tonight and look around in both Rafe's and Jamila's homes this week while they were here at work. Although it had been established that Jamila was Swan's relative, as far as Flipper was concerned, she was still a suspect.

"Yes, I'll still be on the island but I have to concentrate on this project I was sent here to do." No need to tell her that the project involved her.

"I understand how things are when work calls."

He reached up and caressed the side of her face. "We still have a date for the parade tomorrow, right?"

"Yes."

"What about dinner on Friday evening?" he asked her.

Her smile touched something deep within him. "I'd love that, David."

"Good. I'll swing by your shop at closing time Friday and we can go to dinner directly from there. You pick the place."

"All right."

"What time do you want me to come get you for the parade tomorrow?"

"It starts at ten in the morning and we need to get there early to get a good spot. How about if I prepare pancakes for us in the morning around eight?"

"You sure? I wouldn't want you to go to any trouble."

She waved off his words. "No problem. I told you I enjoy cooking."

After they finished dinner, he told her he needed to leave to read some reports for work, which wasn't a lie. She walked him to the door. He leaned down to kiss her, intending for it to be a light touch of their lips.

But the moment his mouth touched hers and she released a breathless sigh, it seemed the most natural thing to slide his tongue inside her mouth and deepen the kiss. Wrapping his arms around her waist, he pulled her tight against him and knew the exact moment the kiss had changed to something more.

It was no longer a *goodbye and I'll see you later* kiss. Instead it was one of those *I need to have you before I go* kind. And Swan seemed to be reciprocating those feelings as she returned the kiss with equal fervor.

The next thing Flipper knew, he was sweeping her off her feet and moving quickly toward her bedroom. When he placed her on the bed, they began stripping off their clothes.

For him, she'd become an itch he couldn't scratch and a craving that wouldn't go away. There was something about making love to her that made every part of his body ache with need. She had imprinted herself on his soul and in every bone in his body and there was nothing he could do about it but savor what they had for as long as he could.

When she was completely naked, his pulse kicked up a notch and his breathing was forced from his lungs when he looked at her. She was beautiful and perfectly made.

He pulled a condom from his wallet in the shorts she'd helped him remove and toss aside. Knowing she was watching his every move, he rolled it over his aroused manhood.

"I want to do that for you the next time."

He looked at Swan. "All right." So she was letting him know she intended there to be a next time for them. He was glad because he wanted a next time, too.

There was a big chance when she found out the truth about why he was here on the island that she wouldn't want to have anything to do with him again. But he forced the thought from his mind.

"You don't have all evening, you know," she teased.

She was right, he didn't and it was a good thing she didn't know why. He moved toward her. "Impatient?"

She smiled up at him. "Yes, you could say that."

"In that case, I can help you with that problem." He leaned in. "I've got to taste you again," was all he said just seconds before his mouth came down on hers.

Swan automatically lifted her arms around his neck the moment his lips touched hers.

Capturing her tongue, David drew it into his mouth. Blood rushed fast and furious to Swan's head, making her feel both light-headed and dazed as his tongue began mating with hers. His technique was rousing her passion to a level that electrified every part of her. Insistent need rushed up her spine, spinning her senses and mesmerizing her with his delectable taste.

He suddenly broke off the kiss and they both panted furiously, drawing deep gulps of air into their lungs.

She rested her head against his chest and inhaled his scent as she continued to catch her breath. She knew she was losing herself to passion again when she felt the hardness of his erection brushing against her thigh, energizing the area between her legs.

Then she heard him whispering erotic details of what he wanted to do to her. His words spread fire through her body and when he gently cupped the area between her legs, she moaned.

"You're torturing me, David," she said, before twisting to push him down on his back so she could straddle him. Before he could react, she lowered her head between his masculine thighs and eased his erection into her mouth.

"Ah, Swan," he growled huskily, gripping her hair. She was fully aware of him expanding and felt a sense of triumph in her ability to get him even more aroused than he already was. The feel of his hands locked in her hair sparked even more passion within her and motivated her to use her mouth in ways she'd never done before.

"Swan!"

She felt his thighs flex beneath her hands before he bucked forward. She wasn't prepared when he quickly switched their positions so that she was the one on her back. The blue eyes staring down at her flared with a passion that sent tremors through her.

Before she could whisper his name, he slid inside

her. He kept going deeper and deeper, stretching her in ways she didn't know she could be spread, inch by inch.

"Wrap your legs around me, baby," he whispered in a throaty voice.

When she did as he asked, he began thrusting hard. It was as if his total concentration was on her, intent on giving her pleasure. She felt every inch of him as he rode her hard, not letting up.

"David!"

She screamed his name as he continued to make love to her, throwing her into a euphoric state that seemed endless. He was using her legs to keep their bodies locked while relentlessly pounding into her. Her world was spinning and she couldn't control the need to moan, moan and moan some more.

She was unable to hold anything back when her body erupted into an orgasm so powerful it propelled her toward utter completeness. She screamed his name once again as a deep feeling of ecstasy ripped through her entire body.

Flipper eased off Swan to lie beside her. Pulling her into his arms, his nostrils flared as he inhaled the scent of sex. The scent of woman, this woman. A woman he still desired even now.

He was not new to lust. Been there, done that and he figured he would be doing it some more. A lot more. With Swan lying in in his arms, snuggled close to him, close to his heart, he knew something had changed between them.

Bottom line, Swan Jamison was not only intoxicating, she was addictive.

"I don't think I'll be able to move again, David."

A smile touched the corners of his lips. He definitely

knew how she felt, but he knew he had to move. He had somewhere to be tonight and as sexually drained as he was, he intended to be there.

"Then don't move. Just lie there. I'll let myself out," he said, reluctant to go, although he knew he must.

"You sure?" she asked in a lethargic voice.

"Positive. I'll be back in the morning for the parade and then we have a date on Friday."

"Yes. I'm going to need it. I'll be working late Wednesday doing inventory. I probably won't leave work until around ten."

"With your worker's help?"

"No. The cruise ship comes in Wednesday."

He released her to ease out of bed and put on his clothes. "What does a cruise ship have to do with anything?" He could feel her gaze on his body. He couldn't disguise the impact of knowing she was watching him. He was getting aroused all over again.

"Jamila dates a guy who works on the cruise ship and they only see each other whenever the ship comes to port. She always requests the day off to spend with him. I guess they made up."

He had planned to check out Jamila's house when he'd assumed she would be at work. Good thing he now knew otherwise.

"Made up?" he asked, pulling his shirt over his head.

"Yes. I got the impression they weren't on good terms last week. Not sure what happened but it's all good now since they've apparently kissed and made up."

He nodded. "How long have they been together?"

"About six months now."

Flipper didn't say anything as he continued dressing. There hadn't been any mention of a boyfriend for

Jamila Fairchild in the report he'd read. Another discrepancy. There were too many inconsistencies for his liking and he was determined to find out why. One thing was certain, he didn't like the idea of Swan being at her shop alone late at night.

He moved back to the bed, leaned down and brushed a kiss across her lips. "I'll see you in the morning."

"Looking forward to it."

He smiled down at her and then turned and left.

Later that night, Flipper, dressed all in black, moved in the shadows, careful to avoid streetlights and security cameras. He had scoped out the area and was familiar with where the cameras were located. More than once, he'd had to dart behind a shrub when people were out for a late-night stroll.

He reached the area where Swan's shop was located and when he heard voices, he darted behind a building to hide in the shadows.

Two men stood not far away. One of them was Rafe. Neither of the men saw Flipper. The other guy was a little taller and appeared to be a foreigner. Their conversation sounded like an argument and was in a language Flipper wasn't familiar with and he spoke four. Most SEALs spoke at least that many, except for Coop, who had mastered seven.

When the men lapsed into English, they lowered their voices and could barely be heard. Flipper did make out the words *ink* and *roses*. Was someone getting a tattoo of roses painted on their body? If so, did it mean anything?

Flipper was glad when the men finally moved on. More than ever, he was determined to check out the tattoo parlor. He waited a half hour to make sure the men didn't return. When he was certain they had gone, he went to work bypassing the security alarms and cameras.

Using a sort of skeleton key, he opened the back door and walked inside the tattoo parlor. Using night goggles, he glanced around.

The place looked like a typical tattoo parlor. He should know since he and his brothers had frequented a number of them. He was proud of the images on his body. Luckily, Swan hadn't asked him about them. He was glad because the last thing he wanted to do was lie about why he was into dolphins.

Pulling off the camera attached to his utility belt, he replaced the night goggles with a high-tech camera, which was his own creation. This particular piece of equipment detected objects underground and under water. Looking through the lens, he scanned the room. It wasn't long before the camera light began blinking.

He moved toward the area and aimed the camera lower, toward the floor, and the blinking increased. Evidently something was buried beneath the wooden floor, a portion covered by a rug. The architectural report he'd been given of Swan's shop had not exposed any secret rooms or closets.

Putting the camera aside, he moved the rug and felt around to find a latch. He opened the trapdoor to find a small compartment beneath the floor. He saw more containers of ink. Why? There was a supply case full of ink on the opposite side of the room. Why was this ink hidden?

The first thing he noticed was the difference in the labeling. Was there something different about this particular ink? There was only one way to find out, he thought, taking one out of the cubby. He would overnight one of the containers to Nick instead of naval intelligence.

At this stage of the game, he wasn't taking any chances about who could be trusted.

Nine

Swan had just finished the last of her inventory when she heard the knock on her shop's door. Crossing the room, she peeped through the blinds to see who it was. A smile touched her lips as she unlocked the door. "David, I didn't think I'd see you until Friday."

He glanced around her empty shop before looking back at her. "I finished work early and remembered you saying you were working late tonight doing inventory. I wanted to make sure you got home okay."

That was really nice of him. "You didn't have to do that." But she was glad he had. They had spent Monday together celebrating Memorial Day. He had arrived at her place for breakfast and then they'd walked to where the start of the parade would take place.

After the parade, they'd gone to the island festival marketplace where various vendors had lined the streets with booths and a huge Ferris wheel. They had taken one of the boat rides around the islands and had ended up eating lunch on Key Largo.

She had thought about him a lot since Monday, remembering in explicit detail how he'd made love to her before leaving.

"I know you said Jamila would be off today," David said. "What about your tattoo guy? Is the parlor closed on Wednesdays as well?"

"Yes, but Rafe dropped by earlier. He was expecting a shipment of more ink to come in today but it didn't. He wasn't happy about that."

"He wasn't?"

"No. He said there was a particular shade of blue he was expecting."

Flipper nodded and checked his watch. "Ready to go?"

"Yes, I just need to grab my purse from my office." She was about to turn to get it when there was another knock at the door.

"Expecting anyone?" David asked her.

"No. I'll see who it is."

She walked to the door and David went with her. After glancing out of the blinds, she turned back to David and smiled. "It's Jamila and Horacio."

She unlocked the door. "Jamila, hi."

"Hey, Swan. Horacio and I were in the neighborhood and I remembered you would be here late. I thought we'd drop by to say hello."

Swan smiled at the man with Jamila. "Horacio, it's good seeing you again."

"Same here, Swan," he said in a heavy accent that Swan always loved hearing.

"And this is my friend David Holloway. David, you

already know Jamila. This is her friend Horacio Jacinto," Swan said, making introductions.

The two men shook hands. Swan wondered if she'd imagined it but she thought David had tensed up when he'd seen Jamila and Horacio. "Nice meeting you, Horacio," David said. "I can't place your accent. Where are you from?"

"Portugal."

"Nice country," David said.

"Thanks."

"I hope you'll leave before it gets too late, Swan," Jamila was saying.

"I will. David came to make sure I got home okay." Usually whenever she worked late, either doing inventory or making her jewelry, she would catch a cab home even though she lived only a few blocks away. But since David was here, she would suggest they walk. It was a nice night and she would love to spend more time with him.

"We'll see you guys later," Jamila said. "We had dinner at Marty's Diner and now we're going to Summer Moon for drinks and live music."

"Okay. Enjoy. And I hope to see you again the next time the ship ports, Horacio," Swan said.

Horacio smiled. "I hope to see you as well."

After they left, Swan went to her office to get her purse. She returned and noticed David was standing in the same spot where she'd left him, staring at the door. "Are you all right?"

He turned to her. "Yes, it's just that Horacio looks familiar and I was trying to remember when I might've seen him. Maybe I've run into him before, here on the island."

She nodded. "That's possible. He's a chef on the Century Cruise Line that docks here once a week. Whenever it does, he comes ashore and meets up with Jamila. I think I mentioned that to you."

"You did, but I could have sworn I saw him a few nights ago. Sunday. After leaving your place."

Swan shook her head. "It wasn't him. The ship didn't arrive in our port until today. But you know what they say about everybody having a twin."

He chuckled. "You're probably right, but I'm sure you don't have one. I'm convinced there's not another woman anywhere who is as beautiful as you."

Swan knew better than to let such compliments go to her head, but she couldn't help the smile that spread across her lips. "You, David Holloway, can make a girl's head swell if she's inclined to believe whatever you say."

"I hope you do believe it because I spoke the truth." He took her hand in his as they headed for the door.

Flipper pulled out his phone the minute he walked into his hotel room later that night. He'd felt it vibrate in his pocket when he was walking Swan home but figured it would be a call he needed to take in private.

Swan had invited him inside but he'd declined, telling her he had a ton of paperwork waiting on him back at his hotel. That wasn't a lie. He'd begun rereading all those naval intelligence reports to see if he could determine why those investigators had failed to do their job and instead intentionally went after Swan as a scapegoat.

He checked his phone and saw Nick had called and Flipper quickly returned the call. "What do you have for me?"

"More than you counted on. All I can say is whoever handled that investigation did a botched-up job."

Or they did the job they'd been expected to do, Flipper thought. "I guess there's a reason you feel that way."

"Yes. That ink you sent to be analyzed isn't what it's supposed to be."

"It's not ink?"

"Yes, it's ink, but coded ink. When applied to the skin as a tattoo, it can be decoded by a special light. It's my guess that's how the classified information is leaving Swan Jamison's shop—with people's tattoos and not with any of her jewelry. Guess where the ink is being shipped from."

"Swan mentioned from some place in California."

"Yes, that's right and the distribution company is a few miles from the naval base in San Diego. That means someone on the base must be passing classified information that's being shipped in the ink."

Flipper frowned. "And because Rafe Duggers is conveniently including Swan's stones with each shipment, it makes sense for her to be suspect."

"Right," Nick agreed. "Someone is setting her up real good, Flipper. They are definitely making her the fall guy."

Flipper wondered who in naval intelligence had targeted Swan and why. "I have another piece of the puzzle I need you to check out."

"What?"

"The guy who was with Rafe Duggers two nights ago. The one I told you he was arguing with. I saw him today."

"You did?"

"Yes. He came into the shop when Swan was closing up. His name is Horacio Jacinto and he's Jamila Fairchild's boyfriend."

"That's interesting. I'll find out what I can about

him," Nick said. "I wonder if Ms. Fairchild knows what's going on or if she's being used as a pawn."

"I don't know, but I'm going to make sure I keep an eye on all of them."

"Be careful, Flipper."

"I will."

A few hours later, after taking a shower, Flipper was sitting at the desk in his hotel room suite when his cell phone went off. Recognizing the ringtone, he clicked on and said, "What's going on, Coop?"

"You tell us."

Us meant Bane, Viper and Mac were also on the phone. "I guess Nick called you guys."

"Yes, he called us earlier today," Bane said. "What's going on with Swan Jamison sounds pretty damn serious. Don't you think it's time to call the CO?"

Flipper ran a hand down his face. He glanced at the clock on the wall. It was close to three in the morning. "If Nick told you everything, then you know it's an inside job at the base. There's a traitor somewhere and until I know who I can trust, then—"

"You know as well as we do that you can trust our CO, Flipper," Viper said. "Once you tell Shields what you've found out, if he suspects Martin or Levart of any wrongdoing, he will know what to do."

"Yes, however, the three of them share a close friendship. What if the CO is blinded due to loyalty?"

"We're talking about our commanding officer, Flipper. Shields would turn his own mother in if he thought she was betraying our country. You know that."

Yes, he knew it. But still… "I don't know if Martin or Levart is really involved. Like Shields, they are Swan's godfathers and I would hate to think they are shady. I just know it's an inside job and right now I'm suspicious of just about everybody."

"We figured you would be, so open the damn door," Mac said.

Flipper frowned. "What?"

"We said open the door," Coop said, knocking.

Flipper heard the knock, clicked off his phone, quickly went to the door and snatched it open. There stood his four best friends.

"What are you guys doing here?"

"What does it look like?" Mac asked as the four moved passed Flipper to enter the hotel room.

"We figured ten pairs of eyes were better than two," Bane said, glancing around. "Besides, we need to keep you objective."

"But what about your families? Viper, your wife is having a baby!"

Viper chuckled. "And I plan to be there when she does. According to Layla's doctor, we still have a couple of months, so I'm good."

"And our families are good, too," Coop said. "They know we look out for each other and they agreed we should be here for you."

"Teri is glad I'm gone," Mac said, grumbling. "Maybe when I go back, she'll have a new attitude."

"Or maybe you'll have one," Bane said, frowning at Mac.

"Whatever," Mac said, picking up the hotel's restaurant menu book. "Is it too late for room service?"

Flipper closed the door and drew in a deep breath as he watched the men gather around the table, already rolling up their sleeves, ready to help him figure things out. They worked together as a team and he would admit that whenever they did so, good things happened.

"There's something all of you should know," he said, getting their attention.

They glanced over at him. "What? No room service at this hour?" Mac asked in a serious tone.

"That, too."

"What's the other thing we should know, Flipper?" Viper asked, sitting back in the chair he'd claimed as soon as he came in.

Flipper leaned against the closed door. "Investigating Swan Jamison is no longer just an assignment for me. It's become personal."

The men nodded. "And you think we don't know that, Flipper?" Coop asked in a steely tone. "That's why we're here. Someone is trying to frame your woman and we're going to help you find out who and why. But first things first. You know what you have to do, right?"

Flipper stared at the four men. Yes, he knew. Instead of answering Coop, he picked up his cell phone from the table and placed a call to his CO.

Ten

As far as Swan was concerned, Friday hadn't arrived fast enough. With every passing hour, she would glance at her shop's door expecting to see David walk in. One would think his surprise visit Wednesday would have sufficed. Unfortunately, it hadn't.

She'd had two days to think about how irrational her thoughts about David were becoming. He didn't come across as a forever sort of guy and she wasn't looking for a forever kind of relationship, so what was up with this urgency to see him?

The only reason she could give herself was that she'd been alone and without a man's attention for so long that now that she had it, she was in greedy mode, lapping it up like a desperate woman. And she had never done the desperate thing before.

The door chimed and she looked up to see that it was Rafe who walked in. Lately she'd noticed him using the front door a lot more, instead of the back door to his parlor. They had decided at the beginning of his lease that the entrance to her shop was off-limits so his customers wouldn't trounce back and forth through her shop on the days Rafe worked late.

"Did your box of ink finally arrive?"

He stopped and looked over at her. "Why would you be asking about my ink?"

Now that, she thought, was a silly question. Did the man have a short memory? "Because you came by Wednesday looking for the shipment and left in a tiff when it hadn't arrived."

"I wasn't in a tiff and yes, I did get my box of ink."

Yes, he had been in a tiff, but if he wouldn't acknowledge it, then she would leave it alone. "Good. I'm glad you got it."

She watched him walk off toward his parlor. He hadn't been in a good mood lately. But then, maybe she'd been in such an extremely good mood that she had a distorted view. In fact, come to think of it, it was pretty normal for him to be moody.

Moments later, while she worked with a customer, Swan watched as Rafe walked back through her shop and toward the front door. She decided if he did that again she would remind him of their agreement about which door he should use whenever he went in or out of his tattoo parlor.

After her customer left, she glanced at her watch. Her shop would be closing in a couple of minutes. David usually arrived early. It would be understandable if he'd gotten detained, but she hoped he hadn't been. She was so anxious to see him.

The thought of how much she was looking forward to being with him should bother her, but for some reason it didn't. Like she'd told Candy, Swan wasn't expecting anything from her relationship with David. There had been no promises made, so none would be broken. The only thing she was expecting was exactly what she was getting—a good time. He was excellent company and great in bed.

It had been almost three years since William, and during that time, although she'd dated, she hadn't allowed herself to get serious over a man. Instead she had concentrated on opening her shop and making it a success.

She had put her mind, heart and soul into Swan's. Especially her heart, deciding that if she put it into her business, she wouldn't run the risk of placing it elsewhere. Now it seemed there might be a risk after all and that risk had a name. David Holloway.

A part of her wanted to protect herself from another possible heartbreak by calling David and canceling any plans for tonight and then to stop sharing any time with him after that. He had given her his number so she could reach him. She could certainly come up with a plausible excuse. But did she really want to do that?

No, she didn't.

David would be her test. If she could handle a casual affair with him, then she would ace the test with flying colors.

The door chimed and she glanced up and there he was. She watched him lock her door and put the Closed sign in place before pulling down the blinds. Then he slowly sauntered toward her wearing a pair of khaki pants and an open white shirt and holding her within the scope of those laser-blue eyes. There was his too-sexy walk and a smile that made her heart beat rapidly.

Suddenly seeing him, when she'd been thinking of

him all day, took complete control of her senses. Without much effort, the man had turned the sensuality up more than a notch. He had his own barometer of hotness.

Finally moving her feet, she strolled across the floor to meet him halfway and walked straight into his arms. The moment he pressed his body to hers, she reached up and looped her arms around his neck. He responded by wrapping his arms around her waist, drawing her even closer so she fit against him.

"I missed you, Swan."

She shouldn't let his words affect her, but they did—to the point where she was having difficulty replying.

"I missed you, too."

And she had, although they'd seen each other Wednesday. Even when she'd tried to convince herself that missing him to such a degree meant nothing. Now, as she stood wrapped in his arms, with her body pressed tight against his, hip to hip and thigh to thigh, she knew it meant everything.

"That's good to know, sweetheart," he said in a throaty voice.

Sweetheart? The endearment left her defenseless. She was trying to summon all her senses to regroup. And it wasn't helping matters that his arousal was cradled in the apex of her thighs. Good Lord, he felt so good there.

"Ready?" she found the voice to ask him.

His gaze studied her face as if he was seeing her for the first time. As if he was trying to record her features to memory. And then a mischievous smile touched his lips. "I'm ready for whatever you have in mind, Swan."

Shivers of desire skittered down her spine and Swan

wished his words hadn't given her ideas, but they had. Ideas that were so bold, brazen and shameless she felt her cheeks staining just thinking about them. But at that moment, she didn't care. She could and would admit to wanting him.

She should wait until later to act on her desires. That would be the safe thing to do. But she knew she would be tortured during dinner whenever she looked at him. The way his mouth moved when he ate, or the way his hands—those hands that could turn her on just by looking at them—gripped his beer bottle. There were so many things about David Holloway that would do her in if she were to wait until later.

"You sure about that, David?"

"Positive. Do you want me to prove it?"

Did she? Yes, she did. "Where?"

"I will prove it anywhere you want. Right here in the middle of the floor if you like," he said. "But I suggest your office."

Flipper could tell by the way she was looking at him that she was giving his offer serious thought. He had no problems tilting the scale in his favor and he decided to do so. Lowering his head, he kissed her, trying to be gentle and finding gentleness hard to achieve. Especially when her taste made him greedy for more.

He knew she'd ceased thinking when she responded to his kiss by sinking her body farther into his embrace and tightening her arms around his neck.

Some things, he decided then and there, were just too mind-blowingly good, and kissing Swan was one of them. What they'd shared these last few days was a dimension of pleasure he hadn't felt in a long time—or maybe ever—while devouring a woman's mouth. And when his hands shifted from around her waist to cup her backside, he groaned at the feel of her body pressed tightly against his erection.

When he finally broke off the kiss, he buried his face in the curve of her neck and drew in a deep breath. This woman was almost too much. She looked good, tasted good and as he drew in another deep breath, he concluded that she smelled good, too.

"You want to come with me, Mr. Holloway?" she asked, stepping out of his arms.

"Yes." The answer was quick off his lips.

She took his hand. "Then follow me."

He had no problem following her and the minute he crossed the threshold into her office, he recalled the last time he'd been in here. Namely, when they'd shared a kiss that had nearly brought him to his knees.

"It appears dinner will have to wait."

He glanced over at her. She had stepped out of her sandals. After locking the office door, he leaned against it and watched her undress. She was wearing a burnt-orange sundress with spaghetti straps. It looked good on her and the color of the dress seemed to highlight her hair and skin tone.

He had gotten little sleep since his friends had arrived in the Keys. But then they hadn't come here to rest. They had left their families to come here and help him solve a sinister plan of espionage against the country they loved.

And to protect the woman *he* loved.

He suddenly swallowed deep when that last thought passed through his mind. As he watched Swan remove her panties, he knew without a doubt that he had fallen in love with her. He wouldn't try to figure out how it happened but just accept that it had. Now more than ever he was determined to make sure whoever was trying to screw her over didn't succeed.

"Are you going to just stand there?" she asked, standing before him completely naked.

"No, that's not my intention at all," he said, moving away from the door to stand a few feet from her in what he considered his safe zone. If he got any closer, he would be tempted to take her with his clothes on. He removed his shirt and eased both his khakis and briefs down his legs at the same time. Quick and easy.

"I love your dolphins," she said. "I meant to ask you about them a number of other times, but always got sidetracked. So I'm asking you now. Any reason you chose dolphins?"

He decided to be as truthful with her as he could. One day he would have to explain to her why he'd lied about so many things. "Like the dolphins, I love being in the water. But this isn't just any dolphin."

"It's not?"

"No. This dolphin's name is Flipper. Surely you've heard of him."

"Not as much as I know Willy from *Free Willy*."

He chuckled as he moved toward her. "Willy was a whale. Flipper was a dolphin. That's what my friends call me. Flipper."

"Flipper?"

"Yes. Like I said, I love being in the water."

"You don't look like a Flipper."

He came to a stop in front of her. "Don't tell that to my family and friends. They wouldn't agree with you."

She reached out and touched the tattoo of the dolphin on his arm. Her fingers felt like fire as she traced along the design with her fingertips. "Beautiful. Not just your tattoos but all of you, David."

"Thanks." And in one smooth sweep, he picked her up and sat her on the desk, spreading her legs in the process.

"Did I tell you how much I missed you?" he asked, running his hands over her arms.

"Yes. Just a few moments ago when you arrived here and I told you I missed you, too. You also told me that you missed me when you walked me home Wednesday night and I invited you to stay."

Flipper heard the disappointment in her voice. If only she knew how much he'd wanted to stay. But once he'd found out Jamila would be out for a while with Horacio, he needed that time to check out her place. "I couldn't, but I intend to make it up to you when we have more time."

He was letting her know this little quickie didn't count. He had something planned for her when all this was over and he could sit her down and tell her everything.

"Not here and not now? What do you call this?" she asked when he reached up and cupped her breasts in his hands, marveling at just how beautiful they were.

"This is an I-can't-wait-until-later quickie."

"Interesting."

Shifting his gaze from her breasts to her eyes, he said, "Let me show you, Swan Jamison, just how interesting it can be." He leaned forward and kissed her while placing the head of his erection against her wet opening. The contact sent heat spiraling through him.

While his tongue mated greedily with hers, he entered her in one hard stroke. Pulling his mouth from hers, he let out a guttural moan when her muscles clamped down on his throbbing erection. That made him push harder and sink deeper.

And when she moaned his name, he knew she could feel the fire of passion spreading between them as much as he could.

Swan wrapped her legs completely around Flipper, loving the feel of him moving inside her. He was giving her body one heck of a workout on her desk. She could feel the heat in his eyes as he stared at her.

He used his hands to lift her hips off the desk's surface for a deeper penetration. When his erection hit a certain part of her, she gasped and arched her back.

"David..."

She whispered his name when she felt him going deeper and deeper. The intensity of their joining sent emotions skyrocketing through her.

She needed this. She wanted this. Like him, she needed it now, not later. This was more than interesting. This was a hot, frenzied, torrid mating. More than a quickie. David was thorough, meticulously so, and not to be rushed. It was as if he intended to savor every stroke.

Suddenly, she felt herself falling. Not off the desk but out of reality when an orgasm rammed through her at the same time as he shuddered with the force of his own release.

They stared at each other, realizing something at the same time. Wanting to make sure he didn't stop, she whispered, "Pill."

It seemed that single word triggered another orgasm and she felt him flooding her insides again while his deep, guttural groan filled the room. His release sparked another within her. His name was torn from her lips when her body shattered in earth-shaking and mind-blowing ecstasy.

As the daze from Swan's orgasmic state receded, she felt David slowly withdraw from inside her. That's when she forced her eyes open to stare at him and accepted the hand he extended to help her off the desk. Once on her feet, she wrapped her arms around his waist, feeling weak in the knees.

"It's okay, baby, I got you. I won't let you fall," he whispered close to her ear as he leaned down.

Too late, she thought. She'd already fallen. Head over heels in love with him. The very thought suddenly sent her mind spinning.

Hadn't she just given herself a good talking to moments before he'd arrived? Told herself he was someone she could enjoy, both in and out of bed and nothing more? That he was someone she knew better than to give her heart to because she hadn't wanted to take the risk?

What on earth had happened?

She knew the answer as she moved closer into the comfort of his warm naked body. David Holloway had happened. As much as she hadn't meant to fall in love with him, she had.

It didn't matter that she had known him less than three weeks. Somehow he had come into her world and turned it upside down, whether that had been his intent or not. When his work on the island was finished, he would move on and not look back. But still, knowing that he would leave hadn't stopped him from winning her heart.

"Ready?"

She lifted her head and look up at him. "You know, David, that lone question will get us in trouble."

He held her gaze for a long moment and then caressed the side of her face. "Or take us to places we really want to go and inspire us to do things that we really want to do."

Then he lowered his mouth to hers and kissed her.

Eleven

"Great work finding out about that ink, Lieutenant Holloway. I knew there was no way Swan would have betrayed her country."

"Yes, sir. Those are my thoughts as well," Flipper said. He had placed his CO on speakerphone so his SEAL teammates could listen to the call. "There's no doubt in my mind the persons naval intelligence should be concentrating on are Rafe Duggers and Horacio Jacinto."

"I agree. I met with Admiral Martin and Director Levart this morning and they concur there's a mole within the organization."

"By meeting with them, sir, does that mean you feel certain they can be totally trusted as well?" Flipper felt he had to ask.

"Yes, Lieutenant Holloway. I do. I know that because of what you discovered and what went down with Lieutenant Westmoreland a few years ago involving those moles at Homeland Security, you're not sure who you can trust. I understand that. However, I assure you that you can trust the three of us to protect Swan with our lives if we have to. We knew she was innocent, which was why we sent you there to prove we were right. You have. Now it's up to us to find out who's behind this and bring them to justice."

"And in the meantime?"

"In the meantime, Lieutenant, you are free to consider this assignment completed. Go home to Texas and enjoy the remainder of your leave."

There was no way he could consider this assignment completed, although under normal circumstances it would be once the CO said so. "I think I'll hang around Key West for a while."

"Why?" Commanding Officer Shields asked. "Do you think Swan's life might be in immediate danger?"

"As long as Duggers and Jacinta don't know they're suspected of anything, then no. However..."

"However what, Lieutenant Holloway?"

Flipper had no problem being truthful to his CO. "However, Swan has come to mean a lot to me, sir."

"Oh, I see."

Flipper figured since his CO knew him so well, he did see. "In that case, Lieutenant Holloway, how you choose to spend the rest of your leave is your decision. But keep in mind, since this is an ongoing investigation, you cannot tell Swan anything, including your reason for being in the Keys in the first place. That in itself will place you in what might be perceived by her as a dishonorable situation."

"I'm aware of that, sir, but I refuse to leave her until I have to. How long do you think it will take to wrap up the investigation?"

"Not sure. We will not only be investigating the original investigators but we'll have to restart the entire case, making Duggers and Jacinta the primary suspects. If you remain in the Keys and notice anything I need to know, don't hesitate to bring it to my attention."

In other words, Commanding Officer Shields was pretty much giving Flipper the green light to do his own thing, unofficially. "Yes, sir."

When Flipper clicked off the phone, he glanced up at his friends. "So what do you guys think?"

"Personally, I think you're doing the right thing not leaving here until you're certain Miss Jamison's life is not in any danger," Bane said.

"And since we don't plan to leave until you do, it's time we figure out just who is behind this," Coop added.

"I agree with all the above," Viper tacked on.

They all looked at Mac, who rubbed his chin as if contemplating something. Then he said, "Someone needs to play devil's advocate, so I guess it has to be me."

"No surprise there," Bane said.

Mac shot Bane a glare and then glanced back at Flipper. "Think about what the CO said. You can't tell Miss Jamison anything. Once she finds out the truth, that she was nothing more than an assignment to you, she's not going to like it, no matter how noble or honorable your intentions might have been."

Flipper drew in a deep breath. He knew Mac's words to be true. Although Swan had yet to tell him anything about her affair with William Connors, it had been in the report. The man had betrayed her and there was a chance she would probably see Flipper as doing the same. "So, Mr. Know-It-All, what do you suggest I do?" he asked.

"Start drawing a line in your relationship and don't cross it. In other words, stop seducing her," Mac said.

Too late for that, Flipper thought. All he had to do was remember what they'd done yesterday in Swan's office and again when he'd taken her home after dinner. Especially when he'd sat in one of her kitchen chairs and she'd straddled his body. The memories of what had started out in that chair and ended up in her bedroom made him feel hot. He hadn't left her place until dawn this morning. There was no way he could put a freeze on his relationship with Swan like Mac was suggesting.

"That's not an option, Mac. I'm going to do what I have to do now and worry about the consequences later."

"What's this about you having a boyfriend? I can't leave you alone for one minute."

Swan smiled when she glanced up at Rosie McCall, one of her frequent customers. Rosie, an older woman in her midforties who'd been away for the past three months visiting her family in Nevada, had returned to the Keys just yesterday. "I see Jamila has been talking again."

"Doesn't matter. So tell me, who is he?"

Swan closed the jewelry case. "First of all, he's not my boyfriend. He's just someone I'm seeing while he's here on the island working, which won't be much longer."

"Um, short meaningless flings are the best kind. What's his name?"

"David. David Holloway."

"Where he is from?"

"Texas."

"You said he's here working. What does he do for a living?"

"Whoa, time-out," Swan said, using her hand for the signal. "You don't need to know all that. David's a nice guy and that's all you really need to know."

She knew how Rosie liked to play matchmaker. She'd been the one who'd introduced Jamila to Horacio. Rosie had met him at one of the nightclubs and thought he was cute, too young for her but just the right age for Swan or Jamila. Swan hadn't been interested in a blind date but Jamila had. Horacio and Jamila met, hit it off and had been an item ever since.

"You can't blame me for being curious, Swan. You seldom date."

"My choice, remember? Besides, you do it enough for the both of us." And that was the truth. After her second divorce, Rosie had made it known she would never marry again but intended to date any man who asked her out as long as they were the right age. Not too old and not too young.

Rosie smiled. "Yes, I do, don't I? But that doesn't mean you shouldn't go out and have fun every once in a while. There's more to life than this shop, Swan. I hope you're finally finding that out."

"Whatever." Swan had heard it before and all from Rosie. She liked the older woman and thought she was a fun person who had a zeal for life. There was never a dull moment around her.

At that moment, the shop's door chimed and Swan knew without looking in that direction that David had walked in. She also knew when he saw her with a customer that he would wait until she finished before approaching her.

Rosie leaned in. "Looks like you have a customer.

Let's hope he buys something since he came in a minute before closing."

Swan inwardly smiled. "We can only hope, right?"

"But then he's such a cutie. Look at him."

Swan didn't have to look at David to know what a cutie he was, but she did so anyway. He was browsing around the store wearing a pair of shorts and a sleeveless T-shirt with flip-flops on his feet. He looked laid-back and sexy as sin. "You're right, he is a cutie."

"I love those tattoos on his upper arms. Nice."

"Yes, they are." She knew Rosie was into tattoos and was one of Rafe's frequent customers. The woman had them everywhere, visible and non-visible.

"You need to go wait on him. See what he wants. If he's not sure, offer him a few things."

Swan smiled. Little did Rosie know, but she intended to offer David a lot. "I will. Come on, I'll walk you to the door. I'm officially closed now," Swan said, coming from around the counter.

"You honestly want me to leave you here with him?" Rosie whispered. "For all you know he's not safe."

Swan chuckled and decided it was time for her to come clean. "He's safe, Rosie. That's David and he's here to walk me home. I'll introduce you on your way out the door."

"You mean that gorgeous hunk is your guy?"

Swan glanced over at David again. He was definitely a gorgeous hunk but she couldn't claim him as her guy. "Yes, he's the guy I've been seeing a lot of lately."

"Smart girl."

David glanced up when they approached and gave her a huge smile. "Hi," he greeted.

"Hi, David. I'd like you to meet Rosie McCall. A friend who has been away for the past few months and just returned back to the island. Rosie, this is David Holloway."

David extended his hand. "Nice meeting you, Rosie."

"Same here, David. I like your tattoos."

"Thanks and I like yours," he responded.

"Thanks. Well, I'll be going. I hope you guys enjoy yourselves."

"We will," Swan said, smiling up at David. "I'll be back after seeing Rosie out," she told him.

He nodded. "Nice meeting you, Rosie."

"Same here."

Swan returned to David a few moments later, after putting up the Closed sign, locking the door and pulling down the shades. She turned and studied him as he stood across the room, looking so amazingly sexy. She felt a lump in her throat. She loved everything about him, especially the muscles beneath his shirt, the masculine thighs and his tanned skin.

"Got more sun today, I see."

"Yes, I had to go out on the boat today."

"One day you're going to have to explain to me in detail just what your ocean duties entail."

"I will. But for now, come here. I missed you today."

She crossed the room to walk into his arms. "I missed you, too."

"That's good to know. Rosie seems like a nice person."

"She is."

"She has a lot of tattoos."

Swan chuckled. "Yes, she does. She's one of Rafe's best customers."

"Is that right?" David asked, still smiling. "He did an awesome job."

She checked her watch. "We can leave as soon as I

grab my purse." They would be having dinner at Nathan Waterway and afterward would attend an art show. "I'll be back in a second."

Flipper watched Swan walk off toward her office while thinking of what she'd told him about Rosie McCall. He recalled what he'd overheard Rafe and Horacio arguing about that night behind this building. Ink and roses. Or had they said Rosie? Was she a part of the group? If she was, that meant she had an ulterior motive for befriending Swan.

Pulling his phone from his pocket he texted Nick. Check out Rosie McCall.

He received an immediate reply. Will do.

He then texted Bane. Excursion tonight.

The reply was quick. On it.

Most of today he and Viper had pretended to go fishing after Mac, who'd been tailing Rafe for the past two days, reported that Rafe had rented a boat and headed in the direction of another island close by. Today Flipper and Viper had also rented a boat, making sure they stayed a good distance behind Duggers.

The man had docked in Fleming Key. Bane and Cooper, who'd arrived ahead of them, picked up the tail on Rafe. It seemed the man had gone into a sports shop where he'd stayed for three hours.

Pretending to be two guys enjoying their time out on their boat, Flipper and Viper had waited at the pier and knew when Rafe had left the island to return to Key West. Mac had been there to pick up the tail and reported that the man had been carrying a package when he went inside his tattoo shop. A package Rafe had gotten from the sports shop, according to Bane and Coop.

"I'm ready."

He looked up and when Swan met his gaze, she quickly clarified, "I'm ready *for dinner*."

He placed his phone back into his pocket and smiled. "That's all?"

The smile she returned made his insides quiver in anticipation. "For now, Mr. Holloway."

Twelve

It was getting harder and harder to leave Swan's bed, Flipper thought as he and his teammates docked at Fleming Key close to two in the morning. But at least he'd left her sleeping with the most peaceful smile on her face.

Without waking her, he had brushed a kiss across her lips and whispered that he loved her, knowing she would remember neither. But he decided to tell her how he felt when he saw her later today. He couldn't hold it inside any longer. She deserved to know. He wanted her to know. And when all this was over and she knew the truth, he would do whatever he needed to do to win her forgiveness and her love.

He jumped when fingers snapped in his face. He glared at Mac, who glared back. "Stay focused. You can daydream later."

"I wasn't daydreaming," Flipper countered. He then

realized he was the only one still in the boat. The others had already gotten out.

"Then night-dreaming. Call it what you want" was Mac's reply. "Just get out of the damn boat."

Flipper didn't have to wonder why Mac was in a rotten mood. Teri had texted him earlier in the day to say the new washer and dryer had been delivered. They were new appliances Mac hadn't known they were buying.

Moments later, dressed in all black military combat gear, the five of them circled around to the back of the sports shop Rafe had frequented lately. Being ever ready and not taking any chances, Glocks were strapped to their hips and high powered tasers to their thighs. Due to Viper's hypersensitive ears—known to pick up sound over long distances away—he would stay outside as the lookout. Flipper, Bane, Cooper and Mac bypassed security cameras to enter the building.

Once inside, they used Flipper's cameras and it didn't take long to find a hidden room. Making swift use of their time, they took pictures of everything. It was obvious this was the group's operation headquarters. More tattoo ink was stored here along with several specific tattoo designs. One design Flipper quickly recalled seeing on the side of Rosie's neck.

Flipper scanned the room with his camera and then opened several drawers in the huge desk and took photos of the contents. When he came across a photo in one of the drawers, he suddenly froze. "Damn."

"What is it, Flipper?" Bane asked.

Instead of saying anything, he motioned his head to the photograph he'd found. Mac, Bane and Coop came around him to see it as well. They looked back at him and Mac said, "We've been royally screwed."

An uneasy feeling settled in the pit of Flipper's stomach. "I need to get back to Swan as soon as possible."

Swan was awakened by the knocking on her door. She glanced at the clock on her nightstand and wondered who on earth would be at her house at four in the morning. Was it David returning? She didn't recall when he'd left but knew it was the norm for him to leave her place around midnight to return to his hotel because of his work. Usually she would be awake when he left but tonight sexual exhaustion had gotten the best of her.

Pulling on her robe, she tied it around her waist as she headed for the door. Looking out the peephole, she saw it was Jamila and Horacio. What were they doing out so late and why were they at her place? She found it odd that Horacio was on the island when the cruise ship wasn't due back in port again until next week.

From the look on Jamila's face, it appeared she wasn't happy about something. In fact, from her reddened eyes, it appeared that she'd been crying. Swan wondered what on earth was wrong. Had something happened?

Suddenly filled with concern, she quickly opened the door. The minute she did so, Jamila was shoved inside, nearly knocking Swan down.

"Hey, wait a minute. What's going on?" Swan asked, fighting to regain her balance.

"Shut the hell up and don't ask questions," Horacio said, quickly coming inside and closing the door behind him.

Swan frowned. "Horacio? What do you mean, I can't ask any questions?"

"Just do what you're told," he barked.

Swan glanced over at Jamila and saw the bruise on

the side of her face. "Did he do this to you?" Swan demanded, getting enraged. At Jamila's nod, Swan then turned to Horacio. How could he have done this when he adored Jamila? "I want you to leave now."

"If I don't, what are you going to do? Call the police? Or call that SEAL you're sleeping with?"

Swan frown deepened. "I don't know what you're talking about. Now leave or I *will* call the police."

"You won't be doing anything other than what I tell you to do. When I get the word, the two of you will be coming with me."

Swan placed her hands on her hips. "We're not going anywhere with you."

A cynical smile touched Horacio's lips as he pulled out a gun from his back pocket. "This says you will."

Swan stared at the gun, not believing Horacio had it pointed at both her and Jamila. She was about to say something when Horacio added, "I'm giving you five minutes to go into your bedroom and put on clothes. Bring me your phone first. I don't want you to get any crazy ideas."

Swan had no idea what was going on, but from the pleading look in Jamila's eyes, she knew it was best to do as she was told. She went and got her cell phone and handed it to him, but not before she noticed several missed calls from David. Why had he been trying to call her? Her mind was filled with so many questions.

"You got five minutes to get dressed. If you're not back in five minutes or try some kind of funny business, your cousin here will pay for it."

Cousin? Why did he refer to Jamila as her cousin? At what was obviously a confused look on her face, he said, "That's right. Secrets. There are plenty more where those came from, Swan, and you'll be finding out about them later. Now go."

Swan got dressed in less than five minutes. If she hadn't thought Horacio was serious about hurting Jamila, she would have escaped through her bedroom window. That bruise along the side of her friend's face indicated the man was serious.

Swan was walking out of her bedroom fully dressed when Horacio's phone rang. Instead of answering it, he said, "That's my signal that things are ready. We'll go out your back door to the beach. The boat is waiting."

"What boat?"

"Please don't ask him anything, Swan," Jamila pleaded, reaching out and grabbing her arm. "All of them are crazy."

Swan wondered just who were *all of them*. But she decided not to ask.

"Move!"

Following Horacio's orders, she and Jamila walked toward Swan's kitchen to go out the back door.

As soon as their boat docked, Flipper raced through the streets of Key West toward Swan's home with his teammates fast on his heels. He had tried reaching her on the phone but didn't get an answer. He immediately knew something was wrong because she kept her phone on the nightstand next to her bed and the ringing would have woken her up. He had tried several more times with no luck, which was why his heart was beating out of control and fear was gripping his insides, especially now that he knew who was involved.

They had contacted their CO and told him what they'd discovered. He was as shocked as they'd been and they knew Shields would be taking the necessary actions on his end. Flipper hadn't had to tell the man there would be hell to pay if anyone hurt one single hair on Swan's head.

When they reached her house, they found the door unlocked. Her cell phone had been tossed on a living room table and a quick search of her bedroom indicated she'd change clothes.

"Take a look at this, Flipper," Mac called out.

When he reached them in the kitchen, Mac pointed out the window. Flipper saw lights from a boat that was sitting idle in the ocean as if waiting to rendezvous with another vessel.

"I traced footprints in the sand that led to the water. A small watercraft probably took them out to that boat," Viper was saying. "There were three sets of shoe prints belonging to two women and a man. And they left around thirty minutes ago."

Flipper raced out Swan's back door and after putting on his night-vision eyewear, he stared out at the ocean.

"Intercept with our boat," he shouted over his shoulder to the others. Quickly dropping to the sand, he began removing his shoes, T-shirt and pants, leaving his body clad in a pair of swimming trunks.

"Don't try it, Flipper. The boat's too far out," Mac said. "It's too dangerous for anyone, even you."

Flipper glanced up at them while putting the waterproof military belt that contained combat gear around his waist. He then put a pair of specially designed water goggles over his eyes. "The woman I love is on that boat and I have no idea what they plan to do, so I have to try. Even if I die trying."

Without saying anything else, he raced toward the water and dived in.

* * *

Horacio had tied their hands before forcing them into a small boat, which carried them out into the ocean to a much bigger boat. Now they were sitting idle in the waves.

Swan wondered why. She glanced around and noticed that, other than the lights on the boat, there was only darkness. They were so far from land she couldn't see the lights from the homes where she lived anymore.

As if Horacio realized she was trying to figure out what was happening, he said, "I'm waiting for the rest of the gang, then we'll decide what we will do with the two of you."

What he said didn't make much sense. "Will someone please tell me what's going on?" Swan asked, getting angrier by the minute. None of this made any sense.

"I'll let your cousin go first since Jamila has a lot of explaining to do," Horacio said, grinning.

Swan turned to Jamila, who was sitting on a bench beside her. "What is he talking about? Why does he keep referring to you as my cousin?"

At first Jamila didn't say anything. In fact, it seemed she was refusing to meet Swan's gaze, but then she finally met Swan's eyes and said, "Because we are cousins, Swan. My mother is your grandfather's youngest sister."

"My grandfather?"

Jamila nodded. "Yes, Lawrence Jamison is my uncle. I knew for years that Uncle Lawrence disowned your father but I didn't know why until I was much older. Then I thought the reason was downright stupid and told the family what I thought. Everyone else in the family thought the same thing but were too afraid to stand up to Uncle Lawrence."

Swan didn't say anything. She was still trying to dissect the fact that she and Jamila were related. She'd known from her father that Lawrence had a sister and another brother. That was all she'd known.

"When I turned twenty-one and finished college, I decided to come find you. Uncle Lawrence didn't like it but I told him I didn't care. I'm one of the few who stands up to him. He said the family would disown me if I came here."

"Yet you came anyway," Swan said.

"Yes, I came anyway."

Swan glanced over at Horacio. He wasn't saying anything and didn't appear to be listening to what they were saying. Instead he stood at the bow of the ship looking through binoculars as if he was searching for someone. He'd said they were waiting for another boat with the gang and Swan couldn't help but wonder who the gang was.

She wanted to ask Jamila how much she knew and why they were being held hostage but figured that although Horacio was pretending not to listen to their conversation, he probably was.

Swan glanced over at Jamila. "Why didn't you tell me who you were when you first came into my shop that day? Why did you keep it a secret all this time?"

"Because I knew how my family had treated you and your mother. I figured the last thing you'd want was to meet a relative from that side of the family. I decided to let you accept me as a friend and then later I would tell you the truth that we were cousins."

"Now isn't that a touching story?" Horacio said, strolling back over to where they sat.

"Yes, it is touching," Swan said, defiantly lifting her chin. "Why are we here?"

He smiled. "You'll find out soon enough. And I hope you're not holding out any hope that your SEAL boyfriend will be coming to rescue you because he won't."

"Why do you keep saying David is a SEAL when he's not? He was in the military once but he was never a SEAL."

"Sounds like you've been conned by him just like your cousin here was conned by me," he said as if it was something to brag about. "Your lover boy *is* a SEAL and he was sent here to get the goods on you. Whether you know it or not, you've been his assignment."

Swan shook her head. "No, that's not true. I don't believe you."

"I don't care if you believe me or not but it's true. I only found out today what he's been doing and why he was sent here by naval intelligence."

Naval intelligence? Swan glanced over at Jamila, who said, "I don't know whether what he's saying is true or not, Swan, but he told me the same thing tonight."

"Why would naval intelligence suspect me of anything? It doesn't make sense." And more than that, she refused to believe David wasn't who and what he said he was.

At that moment, they heard the sound of a boat approaching. Horacio drew his gun and pointed the flashlight toward the oncoming boat. He put his gun back in place. "Hold on to that question, sweetheart. The person who will explain everything just arrived."

Swan kept her gaze trained on the boat that pulled up beside theirs and saw two people onboard. Both of them she knew. What in the world…?

She watched in shock as Rafe and Rosie came aboard. She was so focused on staring at them that she almost missed the third person who also came on board.

She gasped in shock when the person said, “Swan, you look well.”

Suddenly losing her voice, Swan couldn’t do anything but sit there and stare. There had to be some mistake. A very big mistake. There was no way the person standing before her was a part of this craziness.

No way.

She finally found her voice. “Georgianna? What are you doing here? What is this about?”

Thirteen

Flipper reached the boat and attached himself to the ladder on the side. Lucky for him, no one had thought to pull it up. Taking slow, deep breaths, he pulled air into his lungs while ignoring the pain in his arms and legs. He didn't want to think about just how far he'd swum, but like he'd told his friends, he'd had to try.

He quickly eased back into the water when he heard the sound of an approaching boat and was grateful the vessel pulled up on the other side from where he was hiding. He glanced at his watch. It was synchronized with the ones worn by his teammates, and he knew they would do their best to get here soon. In the meantime, there was something he had to do.

Pulling a micro audio recorder off his belt, he moved back up the ladder to peek over the railing and into the boat.

Good. Everyone's attention was on the approaching

vessel and no one saw him when he attached the audio recorder that was no bigger than a dime to the interior wall of the boat. He saw Swan and Jamila seated on a bench with their hands tied behind their backs and Horacio was standing not far away. Other than a man in the cockpit, there was no one else onboard. Flipper knew that was about to change when he heard voices.

Satisfied that the conversations would be recorded, he eased back down the ladder. When his watch began vibrating, he glanced down at the text message from Bane. On our way. Had 2 take care of a little problem 1st.

Flipper wondered what kind of problem his friends had to take care of. No matter. They were on their way and that's what counted. He listened to the conversation going on in the boat as he began pulling items from his belt. He intended to be ready to crash this little party when the time came.

He shook his head, knowing Admiral Martin would be heartbroken to discover his own daughter had sold out their country.

"I hate you," Georgianna said, glaring at Swan.

Swan was taken aback by the woman's words. "Why? What have I ever done to you? To any of you?" she asked, glancing around at the people she'd assumed were friends—Rafe, Horacio and Rosie. She hurt more at seeing Rosie than the others because she'd believed the woman had been a good friend.

"They work for me and did what they were told," Georgianna said.

"Work for you?" Swan was even more confused.

"Yes. I'm in charge of the entire operation. But I'll tell you all about that later. First, let me tell you why

I despise you so much. I've waited a long time to get this out in the open. When your father died and your mother would send you to us for the summer, my parents thought you were golden. They put you on a pedestal, especially my father. Did you know he called you his little island princess?"

Yes, Swan knew but she also knew her godfather hadn't meant anything by it. It was just a nickname he'd given her when she was born. All three of her godfathers called her that sometimes. "It was just a nickname, Georgianna."

"For you, it might only have been a nickname, but for me, it was Dad shifting his attention from me to you."

"Godpop 1 loves you. He wasn't shifting his attention to me, he was just being nice."

"Too nice, and I despised you for it. He had a daughter, yet any time your mother would call, he and Mom would drop everything and take off. Just because your father saved Dad's life—that meant nothing. They were all SEALs and your dad was doing his job when he died. But it was as if Dad blamed himself and he needed to make it up by being nice to you, like you were somebody special. So, with the help of some friends, I decided to change everyone's opinion of you."

It was hard for Swan to believe what she was hearing. She'd never known that Georgianna harbored such feelings. Granted she hadn't always been overnice and had a tendency to be moody, but Swan hadn't detected animosity like this.

"What did you do?" Swan asked her.

Georgianna smiled like she was proud of what she was about to say. "I set up an espionage operation out of your shop with the help of Rafe and Horacio. Then, with Rosie's assistance, I made it appear that the secret information being sent to China was being done through your jewelry."

"What!" Swan couldn't believe it. Her head was spinning from all the shocks she'd received tonight.

"I have to admit I put together a perfect plan. This guy I was sleeping with at the time assisted me by tipping off naval intelligence with what you were supposedly doing. They did their own investigation and my team and I made sure everything pointed at you. It should have been an open and shut case and you were to be arrested and charged with espionage."

As if she was tired of standing, Georgianna moved to sit on one of the benches. She frowned over at Swan. "Everything was going according to plan until the final thread of the investigation reached Director Levart's desk."

"Godpop 3?"

"See what I mean? You have three godfathers and I don't have a one," Georgianna said in a loud voice, pointing a finger at her. "You don't deserve such love and loyalty, and I intended to tarnish their image of you."

Flipper's watch vibrated and he glanced down at the text message. Here. N place. Coop got layout of boat.

He texted them back. 1 N cockpit. 4 others. 2 hostages.

He quickly received a reply from Viper. Eliminating cockpit.

Got 4 in scope. That particular text came from Bane, a master sniper.

Flipper knew that although everyone was in place, timing was everything. Georgianna had no idea her words were being recorded so he wanted to let her talk before making his move. Then there would be no way she could deny anything.

From listening to what the woman was saying, it was obvious she had mental issues. That could be the only reason to have such a deep hatred of Swan that Georgianna would go to such extremes. Georgianna assumed she'd had the perfect plan for Swan's downfall and Flipper was glad things hadn't turned out the way Georgianna intended.

Before inching up the ladder to listen to what else she was confessing, he texted the message: Will give signal.

Swan shook her head. It was obvious Georgianna's jealousy had blinded her senses and fueled her hatred. Didn't the others see it? Why were they following her blindly? Swan glanced over at Jamila and could tell by the look in her cousin's eyes that she was wondering the same thing.

"When Director Levart saw the report, he refused to believe you could be guilty of anything, especially betraying your country."

Thank God for that, Swan thought.

"He requested a thirty-day delay before agreeing to take any actions against you. Even after we made sure the investigation clearly spelled out your role in everything. There was no reason for you not to be charged," Georgianna said.

She paused a moment before continuing. "Unknown to me and the others, Director Levart went to your other two godfathers and they put their heads together to see what they could do to prove your innocence. They decided to send one of their top SEALs to find out what he could and to prove your innocence."

Swan drew in a deep breath. *Oh no, please don't*

let what Horacio said tonight be true. Please don't let David turn out to be someone other than what he said he was.

Georgianna's next words ripped into Swan's heart.

"The SEAL they sent was Lieutenant David Holloway. I guess you didn't know that all the time he spent with you was nothing more than an assignment. You meant nothing to him, Swan." Georgianna laughed as if she found the entire thing amusing while Swan's heart broke.

"Imagine how amused I was to find out just how taken you were with him, while not knowing the true purpose as to why he showed up here on the island. You were played, Swan," Georgianna was saying in between laughter. "But don't worry. I sent some other members of my group to take care of him for you. I think he's dead by now."

Suddenly a deep voice at the back of the boat said, "As you can see, I'm very much alive."

Swan gasped just as the others did. Standing with legs braced apart and wearing only a pair of swim trunks with a utility combat belt around his waist, David looked like a mad badass. It was obvious everyone was shocked to see him, especially Georgianna, who had assumed he was dead.

"Drop your gun," he ordered Horacio, who was still holding his weapon on Swan and Jamila.

"How the hell did you get here?" Horacio asked, enraged.

"I swam from Swan's home."

"That's impossible!"

"Not if you're a SEAL master swimmer," David said. "Now, do like I said and put your gun down."

"And if I don't? It will be a shame if I kill Swan or Jamila before you can get to anything on that belt you're wearing," Horacio sneered.

"Don't try it, Horacio. One of my team members who's a master sniper has all four of you within his scope. Before you could get off the first shot, you'd be dead."

"I don't believe you. There's no one else out here," Horacio said. When he lifted his gun to take aim at Swan, a shot rang out, hitting the man in the chest. The impact toppled him to the floor.

Jamila screamed and Swan understood. Jamila had fallen in love with a man who'd betrayed her and then gotten shot right before her eyes.

Suddenly, Rafe dived for the gun that had dropped from Horacio's hand. Before he could reach it, another shot rang out that hit him in the side. He fell to the floor as well.

"Either of you ladies want to join them?" Flipper asked Georgianna and Rosie.

Rosie looked like she was in shock and ready to pass out.

However, Georgianna looked furious. "You won't get away with this. No matter what you tell my father, he will never believe you over me," she said with absolute certainty. "I'll tell him that you decided to team up with Swan and she turned you against your country."

"I figured you would lie. That's why I've recorded your little confession to Swan detailing everything. I can't wait for your father to listen to it."

Suddenly the boat was surrounded by several naval vessels and sharp beams of light shined on them. A voice through a foghorn said, "Lieutenant Holloway, we are coming aboard."

A dozen men wearing SEAL gear rushed on board with their guns drawn, immediately taking Georgianna and Rosie into custody. Bane, Viper, Coop and Mac boarded the boat as well. Mac rushed over to check Horacio and Rafe. There really was no need since they were both dead.

Flipper rushed over to Swan and Jamila to untie their hands. More than anything, he wanted to pull Swan into his arms and tell her he loved her. He wanted her to put out of her mind what Georgianna had said about him until she'd heard his side of things. However, he knew when she pulled away from him to give her cousin a hug that she didn't want to give him a chance to explain.

He didn't intend to let her walk away.

"We need to talk, Swan," he said, looking down at her.

She glared up at him. "We have nothing to say to each other. Your assignment is over, Lieutenant Holloway. Now leave me alone."

Fourteen

Two weeks later

"How long are you planning to be mad at the world, Swan?"

Swan glanced over at Candy. Her best friend had returned to the Keys after hearing about what happened and she'd decided to stay. Swan was glad Candy had returned home but she was saddened by what had brought her back.

"I am not mad at the world," Swan said, taking a sip of her orange juice.

"But you are still mad at one particular man," Candy said, coming to sit beside Swan on the sofa.

Swan couldn't deny that was true so she didn't. "And what if I am?"

"He had a job to do, Swan. He was given orders. Surely you understand that."

Swan glared at Candy. "I'm sure none of my godfathers' orders included sleeping with me."

"I'm sure they didn't but David didn't force himself on you."

"No, but he deceived me."

"So did the others."

Did Candy have to remind her? "And I'm not talking to them either."

That wasn't totally true since Swan had reached out to Georgianna where she was being held at a federal prison in Orlando. The woman had refused to see her. Swan knew Georgianna was undergoing psychiatric evaluations to see if she was fit to stand trial.

Swan's godparents were heartbroken and she understood how they felt. Like her, they'd had no idea Georgianna harbored such hatred toward Swan, enough to do what she'd done. With both Rafe and Horacio dead, it was Rosie who was singing like a bird, telling everything she knew for a lessened sentence.

According to Rosie, Georgianna had manipulated a number of the men at naval intelligence into doing whatever she wanted them to do. When you were the admiral's daughter, you could wield that kind of power. She had even threatened a few with blackmail. She'd deliberately recorded several of the men having sex with her and then threatened to give the tape to her father and accuse them of rape.

Some of the men were not only married but a number were high-ranking military officers. Fearful of court-martial, the men had done whatever Georgianna asked, including falsifying records. So far, more than twelve men had been named in the scandal.

"I take it David hasn't called."

Swan drew in a deep breath. She had seen him last

week when they'd had to show up at the naval station to give statements. "Yes, he's called. Several times. But I refuse to answer. Like I told him, we have nothing to say to each other. His assignment is over."

"And do you honestly think that's all you were to him, Swan?"

"Yes, but it doesn't matter."

"I think it does," Candy countered.

"And you think too much," Swan said, easing off the sofa.

The first week after the incident on the boat, she had closed her shop while naval investigators did a thorough search of Rafe's tattoo parlor. She had used that time to take care of Jamila, who was still broken up over Horacio. Jamila had loved him and in a single night had seen him become an abusive monster, a man she hadn't known. Then in the end, Jamila had watched him die before her eyes.

Swan knew Jamila was going through something that only time could heal. That's why when Swan had reopened the shop this week and Jamila had asked for extra work hours, Swan had given them to her.

"So what are you going to do?" Candy asked her.

Swan glanced over at her. "About life? Work?"

"No, about David."

Swan just couldn't understand why Candy couldn't accept that David was no longer in the equation. "I'm a survivor, Candy. Although it was hard, I made do after my parents' deaths and I will make do now." She glanced at her watch. "I'm getting dressed to go into the shop today. The cruise ship comes into port tomorrow, so business will pick up. I want to make sure most of my new pieces are on display."

Another thing they had found out was that Horacio

had been fired from the cruise ship months ago but hadn't told Jamila. He had moved into Rosie's place while the woman had been gone. The duplicity of the people she'd thought she knew simply amazed Swan.

"And I need to be on my way," Candy said. "I promised my folks we would go out to dinner tonight. You can join us if you like."

"Thanks for the invite, but I'll pass. I just want to have a relaxing evening here tonight. I might go swimming on the beach later."

Swan had called Jamila and told her she would bring lunch from their favorite sandwich café. However, there were no clients in her shop when Swan got there, so she decided to do something she usually didn't do, which was close for lunch.

Normally, the shop remained open and she and Jamila would alternate lunch duties. But today she wanted to check on Jamila, talk to her to see how she was faring. Although Swan had been there for Jamila last week, they hadn't had a real honest-to-goodness talk since Jamila had admitted to being her cousin.

"What are you doing?" Jamila asked when Swan put up the Closed sign and pulled down the blinds.

Swan smiled over at her. "New store policy. From here on out, we will close at noon for lunch."

"What about the sales you'll lose?"

Swan shrugged. "Sales aren't everything. Besides, it's just for an hour. Come join me in my office."

"All right, let me grab some sodas out of the refrigerator."

A few minutes later, she and Jamila were enjoying their lunch when Swan gave Jamila a long look. "How are you doing?"

Jamila shrugged. "Okay, I guess. Trying to move on.

I loved Horacio so much only to find out he wasn't the man I thought he was."

"I know the feeling."

"No, you don't."

Swan snatched her head up, frowning. "Excuse me?"

"I said you don't know the feeling, Swan. David Holloway was nothing like Horacio. David intended to save you and Horacio would have killed me if that woman had ordered him to do so. Big difference."

"But like you, I was betrayed."

"How?" Jamila countered. "Your godfathers sent David Holloway here to prove your innocence and he did."

Jamila put her soda can down and then added, "And another thing. What man takes a chance and swims across the ocean to save a woman? Do you know how far from land we were? Think about that."

Swan had news for her—she *had* thought about it. She could never forget how David had appeared seemingly out of nowhere on that boat, looking tough and ready to kick asses while wearing nothing more than an outlandishly tight pair of swim trunks with a military belt around his waist. Even when she'd been in what seemed like a dire situation, that hadn't stopped the woman in her from noticing how dangerously sexy he'd looked at that particular moment.

"When I mentioned what an astounding feat he'd accomplished to his friends," Jamila said, reclaiming Swan's attention, "they said that's why they call him Flipper. Did you know that's his code name as a SEAL?"

Swan wiped her mouth with a napkin. "Yes, I knew he was called Flipper. But no, I didn't know it had anything to do with him being a SEAL because I didn't know he was one. I assumed Flipper was his nickname."

Swan forced from her mind the day she'd asked him about those dolphin tattoos. He'd told her then they represented Flipper. That had been the day they'd made love in this office. Right here on this desk.

She wished she wasn't thinking so hard about that now.

She looked over at Jamila. "Why are we talking about me instead of you?"

"Because I think you should and because I think I should," Jamila continued. "Talking about your situation actually helps me believe that not all men are jerks and that there are some who still possess real honor, Swan. Whether you want to admit it or not, David Holloway is an honorable man. He couldn't help being attracted to you any more than you could help being attracted to him."

Swan stuffed the wrappings from her sandwich into the empty bag. "Now you sound like Candy."

"Maybe there's a reason why I do," Jamila said, stuffing her own wrappings into a bag. "It might be because Candy and I can see things that you refuse to see. I often think about what could have happened to us had David and his friends not shown up when they did. Do you ever think of that?"

Swan drew in a deep breath. "I try not to."

"I think you should," Jamila said, standing. "Thanks for bringing lunch. It will be my treat the next time." She then walked out of the office.

Swan stayed in her office after Jamila left, trying to put their conversation out of her mind. She was working on her computer, verifying inventory, when her office phone rang. "Thank you for calling Swan's. How may I help you?"

"Hello, island princess."

She smiled upon hearing her godfather's voice. "Godpop 2. How are you?"

"I'm fine. I just wanted to check on you. So much has happened and I wanted to make sure you're okay."

She had spoken to each of her godfathers and had thanked them for believing in her. They had taken a risk with their individual careers to do that. "I'm fine. How is Godpop 3?"

"He's fine but as the director of naval intelligence, he has his hands full with the investigation. It seems that more names are popping up in this scandal each day."

"And how are Godpop 1 and Barbara?"

"They are as well as can be expected under the circumstances. Learning about Georgianna was a shocker for all of us. We had no idea. When we decided to send Lt. Holloway to prove your innocence, the three of us weren't sure just what he would uncover. The only thing we knew for certain was that you weren't guilty of anything."

"Thanks for believing in me."

"You have Andrew's blood in your veins. You could no more be a traitor to your country than he could. Considering all that happened, I'm glad Holloway remained in Key West when he could have left."

Swan sat up straight. "Wasn't David on assignment?"

"Not the entire time. His assignment officially ended when he sent that ink in to be analyzed and we discovered it was tainted. I told him that he no longer had to stay in the Keys since by then we knew you weren't involved and we would take over the investigation from there."

"Then why did he stay?"

"To protect you."

"He told you that?" she asked.

"Yes. I remember the conversation like it was yesterday. I told him he could consider his job assignment complete and go home to Texas and enjoy the remainder of his leave. But he said he wanted to hang around Key West for a while."

Her godfather paused. "I asked him if the reason he wanted to stay was because he thought your life might be in danger. He said he felt that as long as Duggers and Jacinto didn't know they were suspects, then no, your life wasn't in any immediate danger. He informed me that the reason he wanted to stay was because you had come to mean a lot to him. I told him in that case how he spent the rest of his leave was his decision. And, Swan?"

She drew in a deep breath. "Yes?"

"As his commanding officer, I felt the need to remind him that although he was no longer on assignment, since the issue that had started with you was an ongoing investigation, he could not tell you anything."

When Swan didn't reply, her godfather asked, "You're still there, Swan?"

"Yes, Godpop 2, I'm still here."

"Did you not know how Holloway felt about you?"

"No. I thought I was just an assignment."

"You were at first and I'm glad you were. Otherwise you would be in jail wrongly accused of a crime you hadn't committed. But on the flip side, I'm also glad that when you stopped being an assignment, Holloway had the insight to stay and look out for you because he cared for you."

Long after her telephone conversation with her godfather ended, Swan remained seated at her desk, leaning back in her chair and sitting in silence while thinking about what Candy, Jamila and her godfather had said.

Some people never got betrayed, but she had been,

a lot. William, Rafe, Horacio, Rosie, Georgianna and even Jamila. No one had been who she'd thought.

She remembered David and replayed in her mind all the time she'd spent with him since that day he'd first walked into her shop.

Was anything he'd told her true? Did he really come from a huge family? Was his mother even celebrating a birthday? Did he honestly have three sisters-in-law?

One thing was for certain, both Candy and Jamila were right. David hadn't pushed her into sleeping with him. In fact, Swan was the one who'd invited him to dinner at her place with the full intent of having sex with him.

She got up from her desk and walked over to the window. She knew from Jamila that David had left the island with his friends after that first week, after he'd completed all the questioning by naval intelligence. Was he back home in Texas? Did his parents really own a medical supply company? What parts of what he'd told her were true and what parts were fabricated for his assignment?

And why did she still love him so much it hurt… even when she didn't want to love him? Even when she didn't know how he felt about her? He might have told her godfather he cared for her but David hadn't told her anything. Shouldn't he have? But then, had she given him a chance to do so?

The answer to that flashed in her mind quickly. No, she hadn't.

He had saved her life that night, swam across the ocean to do so, and then she'd told him she didn't want to talk to him. And he had honored her wishes…for that one night. Then he had called her almost every single day since, and yet she had refused to take his calls.

He hadn't called today.

Did that mean he'd given up and wouldn't try contacting her again? Was she ready to put her heart on the line and contact him?

She wasn't sure. But what she *was* certain of was that they needed to do what they hadn't done before. They needed to get to know each other. She needed to know which parts of what he'd told her about himself were true and which were false.

She wanted to get to know the real David Holloway.

Then what?

Hadn't she convinced herself she wanted no part of a man in the military? And what about her decision to never to get seriously involved in an interracial relationship like her parents had? Why did all of that no longer matter to her when she thought about her and David deciding to have a future together?

Maybe that's how love worked. It made you see the possible instead of the impossible. It made you want things you told yourself were not good for you because you were afraid to reach beyond your comfort zone.

Taking a deep a cleansing breath, she decided to call David tonight before going to bed. She had no idea what she would say to him but the words would come.

She doubted he would want to come back to the Keys anytime soon, so she would let him know she would come to him if he still wanted to talk. She would see what he said before asking Jamila if she could take care of the shop while Swan was gone. David might very well tell her that it was too late, that they had nothing to talk about. But there was a chance he would embrace her words. Embrace her.

Her mood suddenly lightened, knowing that was a possibility.

* * *

Flipper entered the hotel room and tossed his luggage on the bed. Different hotel but same city. He had given Swan two weeks and now he was back. They needed to talk and clear up some things. She hadn't accepted his calls, but now he was here and he wouldn't be ignored.

He shook his head when his cell phone rang. "Yes, Coop?"

"Have you seen her yet?"

"No, I just got here. In fact, I walked into my hotel room less than five minutes ago."

"Okay. And there's another reason I called. Bristol is pregnant."

"Wow, man. Congratulations. I didn't know you guys were trying."

Coop laughed. "We're always trying. But seriously, we figured it was time Laramie had a playmate."

"Sounds good to me."

"I hope things work out with you and Swan, Flipper."

"I hope so, too."

"And do me a favor."

"What?"

"For once, open up. Tell her how you feel. Don't beat around the bush. You have a tendency to do that. Women love a man to get straight to the point and share their feelings. I hate to say it, bro, but you're not good at doing that."

Coop was right, he wasn't. "I never had to do that before. I've never truly loved a woman before Swan."

"I understand. But you do love her, so make sure she knows it. A woman has to believe she's loved."

Flipper chuckled.

"What's so funny?" Coop asked him.

"You're giving relationship advice. Do you know how much like Mac you sound?"

Coop chuckled as well. "You would have to point that out. I guess it comes with loving a woman."

"I guess so."

"No guess in it, remember it. Know it. Feel it. Take care and good luck."

After ending the call with Coop, it wasn't long before Flipper got calls from Bane, Viper and Mac as well, all letting him know they hoped things worked out for Flipper and Swan. All giving him advice. They were married men who had the women they loved and they wanted him to have the woman he loved as well.

He appreciated good friends who not only watched his back but who also cared about the condition of his heart. They knew about the pain he had lodged there and it got worse every day he and Swan were apart.

Flipper glanced at his watch. Swan's store would be closing in less than an hour. He would give her time to get home and relax before paying her a visit. He refused to let her put things off any longer. They needed to talk.

He loved her and it was damn time she knew it.

Fifteen

Swan had just poured a glass of wine to enjoy while sitting on the patio when she heard the knock at her door.

She knew Candy had gone out to dinner with her family and Jamila had mentioned she would just stay in tonight and chill. Swan had invited Jamila to join her so maybe her cousin had changed her mind.

Her cousin.

That was taking a lot of getting used to but Swan knew her parents would want a family connection for them. Jamila was the only family Swan had and she appreciated their friendship more than ever.

She reached the door and glanced through the peephole. Her heart nearly stopped.

Was it really David? She blinked and looked again and saw it was really him. Back in Key West. And he was standing in front of her door looking like he always did, sexy as hell.

Drawing in a deep breath, she removed the security lock and opened the door. "David? I thought you'd left the island."

"I had but I returned today. May I come in?"

She nodded and stepped aside. The moment he passed her, she caught a whiff of his masculine scent, the same one she was convinced still lingered in her bedroom.

Swan closed the door and stood to face him. He was standing in the middle of her living room wearing a pair of shorts and a sleeveless shirt with a huge picture of a dolphin. *Flipper.* Her gaze moved beyond the shirt to his face to find his laser-blue eyes staring at her.

She cleared her throat. "I was about to sit out back and drink a glass of wine while enjoying the view. Would you like to have a beer and join me?"

She could tell he was surprised by her invitation. She hadn't bothered to ask why he was there.

"Yes, I'd like that."

Moments later, they were sitting side by side on a bench that overlooked the beach. They had been sipping their drinks for a few moments when he said, "I told you that night two weeks ago that we needed to talk, Swan. I think we still do."

Yes, they did. She would let him go first. "Okay, I'm listening."

"I want you to do more than just listen, Swan. I want you to engage by asking questions, giving me feedback, and I would like to be able to do the same with you."

"Okay, that seems fair because I do have some questions for you."

"Ask away."

She took another sip of her drink. "You didn't tell me you were a SEAL and I'd—"

"I couldn't tell you I was a SEAL, Swan," he interrupted to say. "That's why I lied and said I was no longer in the military."

"Yes, I know that now. I want to tell you, because of what happened to my father, I had made up my mind never to get serious about a military man...especially not a SEAL."

"Oh, I see."

She wouldn't tell him yet that she'd changed her mind about that. "Is your mother's birthday really next month and do you have four brothers?"

"Yes. Everything I told you about my family is true. I never lied to you about anything pertaining to them. I just omitted some details and couldn't elaborate on certain things."

She then put her wineglass down and turned toward him. "Why did you sleep with me, David, when I was just an assignment to you?"

Flipper knew this was the time of reckoning and what he told her would have an impact on their relationship for the rest of their days. He needed her to understand.

"You were supposed to be an assignment, Swan. But honestly, I don't think you ever were. From the moment I walked into your shop and saw you, a part of me knew I had to fight hard to be objective and do the job I'd been sent here to do."

He paused. "I tried to keep my attraction to you out of the picture but found it harder and harder to do. Each time I saw you while getting to know you, I fell deeper under your spell. It was hard pretending with you."

He decided to be totally honest with her. "Just so you know, that day you invited me to your place for dinner wasn't my first time there. I'd been to your home without you knowing anything about it. But at the time, it was just a house I was checking out as part of an investigation. The day you invited me to dinner, I saw it through another pair of eyes. Yours. And for me, it then became your home."

She drew in a deep breath. "You invaded my privacy by letting yourself into my home, but that's not why I'm upset. I accept that you had a job to do and I was your assignment but…"

"But what?"

"You still haven't fully answered my question, David. Why did you make love to me?"

David frowned, realizing that he *hadn't* answered her question. His teammates often teased him about beating around the bush, sometimes providing too much context instead of just sticking with the facts.

"The reason I made love to you, Swan, was because I desired you. Everything about you turned me on. Your looks, your scent, your walk…and then after our first kiss, it was your taste. Fighting my desire for you was no longer an option, although I tried being honorable enough not to seduce you."

"But then I seduced you," she said quietly.

He smiled. "No, I think that night we seduced each other. Everything we did was mutual."

"Yes, it was." She took another sip of her wine. "I spoke with Godpop 2 today and he told me your assignment ended but you decided to stay. Why?"

Okay, no beating around the bush this time, Flipper decided. "The reason is that by then I had fallen in love with you. In all honesty, in my heart you stopped being an assignment the first time I made love to you. I crossed the line of what was honorable, and I knew why. Because I felt you here, Swan," he said, pointing to his heart. "I felt you here in a way I've never felt before. No woman has ever been here, Swan. But during the one time you shouldn't have, you got there anyway."

"And now? How do you feel now?"

He placed his beer bottle aside and turned toward her. "Now you are still in my heart. Even more so. I love you so much I ache on the inside when I'm not with you. I love you so much I think of you even at times I shouldn't."

He reached out and took her hand in his. "Now I need to know, Swan, just how you feel about me."

Swan felt the gentle tug on her hand and, surprising even herself, she moved to sit in his lap.

When he wrapped his arms around her, she felt comfort flow through her. She turned in his lap to look down at him. He'd given her answers to all her questions, now she intended to give him answers to his.

"I love you, David. I fought it at first. I didn't know about you being present-day military, but I also had a problem…not with interracial dating…but with allowing anything to come of it. I saw how others saw my parents at times. Not as a beautiful couple in love but as an interracial couple in love. There should not have been a difference. I never wanted to deal with what they had to deal with in the name of love."

She paused. "But then I moved beyond thinking that way after I fell in love with you. Then I realized how my parents must have felt, believing nothing mattered but their love. Even if the world was against them, as long as they had each other, that's what truly counted."

"So you do love me?" he asked her as if for clarity.

Swan didn't have a problem clarifying anything for

him or anyone else. "Yes, I love you, David Flipper Holloway." And then she lowered her mouth to his.

Shivers of profound pleasure shot through every part of Swan's body when David slid his tongue into her mouth. Sensations bombarded her as she concentrated on his taste, his scent and the way he pulled her tongue into his mouth to mate with his. And when she felt his hands inch upward and slide beneath her top, his touch made her purr.

Both his taste and his touch were awakening parts of her, making her feel alive in a way she hadn't felt since the last time they'd been together. Here at her house. In her bed.

When his fingers touched her bare breasts, using his fingertips to draw circles around her nipples, she oozed deeper into the kiss, almost feeling like melted butter in his arms.

He slowly pulled his mouth from hers and looked at her. His blue eyes were sharp and filled with the same desire she felt. "Any reason why we can't take this inside?"

She wrapped her arms around his waist. "No, there's no reason."

"Good."

And then standing with her in his arms, he carried her into the house.

"Just so you know, David, I didn't ask you all my questions," Swan said when he placed her on the bed.

David glanced down at her. "You didn't?"

"No, but I can wait. None are more earth-shattering than this is going to be. And I need this."

He caressed the side of her face with his finger. "I need this, too. I know why I need it, tell me why you do."

She met his gaze and held it while she said, "I love the feel of you inside of me. I've never felt anything so right before. So pleasurable." She smiled. "Do you know I retired my sex toy?"

He chuckled. "That's good to know."

"Um, not too much information?"

"No. Nice to know what used to be my competition," he said as he began removing her clothes. Lucky for him, she wasn't wearing much. Just a top, shorts and a thong. Flipper had discovered outside earlier that she wasn't wearing a bra. He'd noticed more than once that she liked her breasts being free and so did he.

She reached out and tugged at his T-shirt and he assisted by removing his own shorts. Then he rejoined her on the bed. Reaching out, he lifted her by the waist. "Wrap your legs around me, Swan. I'm about to join our bodies, to make us one."

As soon as her legs were settled around his waist, his shaft touched her core. She was wet and ready. Tilting her hips, he whispered the words, "I love you," before thrusting hard into her.

"David!"

Arching her back off the bed, she provided the prefect position for his penetration to go deeper. They were a perfect fit. They always would be. Not just in lovemaking but in everything they did from here on out. They had become a team.

He began moving, slowly at first and then harder and deeper, over and over again. The only constant sounds in the room were their breathing and flesh slapping against flesh. The air surrounding them was filled with the aroma of sex.

He felt on fire, like his entire body was burning and the flames fueled his need, his desire and his love. She was looking up at him, holding his gaze, and he hoped Swan saw the depth of love in his eyes.

He clenched his jaw when he felt it, the stirring of pleasure in his groin. The feeling was slowly spreading through his body and when Swan gripped his shoulders and dug her fingers into his skin, he continued to thrust inside of her like his life depended on it.

And when she screamed out his name, he knew the same sensations that were taking him were taking her.

He drew in a sharp breath only moments before calling out her name. Multiple sensations tore into him, causing an explosion inside of him that had him bucking his body in an all-consuming orgasm. The sensations kept coming until he let go and his release shot deep inside of her.

He knew right then that he wanted her to have his baby. If not this time, another time. One day, he intended to make it happen.

Moments later, he slumped down beside her and wrapped his arms around her as he tried to get his breathing under control. After recovering from his explosive orgasm, when he was able to talk, he said, "I feel like I've been burned to a crisp."

"Hmm, speaking of burning, do you know what I thought was hot?" she asked, drawing in deep breaths of air into her lungs.

"No, what?"

"You on that boat wearing nothing but swim trunks and that military belt around your waist. Now, that was hot."

He grinned. "You liked that, huh?"

She smirked up at him when he straddled her body again. "I liked it." Then her features became serious. "I still can't believe you swam all that way to save me."

He leaned in and brushed a kiss across her lips. "Believe it."

He then pulled back and looked down at her. His expression was serious. "I'm a damn good swimmer. I'm known to be able to hold my breath underwater for long periods of time. Longer than what most would consider normal. But I wasn't sure I was going to make it to the boat, Swan. I told my friends I had to try even if I died trying because the woman I love was on that boat. That's what kept me going. That's what fueled every stroke I made into the ocean waters. And when my body felt tired, like I couldn't possibly swim another lap, I would think of a life without you and for me that was unacceptable."

He drew in a sharp breath. For a quick minute, he relived the feel of the cold water as he swam nonstop to the boat to save her, not knowing if he would make it in time. "I had to save you."

"And then I rebuffed you. I refused to have that talk you wanted."

"I understood. I had been listening to what Georgianna Martin was saying, the picture she painted. I told myself that once I talked to you and told you the truth that you would believe me. I was just giving you time to think about everything. I figured you would realize that I did care for you."

She reached up and caressed the side of his face. "You never told me you cared."

"I did. Our last night together, when you were asleep, I told you before I left that I loved you. I had planned to tell you the next day when we were together but that's when you were taken."

"And you came back," she said.

"That was always my plan, Swan. I never intended to

let you go. I love you that much. And just so you know, my entire family is rooting for me. I told them about you and they can't wait to meet you. My brothers and I are giving Mom a party for her birthday next week. Will you go to Texas with me?"

When she hesitated, he added, "What I told you about them is true. My parents accept people for who they are and not how they look. Will you trust me about that?"

She met his gaze and nodded. "Yes, I will trust you and yes, I will go."

A huge smile spread across his face. "I can't wait to introduce you to everyone. And I've got the perfect thing for you to wear." He quickly eased off the bed.

She pulled herself up. "What's going on? You plan on dressing me that night?"

He glanced over his shoulder, chuckling as he pulled a small white box out of his shorts. "Something like that."

He returned to the bed and pulled her up to stand her on her feet beside the bed. Then he got down on one knee and looked up at her. "I love you, Swan. I know we have a lot of things we still need to overcome. But I believe we will do so together. Forever. Will you marry me?"

He saw tears form in her eyes when she nodded. "Yes, I will marry you."

He slid the ring on her finger and at that moment Flipper knew he was halfway to having his world complete.

He would get the other half the day she became his wife.

Sixteen

Swan glanced down at the ring David had put on her finger last week. Seeing it gave her strength and she definitely needed strength now, she thought as she entered a huge ballroom on his arm. It was his mother's sixtieth birthday party.

They had flown into Dallas last night so this would be the first time she met his family. Nervous jitters had tried taking over her stomach but a smile from David was keeping most of them at bay. He was convinced his family would love her and he had told her over and over that she was worrying for nothing. She was the woman he wanted and his family would love his choice.

"There's Mom and Dad," he said, with his arms around her shoulders as she carried his mother's gift. The same gift he'd purchased that first day he'd come into her shop.

A man she knew had to be one of David's brothers whispered something to the older couple and they turned with huge smiles on their faces.

At that moment, Swan knew David had inherited his father's eyes and that the smiles on the couple's faces were genuine. She could actually feel their warmth. David's mom was beautiful and did not look like she was sixty or that she had five grown sons.

When they reached his parents, David made the introduction. "Mom. Dad. I want you to meet the woman who has agreed to be my wife, Swan Jamison."

"It's an honor to meet you," Swan said, extending her hand to his mother.

Instead of taking it, the older woman engulfed Swan in a huge hug. "It's wonderful meeting you as well, Swan, and welcome to the family."

"Thank you. Here's your gift. Happy birthday."

"Thank you."

She received a hug from David's father as well. Then suddenly she was surrounded and a laughing David made introductions. All his brothers had those same blue eyes and like David, they were very handsome men. She could see why when she looked at the older Holloways; they were a beautiful couple. And Swan could tell from the way Mr. Holloway looked at his wife and the way Mrs. Holloway would look back at him that the couple was still very much in love.

A few nights ago, David had shared the fact that because his mother had been married to a Navy SEAL for over forty years and had five sons who were SEALs, she counseled a number of SEAL wives who had difficulties with the frequency and longevity of their spouses' missions. Swan had been glad to hear that since she would become a SEAL's wife soon.

Because David would be leaving in less than four

months on anther mission, they hoped to marry within a year. Surprisingly, David wanted a big wedding. She agreed as long as the wedding took place in the Keys.

The logistics of having a big wedding were enormous, given he had four brothers who were SEALs on different teams. Not to mention his closest four friends were SEALs as well. That meant Swan and David had to make sure everyone would be on leave in the States at the same time.

David also introduced Swan to her future sisters-in-law and they loved her engagement ring. The three were friendly and she liked them immediately. She was also introduced to other members of David's family—his grandparents, his niece, nephews, cousins, aunts, uncles—it was obvious the Holloway family was a huge one.

"Now I want to reintroduce you to four guys who are just as close to me as brothers. As you know, they came to the Keys to assist me in proving your innocence. And even when my assignment with you ended, they didn't leave. They stayed."

She had met his four friends that night after the incident on the boat, when they'd had to give statements. She had thanked them for their help but they hadn't been officially introduced.

"Did I tell you how beautiful you look tonight, sweetheart?"

She smiled up at him as they walked across the ballroom floor to the four men and their wives. "Yes, you told me. Thank you." She, Candy and Jamila had gone shopping in Miami. She'd known this was the perfect dress when she'd seen it on a store mannequin.

Within a few minutes, she had been introduced to Brisbane "Bane" Westmoreland and his wife, Crystal; Gavin "Viper" Blake and his very pregnant wife,

Layla; Laramie "Coop" Cooper and his wife, Bristol; and Thurston "Mac" McRoy and his wife, Teri.

After spending time with the couples, Swan felt that just like her future sisters-in-law, the four women were genuinely friendly and Swan looked forward to getting to know them better. They loved her engagement ring as well and told David he'd done a great job in picking it out.

"So what do you think?" David leaned down to ask, taking her hand in his and leading her to where his parents, siblings and their spouses were getting ready to take a group picture.

She grinned up at him. "Um, for starters, I think I need to start calling you Flipper, since everyone else does. And then, *Flipper*, I think I am one of the luckiest women in the world right now. I love you."

He chuckled as he pulled her to the side of the room and wrapped his arms around her waist. "And I, Swan Jamison, think I'm the luckiest man in the world, and I love you."

"A very wise woman, my mother, once told me that when you meet a man who puts that sparkle in your eyes then you'd know he was a keeper. You, Flipper, are a keeper."

He smiled. "You, my beautiful Swan, are a keeper as well."

Flipper then lowered his mouth to hers.

Epilogue

A year later in June

Bane Westmoreland leaned close and whispered to Flipper, "Don't get nervous now. You wanted a big wedding and you got it."

Flipper couldn't say anything because Bane was right. He stood flanked by his father, who was his best man, and twelve groomsmen—namely his brothers, best friends and cousins.

Only his SEAL teammates knew Flipper had a tendency to tap his finger against his thigh when he was nervous. He stopped tapping but not because he noticed that Viper, Mac and Coop were grinning over at him. But then he figured both Viper and Coop had reasons to grin since they'd both become fathers this year. Viper was the proud father of a son, Gavin IV, and Coop had a beautiful daughter they'd named Paris, since that was where he'd first met his wife.

It was a beautiful day for a beach wedding and so far everything was perfect and going according to plan. Swan had hired one of the local wedding planners and the woman had done an awesome job. She had thought of everything, including the super yacht that could hold their five hundred guests that they'd be using for the wedding reception. It was anchored in the ocean near Swan's beachfront home. A fleet of passenger boats had been chartered to transport the wedding guests out to the yacht.

A ten-piece orchestra sat beneath towering balustrades draped from top to bottom in thin white netting. Chairs were set up on the beach, auditorium style, facing the decorative stage where Flipper and the men in the wedding party stood waiting.

Suddenly, the music began and all the ladies strolled down the beach and up the steps.

Swan had chosen her wedding colors of purple and yellow and Flipper had to admit the combination was striking. It took all twelve women long enough to do their stroll. His niece was a flower girl and Coop's son and one of Flipper's nephews were the ring bearers.

Flipper almost held his breath when what looked like a huge forty-foot golden swan was rolled onto the beach. When the orchestra changed their tune for the "Wedding March," the swan opened and his Swan appeared in a beautiful, dazzling white gown. She looked beautiful, stunning and breathtaking all rolled into one.

Flipper stared at the woman who would be his wife and felt so much love in his heart. He hadn't known until now just how much he could feel for one woman. They had spent the past year deepening their friendship and their love. He looked forward to returning from his covert operations, knowing she would be there waiting on him.

He watched as she slowly strolled toward him. All three of her godfathers participated in walking her up the aisle, passing her off to the other so many feet along the way. Then all three of them gave her away. When Swan reached his side and extended her hand to him, he accepted it while thinking she was *his* Swan.

His beautiful Swan.

The wedding ceremony began. What Flipper would remember most when he looked back was when the minister announced them husband and wife and told him he could kiss his bride.

Flipper pulled Swan into his arms and lowered his mouth to hers. She was his and he intended to keep her happy for the rest of his days. They would be flying to Dubai for a two-week honeymoon and then return to the Keys where they planned to make their permanent home.

When David released Swan's mouth, the minister said, "I present to everyone David and Swan Holloway."

Flipper knew they were supposed to exit by walking down the golden steps that led to the boat that would transport them to the yacht. But at that moment, he couldn't deny himself another kiss and lowered his mouth to his wife's again.

* * * * *